ON SHAKY GROUND

Sandy Keranen Grindey

ISBN 979-8-89112-233-8 (Paperback)
ISBN 979-8-89112-234-5 (Digital)

Copyright © 2023 Sandy Keranen Grindey
All rights reserved
First Edition

Disclaimer: This book is based on factual information. The dates have been changed to better reflect the story line.

All rights reserved. No part of this publication may be reproduced, distributed, or transmitted in any form or by any means, including photocopying, recording, or other electronic or mechanical methods without the prior written permission of the publisher. For permission requests, solicit the publisher via the address below.

Covenant Books
11661 Hwy 707
Murrells Inlet, SC 29576
www.covenantbooks.com

To my grandpa, Ernie Johns, my mentor: He survived the harsh times and was my source of information for this story.

Love and thanks to my husband, Gordy, who encouraged me throughout the entire seven years with his "you can do this" attitude.

And heartfelt thanks to my mom, Eleanore, and aunt, Dorothy Henning, for sharing all their early memories with me.

PROLOGUE

Randall Peterson refolded his day-old *Detroit News Press* and slapped it on the wooden end table with a thump. Dated May 6, 1901, it was already obsolete, and every word he'd read was etched into his memory. He looked down as the stale smell of cold coffee drifted upward from the brown-ringed cups piled high at his feet, their scent mingling with the strong medicinal odors permeating the air. Standing up, he shook out the wrinkles from his suitcoat before laying it on the back of the wooden chair, then stretched and resumed his pacing across the small antiseptic room, the walls closing in and feeling more like a stifling prison with every step.

Stopping at the mirrored wall, Randall gazed at his image, aghast to see the facial stubble, the rumpled head and loose tie, giving him a distinctively seedy look. Dark circles under his blue eyes also proclaimed a sleepless night. Raking his fingers through his light golden hair and tugging the tie upward lifted his character a notch, but he *definitely* needed a shave— and a good smoke.

His meanderings were interrupted when a muffled sound from behind made him start. He pivoted swiftly as a nurse, in starchy white, walked through the swinging double doors and stood before him. At last, the nine months of anxious waiting were over. Randall's tired face lit up with excitement. After two daughters, his son, Jessie, had finally arrived!

Smiling eyes peeked up at him from above the surgical face mask, and whispering softly, the obstetric nurse placed a fluffy pink bundle into his arms.

"Congratulations, Mr. Petersen, it's a girl." With a nod, she silently padded back across the vinyl floor and into the concealed birthing area, the swooshing doors closing swiftly behind her.

Randall lifted his stunned head from the baby and gazed at the closed door. "What the...wait a minute!" He thundered. "There must be some mistake! I was supposed to get a *boy*!" But it was too late. With no one to hear, his deep voice just bounced off each wall throughout the vacant room.

But I was supposed to get a boy! Bewildered, he stared back down in disbelief at the warm package nestled in his arms. Carrying his daughter across the room, Randall slowly eased himself into his chair and leaned back against the ugly green wall. *Another girl? Impossible!*

After the initial shock of her late pregnancy, his wife, Lillian, had been so *radiant*, so different from her two previous confinements. *No* morning sickness. *No* backaches. She ate...well, she ate for three! Strength had flowed through her body. Surely, all the signs were there. This time, it *had* to be a boy!

In anticipation, Randall had chosen the name Jessie for his son. Seeing him planning and plotting for the full nine months, Lillian had wisely kept silent. Not wanting to dash Randall's hope of a son (but just in case), she decided on Lynnette for a girl.

The wait had been a long one.

Now what am I going to do? All my plans... Randall was confused, and his eyes searched about the room for answers that eluded him until the baby fussed and his attention turned downward to daughter number three, wriggling in his arms.

Although it was a letdown, Randall loved his two other girls. Both fourteen-year-old Allison and sixteen-year-old Olivia resembled their mama with their thick dark hair and exotic green eyes. Molded in the fashionable norm for proper young ladies, they gracefully adorned his home as their papa beamed with pride. Yes, he adored them, but they were still girls.

Exhausted, he closed his eyes. *Never count your chickens...*he thought. *Well, this egg's been hatched.* His Jessie was gone forever—wasn't he? Randall's blue eyes widened. *Maybe we can still make this* *work,* he thought. *Jessie? Lynnette? Why not Jessica Lynn? Maybe Jessie or even Jess for short?*

Randall sighed. "Okay, sweetie," he said, opening the baby blanket. "Let's take a look at you."

Cautiously, he pulled back on the warm flannel cover, getting a first glimpse of his new daughter. Blue eyes stared back into blue eyes. Taking a deep breath, Randall drew the tiny pink cap gently from her head, then inhaled sharply. Fine, feathery soft hair spilled out, slightly damp, but with a golden hue just like his own. As he folded back the swathing layers, a little arm popped out and five chubby fingers waved aimlessly before gripping tightly onto his index finger. Burning tears filled his tired eyes. Stroking her tiny fist with his thumb, he knew he was hooked. *This* one belonged to him.

Randall swallowed hard. "Hello, Jessie," he whispered.

It was time for a cigar.

CHAPTER 1

Walking through the busy editorial room at the *Detroit News Press*, twenty-four-year-old Jessica Lynn Peterson weaved in, out, and around the busy desks. There were no aisles to speak of as newspaper clippings were strewn haphazardly about, dropping onto the floor and into overflowing wastebaskets. The noisy *clackety-clack* rhythm of typewriters and pungent smell of printer's ink made her pulse dance. *This* was her life's blood, the same as her father's. She squeezed by, waving an occasional hand to anyone who looked up, knowing their busy deadlines received top priority.

Carrying her leather briefcase, she stood silently outside her dad's private office, the little mirror beside his door reflecting a blue-eyed golden-haired blonde of medium height. Short, natural ringlets curled about her head like a halo (a bane for one yearning for straight hair), and her small Scandinavian nose, sprinkled with freckles, was turned up and often referred to as a "ski jump." Her pale skin appeared delicate, creating an illusion of fragility, and although soft to the touch, she had a will of iron formed in her youth as she faced the challenges of living up to her father's expectations. Jessie wasn't the son he had expected but, instead, had become his best buddy and his shadow. His work became her play and under his tutelage, she grew up, first mimicking his ways until reaching out and finding her own. They were two of a kind, carbon copies, and devoted to each other.

Jessie looked up, reading the inscription on the glass window, and proudly reflected on her dad's accomplishments.

Although Randall was chief executive officer of the *Detroit News Press*, his success began in the lowly mail room. He was head strong and driven, advancing through the ranks of copy boy, reporter, and editor with only a high school diploma. He'd spent forty-five successful years in the news world and except for a slight paunch, was svelte from his rigorous afternoon workouts at Louie's Gym. The only hint of his actual age was a slight graying in his temples. Randall was widely known for his integrity and fairness. *Nothing* rivaled his dedication to the field—except his devotion to Jessie.

Raising her arm to knock, she hesitated, wondering what he would think of all this. Then, taking a deep breath, she rapped sharply on the wavy glass window.

With Randall's curt "Enter," Jessie walked into his office and closed the solid door behind her with a firm snap, ensuring their privacy. Confidently strolling across the black and white tiled floor, she placed her briefcase next to the chair before sitting across the desk from her father.

It was now or never.

"You wanna go *where?*" Slouched in his antiquated swiveled chair, Randall Peterson bellowed, his face turning red and his fat Havana cigar dropping from his lips in astonishment. With one hand, he swiftly brushed off the fluffy gray ash from his trousers, smashed the butt into the ashtray, and gave one swift push, spinning the chair's cast-iron wheels in circles and away from his weathered desk. With brows raised and eyes wide in disbelief, Randall sprang to his feet and walked toward his daughter.

"Now, Dad…" Jessie began with a sigh, knowing this was just the reaction she had expected.

Holding up his hand for silence, Randall walked briskly by and headed toward the door. He opened it slightly, poked his head through, and barked orders to his secretary. "Hold all calls, Sadie… and *no* visitors until further notice!" Without waiting for a response, Randall pulled his head back in and slammed the door, causing it to shake and the milky glass to rattle. Pacing back and forth, he pulled out another fat stogie from his pocket, lit it, and puffed out a gray acrid cloud. Stopping suddenly, he pointed the cigar at his daughter.

"Now you listen here, missy. No daughter of mine is going to traipse off hundreds of miles north to a no-man's-land. Upper

Michigan is *barbaric!* Military forts, Indians, brazen miners, snow to the rooftops, and total wilderness. You can go *miles* without seeing another human being. Have you thought about that? I couldn't protect you way up there!"

Standing up, Jessie moved close to her father, waving her hand through the smoke surrounding his head. "Dad, you've got your facts all mixed up. Yes, there *are* Indians, but living on government reservations. Fort Wilkins in Copper Harbor has been abandoned. And miners? What do you expect from the raging copper frenzy? Of *course,* there are miners—"

"Uncouth and uncivilized, that's what *I'd* call it, subjecting my little girl to who knows what!"

Arms clasped behind him, Randall continued his tirade, pacing back and forth and puffing furiously. By now, the entire room was filled with smoke.

Coughing and weaving through the thick haze, Jessie walked toward the nearest window and raised the sash for what little fresh air could be found in downtown Detroit on a hot summer day. Grabbing the old *Merriam-Webster* dictionary, she stood it end up in the open window as rumbles of automobiles, clanging trolleys, and shrill pedestrian voices rushed in. With a frown, she stared at the mayhem below. *Maybe this isn't such a good idea.*

Gazing at her dad with fondness, *and* exasperation, Jessie tried fanning the smoky room out the window with an old newspaper. Randall, getting the hint, settled back down, stubbed out the smelly cigar, and leaned back in his chair. With his hands behind his head, his blue eyes twinkled at her in amusement as the smoke floated out, mixing in with the existing smog.

Putting the paper down, Jessie turned her back on the noise and sat upon the skinny ledge. Fondly caressing the dictionary's spine, now tattered from use and age, she smiled nostalgically.

"Remember this, Dad? Everything I learned came from this book, not just from within, but sitting on top of it while you enlarged my world." Jessie stood up, removed the old book from the sill, and dropped the window back into place, trying to ignore the pungent after-smell still lingering about the room.

Plunking the dictionary down on Randall's desk before seating herself, Jessie continued. "Dad, I grew up under *your* tutelage, free from the stiff rules placed on most women. I learned to think for myself—be myself. And one of the first things you taught me was to be factual. *Never* suppose—*never* listen to hearsay—*never* take anything for granted. Isn't that what you always told me?"

Randall grunted in response. Sometimes, Jess was too smart for her own good. *And my own.* He reached automatically into his pocket for another smoke, but seeing the glint in Jessie's eyes, quickly squelched that idea. Instead, leaning forward and folding his hands in front of him, Randall gave her his undivided attention. "Okay, Jess, let's see what you've got—and it better be good!"

Relaxing back in his chair, Randall focused his eyes on her, his reporter's curiosity now caught by Jessie's avid enthusiasm for her latest pet project. The least he could do was listen.

Jessie lifted the briefcase onto her lap and pulled out several documents with the *Daily Mining Gazette* on top. Randall leaned forward to take a better look of the publication, but Jessie quickly shifted to the last page where a small, neatly typed ad had been circled in red.

Reaching out for the paper, Randall crinkled his forehead in confusion. "This is it? An advertisement for a reporter? Jess, I hate to burst your bubble, sweetie, but they're looking for an experienced newspaper reporter, which, you know, is usually of the male gender."

Jessie rose and walked around the desk, standing quietly behind her father while reading over his shoulder. She emphatically pointed to the insert. "Dad, can you tell me where the ad stipulates a *male* reporter?"

Randall scratched his chin. "Well…no. I guess it's always been assumed that any *normal* female wouldn't do this kind of work." He looked at Jessie, his eyes twinkling. "Now, now—don't give me that look. I'm not implying you're abnormal. But you know reporting has *always* been a man's world, Jess, grueling hours day and night, dirty venues, shady characters—"

"Dad, just what *have* I been doing for the past four years?" Jessie huffed and resumed her seat as she eyed her father. Never expecting any favoritism as his daughter, she had proven herself, time and again, a female competing in a man's world. "Am I or am I *not* a good reporter?"

"Yes, Jess, of course you are. I couldn't be prouder." Randall quickly reached over and patted her hand. "It's just…well, I knew I would always be here for you if you *did* get into a scrape. Remember? I had to bail you out of jail! You were front page news for days!"

Jessie grinned at him, unrepentant.

"Yes, yes, I know," Randall continued. "You ferreted out Sid Brewster's illegal takeover, but the police chief wasn't convinced you were undercover for a story, dressed up as you were. A dancing, cigarette-smoking flapper?" From his middle drawer, he pulled out an old news clipping with her photo and smacked it with his hand. "Jess, you were showing more flesh than when you were born! If I had known what you were up to, girl…" he chided, waving the paper in front of her.

Randall folded the photo and returned it to his drawer. "Thank goodness the chief kept your real name under wraps. No one should connect you with that story unless they personally saw you in that getup. Besides, I made him *very* happy by contributing a good sum of money toward their retirement fund."

He sighed and leaned back. "I don't know, Jess. You'd be hundreds of miles away from me if something did happen. What else have you got there?"

Jessie sifted through the pile of papers in front of her, categorizing the most important on the top.

It was time to test her wings.

"Okay, Dad. Here is the dossier on Houghton and Keweenaw counties. As you can see, it's quite densely populated. Thousands are employed in the copper mines, but the constituency in the sister towns of Hancock and Houghton consists of merchants, restaurants, doctors, health clinics, teachers, lawyers, and law officers. Why, there's even an operatic and two vaudeville theaters in the area!"

Jessie hesitated slightly before going on. "At the present time, though, there's a little controversy between a miners' union and the mining companies. But I'm sure that'll be cleared up shortly." Shrugging, she waited for her dad to respond, but he was busy perusing all the paperwork in front of him.

"And here are pictures and facts about the two local colleges: the Michigan College of Mining and Technology in Houghton and Suomi College in Hancock. It's not a no-man's-land any longer, Dad." Jessie, retrieving two more photos, leaned across the desk, and frowning, handed them to her father. "But I must admit…you *were* right about one thing. It sure does snow!"

One picture captured an unbelievable white downy buildup against a house, drifting up to the second story and hanging off ledges like melted marshmallows. Children were sledding from the garage roof into the fluffy piles below. A wooden walkway from the front door to the street enabled the owners to exit their home without shoveling a mountain of snow. The second photo showed a three-hundred-inch measuring stick with the white stuff piled up 260 inches.

Frustrated, Randall slapped the photos down, causing papers to fall off his desk and float to the floor. Bending over to retrieve them, he questioned her, bewildered. "Jess, why would you even *consider* these conditions? You complain when a few flakes fall, and you hate to drive in the stuff. It's wet, it's dirty, and it sticks to you. It makes your hair frizz, remember?"

Jessie frowned, folding her hands across her stomach. "Dad, I really think this could be my big chance. You mentored me, encouraged me, and challenged me. Why should all that investment go to waste?"

Then, she chuckled. "And who knows…I just might meet a big burly lumberjack and bring him home to meet you and Mom!"

Randall shook his head. "Do that and we'll have to bring out the smelling salts. You know your mother plans to marry you off into a 'fine' family. I'm not bragging, Jess, but as Randall Peterson's daughter, you could have your pick of the marital litter."

Jessie untangled her legs and flew around the desk, wrapping her arms around Randall's neck. "I was only joking, Dad, but it *is* possible. Heaven knows I've had plenty of opportunity with Mom parading every eligible bachelor from here to Chicago through our front door, each wanting to be *your* son-in-law!"

Randall disengaged himself from his daughter and checked over the remaining paperwork while Jessie stared out the window. Glancing over her shoulder, her dad's face was passive, giving no clue to his thoughts. She sighed and continued her outside view in silence.

"What about transportation. How would you get there? Will you take your car? Where will you live?" Randall, rubbing the back of his neck, fired these questions at Jessie, wanting her to be happy but, above all, he wanted her safe.

Jessie left the window and gathered the documents together, the *Daily Mining Gazette* still on top. She reopened it, turning to the classified section. "Here are some rental listings for single family homes or houses with room rentals. All are owned by the mining companies, built for their employees."

Sifting through the portfolio, she pulled out a photo of a large ferry boat. "How am I getting there? First, there's a train right out of Detroit that travels to Mackinac City. On arrival, the railway cars are loaded onto the *Chief Wawatam* ferry and shipped across the Straits of Mackinac to St. Ignace. From there a train travels up to Houghton and the surrounding communities. My car can go as freight."

Both Jessie and Randall sat silently, each engrossed in their own thoughts. Jessie wanted to fly and Randall...well, he wanted to keep her safe in the nest. Most girls her age were already married, many with children. But Jessie's path always seemed to run a different course. Randall couldn't fault her for that—after all, she *was* his daughter.

She broke into his thoughts. "Dad, I'll need a recommendation, too, from the *Detroit News Press*. And the *Gazette* doesn't need to know I'm a woman, do they? I'll just sign my name 'Jessie,' which is a popular name for boys too. They'll never know the difference. With a glowing reference from this newspaper, they're bound to accept me! I mean, how many applicants would consider a job in this location?"

She shook her head. "I'm confident the newspaper will hire me sight unseen." She smiled winningly. "C'mon, Dad, trust me. It'll all work out."

Randall's chair squeaked in protest as he slowly pushed away from his desk and stretched his back. Pacing back and forth, he took a few cursory glances at his daughter, who waited in silence. Once giving his approval, he knew there would be no stopping her. *But how can I disapprove when I'd do the same thing?*

Birds of a feather…maybe it was time to let his fledgling fly.

"Well, when do you wanna leave?"

Jessie shrieked as she flew out of the chair and threw her arms around her dad. Randall said a prayer for her safety, and his own arms tightened around her in a strong embrace, knowing he'd soon have to let her go.

CHAPTER 2

Uh-oh...Did I make the wrong decision?

Jessie braked her 1924 buff Buick Roadster, parked it at the edge of the mud-rutted driveway and stepped onto the hard-packed earth. Squinting, she looked up at the small, faded barn about forty feet ahead wondering if it was safe for her car.

Undecided, she shielded her eyes from the glaring sun and stared at her new home. The two-story salt box was like any other on the block. Rustic, wooden and a weather-beaten grey. Three shallow steps led up to the front door, which was sheltered by a small, peaked roof.

Scuffing the dry grass, Jessie found the lawn crisp, looking like a bad haircut with uneven tufts sticking up here and there. Hemmed in by a five-rail fence, with a rail or two missing, the large, enclosed yard was shared with neighbors on two sides.

Opening the gate at the edge of the drive, she slipped through, its rusty hinges creaking as the door fell back with a clank. Testing the muddy ground, she trudged up the driveway, finding it dry and hard as adobe clay.

At the barn, Jessie pushed up on the crossbar, causing the doors to swing open and her nose to crinkle in distaste at the fetid smell coming from within. Pushing on two heavy rocks, she anchored the doors back and cautiously peeked inside.

Gradually adjusting to the dim interior, she noticed two dusty windows, facing east and west. Untying the cotton scarf from her hat, Jessie rubbed on the glass, watching as sunbeams filtered in, with dust and straw chips dancing in the rays. As the interior lightened, she saw it was empty except for a black iron anvil and a couple of straw bales.

Looking up, she found a few unoccupied bird's nests sitting high on top the wooden beams. She could see—and smell—evidence of mice, most likely living in the straw. Walking outside, Jessie inhaled several deep breaths of fresh air before crunching her way back down the drive.

Reaching the gate, she suddenly felt the ground shifting beneath her, tingling the soles of her feet. Then—it was gone. So barely discernible, she could have imagined it. Startled, she balanced a boot on the lowest rail, lifted one foot, then the other but found nothing amiss. Folding her elbows, she rested her arms on the top tier, and mused over her long journey.

Once the decision to move had been made, plans had accelerated to the point of no return. Train tickets were purchased, trunks were packed, and tearful admonitions were given by her parents and sisters, along with several goodbye hugs. Her excitement had been mixed with sadness and uncertainty; but in the end, a long smoky train had chugged her far to the north.

Jessie sighed as she pulled away from the gate, knowing her fate lay in the hands of tomorrow's appointment. But now was not the time to dwell on uncertainties. First, the house needed to be tackled.

Opening the driver's door, she noticed her rental papers were scattered all over the floor. Knowing she had left them on the seat, she eyed the open window, suspiciously. Reaching over, she gathered the sheets once more, and placed them inside her briefcase. *First the tremor and now this. What next? Ghosts in the house?* Chuckling to herself, she grabbed her handbag, jammed on the floppy hat, and headed toward her new home.

With the blazing sun bearing down, Jessie walked quickly across the crusty grass and mounted the shallow steps, thankful for the little pointed roof that kept the sizzling sun off her head.

Opening the door, she delighted in the cooler air. As she was expected, Jessie knew the wood-box for the stove would be filled, the house swept, electricity turned on and water vessels full. The stove contained an attached water reservoir, while the upstairs tank was used for flushing the commode. The agent said she was one of the *lucky* ones—indoor plumbing! But he stressed, conservancy was a must as water from the community tower was turned on each morning and shut off each night. But with her downhill location in Lower Pewabic, water pressure would be greater, and her vessel should remain filled most of the day. Perfect, because using the old outhouse was *not* an option!

Stepping inside, she found a long narrow hallway with a living room on the left, a dining room on the right, and a stairway to the second story. Jessie was pleasantly surprised as she walked into the living room.

Heavy brocade drapes, waiting to be closed upon nightfall or a chilly winter day, hung from two tall windows and with a push of a button, a round ceiling fixture illuminated the room in a soft glow. Sitting by the center wall was a cast-iron stove just waiting to be shared with someone special on a cold winter's night. Hugging the big, bellied beast, she looked forward to crackling fires, sweet smoky smells, and orange flames dancing through the little glass windows. Standing on four curvy legs, the stove shined like black onyx and would send heat to the second floor through the ceiling's metal grates.

Treading further, she found an oriental rug centered in the middle of the dark hardwood floors, its maroon print complimenting the stove as well as the sofa. A black Edwardian chair, with quilted back, sat to the right of the couch, while a large wooden rocker stood enticingly on the opposite side, beckoning a rider.

Crossing into the dining area, Jessie noted the room was simply furnished, with crème wainscoting throughout, and tiny flowered wallpaper that butted up to the crown molding. Each long window had matching drapes that, when pulled back, let in the bright afternoon sun. A round oak table with six chairs filled the center of the room, with a shiny brass chandelier hanging above.

Noticing a swinging door on the far wall, Jessie pushed through and discovered the kitchen on the other side. A second door also connected the room to the long hallway. A black and white cast-iron cook stove standing against the wall shared with the dining room provided heat for both sides.

Gazing about, an object on the counter caught her attention. Light from the window above fell upon a large metal tool lying next to the sink. Curious, she strolled over and picked up a heavy wrench someone had left behind but glancing about saw nothing broken. The glass-windowed cabinets were in perfect shape, filled with dishes and cooking utensils. Turning on the faucet, the water ran freely into the white iron basin, draining into the pipe below. Squatting down, Jessie pushed aside the muslin curtain, finding a dry floor underneath. Nothing to worry about. *Except...*

...a strange sound coming from the front of the house.

"*Lo-o-o-o-o...*"

Bouncing back up, Jessie quickly turned off the spigot and waited. All was quiet... *I've been alone too long,* she thought.

"*Lo-o-o-o-o...*" There it was, again, and the sound was floating closer to the kitchen.

Jessie felt prickles rising from the back of her neck and up the sides of her face. Ghost or not, she grabbed the wrench, raised it high and edged slowly toward the swinging door. Giving it a hard shove, she slammed into a massive barrier on the other side, bouncing her backward.

"*Ouch!*"

Uh-oh, *that* ghost sounded far too real for her imagination.

Shocked, Jessie let the wrench fall to the floor with a loud clank. Leaning forward, she pulled the door slowly toward her, revealing a very live person on the other side cautiously rubbing his forehead. Not an apparition. He looked slightly taller and a little older than she, but with no graying along his dark temples. A fluffy black mustache curled up slightly above his lip, and his jet-black hair, worn slightly longer than normal, clung to his head where a hat had recently sat. Tan trousers, a light-blue shirt and heavy leather boots completed his attire. Ah, *and* he held a tan flannel cap in his left hand.

Removing his finger from his forehead, the man transferred it to the hat, turning it around with an embarrassed smile as he looked down at Jessie. "Sorry for startling you, miss, but the door was open, so I assumed Mr. Peterson had arrived."

Wow—his dimples were drop-dead gorgeous! Speechless, Jessie gazed up in amazement before peering over his shoulder toward the front door. Had she carelessly left it open?

At first hesitant, she hoped he was harmless enough and took a step closer, the door closing behind her. "*I'm* Jess Peterson." Jessie watched as his eyes widened—beautiful, sparkling deep-blue orbs.

"*You're* Jessie Peterson?" The man took a step backward. "I'm so sorry, but the newspaper said they were expecting a *Mr.* Peterson. I wouldn't have barged in like that, but the *Gazette* sent me over to welcome their new reporter and relay a message." He looked a little sheepish. "I'm sorry. Let's try this again."

Pivoting, he headed for the front door, closing it behind him while Jessie stood speechless, rooted to the floor.

Three loud knocks resonated throughout the house. Shaking her head, Jessie strolled to the door and pulled it open. There he was, again, only this time his hat was placed neatly upon his head. With twinkling eyes, he doffed his cap and gave her a neat little bow.

"Good afternoon, miss. I'm Mitchell O'Brien, looking for a… Jessie Peterson?" He patted the sides of his trousers before reaching into his shirt pocket and pulling out a folded piece of paper. Opening it, he confirmed the name, nodded, and continued. "Yup, Jessie Peterson. And… you…are…?" He lifted his eyebrows and looked down at her expectantly.

With a chuckle, Jessie knew it was time for explanations. "Mr. O'Brien, first, let me apologize for nearly attacking you. Do come in. I was inspecting the house when…when we first met. Sorry about that. Perhaps an ice bag is in order? That is, *if* I have any ice."

"No problem, Ms. Peterson, really. Just a twinge…and, please call me Mitch. Is there anything I can help you with?"

"You said something about a message?" Jessie hoped they hadn't hired someone else. "My appointment is for tomorrow morning, so I hope nothing has changed. Excuse me. My hospitality is slipping. Would you care for some coffee? *Coffee*…Oh, Mitch! I left all my groceries sitting in the car while I was exploring. They've been baking in this heat for the last hour or more. If you're serious, I could use a little help lugging them inside before they rot." Jessie headed out the door and called back over her shoulder. "And please call me Jessie." She ran down the shallow steps, trekking across the baked front yard, with Mitch following at her heels.

Hurrying to the passenger door, Jessie retrieved three large paper sacks from the front and piled them into his outstretched arms. Grabbing the last two, she slammed the door shut with her hip and headed back.

Walking briskly over the dead grass, they climbed up the steps into the house where Mitch kicked the door shut with his heel. Following Jessie toward the kitchen, his mind was spinning with one puzzling question. Did the *Gazette* not know they were hiring a woman?

Mitch watched Jessie walk down the hall before him, with a swing to her hips. She certainly was easy to look at. Great figure, beautiful smile, vibrant personality. With a lack of available females in the area, he wondered if he should stake his claim before others caught wind of her and came prowling around like tom cats.

Unaware of his surveillance, Jessie led the way to a small kitchen table, placing the groceries on top. A white Frigidaire, a few feet away, waited to receive her perishables, and—thank God—it was cold! At her request, Mitch began placing items on its shelves, a jug of milk, cheese, eggs, butter, soda pop and luncheon meat. Jessie took the nonperishable bags and set them down by the sink. They could wait until later.

Pulling up two chairs and sitting across the table from each other, Jessie started in. "As I was saying, you surprised me with your sudden appearance. Since I arrived, my imagination has been playing games with me." She shook her head. "Standing by the driveway, I could have *sworn* the ground was moving, but it was so slight, I thought I imagined it. Then when I returned to my car, the rental papers were strewn all over the floor when they had been on the seat. Naturally, my next thought was a ghost in the house." Jessie chuckled. "Your arrival was the proverbial 'straw that broke the camel's back.' But what I would've accomplished wielding the wrench at a ghost is beyond me!"

Mitch pushed his chair away from the table and grabbed the wrench. "Actually, this is mine, Jess." He laughed. "I'm just grateful you didn't throw it at my head! Last week I was checking the house and must have left it behind."

Pulling the wrinkled paper back out of his shirt pocket and smoothing it out, he handed it to Jessie. "This is why I'm here." Upon reading it, Jessie was relieved to know her appointment with the *Gazette* was still on, but with someone else. Mitch explained. "Curt Johnson, the editor, has been called away for a family emergency, so tomorrow you'll be seeing Brian Mason. He's a nice guy, although a bit conservative."

Mitch hesitated, rubbing the back of his neck before looking straight at her. "Jessie, it's probably none of my business, but does the *Gazette* know they've hired a woman as their reporter?"

CHAPTER 3

Jessie stood up and paced the floor before answering, while Mitch looked up at her expectantly. Coming to a halt, she turned toward him. "Mitch, I came up from Detroit for several reasons. I needed a change in my life, a little peace and quiet, and above all, a little anonymity." She sighed. "Sometimes, it's difficult being Randall Peterson's daughter…"

Mitch's eyes grew wide in astonishment. "Randall Peterson is your *father*?" He was flabbergasted. "I didn't make the connection because there are so many Petersons in this area. But even in Lansing, where I work, your father's a big legend in the newspaper business. *His* name alone would have given you your heart's desire!"

"But that's just it, Mitch! I didn't *want* to trade on my dad's name. So I simply signed the contract as Jessie Peterson, but without any photograph. If the *Gazette* wanted to *assume* I'm a male…" Jessie shrugged then continued softly, but firmly. "I worked hard, Mitch, to get where I am today. I'm *very* qualified and being a woman shouldn't make me any less desirable." Jessie paused, wondering if he was trustworthy.

Nodding to herself, she decided on the truth. "By any chance, Mitch, did you read about a Sid Brewster's attempt to infiltrate a large meat packer in Detroit and was incarcerated?" At his nod, she continued. "His strong mobster connections wanted to unionize the company. To get to the truth, I went undercover to expose his lies—and succeeded. But not without a little controversial effort of my own by portraying myself as a woman of a more, let's say, dubious virtue?" Jessie cast her eyes down, waiting for his response. It didn't take long.

Mitch's blue eyes stared at her in disbelief. "Jess, never tell me *you're* the infamous flapper, Sable, the one they're still looking for?"

Jessie looked up, and flushing a rosy, red, she nodded.

His first thought was for himself. *Great…now all the tomcats will* really *come howling at her door.*

Mitch thought of another very pertinent question he just had to ask. "Jess, I really can't see your father condoning this type of reporting, especially at the physical risk of his daughter. I'm assuming he didn't know what you were up to?"

"You're right, Mitch," Jessie replied, sheepishly. "My dad was clueless until he was called to bail me out of the Wayne County jail. Although I worked for him, our paths didn't cross daily. Off and on, I stayed at the Statler Hotel, wearing several red wigs, heavy makeup, and flashy attire. If *you* didn't recognize me from the photos, I'm hoping no one else will. I'm not even sure if the *Gazette* should know it was me." She sighed, deeply. "But if I need an ace in the hole, I guess this would be it."

Mitch exhaled in relief. Maybe he wouldn't have to guard her door, after all. He reached for her hand across the table. "Jess, you looked astoundingly beautiful and mysterious as Sable. But I find the natural Jessie much more appealing. And don't worry; your secret's safe with me." He raised his eyebrows up and down, giving her a lewd grin. "In fact, I rather like it this way…it gives me a little extra edge."

Laughing, Jessie withdrew her hand. "Thanks, Mitch. Your discretion is appreciated, but only time will tell if it'll be necessary." She stood up. "Meanwhile, you'll have to excuse me as I need to settle in and get ready for my appointment tomorrow. I haven't checked out the bedrooms yet, and my luggage is still in the car. Oh, by the way, can you tell me if there's a washing machine here?"

Mitch pointed toward a little back porch room. "It's in there, Jess. Not like you're probably used to, but two washtubs with an attached electric wringer, all hooked up and ready to go. I promise, it'll do the job for you."

Jessie headed toward the little room to view this strange contraption but stopped short in thought, not realizing Mitch was right behind her until he slammed into her back with a breathless "oomph." Laughing, she turned sharply to apologize as arms entangled with arms. Taking a step back, she looked up at him, her smile dissolving at his intense gaze. Staring at her, his face was dead, dead serious, *and* they were much, much too close. Her lips parted as the air between them became thick, and she struggled to breathe.

Uh-oh. I hope he's not taking this Sable thing to heart.

Turning around, she quickly headed into the little porch, talking to Mitch over her shoulder. "Mitch, you know a lot about me, but what are *you* doing up here?"

Mitch paused in the doorway and took a deep breath, his own heart racing. Leaning against the frame for support, he shoved his hands into his pants pockets and chided himself. Another minute and he would have kissed her. *I'm as bad as the other tom cats! Get a grip, man!*

As she discovered the laundry and bath, Jessie explored both rooms with enthusiasm. Mitch remained silent, hoping to get in a few more 'looks' before she turned back.

With the late afternoon sun beaming through the porch window, Jessie's curls were like golden flames. Never had he felt such an attraction this early in the game. The rays gave her face an ethereal look, but she was no hot house pansy, just a shining gem among the area's gray jagged rock. And of all places, right in his own backyard!

Shaking his head at his musings, Mitch accepted the "olive branch" of questions from Jessie.

"To answer your question, Jess, I was raised up here, but left when I was eighteen. After getting my degree, I accepted a government position in Lansing, and my parents decided to follow me down. My dad's a professor at state, and my mom stays at home, keeping us both in line. Anyway, because I'm familiar with the area, the governor sent me as liaison officer between union and the mining companies to help reach an agreement." He shook his head. "So far, we're not even close." Mitch frowned. "There's talk of sending in the Michigan militia to help keep the peace, but I'm hoping it won't come to that."

Frustrated, Mitch was more than a little concerned. Remaining unbiased had been difficult as many of his boyhood friends were still working in the mines. He knew from experience there were times when nothing could be done but accept the inevitable, and he was very much afraid that *this* was going to be one of those times.

Standing away from the door, he put aside his frustration just as Jessie breezed on through.

Leaning with her back against the kitchen counter, she looked at him thoughtfully. "Hmm, it's been about four weeks since my initial contact with the newspaper. I'd heard stories, of course, but thought the strike would've ended by now."

Jessie stood up, resolutely, and smiled at Mitch. "But speaking of work, I'd better get my luggage inside. Thanks so much for all your help. Do you have far to go home?" She padded down the hall toward the front door with Mitch trailing behind her.

When they reached the front yard, he pointed to a larger weather-beaten house on the left. "Believe it or not, Jess, we're neighbors. I'm renting from the Johns family who take in boarders and gives a guy like me a place to eat and lay his head. Tom and Irma are swell. But they have a *very* precocious, *and* impressionable daughter by the name of Josephine, who's in the eighth grade. She prefers to be called Jo, so there you have it. A kindred spirit of your own." Mitch chuckled.

Reaching the auto, Jessie raised the boot cover and retrieved three large suitcases embedded within. Smiling her thanks at Mitch as he took two of them, she grabbed the third and started back.

"By the way, many thanks, too, Mitch, for checking out the house." She reached the front door, placed her bag in the hallway and indicated for Mitch to do the same. He dropped the bags and turned to say goodbye.

"Well, I guess this is it, but I'm sure we'll be seeing more of each other since we're neighbors. Be sure to let me know if you need anything." Grinning, he took off his hat and bowed in front of her. "Consider me your own personal Sir Galahad." When she laughed, he took a chance and asked, "Would it be alright if I stop by tomorrow afternoon to see how the interview went?"

Jessie gave him a beaming smile. "I'd like that, Mitch. In fact, one way or the other, I'll probably need to let off some steam.

Anytime between four and five o'clock should be fine. It'll give me time to straighten up."

"See you tomorrow, then—*and* watch out for them ghosts!" Chuckling, Mitch bolted down the porch stairs and loped across the barren yard. He turned and waved at her before swinging over the fence to the Johns' residence, thinking tomorrow would be a long time coming.

Jessie closed the front door and gazed up at the staircase. It wasn't too long of a climb, but the steps were steep and narrow. With a sigh, she picked up a suitcase in each hand and slowly mounted the stairs, setting them on the landing with a big *whoosh*.

Exploring the second floor, she found two small bedrooms with a closet in between. The larger room contained a white iron bed, small wooden nightstand, and matching chest of drawers, with a large oval mirror above. A white overstuffed chair with a plump green pillow looked soft and inviting, and the big walk-in closet would hold all her clothes plus storage. The plastered walls were white, and the wooden floor contained two colorful braided rugs, placed on each side of the bed for softness and warmth. A simple pale green bedspread covered the mattress and a matching curtain hung on the small west window. All in all, the room was invitingly tranquil.

Leaving the bedroom, Jessie opened the door of the small closet and poked her head inside. Here was the infamous water tank that filled up each morning. The strange contraption, tall and cylindrical, had a large pipe entering from above with several "spider legs" protruding out of the bottom before disappearing beneath the floor. Jessie knocked on the metal tank, finding the resounding clang reassuring. Good. The vessel was full.

Peeking into the smaller white walled bedroom, Jessie found it empty except for a rolltop desk in one corner and a small chair wheeled underneath. *This* could be useful. The room also had a tiny closet for additional storage.

Taking a deep breath, she quickly skipped downstairs for her last piece of luggage. At the bottom, she stared down at the large bag, then up to the landing. *Just one more trip...* Trudging back up with the suitcase bumping behind her, she brought it into the bedroom along with the other bags and swung them onto the bed. Two more chores and she'd call it a night.

Returning to the kitchen, Jessie stored her remaining groceries from the Quincy Market before strolling out to the car. Her energy spent, just the thought of cleaning out the barn was too daunting. Tomorrow was another day.

Running up to the little building, Jessie lifted the anvil with both arms and puffed her way back down the driveway. Opening the gate, she pushed hard against it with her back until it widened enough to let the automobile through, then braced the anvil against it. Sliding into her car, she slowly edged her way up the drive, the wheels pulverizing the compacted mud underneath. She chugged into the barn, parked the car, then scuffed the two large rocks away from the doors, closing them tight with the crossbar. It was time to call it a day.

CHAPTER 4

Viewing her reflection in the bedroom mirror, Jessie turned back and forth, fingering her mother's favorite pearls wrapped around her neck for good luck. Hoping she looked professional in her white and blue attire, she gazed at herself once more before checking her watch. She gasped. It was time. Grabbing her purse off the bed, she flew down the stairs and out the front door.

Driving cautiously away from the house, Jessie bounced down the dusty road, easing over the potholes and gingerly steering around the larger rocks. Turning left at the end of the street, she drove onto Highway 41 and headed west toward Hancock, the city lying just below. Along the way, she noticed both sides of the road were littered with sister communities, each embracing tall shaft houses and adjacent red stone buildings, with miles of railroad tracks crisscrossing between them.

Through her windows, Jessie could hear the engines chugging—the whistles blowing—the bells clanging. Black smoky plumes puffed up from the locomotives as they trudged back and forth over the rails, carrying their heavy load of raw copper. Although not smoggy like Detroit, she could smell the sooty scent of burning coal floating in the air.

The road suddenly curved and snaked downward, and Jessie's eyes widened in amazement as ridge after ridge of deep green forested hills rose above the shimmering water. Portage Lake, shared by the City of Hancock on the north and Village of Houghton on the south, sparkled as each dancing swell reflected the early morning sun. A portion of the large wooden bridge, connecting the two cities, floated at a right angle, allowing a large freighter to enter the narrow channel that flowed into Lake Superior. Checking her watch, Jessie looked at the bridge hoping it would be closed before she got there.

Pulling into the *Daily Mining Gazette* parking lot with five minutes to spare, Jessie slid her briefcase across the seat and opened the door. Stepping out, she peered up at the red four-story sandstone building, getting a first look at what could be her new workplace. Although small compared to the *Detroit News Press*, it was, nevertheless, impressive, with three large arched windows facing the front and beautiful decorative moldings just beneath the eaves. Dozens of smaller windows, built into every wall, assured an abundance of natural light on every floor. It had promise.

Inspecting her dress once more, Jessie fluffed out some wrinkles of her white shift and brushed off a few imaginary specs of lint from her navy-blue jacket. Head held high, she knew that Sable or not, she *could* handle any situation.

With a positive bounce to her step, she pushed open the office door, then quietly walked inside. The welcoming smell of printer's ink, floating through the vents, made her skin tingle with excitement. For just a moment, she closed her eyes and breathed in deeply, overcome with a sense of belonging.

Stepping across the wide planked floor, Jessie stopped in front of the desk, waiting to be acknowledged by the fluffy brown-haired woman on the telephone. Busy scribbling on her notepad, the receptionist looked up briefly, nodded, and pointed her finger to the chairs along the wall. Jessie turned back and seated herself under one of the windows. Popping open the briefcase, she withdrew a small white business card, with 'Jessie Peterson' printed in dark blue ink, and placed it in her jacket pocket.

The woman ended her phone call and removing the tiny spectacles from the edge of her nose, gave Jessie her undivided attention. Classy women like this one didn't come waltzing into her reception area every day. Intrigued, she stood up and, with an encouraging smile, headed toward her visitor.

"Good morning. I'm Roberta Nutini. How can I help you?" She stretched out a hand, giving Jessie a firm friendly shake.

Jessie rose, taking Roberta's hand in her own, realizing this woman could be an ally or a foe. Reaching into her jacket pocket, she handed her calling card to Roberta. "I'm Jessie Peterson. I believe I have a ten-o'clock appointment with Brian Mason."

Roberta's eyes twinkled. "Well, now, I believe Brian is expecting a *Mr.* Peterson." She held up her hand at Jessie. "I don't want to know…" Crossing the floor, she poked her head through an adjoining door. "Carl?" At her call, a stocky young man in his late teens came running in, looking up at her expectantly. Roberta placed the card in his hand. "Please give this to Brian and tell him his ten-o'clock appointment is in the lobby." She yelled a belated "Thanks!" as Carl tromped up the stairs.

Roberta made her way back to her desk. "Brian's office is on the third floor, so it'll be a few minutes. I hope you don't mind stair climbing." She shook her head, musingly. "I must say, you're the last thing I expected to see this morning. And between you and me, I didn't want to disclose your identity—as a female, that is." She chuckled. "Brian is pretty straitlaced, so I can't wait to see the look on his face when he arrives." She raised her brown mug at Jessie.

"Ms. Peterson, would you care for some water or coffee while you're waiting?"

"Please call me Jessie, and no, I'm fine. Thanks for not betraying me. I'm hoping my contract with the *Gazette* will stand, despite my gender. It was a chance I had to take."

"Well, Jessie—and my name's Bobbie—we sure could use another female around here, so I'll keep my fingers crossed!" Hearing heavy footsteps descending on the wooden stairway, Bobbie quickly sat down and turned her head toward the door, quivering in excitement. *This is going to be fun…*

"Mr. Peterson, welcome! We're so glad you could join our little staff." These words came from a tall, lanky black-haired gentleman as he enthusiastically strode into the reception area. Gazing about the room for his appointment, Brian Mason stopped in his tracks and turned back to Bobbie.

"Roberta, Carl just informed me that our new reporter, Jessie Peterson, had arrived." Frowning, he looked down at the card between his fingers to make sure the name was correct.

Bobbie had to stifle a grin. This was too much fun—a *much* welcomed event in her otherwise ordinary day. Her face was unreadable as she waved a hand toward Jessie, who was now standing.

"Brian, I'd like you to meet Jessie Peterson, your new reporter. Jessie, this is Brian Mason, editor of the *Gazette* and covering for Curt Johnson, our publisher."

In disbelief, Brian looked back over his shoulder. Confused, he turned to Bobbie, then back again to Jessie, acknowledging her for the first time. He was not amused. "Excuse me...but is this some sort of *joke*?" Looking her over, he questioned her caustically. "*Ms.* Peterson? Was there a little something you left out of your application?" He glanced over at Bobbie, who was suddenly very busy at her desk. "I take it, Roberta, you were aware of this little charade before sending Carl up with the card. Sometimes, your sense of humor *quite* amazes me."

Normally, Brian would have enjoyed a good joke. But with Curt out, his responsibilities as both editor and publisher were pushing his button to the limit. Emergencies, tardy deadlines, and equipment breakdowns were playing on his nerves. One thing was correct, though. They *were* in desperate need of a new reporter. He looked at Jessie up and down. Maybe it was time to call her bluff.

"If you'll follow me, *Ms.* Peterson, we'll continue this discussion in my office"—Brian glanced pointedly at Bobbie—"where we'll have a little more privacy." Looking down, he grimaced at Jessie's high navy pumps and commented, "I take it those will carry you up to the third floor?" Without waiting for an answer, he turned and headed toward the doorway.

Jessie looked at Bobbie, grabbed her briefcase, and quickly followed him across the room. As she passed by, Bobbie held up four fingers, crossed for good luck. Jessie smiled her thanks and winked at her.

Stepping through the door, she climbed the stairs behind Brian, stopping at the third floor where Brian waved his hand to an office across the landing and allowed her to enter before him.

As Jessie had surmised, the windows produced a bright natural light which now flooded his workspace. His rugged desk contained several scuffed wooden trays filled with orderly piles of paper, a pencil sharpener, and a black candlestick telephone, along with an old ceramic coffee mug filled with sharpened pencils. The man was neat, with a designated place for everything.

Pulling out a chair, Brian waited for Jessie to sit down. Then, walking around his desk, he sat in his own leather chair, folded his hands across his torso and gave Jessie a quick look over. She had an air of confidence he couldn't fault, a lovely countenance that would provide entry into any interview, *and* they were stuck without a reporter. But her deceit—on purpose—galled him. Oh, yeah, she was playing, but he just wasn't sure of the game.

Reaching into his top desk drawer, Brian pulled out his round spectacles and placed the curved wires around his ears. Pushing up the lenses, he reached for a few sheets of paper from the nearest tray, including a current issue of the *Detroit News Press*. Silently, he perused the information before turning back to Jessie. "Okay, Ms. Peterson. Explain yourself. You know, as well as I do, your credentials are *excellent*, along with the news clippings of your latest written articles and highest recommendations from your employer. Naturally, working for the *Detroit News Press* is a definite plus in your favor. So…why the disguise?"

Jessie was contrite. "I'm sorry, Mr. Mason. I know I owe you an apology, but can you truthfully say you would've hired me as a *miss* instead of a mister?"

Brian shifted in his chair and folded his hands on top of the desk. He was caught, as the saying goes, between a rock and a hard place. *Would* he have hired a woman?

"Truthfully, Ms. Peterson, I'm not sure a female would have been considered at the present time. Not just because of your gender, but because our current coverage deals in hardships, anger, frustration, and fear of the unknown. It might become hostile, even dangerous—no place for a delicate woman like yourself."

Brian stopped, choosing his next words carefully. "However, at the present time, I'm in a quandary. First, we *do* have a signed contract, hiring you as our new reporter. Second, no one else of your caliber has applied for the position. Third, our last employee walked out without notice. So, Ms. Peterson, you see my dilemma. I could fire you for false representation, but our need is greater than retribution."

Giving her a perplexed look, Brian rubbed his chin. "By the way, you look a little familiar, but I know we've never met, and your clippings were minus any photograph which, of course, now I know why. But we do have a lot of Petersons in the area. Any chance you have relatives up here? Or maybe it's just the Swedish look, but I'm feeling a sense of déjà vu. You know…that reporter's gut feeling?" He looked at her expectantly.

Jessie quickly mulled over her options. *Uh-oh. How much do I reveal? If he discovers, later, I was hired on half-truths, he could fire me.* Maybe it was time to lay her cards on the table.

"To my knowledge, Mr. Mason, I haven't any relatives in this area, although we could all be kin to a distant ancestor. As you say, my name and appearance resemble the Swedish culture. My mother, though, is Irish, so I take after my dad." Jessie chuckled. "I was supposed to be a boy at birth, so it was a nasty shock for my parents when I showed up, *and* a big disappointment for my father. He made the best of it though, and I became his sidekick." Jessie gazed intently at the man sitting across from her. "Mr. Mason, I cut my eye teeth in at the *Detroit News Press* and printer's ink runs through my veins. You see, my dad is Randall Peterson, CEO of that newspaper."

Noting first the shocked look on Brian's face, followed by a frown, Jessie quickly continued. "Please understand, Mr. Mason, I *earned* my way…I don't intend cashing in on my father's reputation. My entire life has revolved around the newspaper industry, and I'm good at what I do. Just try me."

Jessie opened her briefcase and pulled out a photograph. "This is an example of one of my assignments. I really didn't want to disclose it to you unless necessary, but it's best to get off on the right foot." Handing Brian the picture, Jessie sat back and waited.

Puzzled, Brian stared down at the picture. Why was she showing him a picture of the notorious Sable who was still missing? From the *Detroit News Press* clippings, he knew Jessie had been the reporter on this case and had done a fantastic job. Almost as though...he looked up at her and back down to the photo once more. Then, he saw it. Despite the pouting red lips, raccoon eyes, short black flapper dress, long silver cigarette holder, and jeweled headband encircling her curly red tresses, it was Jessie with her turned-up nose and sparkling blue eyes peeking out through the kohl. At a loss for words, he silently handed the photo back into her waiting hand.

Jessie smiled fondly at the picture. "It's the only known color photo of her, so I hold on to it for safekeeping. It could be dangerous for me in the wrong hands. You've probably seen the black-and-white newspaper photos that were a bit hazy, and that's why the déjà vu feeling. Hopefully, no one else will make the connection unless I was sitting right in front of them." She looked up at Brian. "I'm trusting, Mr. Mason, that you'll keep my identity a secret. There are probably a few people out there who are, let's say, more than just a little disenchanted with me." Jessie pocketed Sable's photo back into her briefcase and waited for his reaction.

Silent, Brian sat back in his chair and stared at her, baffled. What was a woman of this caliber doing sitting right here in his little office? She was *brilliant*—a fearless reporter willing to risk it all! He sat up straight. No, there had to be an angle. In his experience, there always was...especially with women. One of the reasons he'd never married. Women were like cats, sneaky, first rubbing up against you and then scratching you with their claws. Untrustworthy. *So where do I go from here?*

"Ms. Peterson, or may I call you Jessie? You have me at a definite disadvantage. Although I've worked here for fifteen years, you probably know more about the newspaper business than most of us at the *Gazette*. This reporter's position seems like a step backward."

"Mr. Mason—"

"Please, call me Brian. And as I said before, with the miners on strike, animosity is rife. The men are desperate, holding on to the only way of life they've ever known. On the other hand, with the mining companies, it all boils down to the bottom line. You've met our arbitrator, Mitchell O'Brien?" At Jessie's nod, he continued.

"Mitch is one of the best in his field. If *anyone* can end this strike amicably, it'll be him. He knows this area well, and not just geographically. Some of his boyhood friends still work in the mines, so I'm sure it's difficult for him to remain neutral. To top it all, the companies have imported temporary workers from Russia, Germany, and other countries to keep the mines open. Hiring the Scabs, as they call them, has caused a lot of hostility."

Brian eyed Jessie speculatively. "Just so you know, much of the reporting will consist of interviewing both parties, their points of view, desires, and expected outcome. The venues you enter might not be the most appealing, sometimes vulgar, especially the language, mode of dress, and cleanliness. I'm not questioning your ability to handle the job, Jessie. But I can promise you it can, and will be, unsavory at times."

The shrill ringing of his telephone halted any further discussion. Frowning, Brian apologized for the interruption. "Excuse me, Jessie. I told Roberta to hold all my calls, so this must be important."

Untangling the receiver from its cradle, he barked into the transmitter. "Mason, here..." Brian scrambled for some paper, drew a well sharpened pencil from his mug and started writing furiously. "Okay, got it. Thanks for calling, Bert!" He hung up and turned his attention back to Jessie.

"Like I said, things are heating up fast. That was the editor of the *Register* in Marquette. The Michigan National Guard just passed through on the train and are heading this way. Maybe their presence will keep the hotheads in order."

Brian rose and held out his hand. "Well, Jessie, against my better judgment, I guess it's time to welcome you—again. Things might get a little messy, but it'll never be dull. As today is Friday, how about Monday as a starting date? That'll give you time to settle in." He cleared his throat. "But if you need something to do, please feel free to take a few notes on what's happening in your neighborhood. This weekend ought to be interesting!"

Jessie stood and shook Brian's hand, feeling a little overwhelmed. She had certainly expected more of an interrogation. But as he had pointed out, they *were* without a reporter. As she headed for the stairs, he shouted, "And make sure Roberta puts you on the payroll before you leave!" He stuck his head back in the door, walked briskly to his desk, and swinging one leg over the corner, grabbed the telephone. She could hear him spreading the news before she hit the top step.

Bobbie, hearing Jessie's heels clicking down the stairs, checked her watch. The interview lasted one hour. This was a good sign. She looked up expectantly as Jessie came strolling through the door, smiling.

"So?" Bobbie came straight to the point.

"Well, you said you wanted another woman on the staff…" Jessie dropped her case as Bobbie stood up and gave her a big hug.

"Congratulations!" Bobbie's heartfelt enthusiasm poured over Jessie like a water baptism. "Brian can be funny when it comes to women. I peeked into his personal records and found out he's thirty-five, so probably a confirmed bachelor by now." She shrugged. "Maybe he had a bad relationship at one time. I find him interesting, though"—Bobbie sighed—"but he's never looked at me twice."

Then she gave Jessie a shrewd look. "Maybe it's time he had a wake-up call—and *you* could be just the ticket! The good Lord knows, *I've* tried."

Jessie laughed. "Bobbie, I don't even know the man. My mom's been trying to get me hitched for years, but I've managed to evade every effort on her part. What makes you think I'm on the lookout for a husband? That's not why I'm here, so don't get any silly ideas in your head. I just want to do a good job. Who knows, if Brian trusts me as a female reporter, he just might take another look at *you* and see what he's been missing all these years!"

Jessie picked up her briefcase and placed it on Bobbie's desk. "In the meantime, he wants me on the payroll, beginning Monday. Although, he did ask me to keep my eyes and ears open over the weekend. I'm not sure if you heard, but the militia should be here by tonight, camping out by my house." Jessie chuckled. "Hmm, there you go, Bobbie. You just might find a handsome soldier if they stick around long enough."

"Follow the drum? I don't think so. I've had my share of traveling in the past twenty-eight years. It might be isolated up here, but I'm dug in and have *no* desire to move." Bobbie shook her head resolutely. "But I must admit, my biological clock is ticking, and if someone *should* come along…"

"Oh, well." Bobbie turned to the filing cabinet behind her and pulled open the top drawer. Drawing out some forms, she continued. "Anyway, these are for you to sign if you want to get paid. You can sit at my desk and read them over if you like. The *Gazette* pays its employees every second Friday, in the morning, so you have time to visit the bank during lunch if you need to."

Motioning Jessie to sit, Bobbie grabbed a chair from along the wall and sat across from her in case there were any questions. Jessie had just one.

"By the way, Bobbie, what do you know about Mitchell O'Brien?" Jessie's head was bowed as she signed the few documents. Putting the pen down, she glanced over at Bobbie, who had a twinkle in her eye. Jessie felt her face go warm. "Not that I'm interested, of course…"

"Aha…got your eye on old Mitch, have you? I must say you have great taste. He's dedicated to his job, though, hardworking—and just in case you *are* interested, still single at the age of twenty-nine. I know because I checked out his dossier on file with us. He's been in and out of the office in meetings with Brian, and although he's always been nice to me, he's not exactly my type." She looked at Jessie shrewdly. "You know," she said slowly, "I think you two would do well together. Tell me. Did you feel any of that special, ah, zing when you met him?"

What could she say…Jessie knew there was a strong attraction between her and Mitch. Zing? They practically *sizzled*. "Let's just say I'm keeping my options open, as it's a little early in the day to commit to anything."

"And speaking of which," Jessie said, looking at her watch, "he's coming over later to see how the interview went, so I'd better scoot."

Closing her briefcase, Jessie turned again to Bobbie. "Anyway, I told him I might need to vent…and I've got lots of unpacking to do before then—especially now that I'm going to be here for a while." Smiling, she rose from the desk and handed the signed forms to Bobbie.

"Oh, one more thing. Can you tell me how to get a phone installed?"

"Sure, but let me handle it, Jessie. I've got some pull at the telephone office and can probably get one in much sooner than later. If I call today, you should have one in by Tuesday or Wednesday at the latest."

Before heading to the door, Jessie grabbed Bobbie in one more enthusiastic hug. "I can't tell you how much your support means to me, Bobbie. I feel like we're old friends already."

"Me too. Have a good weekend, Jessie. Oh, and say hi to that good-look'n Mitch when you see him!"

Bobbie, humming to herself, practically skipped back to her desk, already looking forward to Monday. Reaching into her top drawer, she pulled out a hand mirror and gazed at her reflection, fluffing her hair as she mused. *Hmm, maybe a new dress and new hairstyle are in order…after all, what harm could it do? Somehow, I feel our little office is about to turn upside down!*

Closing the door softly behind her, Jessie walked slowly to her car and placed her briefcase through the open window. Amazed, stunned, elated—a myriad of emotions jumbled about her head. Ignoring the dust, she leaned up against the hood of her car and closed her eyes, trying to gather her thoughts together, until a blast from a passing freighter jarred her senses. Steering her eyes beyond the long cargo ship, she gazed up at the sweeping hills rising from Portage Lake.

High above, white fluffy clouds floated from peak to peak. As they dissipated, Jessie saw clusters of mining communities running along the ridges, dipping here and there into the valleys. A murky haze floated between them, possibly remnants of the latest train chugging through. The whole area was teeming with life. *And how will I fit in?* Then, without further ado, she joined her briefcase in the car. Checking her watch, she knew there was plenty of time to tidy up the house before Mitch arrived. Pressing her foot on the accelerator, Jessie smiled in anticipation and started the road back home, crossing over the bridge and into Hancock.

Steering around a sharp corner and heading uphill, she saw the bricked five-story Scott Hotel looming in front of her, while next door, the very ornate Kerredge theater publicized its latest entertainment from glassed-in fliers by the entrance.

Humming to herself, she took a left and started down the main street, noticing the merchants with their colorful candy-striped awnings fluttering in the breeze. A red, white, and blue barber pole swirled to her right, where smoking gentlemen enjoyed their cigars outside on wooden benches, waiting their turn for shaves and haircuts.

A delicious fragrance coming from a nearby restaurant made her nose twitch and her stomach growl. Spotting the diner, she saw a large stand-up easel announcing "today's special" for its hungry noontime guests. *One of these days,* she promised herself, *but not today.* Ignoring her protesting stomach, she continued driving through the throngs of busy pedestrians trying to cross the street, dodging autos, delivery wagons, and clanging street cars.

Life is good. Jessie sighed as she climbed the last hill toward home, peacefully thinking all her dreams were about to come true—and, blissfully unaware of the turmoil boiling just one mile beneath the surface.

Arriving home, she'd unpacked her clothes and hung them in the closet. The barn was swept clean of cobwebs, windows gleamed, and the hay bales had been removed. Tonight, she would drive her little auto inside; but for now, she just stood still, admiring her cleaning efforts before heading back to the house and into the kitchen.

Glancing down at her watch, Jessie saw it was almost four o'clock. Smiling, she placed the potted red geranium she'd purchased on the way home on the windowsill above the sink, creating a splash of color against the pale walls.

Mounting a little stool, she reached up for the dishes, removed them from inside the cabinet and placed them on the counter below. Using a wet rag to wipe down the inside, she hummed to herself with every swipe of the cloth.

Climbing higher to reach the top shelf, Jessie gave it one more swat with an old Turkish towel before feeling a familiar, yet unfamiliar sensation, tingling up her legs. *Now, what?* Closing the cupboard door with a click, she climbed down just as the floor began to rock, shaking the foundation of the house and her heart, as well.

Grabbing the edge of the sink, she clenched her fists, and closing her eyes, whispered a silent prayer. As the thundering vibrations pounded the house, Jessie slipped down to the floor, bracing herself against a cabinet. Drawing her knees close to her body, she wrapped her arms around them for protection.

Above the turbulence, Jessie could hear windows rattling, glass breaking and the thuds of falling objects. The impact seemed to jar every bone in her body, and she tried not to panic by counting. One, two, three…ten seconds.

Then—an eerie silence.

With a racing heart, she waited expectantly for another blow, but except for one more bump, all was still.

Taking a deep breath, Jessie lifted her head and opened her eyes. Then, leaning on the cabinet for support, she pushed herself up on shaky legs to survey the damage.

Her once-spotless kitchen was now in shambles. Trembling, she made a grab for a teetering teacup at the edge of the counter but missed as it tumbled to the floor with a crash. Papers from the table, mixed with specs of ceiling plaster, were scattered across the floor, while millions of dust particles danced in the sunbeam streaming through the kitchen window. Her new geranium lay crushed in the bottom of the deep sink, its petals looking blood red against the white lacquer.

Jessie's dreamy day was over—*this* was a nightmare.

Coughing and sneezing in the floating dust, she stepped gingerly over the cut glass, grabbing a piece of the now-broken broom. Reaching over the sink, she pushed up the window and jammed the wooden dowel under the sash. As fresh air filtered in, the fluffy white curtains began to ruffle in the breeze, and through the window, Jessie could hear crows cawing as they settled back into the tall poplar trees.

Bewildered, she sagged against the sink, wondering what had just happened and where to start when a pounding on the back door jolted her into action. Ignoring the crunch beneath her shoes, she fled through the mudroom, opened the door, and fell into Mitch's waiting arms.

CHAPTER 5

Mitch's day had turned sour. He was tired and dejected. With news of the militia's imminent arrival, all negotiations had ceased with both sides stalking out of the conference room. Although still far from a compromise, he wished the governor would've waited a little longer before sending in the troops. Now it was only a matter of time before the fireworks began.

Shifting his thoughts to Jessie Peterson, Mitch sped around the corner, urging his car to go a little faster as the Johns' house came into view. Pulling into the driveway, he jumped out with unexpected enthusiasm. Suddenly, he didn't feel so tired. After a quick shower, shave, and a change of clothes, he'd head next door.

Whistling a jaunty tune, he leaped up the front steps, practically falling through the door as Irma Johns opened it to welcome him. Grabbing her arms, he continued to whistle his spirited tune as he waltzed her around the living room.

"*Well*, that's as fine an entrance I've seen in a long time! And you're early too. You must be happy about something." Irma laughed as she stopped and fanned herself with a lacy white handkerchief. Although boarders often came through her door, Mitch had quickly become one of the family. "I take it negotiations went well?"

Before he could reply, a clamor rose from above as a young teenage girl sprinted down the stairs, jumped from the second step and vaulted into his arms. "Mitch, you're home!"

Giving the girl a big hug before untangling himself, Mitch chuckled as he set her down. "Josie, what a welcome!" He watched as the high-spirited Josephine, alias Josie, alias Jo (as she preferred) danced around him, her bright carroty braids bouncing on her shoulders. As an only child, Mitch had adopted her as his little sister, adoring her tan freckled face, lively enthusiasm and, sometimes, mischievous antics. She and Jessie both had sparkling personalities. And speaking of Jessie…

"In answer to your question, Irma, an agreement has *not* been reached. I truly wish I had better news for you and Tom. The whole meeting broke up fast when they heard the militia was coming." Mitch checked his watch. "They should be here by tonight, camping in that big empty field south of Highway 41. In the meantime, I'm heading next door to discuss this with Jessie Peterson, the *Gazette's* new reporter, who, by the way, turned out to be a *woman*."

Mitch felt his ears burning as Irma eyed him speculatively but, thankfully, didn't say a word. Josie, however, wouldn't let this juicy tidbit go to waste and started in on Mitch, shaking his arm.

"A woman newspaper reporter? How old is she? Where is she from? Is she pretty? Mitch, can I go and meet her?" Jo stopped to take a breath, dashing to the door, when her mother hushed her.

"For pity's sake, girl, stop your jabbering and give Mitch time to breathe! He just came home and is probably tired. Let him rest." Irma clucked her tongue and shook her head at her daughter.

"No, it's okay, Irma." Mitch turned to Josie with a smile. "Jessie is probably in her midtwenties, has gold, curly hair and a bubbling personality." He flicked Jo's nose with his finger. "I guess you could say, she's a lot like you."

The front door opened, admitting a rather stout gentleman with closed eyes and a long white stick bouncing before him.

"Daddy!" Josie skipped across the floor and grabbed her father's arm, pulling him close. "Mitch is home, and guess what? Never mind—you'll *never* guess, so I'll tell you. The new reporter living next door is a woman! Of all things! *Please* say I can go over and meet her. Mitch says she's bubbly—just like me."

Her father turned his sightless eyes toward his daughter and laughed. "Well, now…I don't know if that's a good thing or not."

After removing her husband's straw hat, and hanging it on the hall tree, Irma placed a warm kiss upon his cheek. "Welcome home, Thomas. Come. Sit down and let Mitch tell you the latest news."

Thomas allowed her to guide him to Mitch and reached out to shake his hand.

"Boy, am I glad to have you here, Mitch! I heard some very disturbing news today. But first, let's sit at the dining room table where we can be more comfortable—*and* you can also tell me about our new neighbor. By the sound of it, she must be something special as Josie's ready to burst!" Thomas grinned as he used his cane, tapping his way through the living room and into the dining area. Before sitting down, he turned to his wife. "Mama, if you'd be so kind, please get us both a cuppa tea. And you, daughter, be a good girl and go help your mother."

Dejectedly, Josie left the men and slumped into the kitchen after her mom, but not before giving Mitch one last beseeching peek over her shoulder. His wink promised more talk later. With a big grin, she obeyed her father with a little more spring to her step.

As Thomas waved both women out the door, he felt for a chair, pulled it out, and sat down, placing his cane alongside for easy access.

"Nothing like a hot cup of tea to settle the nerves, right? Besides, it gives the womenfolk something to do while we talk, man to man." Thomas's ruddy face was anxious as he turned to Mitch. "Now, while I was down at Molly's Pub sharing a pint with my friends, someone came running in shouting about the militia. His panicky announcement stirred up a big hornet's nest, I can tell you! Before I left, rumors were flying of lockdowns, curfews, and armed guards. Got the boys riled up something *fierce*, Mitch! Not a good thing." Tom shook his head in dismay. "Many of the guys went right home to protect their families. Others just talked about getting their *own* army together." He looked at Mitch, expectantly. "So. What can we expect? Do we have a good reason to be worried?"

Mitch rubbed his jaw. "Truthfully, Tom, I don't know much more than you do. According to the governor, the whole idea of a militia was to *keep* the peace, not start riots. But some hot heads will probably use it as a good excuse to cause trouble. You, above most, have a personal interest in the outcome. I know you're glad to be alive, but if safety issues had been addressed earlier, you might still have…uh-oh."

Mitch felt a sudden vibration beneath the house and held his breath as a quake-like tremble suddenly turned into roaring thunder. Windows rattled, walls shook, and rafters sent showers of dust and wood below. Books and nick knacks, falling from the corner cabinet, scattered across the floor. Hearing screams and breaking glass, Mitch jumped up, plunged through the fallen debris, and headed toward the kitchen.

"Tom, stay where you are! I'll check on the women!" Mitch shouted above the mayhem. As he reached the door, he found it jammed, the hinges bent from the jarring impact. "Irma! Josie! Are you alright? Answer me!" He jiggled the door once more.

On the other side, Mitch could hear Josie crying and Irma trying to console her as Jo's wailing grew louder. Then, as quickly as the mayhem began, the commotion stopped. It was over.

His ears echoed in the sudden silence, and he tried pushing the door open with his shoulder.

"It's no use, Mitch. It's stuck." Irma's muffled voice came from the other side. "We'll try going out the back door and meet you in front. Just make sure Thomas stays put." Mitch could hear her coaxing Josie toward the back of the kitchen. "Josephine Helen, you stop your crying and be a big girl for your mama. You're just fine. Come, your daddy needs us."

Making sure Tom was still seated and unhurt, Mitch headed toward the front door, cautiously stepping over the cluttered floor. Waiting for Irma and Josie to round the corner of the house, he leaned up against the porch rail, breathing in deeply. Although he'd experienced these tremors in the past, it had been a while, and his heart was still thudding. He couldn't imagine how Jessie…

"Oh, no…Jessie!" Mitch burst out as he remembered the little vibrations she had experienced yesterday, which must have been a forerunner of today's tremor. *How* could he have forgotten to tell her? She was probably terrified!

Just as Irma and Josie appeared, he bolted off the porch, sprinted across the yard, and leaped over the dividing fence. Mitch tore across the remaining grass, mounted the three sagging back steps in one bound and pounded on the heavy wooden door, scattering gray chips of paint into the air. It was only a second later when Jessie flew through the door and into his arms.

"Mitch! Oh, Mitch…"

"Shh, I know, Jess, I know…"

Mitch held her trembling body close, something he had wanted to do since yesterday, *but* under different circumstances. Still, it gave him a good excuse to touch her, feeling the warmth of her body and sweet clean scent of her soft shiny hair, although now sprinkled with bits of white specs.

Rocking her back and forth, he whispered encouragingly until her shaking subsided.

Jessie looked up with wide eyes.

"Then, it *wasn't* my imagination…I mean, the vibrations I felt yesterday? They really *did* happen, Mitch?"

"Come, Jess, let's sit down, and I'll try to explain." Putting his arm around her shoulders, Mitch led her to the top step where they plopped down, both appreciating the comforting warmth of the afternoon sun.

"Jess, I'm so sorry you had to go through this, alone. I should have explained yesterday when you mentioned the tremor, but I was still in shock finding you here and totally forgot." He shrugged. "Not that it would have made any difference. You can't prepare for these, as each time is different, and some are much worse than others." Reaching up, he picked off a few plaster chips from her hair as he explained the phenomenon of an 'air blast,' the danger of timbers and massive rocks, sometimes falling onto the miners and burying them alive.

Mitch stood up, pulling Jessie with him. "I'll answer more of your questions later, but first, let's go inside and check out the damages. Although the blasts are scary, on the surface they seldom do anything major, except for settling the building's foundation an inch or so." He laughed. "But there's usually a mess to clean up afterward."

Holding tight to his hand, Jessie led Mitch through the back door and into the mudroom, noticing this area was almost free of any damage. A few towels had fallen and lay crinkled at her feet, but her washer stood upright and there was no sign of leakage in the bathroom, which meant, thank goodness, her water tank above was still intact. But her kitchen…

Mitch gaped at the scene in front of him. Dropping Jessie's hand, he slowly entered the room, stepping over the jumbled mixture of broken plates, glasses, cups, and paper, all laced with an icing of plaster. As he gazed up at the ceiling, one last shower of snowy specs fell upon his shoulders. Brushing them off, he grinned at Jessie. "At least I know now that you're not turning white from fright." He pointed to her head.

Jessie picked her way across the room and gazed at her reflection in the cracked mirror against the wall. Laughing, she shook her head, and dozens of white particles flew into the air. Picking up two fluffy towels from the bathroom floor, she handed one to Mitch, then briskly rubbed her head, freeing the embedded debris from her hair.

Setting a couple of chairs upright, Mitch swatted them with the towel. "Come and sit, Jess. After the blast hit, I thought of you and how terrified *you* must have been. I've been through a few of these, in my early days, but this is one of the worst hits I've felt in a long time. The collapsing shaft must have been close to our homes."

Mitch, using his thumb to rub off some white powder from his watch, checked the time with a shocked look on his face. "Jess, I can't believe it's been only a few minutes since the blast." His voice grew urgent. "I *really* need to head back. Irma and Josie sounded fine, but Thomas has special needs and I left him sitting at the dining room table." Scooting his chair back, Mitch stood up.

"I tell you what, Jess. Come and meet your new neighbors. Then, we'll all head back here and help you clean up. I promise." Mitch looked about the kitchen, assessing the damage and what they'd need for repairs, then reached out his hand. Still a bit shaky, Jessie took it to rise, thankful to have a little more time with him.

CHAPTER 6

Irma and Josie stood silently on the front porch, watching two people emerge from the house next door, playfully brushing each other off as they walked across the grass. Dancing with excitement, Josie, leaning over the rail, was anxious to meet the mysterious newspaper lady.

Mitch, much relieved at seeing the women safe on the porch, waved and increased his stride, his hand clasping Jessie's, dragging her right along with him. Slightly out of breath, they climbed the few steps to the landing where Mitch quickly introduced her. "Irma, I'd like you to meet Jessie Peterson, the new reporter for the *Gazette*." He quickly turned to Jessie, dismay written all over his face. "I'm so sorry, Jess. I assume you *are* the new reporter. In all this mess, I forgot to ask how the interview went."

Jessie reassured him with a big smile. "Not to worry, Mitch. And yes, they hired me."

Mitch released a sigh of relief before quickly turning to Irma. "Jessie's offered to help us put things back in order and, of course, I promised we'd help her too."

Smirking inside at his pleading look, Irma held back a chuckle. "Mitch, you'll have to let go of Jessie's hand if you want me to shake it."

Mitch, gazing down and seeing their fingers still entwined, turned red, and quickly let his drop.

"It's a pleasure to meet you, Ms. Peterson." Irma took Jessie's hand, liking the honest direct look she received. "And yes, we certainly could use a little help." She reached out and protectively placed her arm around Josie. "This is my daughter, Josephine, but she'll tell you to call her Josie. She can be a big help, too…when not getting into mischief." Irma gazed fondly at her daughter, who was red with embarrassment.

"Ah, Ma." Then, looking up, Josie was relieved to see a twinkle of understanding in Jessie's sparkling blue eyes.

Jessie smiled warmly at each of them, taking their hands in her own. "Please call me Jessie." She looked inquiringly at Irma. "If that's alright with you, Mrs. Johns? After all, Josie's *almost* a grown woman." Understandingly, this remark brought a beaming response from the young girl and approval from her mother.

"Ir-r-ma?" a petulant voice shouted from within the house.

"We're coming, dear!" Answering the call, Irma turned to Jessie. "That's my Thomas. It's only during times like this that he gets peevish." She padded Jessie's arm reassuringly before herding the small group together over the threshold and into the living room.

Jessie entered their house, finding it in disarray, the littered floor mirroring her own. There'd be a lot of cleanups ahead, but right now her focus was on the white-haired gentleman fidgeting at the dining room table. She was confused until noticing a cane lying on the floor that was out of his reach.

"Come. Meet my husband." Irma cautiously led the way across the room and standing behind him, squeezed his shoulders with both hands. "Thomas, this is Jessie Peterson, the new reporter who lives next door." Irma turned her head toward Jessie. "And please, call us Thomas and Irma. I'm sure we'll be seeing quite a bit of each other." She glanced behind her at Mitch and gave him a big smile before turning back to her husband. "Jessie has offered to help clean up this mess, but if you don't mind, Thomas, I'd like her to get acquainted with you, first. Maybe you can give her some insight into all this chaos." Irma bent down, retrieved his cane from below and stood it next to his chair. Placing a quick peck on his cheek, she headed over to Mitch and Josie, who were already trying to put things in order.

Left alone with the blind man, Jessie hovered above, anxiously wondering what to do next. But Thomas came to the rescue.

"So it's Jessie, is it?" He gazed up at her through tightly closed eyes, as though he could see through the lids. "I always like to know who I'm talking to. Do you mind if I see your face with my hands?"

Moved by this unusual request, Jessie swallowed hard before kneeling beside him. "Thomas, I'd be *honored* for you see me." Taking his hands, she placed them on each side of her jaw, and with precision, he moved them about, feeling her chin, nose, eyebrows, high boned cheeks, and forehead, before gently touching her soft curly locks above.

Smiling, he spoke to her softly. "Well, well, now I know why Mitch seems smitten with you." He touched her shoulder lightly. "Please, sit down and keep me company."

Jessie stood up, blushing, even though she knew Thomas couldn't see her. Peeking across the room at Mitch, she saw he was out of range and not privy to their conversation. Feeling a little more at ease, she rounded the table and sat directly across from Thomas.

Irma, watching her husband getting acquainted with Jessie, looked up at Mitch and nodded. Mitch grinned with satisfaction and turned back to reshelving the fallen books.

Facing Jessie, Thomas folded his hands on the table. "Let's tackle the most direct issue first…my blindness. Don't be afraid to ask me anything. In fact, sometimes it helps discussing my disability with others. Addressing a handicap up front makes everyone feel more comfortable. And you can call me Tom if you like. Mitch always does even though Irma calls me Thomas." He grinned at her, his friendly smile lighting up his weather-beaten face.

Jessie smiled at his bravado. "I must admit, I *am* curious, Tom. I assumed you were blind from birth."

"Nope," Tom replied with a shake of his head. "I was injured in a mining blast some twenty years ago, long before Josie was born. That's when I lost my eyesight, and along with some internal injuries, wasn't expected to live. But miraculously I did, and Josie came along six years after that, another miracle. I admit, not being able to see my baby growing up has been frustrating, but Josie loves her daddy, just as he is, and in some ways, I'm more in tune with her thoughts, the tone of her voice, and her concerns than I might be otherwise. No, Jessie, I'm a blessed man to be here when I should have died. I've had my Irma, my daughter, and many friends to see me through the difficult times."

Jessie spoke, hesitantly. "Tom, I know it's probably old hat, and maybe you don't like to rehash it, but from a reporter's point of view, I'd like to hear your version of the accident."

"No, it's okay, Jessie. What happened was a long time ago…and to be fair, some of the working conditions *have* changed for the better. Back then, candles were all we had for light, whether on our helmets or placed by a drilling site. The mining companies purchased them by the thousands instead of installing electricity in the lower shafts." Tom gave a snort. "They called it being 'frugal.' Nowadays, miners have the brighter carbide lamps on their helmets. But like candles, if the carbides go out by default, you're lost in total darkness, and you need to *feel* your way out to the entrance. A few miners have made it, but others, losing their bearings, have fallen into deep pits. But candles or carbides—it makes no difference when the light goes out. *Black is black*."

"As for my story"—Thomas shifted in his chair—"it must have been, oh, about twelve thirty, just after midnight. The shift had been quiet. For protection, we always had two men working together in case of an emergency. But on that night, we were very lucky—there were three of us—Eli, Jake, and me.

"The blasting was going well until we drilled the last hole. We put in the charge, lit the fuse, and backed away, waiting for it to ignite. But nothing happened. It was a dud. Jake left us to locate another fuse so we could try again. While he was gone, Eli and I went back to prepare the hole, and that's the last thing I remember. As soon as the old fuse was touched, it must have exploded, crushing us up against the wall."

Thomas leaned comfortably back into his chair. "I heard I was unconscious for several days. We both lost our eyes, but Eli also lost an arm and part of his other hand. We also had numerous internal injuries, cuts, and bruises. But I was the lucky one. Although the newspaper was doubtful of our recovery, I made it through."

Turning around, Tom called for Mitch to come over. "Along with safety, there are several other issues that need to be resolved, especially the introduction of the one-man drill."

Mitch sat down next to Tom and took over the conversation.

"The mining companies highly favor this drill, Jessie. Although working alone could be dangerous, it would decrease the number of miners, thus lessening their labor costs. Second, the efficiency of the drill would increase production and profits for the companies and their stockholders. It's a win all situation for them."

Mitch leaned across the table. "Right now, the union is also fighting for higher wages, shorter work periods, which are now ten-to-twelve-hour shifts, six days a week, and elimination of child labor. The miners have no rights voicing their concerns and can be fired for the least negative comment about the mining companies.

Jessie's forehead wrinkled in confusion. "But, Mitch, how can the mines be operating with the strike on? I've seen trains loaded with ore and men with lunch pails walking toward the shaft houses."

Mitch grimaced. "That's a big part of the problem, Jess. Some desperate miners, out of money, tore up their union cards and headed back to work. The other strikers feel they're deserters. Although deputies have been on hand to escort the men to work, they can't be at all mine entrances all the time. Several workers have been attacked, even away from the mines, just for carrying lunch pails!"

He shook his head. "Now, requested by the mining companies and local sheriffs, the whole Michigan National Guard is en route. Who knows what will happen?"

Standing up, Mitch reached for Jessie's hand, pulling her to her feet and with a forced laugh, placed a heavy hand on Tom's shoulder. "Hey, there's nothing we can do about that right now, so let's say we put this house back together, then try to clean up Jessie's."

CHAPTER 7

Before closing her back door, Jessie gazed at the diffused red sun slipping beneath the horizon, spreading its gold, pink, and mauve colors against the deepening blue sky. Through the waning light, a full moon already visible overhead cast a filmy white glow on her watch as she checked the time. Ten o'clock. *And all's well,* she thought. Lifting her face to the night, a cool gentle breeze caressed her flushed cheeks with the first promise of fall, but for now she was thankful for the longer summer days.

Locking the door behind her, Jessie gazed fondly at her freshly cleaned home with appreciation before turning off the lights and heading up the narrow staircase, every part of her aching body crying out for rest.

Beginning with her interview at the *Gazette*, which now seemed eons away, her day had been filled with anxiety, excitement, and joy, followed by pure terror, before settling into peace and extreme tiredness. Jessie yawned sleepily as she rolled up her dirty clothes and placed them on the chair. She'd deal with them in the morning. Donning a long silky nightgown, she slipped into bed, drawing the soft blankets around her, and snuggling deep within them. Morning would come soon enough with its own challenges. *Although what could be more surprising than today...* Her last thoughts were positive as she drifted off.

Suddenly interrupted, Jessie woke up with a start, her heart racing. Disoriented, she sat up and leaned groggily against the pillows. *Was it just a bad dream?* Turning her head toward the window, she saw a faint glow of flickering lights just down the road. Throwing back the covers, she rose shakily from the bed and staggered to the window. She pushed up the sash and peered into the darkness, hearing the muffled voices of men as shadows appeared and disappeared in the wavering light. White apparitions with circus peaks reflected the moon's milky light as dozens of tents now occupied the empty field close to her home.

The militia had arrived.

Instead of feeling secure in their presence, Jessie felt a shiver of apprehension trickling down her spine. Premonition or reporter's gut feeling, she knew this wasn't a good thing.

Raising her arms to close the window, she saw a bright flash of light before hearing an explosive boom. Mesmerized, she watched as three or four more flares lit up the inky black sky before realizing the loud resonant blasts were gunshots.

The party had begun.

With difficulty, she pulled back on the reins urging her to jump into the fray. Although her heart tugged her forward, she would be foolhardy to wade into an unknown sortie and be caught in a crossfire of flying bullets. *No*, she decided, slamming the window down and pulling the curtain across. Sacrificing her life was *not* part of her contract with the *Gazette*! When the veil of darkness lifted with the dawn, she'd be ready. But for now, she crawled back into bed, willing to give sleep time to heal her foggy brain and tired body.

Waking to silence in the early morning, Jessie tossed back the warm blankets and sitting at the edge of the bed, slid her bare feet into a pair of white fluffy mules. Reaching for her furry pink robe, she slipped her arms through the long sleeves and pulled the belt snugly around her. Padding to the window, she drew the curtain aside, expecting to see bodies scattered across the road or in the ditches. However, the military encampment was completely hidden by a heavy mist of the cool autumn morning.

Curious, Jessie pushed up the window, but except for a few twittering birds, all was still. The heavy air sucked into the room was thick with the pungent scent of dried leaves mixed in with the earthy smell of damp soil. Breathing in deeply, she felt invigorated, excited, and ready to tackle her first unofficial assignment.

Quickly throwing on a sleeveless black shift, she reached down and tied the laces of her black and white oxfords before racing down the stairs and into the kitchen. It took but a minute to wolf down half of a peanut butter sandwich with a gulp of cold milk, before running for the door. Stopping to fluff up her curls, she stared at her garb, satisfied her bland attire wouldn't draw notice, not realizing her natural beauty was enough honey to catch the bees.

Grabbing a notebook and pencil, Jessie placed them into a canvas tote before starting up the road toward the military camp. Looking down, she noticed the dewy brown dirt already clinging to the soles and up the sides of her shoes and was thankful she hadn't scrapped the grubby pair before now. *You never know when you might need them,* her mother's voice echoed in her ear. Jessie grinned. *Thanks, Mom!*

Fading into the fog, she walked toward the encampment and shivered as the cool mist slid down her bare arms. Along the road, sparkling spider webs, connecting plant to plant, waited for their unsuspecting catch of the morning. Edging the ditches were blue Iron Weed, snowy white Queen Ann's Lace and Black-Eyed Susan's with their golden petals, adding splashes of color along the dusty road. Robins called to each other, and Meadow Larks sang, unseen, in the veiled grasses.

Walking further into the haze, Jessie glanced over her shoulder, finding her house now obliterated behind her. She heard a distant chugging of engines, muffled by the murky air, and then low voices penetrating the gloom as the encampment came into focus. Hundreds of uniformed men were busily pounding stakes into the ground, reenforcing their makeshift canvas city, while supply vehicles unloaded their cache into the larger storage tents.

Jessie paused at the nearest entrance where two soldiers stood deep in conversation guarding the road and the field. Putting on her sunniest smile, she called out to them as she approached.

"Good morning!"

Noticing their visitor for the first time, the guards walked warily her way. The first to approach took off his hat and eyed her suspiciously, but his partner came forward amicably.

"Good morning, miss." He touched the rim of his hat with a brief salute. "I'm Corporal Cameron, and this is Private Richards. Is there something we can help you with?"

"Thank you, Corporal, Private, and yes, there is. My name is Jessie Peterson, and I'm a reporter for the *Daily Mining Gazette*. Yesterday, we heard you were coming, so if you don't mind, I'd like to ask a few questions." Jessie noticed the men were dressed in full khaki uniform—rifle and bayonet included.

"Ms. Peterson, that would be up to Sergeant Andrews, our present bivouac commander." Corporal Cameron raised his hand to his forehead and searched the grounds before pointing to a larger tent to the East. "You'll find him in that area, miss." He turned to Private Richards. "Please escort Ms. Peterson to the command tent and then return to your post."

"Yes, *sir*!" Private Richard saluted his corporal, and his eyes scanned Jessie from head to toe, hesitating before questioning her.

"Ah, miss, you're not carrying any dangerous weapons, are you?" He looked sheepish having to ask the question. But apart from physically searching her, it was the best he could do.

Jessie's tinkling laugh was as sparkling as the dewy grass, prompting the two men to take another look. Even with her drab mode of dress, her refinement was obvious through her confidence, stature, and intelligence.

"I promise you, gentlemen, I'm harmless," Jessie said with a reassuring smile and purposefully started forward.

Private Richards, with a backward glance at his corporal, skipped to catch up with her. Several heads swiveled their way, and conversations halted as they watched the unusual pair walk across the grounds. The private, seeing their interest, felt his male ego inch up a bit as he escorted this beautiful woman into the camp.

Jessie, with her mind clear from a restful night's sleep, mentally surveyed the encampment, taking notes with her eyes. Despite the previous night's fireworks, the camp's operations seemed to be normal. In one end of the field, soldiers practiced marching while others bent over make-shift kitchens outside a mess tent. She could smell the remains of their breakfast, and...ah, yes, horses, corralled in the farthest corner of the field, next to a few motorized vehicles and a large wagon.

"Please stay here, miss, while I inform Sergeant Andrews of your presence." Private Richards halted in front of a large brown tent and pulled back on the canvas flap. Taking a quick glance at Jessie, making sure she was secure, he entered the large enclosure and closed the flap behind him.

Jessie, hearing murmurs from inside, prepared herself for either a welcome or a rebuke. Refusals were often a part of her job, but one couldn't take them personally or you'd lose before you started.

The tent flap reopened. Private Richards held back the canvas, allowing a tall slender gentleman to exit. Where the private had none, this man sported an insignia of higher rank on the upper part of his left sleeve. Jessie also noticed the slight graying of his black sideburns and thick salt and pepper mustache, evidence of his maturity. Gazing at him, she saw the look of authority on his face when his cool gray eyes held hers for a moment as through assessing her real motive for entering the campground. He turned to Private Richards.

"Private, you're dismissed. You may return to your duties."

Acknowledging this command, Private Richards came to attention, saluted, and taking a quick last look at Jessie, strolled off across the field.

Jessie sighed in relief. At least she wasn't being booted out of the camp. Yet. A thought occurred to her, though. Did one offer a handshake to a soldier? Especially an officer?

"Ms. Peterson?" He extended his hand. "I'm Sergeant Andrews. I'm told you're a newspaper reporter?" He scanned her up and down. "Forgive my skepticism, but in my experience, that's highly unlikely, especially, if I might say, one with your looks."

With a rueful smile, Jessie shook his hand. "Thank you...I *think*. But in this case, your men were correct. The *Daily Mining Gazette* hired me just last week. Interviewing you is my first assignment up here, although I've been a reporter in Detroit for the past four years."

Sergeant Andrews silently took in her honest face, steady blue eyes, and erect posture. He nodded to himself, satisfied. "Ms.

Peterson, I understand you have some questions? Perhaps we can walk the grounds together." As a gentleman, he offered his arm to Jessie. "Shall we?"

Jessie took the distended elbow, feeling the rough material of his uniform beneath her fingers. Walking sedately, they headed away from the command tent.

"Sergeant Andrews, although you can't see it, my house is just down the road. Last night I awoke to your arrival, seeing the lights and movements from my window." Jessie looked up at him. "A few minutes later, I heard…gunfire?"

He turned to her, a wry smile crinkling his face, making him look younger than when he first appeared. "You don't miss much. What you heard last night, Ms. Peterson, was just a little *welcome* from a couple of locals shooting off their guns." He shrugged. "It was to be expected, I suppose. But we'd hoped to get a bit more settled in before any showdowns. As it was, the only things they frightened were the horses, and luckily, they were already penned in."

By now, they were alongside the corral. Removing her hand, Jessie leaned up against the fence, watching the soldiers drill their mounts. The bonding between man and the chestnut beasts was obvious as hairy noses were fondly scratched, and big ears rubbed. But the horses, knowing their masters, responded instantly to their commands.

Jessie reached into her tote and pulled out the notebook and pencil. Although Mitch had explained the presence of the Guard, Jessie still wanted more information. "Sergeant Andrews, from what I hear, the miners are getting desperate. Knowing you were coming has just added fuel to their fire. They're *scared*, not knowing what to expect from you."

Sergeant Andrews frowned. "Ms. Peterson, our purpose is to keep the peace until the issues are resolved." With a sweep of his arm, he waved Jessie back toward the command post. "We'll be guarding the mine entrances, helping any miners who *want* to work. We'll be a buffer between the strikers and the workers, to protect—*not* attack." He stopped suddenly, his expression serious. "Believe me, no matter what you've heard, we're not here to start a war. It's not our intent to injure or arrest, that being left up to the local authorities." He looked down at Jessie, who was busy taking notes. "It's our understanding the mining companies and sheriff's department have hired private guards from New York to be enforcers. You might want to confirm that with the local police."

By now, they were back at the big tent.

"Now, if you'll excuse me, Ms. Peterson, Major Washburn is expected today, and I have lots of organizing to do. I wish you well in your new position." Clicking his heels together, he bowed and headed in the opposite direction.

With this abrupt dismissal, Jessie stood uncertainly for a moment, perusing the camp, before Private Richards hurried to her side.

"Miss, I'd be happy to escort you back to the road. You'll have to excuse the sergeant, but he's under a lot of pressure right now."

Jessie looked understandingly into the private's eyes. "No, that's fine. And you don't have to apologize for him. I really appreciated the time he *gave* me. And yes, Private, thank you for your escort."

With his chest puffed up, Private Richards led her back across the grounds to the exit, fully aware of the second looks they were getting. As they approached the road, Corporal Cameron walked briskly toward them.

"Ms. Peterson, pending approval of Major Washburn, Sergeant Andrews said you're welcome to return for more information. Please check back with us in another day or so and we'll verify his consent."

Jessie, pleased at this offer, nodded. "Corporal, please convey my gratitude to Sergeant Andrews. I'm sure the *Gazette* will want to keep up on your activities." She enveloped them in a beaming smile. "And many thanks to both of you for helping me today." With a wave of her hand, she mentally dismissed them and started back down the road, unaware of being watched until she disappeared into the mist.

CHAPTER 8

"You wanna go *where*?" Mitch was stumped, staring at Jessie in horror as well as disbelief.

Now, why does that sound so familiar? Jessie mused.

It was Saturday. Mitch had arrived shortly after lunch hoping to find Jessie alone and needing some company—mainly his. Expecting her to be anxious about her new job, he found her competently sitting at the table writing an article for the *Gazette*. So much for pining away for his attention. Swallowing his bruised ego, he helped himself to a cup of coffee and leaned up against the kitchen counter, watching her write furiously.

Finally, satisfied with the contents, Jessie put down her pencil and grinned at Mitch. "Sorry about that, but I have to get this finished before Monday."

Mitch pulled up a chair, and looking at his watch, raised his eyebrows at Jessie. "May I ask what you found to write about in the last sixteen hours? Here I thought you might want to visit the National Guard with me this afternoon and do some interviewing for your first article."

Jessie smiled unabashedly at Mitch. "Beat you to it! I was up early this morning, walked up to the camp and spoke to the sergeant in charge. I was especially curious about the gun shots I heard last night."

Mitch frowned as he put down his coffee cup and leaned forward, his attention caught. "Gunfire? I didn't hear anything, but I must admit I'm a sound sleeper. Are you sure that's what you heard?"

Jessie nodded. "As the sergeant put it, a couple of locals were just warning them that the militia was being watched. But whatever, it put the militia on their guard, so to speak. Thankfully, no one was injured."

Standing up, she walked over to the counter and, after pouring herself a cup of the hot brew, sat down across from him. Holding the cup in both hands, she blew on the steaming liquid and gazed intently over the rim.

"Mitch, I really need to get some firsthand information, and if anyone can make it possible, it would be you." She took a deep breath and continued.

"I want to go down into the mine and see the working conditions, interview some of the miners and check out the infamous one-man drill."

In the middle of another sip, Mitch choked on his coffee before slamming the cup on the table, sloshing the liquid over the brim.

"You wanna go *where?*" Mitch stared at her in disbelief.

"You heard me. I need to know what I'm writing about. Good reporters need firsthand experience." Jessie was insistent.

"Come on, Jess, you're being unrealistic. First, there's no way they'd let a woman down there. Second, just trying to enter the shaft itself is pure folly. Even with the Guards monitoring the site, someone could take a pot shot at you." Mitch, with a negative shake of his head, dismissed her request. "Nope. Sorry, Jess, but it's for your own safety." He took another sip of his coffee, dismissing her request with a wave of his hand. "I'm sure, though, all parties would be more than happy to be interviewed—*aboveground*. You'll just have to settle for the information they give you. If you like, I can even arrange for you to sit in on one of our meetings."

Gazing down at his cup, Mitch neglected to see the glare of ire and challenge in Jessie's sparkling blue eyes.

Silently she stood up, turning her back on Mitch. Bringing her cup to the counter, Jessie slowly poured the coffee down the drain, taking her time and a few deep breaths as well. Placing her mug in the sink, she turned to him with a look of disappointment, as well as betrayal.

"Mitch, as you come to know me better, you'll discover I never *'settle'* for anything. If you won't help me, then I'll find another way."

Jessie spoke softly but had a glint in her eye that always made her dad apprehensive. Unfortunately, Mitch was not yet privy to her stubborn will.

Leaning back against the counter, Jessie tried to make light of the thickening atmosphere. "So whatever happened to Sir Galahad? I thought you wanted to be my knight in shining armor."

Mitch calmly set his mug on the table and rose, unsmiling, from his chair. Facing Jessie, the grim look on his face brooked no argument.

"And that's exactly what I *am* being, Jess, saving you from pitfalls and dangers you couldn't possibly imagine." He stood before her, gazing at her eyes, nose, and mouth before bending his head and placing a soft kiss on her lips. He heard Jessie inhale sharply. Knowing it was time to leave before engaging in a battle of wits that could injure their blossoming relationship, Mitch headed toward the door with a parting comment. "Believe me, Jess, if there was any way…but please don't ask me to *deliberately* place you in a life-threatening situation." With that he walked down the hall to the front porch, closing the door quietly behind him.

In a stupor, Jessie remained where she was, digesting both his kiss and his refusal to help. Her thoughts floundered, battling back and forth. Okay, Mitch was probably right about the danger part, but that hadn't stopped her before. Now an unknown story lay hidden deep below, beckoning her, along with the delicious excitement of living close to the edge, which she had experienced before as "Sable." But although Sable had been put in a precarious position, she had known all her facts before stepping into such a role. Well, *almost* all of them.

Hmm. Sable—now there's a thought. Jessie pondered, tapping her chin with her index finger. A disguise had worked once before. Why not again? Her short hair could easily be covered up by a miner's cap. With a little dirt on her face and bulky miner's garb…

Could she go to Thomas for help without him telling Mitch? No. She would wait and talk to Bobbie on Monday morning. In the meantime, she'd edit her report and catch up on some much-needed rest. From the stubborn look on Mitch's face, he probably wouldn't be back today, anyway.

Sighing, Jessie lightly touched her lips with the tip of her fingers, brooding over the lingering memory of his kiss. It wasn't the first one she'd received—but, oh yes, it was the best. *Of all people, why did it have to be him?*

Disgusted with her flip-flopping emotions, Jessie chastised herself for mooning over someone she barely knew. What she needed was a diversion. Editing could wait. Gathering her papers, she piled them neatly on the table, then grabbed an orange soda out of the Frigidaire. Putting on a floppy straw hat, she headed out the door, needing to clear her boggling mind—which was already racing with possibilities.

Mitch, in the meantime, feeling bewildered and anxious, trampled across the Johns' yard in frustration. A woman in the mines? Unthinkable! Jessie's request had caught him off guard. It was unreasonable, irrational, and downright ridiculous! There was no way he was going to support or encourage her. Then he smiled grimly. *On the other hand, I couldn't discourage her, either.*

A movement caught his eye, and he watched Jessie leave her house, heading below toward the wooded hills above Ripley. *Guess she needs some air too.* But what he needed right now was an ally, someone who could talk some sense into her.

Sitting on top the little telephone table in the Johns' hallway, Mitch dangled a leg over the edge, clicking the receiver button up and down.

"Operator? Operator? Hello? Yes, would you please connect me with Randall Peterson in the Detroit area? Yes, I'll wait." Mitch, hoping there weren't many other Randall Peterson's in that area, held on patiently. It was the weekend. Peterson should be home. "What's that? You have two… Okay, Operator, please connect me to the one in Farmington Hills. Thanks." Mitch was confident he'd find his man in this wealthy Detroit area.

A minute went by, then two. While he waited, the silence on the other end occasionally gave way to the crackling sound of long-distance service. Finally, a low masculine voice sounded on the other end.

"Randall Peterson speaking."

Hearing his voice, Mitch floundered. *I really should have thought this over before calling.*

"*Hello!*" Randall's voice was now impatient.

Hurriedly, Mitch replied. "Ah, yes. Hello, Mr. Peterson. First, I feel awkward calling you like this, but I need to talk to you about your daughter, Jessie. My name is Mitchell O'Brien and—"

"And just how do you know my daughter, Mr. O'Brien? Are you from the *Gazette*?" Randall scratched his head, wondering who this man could be and what could be so urgent—*unless* Jess got into another one of her scrapes. But surely, it was too early for that?

"Please call me Mitch. No, sir, Jessie doesn't work for me. I'm the Michigan state liaison officer between the local mining companies and the union. I met Jess while passing on a message to her from the *Gazette*." Mitch chuckled in remembrance. "I must admit, Mr. Peterson, our initial meeting was a bit unconventional. Your daughter came at me with a wrench, but then, that's another story."

Mitch swung the black phone cord back and forth, before finally sitting down in the attached chair. "So, Mr. Peterson, here's my problem."

This time, Randall waited patiently for Mitch to continue.

"Yesterday, Jessie was hired by the *Gazette* and starts working on Monday. She heard about the strike and wants to write an article about the issues. But unbelievably, she's got this *crazy* notion about going down into the mines and seeing the problems for herself. *And she wants my help to do it!* Believe me, Mr. Peterson, I told her in no uncertain terms I would never deliberately place her in a hazardous position." Mitch stopped as he heard a large snort across the line.

"I take it she didn't like your answer." Randall grimaced to himself.

"No, sir. Not at all. She stated if I didn't help, she'd find another way. And from what little I know of your daughter, she probably will. She's already walked into the militia encampment this morning, unaccompanied, after shots were fired over the compound!" Mitch shook his head in dismay. "Mr. Peterson, I'm concerned for Jessie's safety, so I called hoping you'd be more successful in talking some sense into her. Obviously, I've failed."

Feeling older by the minute, Randall decided it was time to sit down—this conversation would probably take a while, anyway. "Mitch, as you've probably discovered, my daughter has a mind of her own. She's different—not that I would change her—but when she gets an idea in that curly head of hers, well...nothing gets my girl's blood racing like a good challenge."

Randall crossed his legs, lit up a fat cigar, and thoughtfully blew a gray cloud into the air before continuing. "By the way, not that I'm changing the subject, Mitch, but she attacked you with a wrench. I assume she had good cause?" Then he chuckled. "Or it is better that I don't know?" Although he knew Jessie could take care of herself, thoughts of "brazen, uncouth, and uncivilized" popped back into his mind from their previous conversation.

Hmm...and *why* was Mitch so interested in his daughter's affairs, anyway?

"Well, it's a long story. Jessie thought I was a ghost. She'd had a long, mysterious day, then heard bumps and grinds when I entered the house, unannounced. My 'hello-o-o' drifting down the hallway must have sounded like a wailing banshee. Any other female would have probably screamed or fainted dead away, but not Jess. She just grabbed the heavy wrench I'd left behind and went after the noise. Lucky for me, all I ended up with was a bump on my forehead." With his fingers, Mitch gingerly touched the purple bruise, a souvenir of their first meeting.

"Nothing against your daughter, Mr. Peterson, but she's a very impetuous, strong-minded young woman."

Randall laughed. "That's my girl! Takes after her daddy. Not that I've approved of all her schemes, mind you, but Jess can usually take care of herself. I wouldn't worry if I were you, Mitch." He tapped off a fluffy gray ash into the tray before continuing. "Take it from me, son. Saying 'no' to Jess will just get her dander up. It's like waving a red flag at a bull!"

Hmm. Interesting. Mitch drummed his fingers against the table in frustration. This was not going as he had planned. Instead of worrying, Randall Peterson seemed right *proud* of his daughter.

Mitch tried again to get his point across. "Mr. Peterson, I don't mean to be disrespectful, but you have no idea how dangerous this situation can be."

"That's very true, Mitch, but I *do* know my daughter. She's going to do what she wants, anyway."

Silence.

Randall sighed. "Mitch, can I give you a piece of advice?"

"Anything."

Randall leaned forward, stubbing out his cigar before settling himself comfortably against the back of the chair. "First, I need to ask…can you protect her if she decides to go through with this? Second, from a father's point of view, I need to know why you're so concerned about a woman you barely know."

Now, that's a good question, Mitch mused.

"Mr. Peterson…"

"Mitch, just call me Randall. I'm sure I'll be hearing from you, again, at least where my Jess is concerned. But sorry to interrupt. Please go on."

"Thanks, Randall. As I see it, the only way I can try and protect Jessie is by taking her down myself and keeping her close. But even then, there's no guarantee she won't be hurt in some way. It's a dangerous place for a man, let alone a woman. Tripping over fallen rock, bad air, piercing drills, mine quakes, collapsed timbers, slippery paths. Although it might not happen, *anything's* possible. And of course, she'll need to be disguised. But if that's what it takes, and I have your permission, I'll try to make it happen."

Mitch swallowed hard before answering the second question. How do you tell a girl's father you're stuck on her? "Regarding your second question, Randall, I know it hasn't been that long since I met Jessie, but I already feel an attraction that I've never felt before—and I'm quite sure she feels the same way. Honestly, she's unlike any woman I've ever met!"

Randall grinned, surprised at the guy's honesty. Reading between the lines, Mitch sounded well educated, confident in his abilities and had integrity. His voice carried strength, but was also caring, which was a big plus in his favor. Nodding to himself, Randall gave his approval. "Alright, Mitch, go ahead and see what you can do. I realize nothing is foolproof, but if you do your best, I'll be satisfied. Just give me a call when it's all over."

Putting the phone back in its cradle, Randall smiled to himself. By the sound of it, his daughter had finally met her match! He jumped up and yelled to his wife.

"Hey, Lillian, guess what!"

CHAPTER 9

Jessie walked into the *Gazette* on Monday morning expecting to find Bobbie behind her desk. Instead, an unknown woman stood at the filing cabinet, her back toward Jessie.

"Excuse me, but I'm looking for Bobbie...*Bobbie?*" Jessie gasped as the unfamiliar woman turned to face her. Gone was the drab fluffy brown hair—instead she stared at a sleek redhead, with a Dutch boy haircut curving the line of her jaw, dressed in a striped lime green sheath. Speechless, Jessie turned Bobbie in a circle. "Yikes! Look at you! You're stunning!"

Bobbie laughed, a little embarrassed. "Well, it wasn't all me. My hairdresser had something to do with it. And of course, once my style changed, I needed new clothes too. Besides, it was time for an update." She looked at Jessie up and down. "I can't have you getting all the attention around here, can I? Also, I remembered your words of encouragement regarding Brian. I guess I had thrown in the towel a long time ago, but maybe he just needs a little shaking up."

At that moment, the object of her interest entered the room, gazing down at the paperwork in his hands. As usual, he was engrossed with his current task and failed to see two women in the office.

"Roberta, will you...?" Brian looked up at that moment, stopped, and took a step backward. For a few seconds, he was speechless as he stared at the unfamiliar woman standing before him. Then, realizing there were two women in the room, he turned to Jessie. "Oh...g-good morning, Ms. Peterson. I didn't see you there. I was just going to ask Roberta to have you sign this extra form when you came in today. There's no rush, just when you have time..."

Taking another peek at Bobbie, he mumbled something, then, giving her a wide berth, quickly strode forward. In his rush to put the paper on her desk, Brian bumped his knee against her wooden chair, twirling it around and knocking his glasses off his nose. Bending over, he picked them off the floor, giving both women another swift glance before limping out the door.

Jessie and Bobbie looked at each other, their eyes sparkling with mirth. Then, knowing Brian was out of ear shot, they burst out laughing. Catching her breath, Jessie gave Bobbie a wink. "*That* went well, don't you think? At least you got his attention."

Bobbie reached down to her desk and handed Jessie a pen for signing the extra form. "Yes, well, at least he looked at me." Her attention was caught by a movement outside the door, and she leaned sideways to get a better look. "And unless I miss my guess, your handsome neighbor is about to make an appearance."

Jessie whirled around to see Mitch in an animated conversation in front of the office. Clapping an unknown gentleman on his shoulder, he threw back his head and laughed, then shook the man's hand before entering the *Gazette* office. Jessie blushed remembering their last encounter. Mitch had not returned since she'd handed him her ultimatum. Not knowing if he was still angry, she leaned over and slowly signed the document, stalling for time.

A cool wave of fresh morning air whooshed across the room as Mitch entered the office. He glanced at the women inside before taking a double look at Bobbie. Swiftly closing the door behind him, he strode across the room and stood in front of her desk. "Well, Roberta, I must say the scenery in this office has definitely improved!"

"And how am I supposed to take *that*, Mr. O'Brien?" Bobbie arched a tweezed brow, throwing him a sassy look. Seeing the chagrined expression on his face, she had pity on him and laughed. "I'm just teasing you, Mitch." She dipped her head and sank into a shallow curtsy. "Thanks for the compliment." Then, she added, "It *was* a compliment, wasn't it?"

Mitch laughed and bowed down, taking her hand, and grazing it with his lips. Looking into her sparkling brown eyes, he reassured her. "Bobbie, you look gorgeous, and you know it. Not that you didn't before, but now you look positively amazing!" He stood up, his eyes flitting back and forth between her and Jessie. "Well, ladies, between the two of you, you're going to set this town back on its heels."

Jessie, sensing his warm lingering gaze, felt her already hot cheeks notch up a degree, their deep pink hue matching the dress she was wearing. At least Mitch wasn't angry. Relief flooded her heart as she gazed up into his twinkling eyes.

"I was hoping to catch you here, Jess. Can we step outside for a moment?" He turned to Bobbie. "Would you excuse us for a few minutes?"

"Sure, Mitch. But you don't have to leave. I was just going in back for a cup of coffee, anyway." As Bobbie headed toward the rear of the building, Mitch turned back to Jessie.

Here it comes. Jessie knew it was too good to last. She led the way to a couple of chairs against the windows and sat down, inviting him to sit beside her. Turning toward Mitch, she gave him a reproachful look and waited for his reproof. But his response was not as she expected.

"Jess, I've changed my mind. If you're still determined, I'll find a way to take you underground."

What? Staring blankly into his face, Jessie was momentarily stunned. Had she heard him right? Then, jumping up, she threw her arms around his neck. Mitch held her for a brief second before putting a stop to her exuberance. Taking her arms from around his neck, he stood up and gently set her in front of him.

"Now, now, don't get all excited. First hear me out." Mitch looked at her sternly and shook her arms a little, making sure he had her full attention. "This venture will be on *my* terms, only. Even then, it'll be a miracle if we come out in one piece. Jessie, you must promise to do what I say without question."

"Anything, Mitch! I'll let you call all the shots." Stopping short of dancing around the room, Jessie launched herself at Mitch once more.

Bobbie, coming back into the reception area, witnessed this display of affection as she placed a tray of three steaming mugs on her desk. "Well!" Focusing on the couple, she stood with hands on her hips in mock disapproval. "Will someone tell me what's going on?"

Separating herself from Mitch, Jessie turned her glowing face to Bobbie. "Mitch just promised to help me with a *very* important assignment." She turned to Mitch. "Can I tell her?"

Mitch sighed. "Yes, Jess. But before you get all excited, I need to clear this with Brian. If he gives his approval, we'll start on the details."

Glancing at his watch, Mitch questioned Bobbie. "Has Brian come in yet?" At her affirmative nod, he headed for the stairs, taking them two at a time.

Bobbie couldn't contain her curiosity. "So?"

"Oh, Bobbie!" Jessie gushed. "I'm so excited! Mitch has agreed to take me down into one of the mines so I can get some real experience..."

"What? Are you crazy?" Bobbie exploded, gaping at Jessie like she had two heads.

"No, really." Jessie tried reassuring Bobbie. "I told Mitch on Saturday I needed some firsthand information—you know, getting to the core of this mining situation so I could write a good article. Seeing the working conditions, myself, would be a great place to start." She frowned, thoughtfully. "Funny, though. When I first asked Mitch for his help, he refused, saying it was far too dangerous. I wonder what changed his mind?"

"Mitch is as crazy as you are if he goes through with this, Jessie. The mine's no place for a woman." Bobbie shook her head and withdrew to her chair. She sat in silence, whipping a pencil back and forth in consternation. "Look, Jess, I knew right away there'd be a change in the office when you came on the scene. You're a head turner, with a mind to boot! How could you not make a difference! But I must admit, this isn't what I expected."

Grabbing the newly signed form, Bobbie got up, filed it in the cabinet and pushed the drawer shut with a bang before turning back to Jessie. "Anyway, Brian will most likely say no. His idea of a woman's place—"

"Come on, Bobbie. This is a great opportunity to show the *Gazette* how capable their new reporter is!" Some of Jessie's ballooned enthusiasm deflated. She had been counting on Bobbie for support. "Can't you see how exciting this will be?"

"What I *can* see is you being dead—or badly hurt. Be reasonable, Jess. It's not like you need to prove anything. You already did that in Detroit!" At Jessie's sharp glance, Bobbie looked horrified.

"And what's that supposed to mean?"

"Oh, Jess, I'm *so* sorry. But when I went to file some papers in Brian's office late Friday, I found an older newspaper clipping on his desk and wondered if he had left it out by mistake." Bobbie wrung her hands together. "Naturally, when I picked it up, I had to read it…" She turned up her mouth in a placating smile. "I'm sorry if you didn't want me to know about it. But I must admit—you looked *awesome*!" Then her eyes widened. "Jess, is there any chance someone could be looking for you?"

Jessie shook her head, negatively. "As far as I know, Sid Brewster will be occupying a little room in the Jackson Penitentiary for some time to come. Anyway, it's highly unlikely I'd be traced up here. My real name was never disclosed in the newspaper, and after the arrest, Sable simply disappeared." Jessie's shoulders drooped. "I'm sorry I didn't tell you, Bobbie. It's not that I was trying to hide it from you, but with the move and then getting the job…I guess it's something I'd just put behind me. Brian *did* make the connection, though, so I had to disclose Sable to him. He must have dug up the old news article and photo after I left his office."

Bobbie came around the desk and enveloped Jessie in a big hug. "I just don't want you getting hurt, okay?" She turned and eyed the stairs. "I wonder what's taking Mitch so long?"

Even as she spoke, thudding footsteps came from above, gaining momentum as they sped down the wooden stairway.

Both women stared as Mitch, with a big grin on his face, burst excitedly through the doorway.

CHAPTER 10

"Are you sure you want to go through with this?" Mitch stopped Jessie from getting in line with the other miners, giving her one last chance to back out.

Jessie nodded and took a deep breath. The heavy canvas jacket, leggings, and leather boots she wore weighed her down, and the hard helmet squeezed her skull; but clothed as she was from head to toe, no one would suspect her sex.

Giving her appearance one last glance, Mitch led Jessie to the end of the line as they waited to enter the shaft. Amazed at Brian's consent to this scheme, he had managed to procure all the proper garb for the journey and Jessie was attired like everyone else, including lunch pail in hand—for show, of course.

Peering into the shadowy morning light, Mitch scanned the area for anything unusual—like a disgruntled, trigger-happy intruder. Although feeling secure while hired guards created a buffer for those who wanted to work, he knew they'd be walking through a gauntlet of angry strikers before entering the shaft house. As a liaison official, he had previously gone safely below, but now he was dressed like the others. This, and being responsible for Jessie's safety, kept his heart thumping. Mitch glanced at her cool countenance and wondered what she was thinking. Her natural pale complexion was smeared with coal dirt, and although she was a little shorter than most workers, he didn't think she would cause any undue attention.

Jessie jumped as a shrill whistle announced the opening of the gate, and they followed twenty-five others marching their way to the shaft. Hearing the jeers, foul language, and accusations of the enraged strikers, she ducked her head in embarrassment, but understood their frustrations.

Feeling a thud on her back, Jessie glanced over her shoulder where a red tomato stain was ominously bleeding into her tan jacket. Mitch, reaching over, brushed off the messy pulp with his hand, then continued forward as guards searched the crowd for the irate attacker.

Gazing ahead, Jessie could see the towering shaft house silhouetted against the breaking dawn, with light reflecting in its many tiered windows and bouncing off the corrugated metal sheeting. Drawing nearer, the group halted as the night shift began drifting slowly through the exit, their silence a testimony to their exhaustion. Jessie watched as they made up a solemn two-column formation, waiting for the guard's escort back to safety.

Jessie and Mitch were the last two through the door, and Jessie's heart pounded as she heard the whining spin of the hoist readying itself for their descent. She gulped, knowing it was too late to turn back, and suppressed the desire to grab Mitch's hand for support. Instead, she glanced up at the steep wooden man car and watched as miners started climbing to the top step, one by one, before settling themselves in rows of three. She and Mitch would occupy the bottom rung as they would be one of the first to depart some 1,200 feet below the surface.

As the last man took his seat, Mitch motioned for Jessie to sit next to the miner, then settled himself against her, hip to hip, metal lunch pails looped over their arms and elbows in. He nudged her with his foot, reassuring her of his presence as a shrill whistle pierced the air. Then, with a sudden jerk, the car plunged them below into total darkness.

Clutching the edge of her seat, Jessie's stomach lurched upward as the car sped downward, deep into the pit at twenty miles per hour. She swallowed hard, clenching her teeth as she questioned her own sanity, or—insanity. Oppressed, suffocating, claustrophobic…she wanted to scream as the walls within the chute seemed to close in on her.

Ten seconds…twenty seconds…thirty seconds…

Fighting for breath, Jessie panicked and reached over to grab Mitch just as a dim glimmer of light floated beneath them. She could feel the car slowing down, each second bringing them closer to the wavering glow. Blinking her eyes in adjustment, Jessie welcomed the contrast from the jet-black vacuum into the soft light radiating up the walls of the shaft. She removed her frantic clutch of Mitch's hand and began breathing again just as the landing became visible and they jolted to a stop.

Standing up, Jessie and Mitch joined four other miners, stepping away from the man car as it slid the remaining men deeper into the shaft. As they vanished, she sighed with relief, all her excitement fading as fast as the men before her. She turned to Mitch who was watching her carefully.

With a nod, he pointed to a tunnel to the left, while the four miners followed a railed track to the right, their voices becoming muffled as they disappeared into the long rocky cavern. Except for an occasional drip-drip of water trickling off the slippery walls, this level was eerily silent, at least for now.

Jessie stumbled into the jagged crevice and turned to Mitch, who had stooped to place his heavy metal pail down on the damp floor.

"Here, Jess. Let's put this down." Mitch tried taking the bucket from Jessie's hand, finding it clenched in a death grip. "Come on, easy now," he said softly. He worked her fingers until they unlatched, and with a shudder, Jessie let go.

Glancing over his shoulder, Mitch found the corridor empty. Drawing her close, he gazed into her pale face, and chuckled softly. "Come now…where is that fearless Sable I've heard so much about?"

Jessie looked up at Mitch and choked back a sob. She knew he was right, but Sable had been in control of the situation. Well, sort of. Kind of. But this was different. Or was it? Shaking out of her stupor, she stepped back, stood resolute, and locked her wobbly knees into place. Taking a deep breath, she picked up her pail and looked at Mitch for further instructions.

Inwardly, Mitch sighed with relief. A deep mine shaft was no place for a hysterical female. Grabbing the handle of his own pail, he turned and headed back down the track, following the path of the other four.

Trailing a few feet behind, Jessie faltered occasionally as she tripped here and there over the uneven ground. Her shuffle was slow but steady, occasionally slipping on a bed of rocky shrapnel left behind from the last shift.

Gaining confidence, she surveyed her surroundings, gazing overhead at the hanging rock walls awkwardly supported by wooden timbers propped up here and there at crazy angles. Dim electric bulbs, widely spaced along a wire running through the passageway, created eerie shadows that danced up and down upon the walls before disappearing around the corners, uh-oh, just like Mitch.

Stepping up her pace, Jessie headed for the corridor. Hearing a shrill whine, followed by the reverberating clamor of heavy metal meeting solid rock, she stepped off the track, bracing her hand against the wall as vibrations bounced off, rat-a-tatting down her arm and through the rest of her body.

The thunderous noise grew nearer as she rounded the corner. There, appearing through the wavering light, was Mitch with another miner, both looking ghostly as they moved about in the dim haze.

Breathing in a bit of dust, she sneezed, catching Mitch's attention. Waving, Jessie watched him become more visible as he walked out of the shadows and hustled toward her.

"Jess, I'm sorry for going ahead of you, but I needed to explain to Jacob what we're doing down here and ask if he'd speak with you. He's agreed to the interview, but we'll only have a few minutes as he has a quota to meet." Mitch caught her arm and propelled her toward the miner, who shut down the powerful drill, set it at his feet, and watched their approach with caution as well as curiosity. His look was incredulous as Jessie removed her helmet, revealing a halo of golden curls.

"Jessie, this is Jacob Pascoe, who has agreed to let you interview him. Jacob, this is Jessie Peterson, the reporter I was telling you about from the *Gazette*." Mitch made the introductions. "Like I told you, she's very interested in the special one-man drill, your feelings about it and the strike.

Jessie held out her hand. Jacob, caught staring in disbelief, then embarrassed, rubbed a muddy hand against his threadbare trousers before clasping her own. He swallowed hard. "'Tis a pleasure, miss. Thought I was dreaming when I first saw you. Bit of a shock, you know." He spoke with a distinct English brogue, probably an immigrant from the Cornish mines in the 'old country.'

Good grief. He can't be more than twenty years old. Now it was Jessie's turn to be embarrassed, as close-up she studied his grimy face, coarse with premature aging. His eyes were sad and old beyond his years.

Grabbing a notebook from her pocket, Jessie wrote furiously as Jacob answered her barrage of questions. Then, as Mitch tapped his watch, she flipped the cover back over her notes and returned the book to her jacket. Meeting over. With a heavy heart, she summoned up a little smile and thanked Jacob for his time, wanting to wish him well, but knowing how fruitless that would be.

Aligning the drill into position, Jacob halted a moment before turning back to Jessie. "What ya gonna do with those things I told ya, miss?" Jacob's voice was edged with fear as well as doubt. "I don't want no trouble with the companies. It ain't likely they'd favor me none and I have my family to consider. Pa's been dead for two years and we need the income. Ma does for people, but it don't pay much." His forehead wrinkled in a frown. "Winter's coming. We need fuel to keep us warm and food. Got six to feed with Ma and me." Jacob shook his head. "Truth be told, miss, I'd hate to lose my job."

Jessie looked over at Mitch before answering carefully. "Jacob, I appreciate all you've told me. Please believe me, I will keep your confidence, and your name won't be mentioned. I have enough material here that's common knowledge so exposing you won't be necessary." She reached out her hand toward him, again. Jacob swallowed hard, his Adam's apple moving up and down. Then, releasing the drill once more, he reached over with both hands. "My thanks to you, Ms. Jessie. And to you, Mr. O'Brien. Can't say our lives down here don't need a change and anything you can do to make it better …well, we'd all be mighty grateful." With a sigh of resignation, he repositioned the drill into the rocky surface, pushed the button, and became lost, once again, in the intensity of his job. Holding steady, he pushed against the wall, sending a barrage of rocks flying in all directions.

With a "Keep safe" whisper to Jacob and pushing down her desire to cry, Jessie slammed the helmet back onto her head, turned and walked swiftly back toward their tunnel entrance. It was all so hopeless and not what she'd expected.

Picking up her speed, she heard Mitch's footsteps echoing behind as he caught up. Face-to-face, he saw the anguish in Jessie's eyes and with his thumb, wiped off a glittery tear that rolled down her cheek. Looking about and finding the area empty of witnesses, he drew her gently toward him, drawing her head against his chest. Then, not wanting to linger, lead her into the little alcove by the car depot.

Despite the dampness, Jessie sank to the ground as they entered the little shelter. Raising her knees, she buried her head in her arms. Had she only "played" reporter for the past four years? Where had she been? How could she have missed all the despair, frustration, and loneliness in the troubled faces of others? Although Detroit had its own problems, her assignments had led her into the areas of society's upper crust. Dinners, politics, promotions, births… Yes, she was a good reporter and did her job well, but she'd never come face-to-face with the gut-retching reality of 'life on the other side.' Suddenly, the importance of gaining information and facts on the drill and strike changed from impersonal to personal as Jacob's eyes had imprinted into her own, conveying trust and appreciation, along with a little hope for any effort she could make on his behalf.

Mitch saw the change in Jessie's countenance as she raised her head and looked at him. The tears had stopped but the glitter remained in her eyes, shining, determined, unafraid. Although relieved at her change in attitude, he felt a quiver of apprehension, knowing he was staring straight into the eyes of…Sable.

Unaware of his concern, Jessie stood up and pointed to a small opening in the ceiling above. "What's that, Mitch?" Curious, she moved toward the hole in the rocky dome across from the alcove.

"I'd forgotten all about this, Jess." Reaching overhead, Mitch touched the rough, wooden rungs of a ladder. He stared up into the dark opening which was wide enough to accommodate the width of one man, but no more. Wisps of dirt and splinters fell into his hand as he rubbed his palm across the lowest bar. Turning to Jessie, Mitch gave a short laugh. "No matter how you feel about it, Jess, be thankful for the man car. This hatch was probably one of the main entrances into the shaft many years ago. Imagine climbing down into the mine, working your shift, and then having to climb back out again at the end of the day." Musingly, he shook his head. "It must have been exhausting. But I also heard it later served as an emergency escape route to the surface if you couldn't get back to the car. Obviously, this one hasn't been used in some time."

Mitch glanced at his watch. "And speaking of which, I think it's time I rang for the car to come down and pick us up." Mitch looked expectantly at Jessie. "If you're finished, that is." He didn't want to keep her down here for any time longer than necessary. No sense pressing their luck.

Nodding, Jessie headed over to the depot area, her eyes recording every sight as she moved forward. Although slightly muffled, she could still hear the shrill grinding sound of Jacob's drill spitting out rock, reminding her that while she had the freedom to leave, he didn't.

Picking up their pails, Mitch pressed the button on the wall, signaling they were ready to come back up. He knew the ring would alert the engineer to send the man car down, just as he had promised. As they waited, he and Jessie were both quiet, each engrossed in their own thoughts. Mitch was just anxious to leave the dangerous area, but Jessie's mind was bombarded with feelings of depression, frustration, anger—and some guilt. Her life was easy compared to Jacob's and all the others below.

A slight rumble came from above and an empty car slid slowly to a stop. Climbing aboard, she felt no apprehension this time as the car whizzed her upward to the surface. Rising closer to the top, fresh air filled her nose, and she breathed in deeply. As light appeared above, she sighed in relief and, feeling slightly weak, hoped she could stand without assistance. When they halted, Mitch turned his head toward her and winked. Jessie fought the urge to laugh as she pulled the helmet further down on her forehead and leaned her chin against her chest. With her eyes to the floor, she slowly stood up, locked her knees, and took a tentative step forward, determined to make her own way across the floor and out into the bright morning sun.

Mitch, turning to the engineer, pressed a few large bills into his calloused hand. "Thanks, Wes. We couldn't have done it without you." Grinning, Wesley nodded as he took the money and with his four-fingered hand, shoved it into a grimy shirt pocket. "Thanks, Mitch. You know I'm always glad to help whenever I can." He glanced over at Jessie standing by the door and chuckled. "She's got grit, that one."

"You don't know the *half* of it!" Mitch grinned at Wesley.

"Well, I'm just thankful we were able to pull it off." The engineer reached over and shook Mitch's extended hand. "And don't worry, Mitch, your secret's safe with me." He turned toward the shaft as the bell rang again. This time several times. "Gotta go. They need to ship some ore to the surface."

Jessie stepped through the doorway, adjusted her eyes, and squinted into the bright morning sun. As its warm rays fell upon her, she felt cleansed from the cold physical and emotional darkness below. Checking the face on her watch, she was amazed to see it was only ten fifteen. Three hours had passed since their entrance into the shaft. Only three hours, but in some ways, a lifetime. Gazing about the area, she noted all the strikers had left, although several guards were still milling about. Later that day, a new crew of hecklers would arrive, filling the air with their jeers as the second shift sought entrance into the mine. There was so much to digest, but right now all she could think about was a hot shower and some clean clothes. Her notes would have to wait.

CHAPTER 11

"What da'ya mean...ya can't find her?" Sid Bruster's pasty countenance turned a blotchy red as he rose slowly, pounding his fist against the old desk, making it wobble. Planting his pudgy fingers down, he leaned across and spoke to his two anxious cohorts in a low deadly voice. "Vinnie, get over here and tell me I didn't hear ya right!"

As both men shuffled across the room, Sid looked them over, knowing his life depended on these two. The tallest, Vinnie, was lean with wavy black hair, and would've been handsome if not for the deep pockmarks on his swarthy face from a childhood disease—and a few knife wounds. Then there was Eddy, the quiet one, a head shorter than his partner but carrying an extra fifty pounds around his middle. That flaming red hair and freckled face did nothing to endear him to the ladies, either. Sid shook his head. Maybe they weren't the best in looks or brains, but they were all he had.

Vinnie glanced at his partner before creeping forward, putting up his right hand. "I swear, boss, we're telling you the truth. Honest. She's just *disappeared!*

Sid was livid. "I didn't spend six stinking months rotting in that hell hole of a jail just for you to tell me she's gone; vanished into thin air—*poof*, like magic." He raised both arms. "Hallelujah! It's a miracle!" He glared up at Vinnie, who took a step backward, and pounded again. "I tell you, it *had* to be Sable. She was listening in on our conversation after I told her to stay put at the bar. Then, as I walked toward her, she spooked and ran into the crowd. She's guilty, I tell you! Why else would she run?"

Sid looked down, pushed his sleeve up and checked the time on his watch. 3:30 AM. Thanks to a greedy prison guard, they wouldn't miss him until the early-morning roll call. He heaved his chest and grimaced as he recalled the filth, the smells, and the sounds of the Jackson Penitentiary. *Never again*, he vowed. Taking a quick look around his current 'prison', a tiny room in an old, abandoned warehouse on Detroit's south side, it was a palace compared to the cell he had inhabited. With a slim chance of discovery in this rat-eaten sanctuary, it provided a secure cover while planning his next move.

Scratching away at his balding head, Sid weighed the alternatives for locating a person who didn't want to be located; and, how he was going to deal with her. Walking across the room and grabbing two dilapidated chairs resting against the wall, he shoved them by his desk, sliding them into position with his foot before sitting down. Then, leaning back in his own chair, he reached into his pocket for a pack of cigarettes and a book of matches. Bending over, he struck the head against his heel, lit the butt and with a quick puff, blew out the match. Sid inhaled deeply, then exhaled with a contented sigh as the sulfurous smell encircled the air in a transparent white cloud. Smokes had been scarce in jail. Contraband, they called it. But guards could be bribed—with the cost of each precious butt exorbitant. *Ha—and they called* me *a crook*. Sid snorted, then slowly inhaled again, closing his eyes in deep satisfaction.

"Okay, boys. Take a load off." With a wave of his cigarette, Sid motioned for the guys to fill the chairs in front of him.

"Here's what we're gonna do." Sid pulled out a stubby pencil and began scribbling on a wrinkly piece of paper. "Vinnie, I want you to check out Detroit's finest and see who needs some extra cash to do a little 'in-house' snooping. Someone's gotta know where she is." He turned to Ed. "Eddy, you go back to the old bar and hang out a bit. Keep your ears open but act casual. We don't want anyone gett'n suspicious. It's been a several months since the raid and, hopefully, things have quieted down, and someone just might talk. You guys hear anything, you report back to me."

Squinting his eyes, Sid slid his head back and forth between the two. "Ya got me?"

"Sure, Sid, sure." Vinnie quickly replied without glancing at Eddy. "What about money, boss? It's gonna take a bit of greasing, you know, to get the wheels in motion."

Sid bent down and pulled open a rusty bottom drawer. Lifting out a green metal box, he placed it in the middle of the desk and opened the lid. Retrieving several large bills, he handed a fat wad to Vinnie, with a smaller amount to Eddy. "That should take care of it. If you need more, boys, come 'n see me. I expect some answers—and soon!" He turned to Ed. "Buy some rounds and see if any tongues start flapping, will ya, Eddy? If you hear anything, get over here fast."

Dismissed, the two stood up with relief and scooted out of the dingy room. Sid, putting an arm behind his head, leaned back gingerly in the squeaky chair until he was sure it would hold his heavy weight. Blowing clouds of smoke toward the ceiling, he looked up and smiled. She would pay…oh, yeah…she would pay.

CHAPTER 12

After reading her notes for a third time, Jessie sighed with satisfaction as she put down her pencil and leaned back against the top step. Closing her eyes against the hazy afternoon sun, she relaxed as a cooling breeze from the early fall air blew across her face, lifting curly wisps of hair from her sweaty forehead. There. It was finished. After several days of rewrites, as well as time-consuming interviews with several union members and company personnel, her article on the strike would be delivered to the *Gazette* in the morning. *Not* that it would please everyone. In fact, Jessie experienced little pleasure from her editorial as she fought to remain unbiased. Thinking of Jacob and the others, she felt overwhelmed, but training had won out as she stuck to the facts. As much as she would've liked a miracle, waving a magic wand was not going to happen. Chances were many would lose in this battle.

Surprisingly, the nightmares of her mine descent never materialized as she had expected, and the ground remained silent. A calm before the storm? Not that Jessie believed in it. Two weeks had passed without incident, although the hecklers appeared and disappeared at will. A few more striking miners, finding it difficult to care for their families, had ripped up their union cards and returned to the mines, creating enemies of old friends. Others remained adamant in fighting for their cause.

But it was more than that. As the chilly autumn winds swept in, frustrations mounted and tempers grew short knowing winter was on its way, a reminder of the coming snow and freezing temperatures. Winters in this "northern tundra" were difficult enough without the added mental and physical stress of providing for their families during the stalemate. Right now, Jessie almost wished she had never ventured into this mess, sometimes longing for the 'peace' of a busy downtown Detroit street where she could just close the window and, with a click, get away from it all.

"Je-ssie?" Her meanderings were interrupted at the urgent calling of her name. She straightened up and turned her head toward the front of the house.

"I'm back here, Jo!" she called, waiting as Josephine came running from the other side. "Hey, slow down, there. What's going on?" Jessie smiled as Josie panted, trying to catch her breath and her eyes wide with excitement.

"Mitch's been trying to *call* you, Jess, but you didn't answer, so he called us instead. Said there's trouble, I should try to find you and that he's on his way over to pick you up."

Hurriedly, Jessie stashed all her notes into the briefcase and dashed through the back door, with Jo on her heels. Dropping the case on the kitchen table, she turned to the younger girl. "Did he say what it's all about?"

Josie shook her head vehemently and repeated what she'd been told. Just as she finished speaking, a honking sounded out front. Walking briskly down the hallway, Jessie opened the door just as Mitch jumped out of his car and leaped up the stairs.

"There's been two murders, Jess!" His face was ashen with disbelief. "Come on. We need to go—*now!*"

Without question, Jessie darted back into the house and within seconds dashed out with her briefcase. Mitch turned to Josie as all three rushed down the stairs toward the car. "Josie, go back home and *stay* there. Tell your parents not to leave the house until I get back."

Josie, hearing the urgency in his voice, obeyed at once, racing across the yard to her own home just as Mitch and Jessie sped out of the driveway.

"What's happened, Mitch? Where are we going?" Jessie placed her hands on the dashboard and held on as the car bumped over the rocks and potholes, speeding toward Highway 41.

With his eyes focused on the road, Mitch answered without turning in her direction, as he concentrated on his driving. "All I know is two men have been shot by some of the imported guards from New York and I'm supposed to get the facts back to the companies before anyone else gets hurt."

Mitch turned to face Jessie. "Just thought you might want to come along for the questioning and take some notes?" At her nod, he turned back, looking straight ahead through the windshield before continuing. "I know it's been pretty quiet, but haven't we all been expecting something to happen?" He shook his head.

Steering his car down Quincy Hill, Mitch drove through Hancock and around several curves before crossing over the bridge into Houghton. Turning right, he shifted gears and chugged up the steep curvy incline leading out of town toward the small mining communities of Trimountain and Painesdale.

Jessie, letting Mitch expertly navigate the road, remained silent, but wondered what lay ahead. She bit her lower lip. Murder was common in Detroit, but up here? Opening her briefcase, she pulled out a notepad and pencil, ready to record the facts.

As they turned into the little town, a noisy group of spectators blocked the road ahead. Pulling over and parking the auto just short of the crowd, Mitch switched off the ignition before reaching over and grasping Jessie's arm, restraining her from leaping out of the car. She looked down at his hand, turning to him with a frown.

"*No*, Jess. I want you to stay put until I see if it's safe." As she started to protest, he placed his fingers firmly against her lips. "Shh! No arguments. Not this time. I promised your father I'd keep you safe, so please—let me clear things first."

With that, he released her, hoping she would obey him—at least for a few minutes. Mitch sighed with resignation knowing her reporter's curiosity would probably get the best of her. Time was not on his side. Swiftly scanning the crowd for any threatening signs, Mitch got out and walked toward the mass, disappearing into the throng of people as they parted to let him pass.

Impatient and fuming, Jessie hugged the briefcase against her chest, drumming her fingers against the hard cover. Waiting for his return, she suddenly remembered his last words.

Wait a minute…he promised my dad? Since when?

Slipping out of her seat, Jessie quickly strode toward the noisy cacophony determined to hunt down Mitch. He had some explaining to do.

"Excuse me." As she squeezed through the thickening crowd, Jessie heard snatches of conversation from the men and soft murmurs from the women as she made her way to the crime scene. Stopping just at the edge of the private yard, she spotted Mitch in conversation with two blue uniformed officers. Gazing about, her eyes fell upon the two bodies hastily covered with white sheets, obscuring the gory scene from the gawkers. Even so, blood red stains began slowly seeping through as Jessie viewed the stilled victims in disbelief. Looking up, she saw two hearses parked in the backyard and gasped at the house with its broken glass windows and multiple bullet holes.

Mitch, as if sensing her presence, looked behind him and sighed. "Excuse me, gentlemen. I'll be right back."

"Jess," he hissed when he reached her side, "just what do you think you're doing? I thought I told you to stay put." He took her arm, pulling her aside as the hearses pulled up to transport the victims to the hospital morgue. Silently, they watched as the officers lifted the bodies, and slid them into the back end of the vehicles.

Turning back to Jessie, Mitch continued his tirade. "What were you thinking, barging through like this?"

Jessie opened her mouth to speak but was forestalled as one officer entered his car and with sirens wailing, guided the transports back down the hill. With the exit of the bodies, the crowd began to disperse, their silence now deafening. Taking a final look at the trampled front yard, they walked back to their homes, shaking their heads, and sending up thankful prayers. It could have been any of them.

Mitch let go of Jessie's arm as the second policeman approached them.

"Hey, Pete," Mitch spoke to the remaining officer. "Any idea what happened here? The companies are outraged and want answers right away." He turned to introduce Jessie. "This is Ms. Peterson, a reporter from the *Gazette*. Anything you say to me can be said in front of her, also."

"Nice to meet you, Ms. Peterson." He shook Jessie's outstretched hand and then turned back to Mitch. "Just so you know, the house is empty. A woman carrying a baby ran out the back door when the shooting began; others are waiting on the front lawn for questioning." He removed his hat and scratched his head. "What we have so far is two striking miners were taking a shortcut across some mining property, which is illegal during the strike. They were warned but didn't understand English. Heading back to their boarding house, they were confronted by two New York thuds, a guard and deputy. When the miners tried entering the house, the gunmen just opened fire. Unfortunately, the two men who *were* hit were just innocent bystanders."

By now, Jessie was scribbling fast as they went over the horrific details. Listening as the officer questioned all those involved, she jotted down her notes, concluding that all agreed upon what they had seen, accusing the New York thugs as the murderers.

Jessie remained silent until Mitch led her back to his car; but once inside, wanted answers to his earlier statement.

"Just what did you mean, Mitch, by saying you promised my father you'd keep me safe?"

Mitch groaned, inwardly, at his earlier slip-up. "To be truthful, Jess, I called your dad *before* going down into the mine. I just wanted him to know how dangerous it was and to get his permission. Then I called again to let him know you were safe."

Silence.

"Come on, Jess. I was *worried* about you. You know as well as I do it wasn't something any father would want for his little girl. At least *I* didn't think so. I just needed to get his approval and promised him I would do everything to keep you safe. To be truthful, his reaction wasn't exactly what I expected. Instead of disapproving, he told me you'd probably do it, *anyway*, so it may as well be with me." He shook his head. What kind of father was he, anyway?

Jessie was angry. Very angry. Mitch had no right interfering. It was *her* business what she did, not her father's and not Mitch's.

"I will say this just once, Mitch, so listen carefully." Jessie was dead serious, and he cringed at the icy calm of her voice. "*I* am my own person. *I* am a reporter. *And* I will do as *I* see fit without seeking the approval of my dad, you, or anyone else not connected with my job. Do I make myself clear?"

Not just the words, but the tone of her voice gave Mitch shivers up his spine. How was he going to keep protecting her if she didn't confide in him?

He briefly raised his right hand from the steering wheel. "Alright, Jess, we'll do it your way. I'm sorry if I butted in, but please know that you can count on me if you need anything. Fair enough?"

Jessie nodded. "Now, please drive me home while this is fresh in my mind. And, Mitch, I'll need some time to compose this information, so would appreciate some privacy. In other words, I need a little room to myself right now. Understand?"

She spoke softly but didn't look at him, again, checking her notes as they headed back down the hill.

It was a silent ride back to Quincy.

CHAPTER 13

Bobbie placed her elbows on the desk with a sigh after receiving Jessie's latest editorial from Brian. With a "Please note the changes and retype this page, Roberta." He exited without further ado. No *"Thanks"* or *"How are you doing?"* or *"Have a good night."* She closed her eyes, laid the copy in her basket, and considered her options.

It had been almost two months since Jessie's arrival. Despite her stylish hairdo and dresses, Bobbie was no closer to attracting Brian than before. In fact, he seemed to be more elusive than ever, communicating only, when necessary, and mostly through Carl, who's thumping footsteps could be heard darting up and down the wooden stairway several times a day.

Bobbie felt ignored and frustrated to the point of giving up. *"Maybe he's just not interested. Maybe it's just me. Maybe…?"* Glancing up at the clock, she noted the time and began clearing her desk for the evening. Sure, she enjoyed her single life, but a little admiration would boost any girl's ego, *if* coming from the right man. As it was, the admiring glances, cat calls and whistles she received walking down Sheldon Avenue pumped up her self-esteem but did nothing to further her relationship with Brian.

Briefly glancing down, she caught the headlines. "Accused Murderers Arrested." Now that *did* get her attention. Pulling the report back out and scanning through the script, she found that the New York thuds who had shot down the two miners in Painesdale had been taken into custody, along with a deputy. The company had hired special lawyers to defend the men, but the outcome of a trial was uncertain. Evidence had been tampered with before the arrival of authorities but witnesses to the crime stated the thugs had just started shooting randomly at the house and windows.

Bobbie shook her head. Two men dead, a house in shambles, and horrific memories for those who had witnessed the shooting. What next? The miners were already keyed up. Something or someone would have to give, and soon.

"Bobbie, are you ready?"

Jessie checked in with a cheerful voice as she poked her head into the reception area. Surprised to see Bobbie's desk still in disarray, she entered the room and stood behind her. "What's up? The show starts at seven, and we need to get a bite to eat first." Friday was celebration time for the end of the week, and they had plans for the evening.

Bobbie looked up in disbelief. "Jess, Brian just handed me your editorial with an additional comment. Have you heard about this? Those New York thugs and a deputy were arrested for murdering those miners, but the companies have hired special lawyers to defend them. Can you believe that?"

Wide-eyed, Jessie snatched the papers from Bobbie, read the headline, and immediately scanned to the bottom where Brian had added the conclusion.

She was still shaken from the scene she'd witnessed earlier. Sticking to the facts as she had known them, she tried keeping her own personal horror from filtering into the editorial.

Plopping down onto the nearest chair, Jessie reread the notes Brian had made. Special lawyers, indeed. Shaking her head in denial, anger, and frustration, she slammed her palm down on the desk causing Bobbie's paperweight to fall onto the floor with a big thud, shattering the glass and spilling the liquid into the wooden grooves.

Dismayed, Jessie jumped up with a start. "Oh, Bobbie, I'm *so* sorry." She grabbed some tissues and began mopping up the floor. "But I was there, directly after the shootings. I saw the house myself, covered with holes, and my notes included testimonies from witnesses. How could they do this?"

She handed the largest piece of glass to Bobbie. "Oh, dear. I hope this wasn't a priceless heirloom or something."

"Not to worry, Jess. Just a little souvenir from a trip I took a while ago. Now I have a good reason to go back and get another one." Bobbie's smile was reassuring.

Hearing the clopping of heavy footsteps scurrying their way, both women looked to the doorway as Brian entered with concern on his face. He glanced down at the floor and back to the girls.

"Is everything alright?" Brian directed his question to Jessie first, but then gave Bobbie a quick peek, his face reddening. Jessie looked up at him before replying. *Hmm, interesting.*

"Everything's fine, Brian. We were discussing your latest revision, and my emotions got the best of me. I guess the arrest happened late this afternoon while I was at another interview. Needless to say, the news of the special defenders *really* upsets me. And when I think how the victim's families are going to feel—"

"Knock, knock!" Mitch poked his head through the front door, looking surprised to see everyone together. He'd wanted to catch up with Jessie at the end of the day before she left. It had been a long wait without seeing her as he'd given her the time she requested. Now he hoped she was in a better frame of mind. Especially about *him*.

"Hey, Mitch! Come on in," Brian called enthusiastically, seeming relieved at the distraction and beckoned Mitch to join him and the girls. "We were just discussing the arrest of the shooters. I guess the companies have hired some big law firm to defend them. What have you heard?"

"As a matter of fact, I was just about to ask Jessie out for supper to discuss this." Mitch looked hopefully at her and received a soft smile in response.

"What a *great* idea, Mitch! In fact, this being Friday, Bobbie and I were going out to eat and celebrate the week's end." Then, with a big grin, she added, "But I have a better idea. Why don't we *all* go out together? I'm starving, it's been a busy day, and I'm sure everyone else is hungry too. What do you say, Brian? Do you have any other plans for tonight?" She turned to Bobbie. "You don't mind the men joining us, do you?"

Bobbie looked at Jessie like she'd lost her mind. *Brian?* Go out with them? Huh! That would be the day. But she only shook her head, saying it would be fine with her. Now it was Brian's turn.

While everyone waited for his response, his red face deepened as he gazed at his shoes. Then he cleared his throat and spoke, without looking at anyone.

"I suppose that would be alright." He looked up at Mitch and nodded. "Okay. Just let me run back upstairs and grab my jacket." Brian headed out the door, then took the stairs two at a time. Bobbie just stared after him wide eyed in disbelief.

"Okay, Jess, what was that all about and why is Brian looking so uncomfortable?" Mitch knew something was up. She had that look on her face and a twinkle in her eye.

Jessie looked up at him innocently and shook her head. Honestly, guys could be so dense. "What are you talking about, Mitch? I merely suggested a few friends having supper together so we can talk without interruption."

"Ah, I'll just go and get my coat." Bobbie retreated to the back room, leaving the two of them alone.

Jessie reached for her jacket just as Mitch picked it up and helped her into it. Leaning close, he whispered. "I know you're up to something, so spill. Why have all of us suddenly become such good buddies?"

Peeking up at him, Jessie whispered. "Bobbie's been trying hard to get Brian's attention for months, now, and failing miserably. I just thought this would be a great opportunity for them. Brian couldn't very well say no when we're all going, right? So maybe he'll finally see Bobbie in a different light."

Mitch's look was skeptical. "So now you're playing matchmaker? Maybe Brian's not interested in her."

"Come on, Mitch. You saw how he looked at her, didn't you? He's interested, all right, but too shy. Let's just see how it goes, okay?" Jessie nodded toward the hallway as Bobbie was coming back, ending any further conversation.

A shuffling on the stairway indicated Brian's return, also.

Mitch cleared his throat. "How about the Douglas House? Food's good, and it shouldn't be too busy yet." At their affirmative nods, he continued. "And since it's only a couple of blocks away, why don't we just walk and work up an appetite? The brisk air will be invigorating. We can come back here for our cars later."

With everyone in agreement, they headed out the door, Brian stopping long enough to ensure the building was locked up tight for the night.

Stepping out into the late-afternoon air, it was cool as expected for early October, but refreshing as Mitch had said. Across Portage Lake, the Ripley hills were glorious in their autumn dressing of gold, red, and orange hardwoods, accented by the deep-green fir trees in between.

Tucking Jessie's arm in his, Mitch slowly led the way up the hill to the main street, pausing for a streetcar filled with passengers. With the clang of its bell, it rolled down the tracks to its next stop.

Holding onto Mitch, Jessie turned for a quick peek behind to see how the other couple was doing and smirked with satisfaction as Brian hesitantly took Bobbie's arm and assisted her across the street and up the sidewalk. At least he had good manners. She saw Bobbie smile at him in appreciation. So far, so good!

Jessie glanced up at the impressive four-story Douglas House, eyeing the buff-colored brick with its striped awnings draping over each window, and gold cupolas crowning each of the corners. Anyone who was anybody stayed at this luxurious hotel during their visit.

The foursome crossed over Sheldon Avenue and entered the building on the second floor. After discarding their wraps, a bus boy directed them to a table overlooking the busy street below. The waiter handed menus to each one as Mitch checked over the sparsely occupied restaurant with satisfaction. He'd been right. It was early, yet for regular customers, so quiet talk was possible. Satisfied, he turned back to the selection of entrées looking forward to a good meal and special time with friends.

Glancing up from her menu, Jessie had time to eye Mitch as he studied the various options. She'd had a long time alone to consider their relationship—if they had one. The killings had provoked some deep thinking on her part, and she knew how lucky she was to know someone like Mitch. He was honest, fearless, hardworking as well as good-looking, and she'd enjoyed their time together. He hadn't forced their relationship which was another point in his favor. And she had to admit, she had *really* missed his presence.

Mitch caught her staring at him and gave her a quizzical smile. Now, what was she thinking? He took a sip from his water glass and turned to Brian and Bobbie. "Have you two decided what you'd like to eat? I see the Trout and Whitefish are specials for today. And of course, you wouldn't go wrong with a Cornish pasty." He could already taste the rich crust and juicy filling inside. Maybe it would be good for tonight, some comfort food. Yes. They all needed that.

After the two funerals, tension hovered over them like a clawed predator. Many miners, fearing for their families, had torn up their union cards and headed back to work. But others persisted in marching, now including women and children as they paraded through the towns. It had made bitter enemies of old friends.

After the waiter took their orders, Mitch reached into his pocket and pulled out a photo.

"I had an extra copy made for me," he said as he passed it around to the others. Sadness seized him. He was no closer to a compromise and things had only gotten worse.

Jessie gazed down at the photo. "I was there for this procession. These young girls in their white dresses and flowing veils were walking behind the hearses." She looked up at the others and passed the picture to Bobbie. "Do you know what this means?"

Bobbie nodded, sadly. "It's a Croatian tradition for girls to dress up like brides, honoring those who will never be married." Her eyes filling up, she sniffed and looked over at Jessie, her soft heart causing a tear to trail down her cheek.

"Here, Roberta, take this." Brian hastily reached into his pocket, pulled out a handkerchief and handed it across the table to Bobbie. Dabbing at her eyes, she gave him a shaky smile of thanks in return.

He turned to Mitch. "I heard some strikers have been locked up and the companies are using imported workers in their place. Is it true, Mitch?"

"I'm afraid so," Mitch replied, sadly. "Not only that, but they've sent out eviction notices to the strikers. I haven't seen it enforced, but several families have packed up and moved away. The union finally backed down, asking the companies if they would allow the miners to return but let them keep their union cards. They refused. They want all or nothing."

Mitch looked across the room at an approaching waiter. "Ah, good. Here comes our food." He leaned forward and sniffed in appreciation as the aromatic dishes were placed before them. Noting his pasty was steaming hot, he spread a large pat of butter over the top and watched as a golden stream melted down the sides and onto his plate. With a "thank you" to the waiter, he waited until the others were served before diving in.

"How about we change the subject for a while and talk about something cheerful. I hear the Kerredge theater is beautiful inside. Is it true Caruso and Sarah Bernhardt performed here?"

Bobbie's bright eyes now glowed with enthusiasm. "Yes, and John Philip Sousa too! It *is* beautiful, Mitch! There are tiered circular box seats above the main audience, and the walls and ceilings are very ornate. It's a perfect setting for a play or a musical." She looked up and smiled her thanks at the hovering waiter as he placed a steaming plate before her.

Seeing the others were served, Mitch closed his eyes with pleasure as he took his first succulent bite of the flaky pasty. The rich buttery crust melted in his mouth and the combined flavors of beef, potatoes, carrots, onions, and rutabaga teased his taste buds with every forkful. He sighed with satisfaction as he dove in again thinking how it was the little things in life that sometimes made it all worthwhile.

As they ate, conversation flowed easily, and if Brian didn't contribute much, no one noticed. Occasionally he looked over at Bobbie as if seeing her for the first time and didn't quite know what to make of it. Jessie saw the inquiring look in his eye, though, and was happy for her friend. If Bobbie observed him sneaking a peak or two, she didn't let on.

Finishing their meal, Mitch signaled the waiter for their check. "This one's on me," he said with a smile. "It's been great having some down time with my friends after this dismal week."

Brian started to protest, but Mitch waved him off with a chuckle. "Just don't expect it every time, but tonight's been special. I can't remember being so relaxed, especially with two beautiful women sharing our table. Don't you agree, Brian?"

His face coloring, Brian nodded and became busy folding his napkin before placing it on the table.

The girls excused themselves while Mitch paid for the meals.

"Thanks, Mitch, for inviting me." Brian smiled as he pulled on his jacket. "I enjoyed both the food *and* the company."

Mitch nodded and pocketed some change as he looked at his friend. Jessie had been right. Brian *did* have some interest in Bobbie.

Just then the girls came through the door and reached for their coats. Mitch helped Jessie into hers while Brian held out Bobbie's as she put her arms through the sleeves.

"Thank you, Brian." Bobbie beamed up at him.

"My pleasure." He escorted her through the door and out into the chilly air.

The walk back to their vehicles was silent and hurried, as each huddled into their clothing for additional warmth. With a full moon and northwest wind blowing off the "big lake," a steady fall in temperature was bound to occur over night. Snow was even possible in October, although usually later in the month. The old-timers even spoke of snow in July! Right now, the air was crisp and fragrant from the wind blowing through the pines.

Jessie held onto Mitch's hand while pulling the collar of her jacket snugly around her neck. "Brrr. Even though it's over two months away, it already smells and feels like Christmas around here." She'd have to get her hats, scarves, and gloves out soon unless they got a late Indian summer. She glanced at Bobbie to see Brian leading her down the hill to the office building.

As they approached the parking lot, it was empty except for three vehicles.

"Jess, I'm going to follow you home to make sure you get there." Mitch opened the door of Jessie's car and let her slip in. She rolled down the window and, surprisingly, agreed.

"Thanks, Mitch. It's dark on the Hill and I haven't driven at night for a while."

She waved at Bobbie and Brian, rolled up the window and started her car.

Mitch looked around and then at the other couple in surprise. "Bobbie, where's your car?"

"I usually take the streetcar since I live close to town. Don't worry about me. There are lots of people around." Bobbie hoped she sounded more confident than she was feeling.

"Roberta, if you like, I'd be happy to drive you home." Surprisingly, this came from Brian. He added hesitantly, "That is, of course, if you don't mind riding in a truck. It bucks and bounces at times. But it'd probably be a lot quicker and warmer than the trolley, especially this time of night."

Brian swallowed hard and glanced hesitantly at Bobbie.

I can't believe I just did that.

I can't believe he just did that.

It was Bobbie's turn to be shy as she looked at him to see if he really meant it. At his earnest look, she sighed with relief.

"Sure, Brian. I'd really appreciate a lift home." She looked over at Mitch. "Guess I'm taken care of. Thanks, again, Mitch, for everything." She laughed. "Better hurry and catch up with Jessie, though. She's got a lead foot!"

Mitch took off after Jessie as Brian walked Bobbie to his truck, a black 1925 Ford Model TT with flat bed. After assisting her into the passenger seat, he climbed onto the driver's side and started up the engine. "There's a blanket behind you if you want extra warmth. I keep it handy in case I get stuck somewhere, especially in winter." Before she could respond, he reached behind her, retrieved a red woolen blanket, and placed it in her lap. "Here you go. There, that ought to help." He shifted gears and started up the hill.

Bobbie tucked the heavy cover over her legs and sighed with relief. The wool was scratchy but kept the cold air from seeping through. "Thanks, Brian. This feels marvelous. Do you need directions?" At his nod, she instructed him. "Okay. Just turn left here at the stop sign and keep driving until you're past the college. After that, my house is about one-quarter mile on the right side."

Driving as she instructed, Brian passed the college and continued until a short distance later when Bobbie pointed to a small stone bungalow that was built on a hill overlooking the road. Slowing down, he pulled over to a parking spot on the side of the road. From what he could see by moonlight, the home was built from a neutral-colored stone, had a circular room to one side, and was surrounded by trees. It was beautiful.

Brian commented, "You're lucky to have such a lovely home, especially for a single woman." He smiled at her. "I hope you don't take that wrong way. I meant it as a compliment."

"My parents built this for their retirement," Bobbie explained. "Dad was a professor at the mining school, and Mom taught sixth grade in Houghton. They'd hoped to live in it for some time." She looked sadly at Brian. "Five years ago, in late spring, they decided to take their boat out. It was always a tradition for them on the first warm day of the year, celebrating the end of winter. But this time, while out on Superior, clouds blew in from the north, and a sudden storm capsized the boat. They both went over." Her eyes glittered. "You know how long anyone would last in that freezing water." She shook her head. "Thankfully, their bodies came ashore, and at least I was able to say goodbye to them."

Bobbie sighed and brushed her palms against her eyes. "Anyway, that's enough morose information about me." She shook her head. "Sorry. Not the best way to end such a nice evening."

"Not to worry." Brian quickly assured her. "Not a day goes by when I don't think about my own folks. They were both taken by influenza ten years ago. It happened so fast when I was in college that I never got to say goodbye. But I do know that one would have been miserable without the other, so perhaps they would have wanted it that way."

Brian cleared his throat and gave a short laugh. "Well, we've certainly covered a lot of territory tonight. You're so easy to talk to,

Roberta," he added shyly. "It's been a very nice evening, and I'm glad we were able to share it.

Swinging the blanket off her lap and folding it up, she placed it behind her seat and smiled at Brian, hating to call it a night.

"It *was* fun, Brian. Thanks, again, for the ride home, *and* the warm blanket. You were right. It was much nicer than the trolley. Well, guess I'll see you bright and early on Monday morning."

She moved to open the car door when Brian coughed. "Bobbie, excuse me, Roberta…"

She smiled and held out her hand to him. "Bobbie is just fine, Brian, especially among friends. And I hope we'll be friends?"

Brian took her hand and colored up, relieved that she couldn't see in the shadowy truck.

"And when we go back to work on Monday, I hope you'll continue to call me Bobbie." She laughed. "That is, unless I mess up and you must yell at me. Then you can call me Roberta!"

Brian chuckled. "It's a deal. And, Bobbie, I hope you won't think me forward if I say I'm very much looking forward to Monday morning."

Now it was Bobbie's turn to blush.

CHAPTER 14

Blinking her headlights, Jessie let Mitch know she was safe in her driveway, but instead of pulling into the Johns' house next door, he drove in behind her and jumped out. Opening her car door, he took her hand and helped her out of the vehicle.

Jessie stood up with a quizzical look. "Is something wrong, Mitch? I usually park the car in the garage overnight."

"No, but..."

"Well, in that case, would you please open the doors for me so I can drive in?" She climbed back in, gazing up at him with a blink of her lashes.

"Sure thing, Jess." Mitch hurried to the front of her car. In the beaming headlights, he found the bar on the doors, and pushed up with both hands. As they swung open, he motioned her to drive forward, stepping to one side as she maneuvered the car into the small building.

Jessie had one thought as she drove into the little barn. *I wonder if Mitch would be interested in sharing a little warmth with me.*

Stepping outside and looking up at the bright moon in the clear sky, Jessie shivered. "Unless I'm wrong, I think we're in for a freeze tonight." She smiled at Mitch. "So how about coming inside for a hot cup of coffee. It's the least I can do after such a lovely dinner."

Mitch pulled the bar into place and grinned. "Lead the way."

Jessie inserted the key into the front door, and Mitch, pushing it open, felt a beckoning warmth radiating from the living room.

After hanging up their coats on the hall tree, Jessie led the way, pausing by the potbellied stove as she reached out for its emitting waves of heat. Mitch did the same, and they shared a few quiet moments together gazing into the glowing embers.

Removing a log from the metal box that lay a few feet away, she opened the little stove door and added the wood into the fire. Prodding it to the bottom with a brass poker, she pushed the bright ashes around and shut the door. Immediately, little flames touched off the dry timber, sending wavy orange beams that glowed through the windows. As the sweet smell of hardwood floated into the room, Jessie sighed with pleasure.

"You know, Mitch, it was love at first sight when I saw this pot-bellied stove." Jessie spoke softly, gazing at the mesmerizing flicker of light. "My first thought was how very much I wanted to share it with someone." She turned to look up at him. "And I can't think of anyone else I'd rather share it with but you."

Mitch stared into Jessie's eyes, which spoke of yearning but mixed with uncertainty. Lifting his hand, he trailed his thumb down from her temple to jaw, feeling her silky soft skin warming under his touch.

"Jess," he breathed. Leaning in slowly, Mitch watched as her eyes fluttered closed in anticipation. The tender touch of her lips created a shock through his stomach, spreading like wildfire through his entire body. He shuddered, yearning for more and wondered when the last time was he'd felt this way, if ever.

Jessie leaned into his kiss, a moment she had been waiting for. Just the gentle touch of his lips on hers created not the sizzle she had anticipated, but an explosion. Uncertain, she moved back an inch, and staring into his eyes was struck by the intense fire she saw in them. Then, lifting her arms around Mitch's neck, she closed her eyes and drew him closer for another taste.

"Hmm."

Responding to her invitation, Mitch deepened the kiss. A startling vision of Sable popped into his head as he wondered who was the reality and who was the illusion. Shaken by his thoughts, he became aware it wasn't just the stove creating all the heat. Drawing back, Mitch ended the embrace with a sigh and a chuckle.

"Well, I promised your dad I'd keep you safe, and I guess that includes from *me* too." He slowly withdrew her arms from around his neck and, taking a dazed Jessie by the hand, led her over to the sofa.

Sitting down, she turned and angled her body to get a better look at him. Reflecting in the firelight, Mitch looked as overwhelmed as she felt. She waved an imaginary fan and smiled. "Whew. That stove must be hotter than I thought."

Mitch chuckled. "Well, Jess, I don't think we can blame it all on the stove. I think a little bit was me and a little bit was you." He smiled at Jessie's face, now burning with embarrassment.

Jessie slid her hands down into her lap, overcome by her boldness. What if Mitch didn't feel the same way? "I don't know what to say, Mitch. It was very forward of me to, well, you know."

He recaptured her fingers between his and raised them to his lips, kissing them one at a time. She murmured and tried to pull back, but he held on and drew her nearer.

"Don't say anything, Jess. I know we haven't known each other very long, but these feelings I have for you are very strong." He lifted her chin to look at him. "And I'm hoping you feel the same way."

Lifting his hand to her lips, she placed a kiss against his knuckles. "I'd be a liar if I said no, Mitch." Jessie leaned toward him, her eyes dark with emotion. "But just to be sure…"

"Anything to please my lady…"

Just as Mitch reached out to draw her back into his arms, the phone rang.

With a shaky grin, Jessie shook her head and laughed. "Saved by the bell." She looked at her watch. "That'll be my dad. He always calls me on Friday night. Maybe you'd like to say hello?"

Jessie extracted herself from Mitch and hurried into the kitchen, grabbing the mouthpiece just as the phone rang again.

"Hi, Dad. Yes, I knew it must be you."

Mitch followed her through the doorway and put his arm around her shoulders causing Jessie to feel slightly breathless as she continued. "What's that? Oh, I had just got in the door when the phone rang. You called earlier? Sorry you missed me, but I was out for dinner with friends. Who was I with?" She chuckled. "Come on, Dad, are you checking up on me? Yes, I know you worry, but I'm fine and keeping busy."

She was silent for a moment, listening to her dad on the other end, then sighed. "Okay, Dad. If you must know, I was having dinner with Mitch O'Brien and two friends from the *Gazette*. We were discussing work, mostly." Jessie wound the tangled cord around her fingers. "Uh-huh. The strike is still on. Not even close to any solution. Did you read the copy of my latest editorial I sent? Well, nothing has changed since then. The militia is still here, and the companies won't budge. Dad, would you like to say hello to Mitch? He's right here. And say hi to Mom. Give her my love, and tell her I'll talk to her next week."

Jessie passed the phone to Mitch and stepped away. She busied herself by filling the coffeepot full of water, and after adding the grounds, set it on the stove to perk. After all, she did promise him a hot cup. But whether they needed any more heat was debatable.

As she listened in, Mitch spoke to Randall for a few minutes and answered all his questions, nodding on occasion. Then, with a frown on his face, he turned and looked at Jessie. "Are you sure? Do you want me to tell her? Alright. Yes, I'll keep a close watch but can't imagine her being in danger up here. Sure, I'll let you know if I hear anything."

Then he gave a short laugh. "Yes, Randall, I *know* what time it is, and I'll be leaving shortly. It's freezing up here, and Jessie just invited me in for a hot cup of coffee. Okay, I'll be in touch and let you know if I hear or see anything suspicious."

He hung up and turned to Jessie who was looking at him questionably.

"What is, Mitch? Why would my dad think I was in any danger?" Jessie pushed the coffeepot to the side as it began to bubble and walked over to him.

"You'd best sit down, Jess." Mitch pulled out a kitchen chair, then placed another one close to her as he reached for her hand. "You're not going to believe this, but Sid Brewster has escaped from prison." He watched her face go pale in response to this unexpected news. "The press wasn't notified right away as the warden wanted to keep it under wraps, hoping to capture him before the word got out. Your dad was just informed and is trying to get more details."

"But, Mitch, how could he possibly escape? Jackson is a maximum-security prison where only the hard-core criminals are sent. I know because I did a piece on it last year and guards are supposed to be everywhere!"

Mitch leaned back in his chair. "Well, according to your dad, *one* of those guards got greedy and took a bribe. It happened late at night, so a missing prisoner wouldn't be discovered until bed check in the morning."

Jessie rose from her chair and began pacing the room. This was not good news. As she thought it over, questions whirled through her mind. Would he come looking for her or just leave the country? What were the chances he'd ever find her? Should she leave? *No. I'm probably getting excited about nothing. There is no way he can connect Sable to Jessica Peterson.* Mitch stood silent, watching her face as she digested this latest information and wondering what was going through her mind. Shaking her head, Jessie poured two cups of coffee and sat back down.

"Mitch, I don't see how Sid could possibly know who I really am or where I am. My dad paid *royally* to keep my identity under wraps. Even my friends think I'm on a sabbatical somewhere private."

"Regardless, Jess, we need to be diligent, keeping our eyes and ears open to anything unusual." He stroked her hand. "This area is teeming with foreigners, and with most of them being men, someone could easily slip in among them. As far as I know, you're the only female newcomer to this area." He eyed her seriously. "Promise me, Jess, you won't take any unnecessary chances."

Mitch thought for a moment as he sipped on the hot brew. "You know, Jess? I think we should let Brian and Bobbie in on this, and if you don't mind, I would like to tell Thomas. Because of his blindness, he picks up on things faster than we do with his other senses. He won't speak of this to anyone else, but his friends down at Molly's Pub just might gossip about any strangers they've seen."

He heaved a heavy sigh and patted her hand. "I guess it's the best we can do for now. Naturally, your dad is concerned about you and will keep us updated. He just wanted me to tell you as he can't be here to protect you." Then he laughed. "I guess that means he trusts me to take care of you, Jess."

He leaned over and kissed her cheek. "Now, that I've had some coffee, I'd better leave before your dad calls again."
But it was another hour before Jessie walked Mitch to the front porch where they shared one more good night kiss. Locking up behind him, she moved slowly through the house, checking every window and the back door, finding them secure. After all, you couldn't be too careful.
Turning off the lights, she headed upstairs, hurriedly donning a warm flannel nightgown and quilted robe in her chilly bedroom. Walking to the window in her fluffy mules, she parted the curtain and watched as the full moon created shadows that floated swiftly across her yard. Although not prone to imagination, Jessie quickly pushed the curtain closed before seeing things that weren't there.
Shivering, she dove under the covers thankful she had had the foresight to put another quilt on the bed this morning. Blustery winds were beginning to slam against the house, shaking the glass windows and whistling through the loosely sealed frames. She snuggled deeper into the blankets searching for some warmth, for although some heat rose through the floor vent, it still wasn't enough to keep the chill out.
Tossing back and forth, she tried getting comfortable, but it was no use. With a sigh, Jessie rolled onto her back, placing her arms under her head. Staring up at the ceiling, she knew it was going to be one of those nights. Between the bad news from her dad and now the eerie sounds floating around her bedroom, sleep was elusive. Or maybe it was the late-night coffee she shared with Mitch, among other things. With a groan, Jessie slid beneath the blankets and pulled them over her head. Great. Now her nose was cold. She'd never get to sleep.
It was going to be a long winter.

CHAPTER 15

Jessie entered the *Gazette* office Monday morning filled with anticipation. Giving herself a good talking to, she was now convinced her fears were all for naught. *Mountains out of molehills,* she thought. Now all she had to do was convince Mitch when he came in to discuss her predicament with Brian and Bobbie.

Coming through the door, Jessie saw Bobbie at her desk with Brian perched on its edge, both enjoying their coffee and deep in conversation. Obviously, the Friday night ride home had done the trick.

Clearing her throat, she closed the door behind her. Swiveling around, Brian's face turned red at being caught in such an awkward position, but Bobbie was glowing.

"Good morning to you both!" she casually called out, walking briskly across the floor toward the closet where she hung up her coat and hat. After fluffing out her hair and preening into the little mirror hanging on the door, she headed in their direction.

Brian greeted her with his usual, "Good morning, Jessie." Then he said, "Bobbie, I'll take care of that matter we were talking about as soon as I get to my office." Slipping off her desk, he was about to leave the room when Jessie stopped him.

"Please stay, Brian. Something's come up since I saw you two on Friday night, and Mitch promised to be here when the office opened. Personally, I think it's much to do about nothing, but he felt you needed to be aware of it." She peered behind her to see Mitch walking past the window. "Oh good, here he comes now." Jessie headed to the door and opened it just as Mitch appeared on the other side.

Both Brian and Bobbie looked at each other, mystified, as Mitch shed his jacket, hat, and gloves onto the nearest chair.

"Did you tell them?" he asked softly. At Jessie's negative shake of her head, he took her hand and strolled over to the waiting couple.

Mitch charged right in. "I'm glad you're both here. It's like this. Jess received a phone call from her dad late Friday night with news that Sid Brewster's escaped the Jackson maximum security prison. Although it happened some time ago, it was hushed up while they were searching for their missing prisoner. Right now, his trail is cold. Naturally, Randall is concerned for his daughter's safety, and I promised him we would all be on the alert for anything suspicious."

Bobbie rushed forward and put her arms around Jessie. "See? I had a feeling something like this was going to happen! Remember when you first came, we talked about it."

Jessie hugged her in return. "I still find it hard to believe he'll discover who I am, much less find me. This is *way* out of his comfort zone." She shrugged. "Hopefully, he fled to Mexico or some remote island where no one will ever find him."

Unconvinced, Bobbie looked at Mitch. "What do you want us to do? Should she be living alone? Do we get the police involved?"

"Right now, Bobbie, I think we just need to be vigilant until we get further news. Brian, can you pull some strings and see what you can come up with? Surely you know some newspaper editors that might have more detailed information. Her dad will head up an investigation on the home front, too, but he's got to keep Jessie's name out of it. Too much personal interest on his part could raise a red flag for anyone who's looking for her. Other than that, there's not much we can do until we get more facts. But we need to keep our eyes and ears open for any strange inquiries of Jessie, where she lives, her work schedule, etc."

Brian, recovering from his earlier embarrassment, looked horrified and hastened to assure Mitch of his full cooperation. "Of course, Mitch! I'll get on the phone right away. A few guys I know down there owe me some favors, anyway, so I guess it's time to collect." Brian smiled reassuringly at Jessie. "We don't want anything happening to our *best* reporter, do we?" At this remark, he grabbed his coffee cup, took one lingering look at Bobbie, and headed for the stairs.

Mitch spoke softly to Jessie.

"I spoke to Tom over the weekend, and he'll be listening for any strange voices or unusual talk while at the Pub. Irma knows, too, but not Josephine. As much as I trust her, she's too young and innocent to get involved. And as friendly as she is, someone could try to manipulate her."

Bobbie gave her arm a gentle tug. "Jessie, please come and stay with me. I have a big house and it would be so much fun having you. I'm sure you'd feel safer than in that old house all by yourself."

Mitch agreed, but also had another suggestion. "Bobbie's right about you not being alone, Jess. But if you insist, maybe you should get a dog for protection, one that will alert you if someone comes or if it hears any strange noises."

"And what would I do with a dog when I'm gone all day?" Jessie asked. "Or with special assignments at night? It just wouldn't be fair to the poor thing to be left alone so much." Then she added fondly. "You see, all this commotion is *just* what I anticipated. Really, I appreciate your concerns. But over this weekend, I convinced myself this worry is all for nothing. Even *if* Sid does find out who I am, it'll take him ages to track me down. Time is on our side and in the meantime, it's possible he'll get caught again. Or maybe he'll just think it's a waste of time and too much effort on his part to come after me. So let's just wait and see what Brian finds out and what my dad comes up with."

With that remark, Jessie tried inserting a positive attitude. "Come on, you two. You know the paper's not going to wait for any of 'ole' Sid's decisions. We all have work to do, so let's go do it."

Mitch looked at his watch. "Well, with that note, I'm off for another company meeting. Jess, I'll check in with you later to see if Brian's come up with anything. You girls have a nice day; just remember what I said about keeping eyes and ears open, okay?" He gave Jessie a peck on the cheek, despite Bobbie's presence, and walked out the door.

"Well, that looked promising." Bobbie teased. She walked over to her desk, sat down, and looked up at her friend expectantly.

Jessie was quick to reply. "Ah-ha. And since when did Brian start calling you Bobbie instead of Roberta? You got something to tell me, girl?" She plopped down across from her.

Bobbie folded her hands in front of her, happiness radiating from her face. "I can't thank you and Mitch enough. It's like a miracle. As we were driving home, he warmed me up—" At Jessie's raised eyebrow, she continued, "With a woolly blanket." Then she went on dreamily, "It was like we were in a cocoon of our own. He liked my house, and I started telling him about my parents and their accident. We parked on the roadside and talked for a long time."

She looked at Jess in amazement. "What's taken me years of trying to get his attention, without success, happened in just a few short hours. If you don't call *that* a miracle, I don't know what is!" Her face warmed as she recalled their special time. "He's so nice, Jess…"

Then she sat up straight. "But enough of me. Something's happened between you and Mitch, too, since Friday. I can see it. Maybe it was the full moon?"

"I don't care what it was, Bobbie, but I'm hoping for a double dose!" Jessie smiled slyly. "We were just getting, ah, better acquainted when my dad called. Talk about bad timing! And then, of course, came the ugly news about Sid Brewster. Sort of put a damper on things as I thought I was done with him." She stretched her legs out in front of her.

Bobbie took a sip of her now lukewarm drink, made a face, and set the cup on top the desk. "I'm for a warmer upper on my coffee. How about you? Want a cup?"

"Sure. Grab a hot one for me." Jessie looked at her watch. "I don't have to be at my interview this morning until ten o'clock."

As Bobbie walked into the back room, Jessie called out, "And see if there are any pastries left, would you? It was Carl's turn to bring them in today. I couldn't eat a thing this morning knowing Mitch was coming in to talk with you and Brian, so now I'm starving."

Jessie crossed her legs, leaned back in an unladylike position, and considered her options. Not that she was fearful, but logic demanded caution. What should she do now that Sid was on the loose?

Coming through the door, Bobbie mirrored her thoughts "Seriously, Jess, maybe you should reconsider the dog idea. At least it could act as some sort of warning signal if a stranger approached the house."

Jessie grabbed an iced Danish from the plate Bobbie held out and slowly sipped from her steaming mug. Biting into the confection, she closed her eyes in pure delight as she savored the fresh, gooey roll, with its fruity sweetness, wishing her problems could dissolve as fast as the flaky pastry.

Bobbie, too, sat down, enjoying her second cup with a sugary raised doughnut. Both had much to think about.

Some good, some bad.

Dusting the granules off her fingers, Bobbie passed a napkin to Jessie and leaned on her elbows. "So what's the latest on the strike? You've covered just about every angle, so I can't think where you'd be heading next."

Jessie set her cup on the desk. "Well, you're right about that. So I'm headed up to one of the, ah, joy houses, close to the mines, to get a different perspective. You know, their involvement with the miners can put a new twist on the same old story. I'm sure some of the men are more open to talking while they are, shall we say, more relaxed."

"No!" Bobbie's cup hit the desktop with such force, the coffee sloshed over the brim. She grabbed a napkin and quickly blotted the liquid before it ran onto the floor. "You just can't walk into one of those houses! What will people think?"

"Well, they're not a big kept secret, are they?" Jessie smirked. "You know as well as I do that men have needs that can't be solved anywhere else. And with the amount of 'houses' in that area I'd say the 'ladies' are pretty busy keeping the miners happy." Jessie's tone became more thoughtful, though, as she held her cup with both hands, staring over the top. "I'm curious, Bobbie, to see how they live and think, and what kind of impact the miners have on their lives, especially with the strike going on. I feel sorry for them. I mean, what kind of life is that?"

Bobbie shook her head. "Now, Jess," she chided, "there's got to be a better way to get that information. We women just pretend we don't know what's going on inside, like they don't exist. Gosh, Jess, who knows what kind of disease you can catch just by walking through the door." She shivered. "Ugh. You wouldn't get me *near* one of those places!"

After finishing their coffee and rinsing out their cups, both women returned to their desks to work until Jessie left for her first appointment.

It could be Bobbie was right about this. Jessie was having second thoughts as she approached the two-story building. Pulling off the road, she parked behind a row of ancient poplar trees that provided camouflage for her auto and stepped outside. Leaning against the hood, she peered between the trunks searching for any activity while considering her next move.

The house, itself, looked innocent enough. In fact, it was a close resemblance of her own. *Well, what did you expect, blinking red lights and a waiting line?* As she watched, the side door opened exposing two people. The woman was dressed in a shiny pink dressing gown; the man in typical miner's garb, carrying his hat and coat. Leaning forward, she placed a kiss on his lips as he slipped a few bills into her hands. His mouth moved and whatever he said must have pleased her for she kissed him again. Looking over her shoulder, she shoved the bills inside a pocket before sending him on his way.

Jessie quickly popped behind one of the tall trees as the man headed her direction but peeked slowly around the trunk to get a better look as the miner hitched up his suspenders and shrugged into the worn tan jacket. Placing the cap over his head, he strolled toward her, staring down at the ground. Although unable to see his face, Jessie was puzzled at the tingling déjà vu feeling. And as if feeling her scrutiny, he suddenly looked up and spotted her among the trees.

It was Jacob.

There was no way to escape. Knowing he had seen her, Jessie stepped away from her cover as he approached.

"Ms. Peterson!" His tone was puzzled yet respectful. "What are ya *doing* here? He quickly glanced around him but saw no one.

With a smile, Jessie reached out her hand. "How are you, Jacob? I'm sorry for startling you…"

"This is no place for a lady like you," he hissed, ignoring her hand. "Quick! You need to get out of here before someone sees you."

Jessie dropped her hand and frowned at him. "Jacob, I appreciate your concern for my reputation, but no one else has noticed me. The only person I've seen so far is you."

Jacob was firm, saying in a no-nonsense voice, "And that's all you're going to see. Now, hurry, get back into your car and—"

Grabbing her arm suddenly, he dragged Jessie behind the tree line, motioning her to keep quiet. At his nod, Jessie glanced across the road to see two other patrons leaving the same house, both in military uniform. Stunned, she froze as their loud voices shot across the highway and cringed at their crude vocabulary. Although not familiar with all their racy cant, Jessie concluded that their rendezvous at the house must have been *very* satisfying.

She held her breath as they approached, but just before reaching the road, the two turned right, walking down a dirt path leading back to their barracks, their raucous laughter fading in the distance.

"Sorry you had to hear that, miss," Jacob apologized as he shook his head. "But that's what you get for being where you shouldn't be."

"Well, let's look at it this way. I've *definitely* increased my vocabulary today!" Jessie tried inserting a little humor into an embarrassing situation.

Jacob hung his head down. "I'm ashamed for you to see me here, but Fannie and I, well, we got this thing going, and I'm wanting to earn enough money to get her out of there. She's tried to get different jobs, miss, really, she has. But no one wanted ta hire her. You see, Fannie's an orphan, come up from down state hoping to cash in on the copper rush. But so far, this is all she could find. And now with the strike going on, money's gett'n scarce."

He took off his hat and scratched his head. "Don't know what to do, Ms. Peterson. We enjoy what little time we have together. They keep her busy, though, and some of the guys, well, they don't treat the girls too well. Fannie has even had an occasional bruise or two."

Jacob looked forlorn. "I can get past what she does, knowing how sweet she really is, but other guys, they have no right treating her that way. I sure wish there was something I could do."

Jessie was pensive. "Jacob, let me think about this. I came here looking for a story, and you've filled in a lot of blanks, putting me on another trail, so to speak."

She thought for a moment. "Do you think Fannie would come and talk to me about what goes on inside and what the strike is doing to their business? You could bring her to my house so we can be private. No one would see us. And in the meantime, I'll try and think of some way she can better her life."

Jacob's eyes widened at her suggestion. "Gosh, I don't know, Ms. Peterson. I mean, I think the world of Fannie, an all, but what if someone sees us walking into your house? Not a good thing for you." He rubbed the back of his neck. "Could cause a lot of trouble for her, too, just trying to get her out of there. You see, they only let the girls leave for an emergency, like a doctor's appointment and then, always guarded. Guess they're scared some won't return. Many guys have their favorites, too, and pay a high price for their services. Anyway, from what Fannie tells me, the girls are too scared to be seen in public. The ladies don't treat them well, and the men pretend like they've never seen 'em before. I have heard of some fellas buying a full night out with their favorite girl, but most of us can't afford anything like that." He shrugged. "It's pretty hopeless."

Jessie clapped him on the shoulder. "No, Jacob, it *isn't*. Believe it or not, you just handed me the solution." She was excited now. "All we must do is, how do they put it, buy her off the floor? That way it'll give you two more time together and I'll get my interview."

Jacob shook his head. "Now, Ms. Peterson, you know I can't afford nothing like that! Not that I don't want to spend more time with Fannie, but even if I had it, what would my mam say to spending money so foolishly?"

"Maybe *you* can't, Jacob, but I can. And I promise you, I'll think of a better way for Fannie to live." She held out her hand. "What do you say?"

Still hesitant, Jacob rubbed his hands on his hat and plopped it on his head. He cocked his head and stared at Jessie's face, then down at her outreached palm. Reaching out, he grasped it with his own and shook on the deal. In for a buck or, in this case, a hundred bucks. He wasn't going to ask where she'd get the money, but for the first time in a long while, his soul felt uplifted. Maybe, just maybe, she could pull this off.

Jacob refused a lift home, saying the walk would help him think. Reassuring him that she would be in touch, Jessie watched him walk away, his stride jauntier than before.

She, too, was thinking. Without knowing all the facts, Jessie knew this was going to take some doing. But then, wasn't life supposed to be full of hope? She smiled, knowing just the right person to tackle the job.

CHAPTER 16

"I feel like I'm being led to the gallows, or you're fattening me up for the kill!" Mitch said, patting his bulging stomach.

He sat next to Jessie on the sofa, basking in the heat of the potbellied stove as well as her warm body snuggled up beside him. They had just finished one of the best suppers he'd ever eaten, succulent roast beef, creamy mashed potatoes with silky smooth gravy, homemade yeast rolls with melted butter and cheesy asparagus. Other than sending inquiring looks her way, he had said nothing until they moved into the living room for their coffee and dessert.

"Why, Mitch, what makes you think that?" Jessie, looking completely innocent, batted her eyelashes. Was the way to a man's heart truly through his stomach? She hoped so, her meal being along the lines of the fattened calf. Would his mellow mood sour when she brought up Jacob and Fannie?

Well, I've had a lot of now or never, so why stop now. Taking a deep breath, she reached over and poured out two steaming cups, handing one to Mitch before settling back against the cushions with the other. A strawberry-rhubarb pie, ready to be cut, sat between them on the little table.

"Well, there *is* a little situation I've got myself into that could use a bit of your expertise." Jessie said cautiously.

"Okay, let's have it." Mitch took a sip of the rich brew, put his cup back down on the table and settled back, giving her his full attention. For him, nothing could be worse than taking her down into the mine shaft, so he was willing to listen to her latest dilemma.

Encouraged by his attitude, Jessie blew on her cup, taking a small sip before setting it down next to his. Grabbing his hand, she looked into his eyes and began her spiel.

"Yesterday, I drove up to the red-light district on top of the hill hoping to get a different perspective on how the strike is affecting the residents of that community. You know, a different slant on the story. The miners are probably less inhibited when talking to the girls, so there might be another angle we're not aware of. By now, our readers must be tired of hearing the same old thing, as there's nothing new to report. It's depressing. I thought this would brighten their horizons."

Oh, it would brighten their horizons, alright. Mitch, overcome, pulled back his hand and looked at her like she was crazy. Was she so naive not to realize how tainted she could have become? Or the danger she could have encountered? He shook his head. No, this wasn't like the mine venture; it was worse.

"Now, Mitch, don't look at me like that." Jessie stood up, facing him. "I know it was a far-fetched notion, even for me, but this extended strike is trickling down into so many different areas. Life is *never* going to be the same for anyone, not just the miners. These girls aren't any different. But don't worry," she assured him. "I never got into a house. Not even close. I did encounter a patron of one of the, ah, establishments, though. It was Jacob. Remember? The young miner who gave me the interview?" At his nod, she continued. "Well, I was parked behind that big row of Poplar trees. You know, the ones on top the hill. I thought I was cleverly camouflaged, but he must have felt me watching him and came over."

"I hope he was smart enough to make you drive away from there. If not, I've lost all respect for him." Mitch folded his arms across his chest and glared up at Jessie.

Jessie looked sheepish. "Well, he *tried* talking me into leaving immediately, but just then two other guys walked out of the same house and headed toward us. Jacob grabbed my arm and pulled me behind the tall trees so they wouldn't notice us. As it was, they were soldiers. Thankfully, they turned before reaching the road and headed back to their camp."

She held her hand up. "No one saw me, I promise."

Mitch, shaking his head, wasn't pacified, and chided her. "Don't you *ever* think before you act, Jess? Even being near that area could have been dangerous. Don't kid yourself. That location isn't any different than in Detroit. Any guy could have taken you for one of the 'ladies' and approached you with physical intent. And don't you realize just being seen there could ruin your reputation? Thank goodness Jacob had brains enough to get you out of there."

At her silence, he squinted his eyes and looked up at her for confirmation. "He *did* get you out of there?"

"Well, yes, of course he did, Mitch, but you see, there's a little hitch." Jessie leaned forward and reached for both coffee cups before sitting back down beside him. He accepted the cup she handed, took a little sip, and raised his arm in a salute.

"Well, let's have it. Here's to your latest project. I might as well listen, now, knowing I'll probably be in the thick of it before long." Mitch ached a skeptical eyebrow. "Not saying I'll approve, mind you, but at least I can be prepared."

Balancing her coffee with both hands, she swiftly leaned over and pecked him on the cheek. "Thanks, Mitch. You're *such* a sweetie! I *knew* I could count on you." Now that she had his support, Jessie was exuberant. Helping someone else would take her mind off her own problems too.

"Remember how bad I felt after I interviewed Jacob?" Remembering her tears, Mitch nodded. "Well, now there *is* a way I can help him. Not necessarily out of the mines, but better his life in a different sort of way."

Jessie frowned. "But how to go about it is still foggy, and that's where you come in, Mitch. You see, Jacob visits that house to be with his friend, Fannie." She shuddered, thinking of the horrors Jacob had told her about. "Anyway, Fannie came up state when she heard about the copper explosion and thought she could improve her circumstances by being where the money was. Unfortunately, she was unable to find any employment except for being one of the 'ladies.' She *wanted* to work somewhere else, but no one would hire her; and Jacob, of course, wants to spend more time with her."

She looked at him with misty eyes and whispered, "Oh, Mitch, if only you knew the conditions those poor girls live in every day. Jacob told me some shocking stories. It's like they're in prison. Many aren't there because they want to be but because they have no other place to go. And it can be physically brutal at times. The girls bring in lots of money for their proprietors, so they don't want to lose any of them. Getting her out might be difficult."

Jessie sniffed, then with glistening eyes and a winning smile, she patted his leg. "But that's where *you* come in, Mitch. You must have some idea how to go about this. Not that I care to know, mind you, but you must have more knowledge about the red-light district than I do."

Mitch chuckled. "Are you asking me if I ever visit the girls?"

Jessie turned red. "As I said, Mitch, I'd rather not know all the juicy details; but I'm sure as a guy you have more inside information than I could ever obtain."

Mitch was amused. "Maybe it'll be my little secret to keep you guessing for a while." Inward, he chuckled, amazed that she could be such an innocent at times. No way would he take a chance on getting a disease they probably housed in there, but she didn't have to know that. Now the ball was in his court, and he was ready to play.

"By my rules, Jess?"

"By your rules, Mitch. I promise." Jessie made the vow, crossing her heart, and *hoping* that in the future she'd remember to keep it.

"First, what to do about Fannie. We'll need to find her gainful employment and then, of course, another place to live." Sensing where her wheels were spinning, he quickly added, "And don't you even think about it. She *cannot* live with you, Jess. It wouldn't be proper, at least for now."

Jessie slumped back in disappointment. He was beginning to read her all too well. She *was* going to suggest that Fannie live with her while looking for employment. It would be a quick solution. But Mitch was right about the proprieties. Even though she knew Fannie *wanted* to make a change in her life, she really didn't know her at all. Jessie had another idea, though.

"How about if I hire her as my housekeeper? With all my crazy hours, there's not enough time to keep up with everything. She'd also be a good babysitter for the house, too, in case someone comes snooping about. That is, if you don't think it would be too dangerous for her?"

Mitch thought for a moment, then nodded. "That would probably work, providing she understands there wouldn't be any secret trysts with Jacob or anyone else at your home. I won't have any shenanigans going on while you're out."

"From what Jacob told me, Fannie will do anything to get out of the business, so I'm sure she'll agree to the terms. That's the easy part." Jessie thoughtfully tapped her chin with her finger. "The plan to get her out might be more difficult, though. I understand the girls are watched very carefully; but with enough money, they can be bought off the floor for a night. I can pay for this service, Mitch, but can't just hand over a wad of money to Jacob. Can you do this if I give it to you?"

Mitch silently absorbed this suggestion. "It's a workable solution as I can get below and hand over the cash to him. I'd approach his home, but everyone would wonder why I was selecting him for a special visit. I don't think the companies, or the union would appreciate it."

"Now, where to put Fannie..." He snapped his fingers. "I've got it! One of the boarders left to go back home last week and Irma needs to fill that vacancy. You know what a soft heart she has. And the money you pay Fannie can go for her room and board." Then he grimaced. "Hmm, what to do about Josie, though. Knowing her, she'll probably adopt her as one of the hurt creatures she's constantly bringing home." He smiled. "Yes, Jess, it *just* might work!"

Mitch was getting excited, now, catching on to Jessie's enthusiasm as they drew up their plans together.

"Jessie, first I'll have to speak to Irma and Tom and clue them in. If they have any objections, we'll have to start over. But I think Irma will agree with me that it will be good for Fannie to see how a normal functioning family works. Irma might even teach her a thing or two in the kitchen."

Jessie grabbed his hands excitedly.

"When can we start?"

CHAPTER 17

Mitch had been lucky. It was a beautiful Indian summer day. Although many of the trees had lost their brilliance, a few hung on to their faded orange, gold, and reds, now reflecting the sun's bright afternoon rays. Overhead, squawking geese in large Vs were heading south, a reminder that the cold days of winter were not far behind. He hummed as he parked his car outside the mine perimeter and walked toward the hoist building.

He had good news for Jacob. Irma and Tom had agreed to their scheme, albeit the latter with reservations, especially when subjecting his daughter to a "tainted lady." But after hearing Mitch's spiel, agreed that Fannie should have a chance to better herself…if she didn't entertain Josie with stories of living in a bordello. Mitch grinned in satisfaction. Not only had he secured a job and room for Fannie, but also a possible position for Jacob at Kirkish Furniture in Houghton, where work was a lot less dangerous.

Clutching a paper bearing the good news, he strode toward the first striking group milling about with picket signs. As he approached, Mitch could see only a few hecklers remaining for the small afternoon shift. The numbers had dwindled during the past week, for although the parades and marches continued, some of the original steam had evaporated.

As Mitch drew closer, some strikers raised their hands in greeting, knowing Mitch was not their enemy and feeling no animosity toward him. He, with diplomacy, greeted each one, inquiring about their families, health and discussing the unusual warm weather they were having. One man pulled a flask from his pocket and offered it to Mitch. Clapping the man on his shoulder, he declined with a smile, saying he was still on duty. Waving goodbye, he continued toward the small circle of miners who were still aboveground. Good, he wouldn't have to try and find Jacob below the surface. It wasn't his favorite place to be.

As it was, the few miners on second shift were delayed, waiting for inspections to be completed by a timber crew who were working on some damaged areas below. He spotted Jacob about halfway down the short line of workers and made his way toward him, camouflaging the rendezvous by stopping and asking questions of a few other men. As he approached, Jacob's eyes widened with surprise, mixed with hope. As with the other workers, Mitch pulled him aside for a few private questions, but also slipped a note into his palm as they shook hands. Jacob's fist closed over the paper just as they started moving forward. With a nod and a wink, Mitch stepped aside as the men headed for the mine entrance. After marching through the door of the shaft house, they climbed onto the man car, preparing to descend into another day of darkness. Mitch waved and turned back, knowing that for Jacob, at least, the day would be a little brighter.

Approaching his car, Mitch was about to step in when a heavy rumble of the earth shook him off balance. He spun and started running back toward the hoist when the whistles began to blow. As plumes of dust shot through the doorway, he saw the engineer stagger out, coughing violently until he fell to the ground, blood streaming from an ugly gash on his forehead. Hurrying to his side, Mitch half lifted the man and pulled him away from the entrance, exposing him to the much-needed fresh air. No one else came through the door, which meant that the miners were already down. But how far?

"Oh god. Not Jacob, please," Mitch sent a heartfelt prayer upward. By now, all the strikers surrounding the area came running to assist, strike or no strike. It could have been any one of them down there. And many still had friends who worked below.

Pulling out a large handkerchief, Mitch tied it around the man's head trying to stop the red flow. But the engineer waved aside his attempt to help him and tried to sit up. "Let me go! There are men in there!" he shouted. The exertion was too much, and he fell back to the ground, pointing to one of the side buildings. "There are shovels and picks inside." He rasped. "Blinded by all the smoke, I couldn't see if the hoist is still intact." He coughed again, spitting out tiny pieces of rock and other debris.

"Easy now," Mitch tried to comfort him, then yelled at one of the men close by. "Quick. There's a canteen of water in my car, parked outside the fence." The striker went running in the direction of the road as others ran to the shed to get the tools needed for digging.

As they loaded up, many neighbors who had felt the blast, came running, anxious to find out what had happened. How many were down there, at what levels, what shafts? How to locate them? The families of the afternoon shift arrived first, each fearing it was one of their own. Although always a daily hazard, no one ever wanted to believe it would happen to them. Twisting their hands around their handkerchiefs, the women waited, each with hope and prayers for their own as well as others trapped below. Their silent vigil was short lived as a wailing young wife came running up the road, knowing her husband had been in the second shift. They immediately surrounded her, offering words of support. Hushed whispers and loud sobbing comingled as each tried to console the other.

Within a few minutes, trucks arrived with the rescue team, about forty men trained to seek out the injured and bring them back to the surface. The leader pulled out prints of the entire mine pointing out several possibilities for locating the men. Mitch joined them, finding out where the timber crew had been working, bracing up walls that had been weakened by a recent fire. He listened attentively, not knowing where Jacob was stationed.

Pulling on their heavy jackets and thick helmets, the team picked up their tools and headed into the opening where the dust was finally dissipating. To their relief, they could see the hoist was still in working order. Just outside, Mitch watched as the men jumped onto the car with shovels, picks, axes and whatever else could cut through the solid rock. He knew blasting would be the quickest way, but also the most dangerous. However, the longer it took to find the victims, the less chance they had of surviving. Just as they were debating, another blast shook the ground, causing more debris to fall from the ceiling and float up from the deep crevice. Holding on to their helmets, the men hunkered down, waiting for the debris and dusty smoke to settle. Going underground was not going to be an easy decision.

As the dust lessened, the team captain held up his hand. "Men, you know the hidden dangers below. There could be more blasts, falling rocks, timbers, and who knows what else; but if we don't act now, *all* lives might be lost. Time's not on our side." He paused, looking into each face. "If any of you want to stay behind, just say so as we're all volunteers." He waited but, by their silence, knew they would go. This is what they had been trained for, although probably hoping it would never be necessary. The hoist was engaged, and the men slid down into the shaft.

Sending up a prayer for both the injured and rescuers, Mitch returned to the engineer to see how he was faring. By now, the man was standing with the assistance of those around him. Despite his affliction, desperate loved ones were pelting him with questions, seeking answers he couldn't give them. Mitch had only one question to ask him. Did he know at what level Jacob was working in?

Inhaling deeply, the man thought for a moment. "Young Jacob? I think he was supposed to be drilling somewhere above the timber crew, who were way down on the forty-first level." He nodded. "Yup, that's the level still workable after the fire, so they were to set up there." Leaning forward, his body convulsed with violent coughs, leaving him weak and unable to continue standing.

Lowering him to the ground, Mitch could hear sirens blaring a short distance away and within a minute, two fire trucks and an ambulance pulled close to the spectators. As severe air blasts could be felt miles away, he wasn't surprised to see the vehicles arrive. He stood up as a couple of white garbed men jumped out. Carrying a stretcher, they pushed through the crowd to tend to the wounded.

Mitch hailed them. "Over here, guys!"

They hurried to his side just as the engineer had another spasm. When it passed, they gently picked him up and laid him on the stretcher. One medic checked his eyes and throat while the other prodded his body for any painful areas. "George, this one needs to get to the hospital stat." He looked down at the patient. "No broken bones that I can feel, but if blood is any indication, that bad gash on your head will probably need some stitching. And I guarantee, you'll be sore for a while." He unwound Mitch's red-soaked handkerchief, poured a little antiseptic onto a cotton batting square, and padded the open wound. The engineer winced as he touched the raw area but submitted to the medic who then wrapped a white gauze bandage around his head several times.

"There. That should keep you from bleeding until you get to the hospital. When you arrive, they'll probably want to monitor your breathing, too, to make sure you're getting enough oxygen in your lungs." He smiled down encouragingly at the engineer before looking up at Mitch. "Were there any others hurt?"

Mitch shook his head. "Right now, it's unknown," he replied sadly, thinking of Jacob. "But both a timber crew and some miners are still down there. We don't know their whereabouts or if there are injuries. The rescue crew just went down to search for them."

The medic nodded. "All right. I'll stay behind, then, in case I'm needed. My name's Don, by the way." He shook hands with Mitch and then spoke to George. "I'll empty out all the equipment we might need here, and you take the patient to the hospital. Before coming back, load all the medical supplies you can into the ambulance and see if there's another vehicle we can use, too, plus a couple more medics. Get back here in a hurry. If there are casualties, we'll need to be ready for them when they surface."

Carefully, George and Don hoisted the stretcher and placed it in back of the emergency van. After securing the patient, George ran around to the front and with sirens blaring and lights flashing, headed down hill to St. Joseph's hospital in Hancock.

Mitch was in turmoil. What he *wanted* to do was run into the mine shaft and start digging for Jacob or any other lost souls. But logically, there was nothing more he *could* do except, like the others, wait. Feeling emotionally drained, he shuffled toward the group of strikers. What had started out as a helping hand for Jacob, had ended up as a full-blown rescue mission. Glancing at his watch, he knew he was late. Jessie would be expecting him, but there was no way he could contact her now. His concern for Jacob overshadowed any other issues and he was sure she would understand, considering he was there on her behalf.

But back at the *Gazette*, Jessie frowned and checked her watch… *again*. Confirming it hadn't stopped, she stood up by her desk and peered out of the window into the parking lot. *Mitch must have a good reason for being late. It isn't like him to keep me in suspense.* She knew today was the day he would get word to Jacob and start the ball rolling for him and Fannie. With a sigh, she sat back down and tried to concentrate on her weekly editorial, using an eraser for the third time.

"Knock, knock." Jessie looked up as Bobbie poked her head inside the door of her office. Great! A much-needed distraction. She pushed her chair back, the wheels wobbling against the hardwood floor. "Come on in, Bobbie."

"Am I disturbing you?" Bobbie asked.

"Not in the least. Come. Sit. My mind can't seem to settle down today. I've been waiting for Mitch and he's way overdue." Jessie looked up at Bobbie who had carried in two steaming mugs.

"Hmm, what have we here?" It certainly didn't look like the usual coffee, but by now, anything sounded good. Reaching up for a cup, she sniffed and tentatively took a sip. Hot cocoa!

"Mmm, delicious." Jessie took another sip, closed her eyes, and settled back into her chair. "You're a mind reader, Bobbie. How did you know I needed a diversion this afternoon?"

"Well, you've seemed a little bit distracted today, not your usual bubbly self. Wanna talk about it? You and Mitch haven't quarreled, have you?" Pulling over a nearby chair, Bobbie settled down for a cozy chat.

"No, no. Nothing like that." With elbows on her desk, Jessie grasped the cup with both hands, taking another satisfying drink and sighed. What was it about chocolate that made you feel so good? "Bobbie, this is awesome. Hershey's?" It was her favorite.

"What else?" Bobbie answered with a smug smile. "Now, tell me what's going on." She was curious as well as concerned about her friend.

"Okay. But I hope you'll keep an open mind." With a prayer that Bobbie would understand, Jessie started in. "Remember when I wanted to interview the red-light district on the hill, and you advised me against it?"

Bobbie vehemently shook her head. "Of course, I remember. I had nightmares just thinking about it."

"Well..."

Bobbie's eyebrows shot up. "Jessie, you *didn't*!"

"I didn't get my interview if that's what you're thinking. Didn't even get inside. But yes, I did go there, and something good did come out of it."

Bobbie was silent, but as she raised a skeptical eye, Jessie continued.

"The miner I had interviewed when I went below was coming out of one of the houses and, unfortunately, spotted me. He hurried across the street and tried to persuade me to leave immediately before anyone else saw me."

"Well, at least someone had good sense, but go on, Jess. I'm listening."

"Anyway, Jacob, that's his name, has been visiting one of the girls by the name of Fannie. They've become more than good friends and he's been trying to think of a way to get her out. Fannie is obligated to the owner for providing for her when she had no place else to go, but now she wants to leave the brothel. Unfortunately, the monies received from their patrons make it difficult." Jessie sighed. "And from what Jacob was telling me, it can be pretty rough at times if the men get overly physical."

Jessie leaned earnestly across the desk. "I've *got* to try and help her, Bobbie. Mitch was supposed to catch Jacob today and let him in on our little scheme. I've been preoccupied all day waiting for him to return and fill me in." She glanced at her watch. "He's an hour overdue, which isn't like him at all. I just hope everything's okay."

A movement in the doorway caught the girls' attention, but instead of Mitch, it was Brian coming through the door looking for Bobbie.

"There you are!" Brian, smiling, addressed Bobbie, first, before turning his attention to Jessie. "Hey, Jess. What are you girls cooking up now?" he teased.

As she watched, Jessie saw Bobbie blush at his flattering attention. Since the foursome had dinner, he'd found many occasions to just grace her desk with his presence, complimenting her outfit and typing skills or just asking her opinion on an article going to print. Brian had certainly come out of his shell. On a few occasions, the four of them had ventured out together for dinner or the theater with Brian driving Bobbie home, afterward, in his truck. The next morning, she would come in all dreamy eyed before settling into her daily routine.

Jessie chuckled as she held out her cup. "The only thing we're cooking up right now is hot cocoa. Want some, Brian?"

He shook his head. "Sorry, I'd love to, but I have a mechanic coming in shortly to check one of the printers that's been giving me trouble." He turned back to Bobbie and said softly, "I was just checking to see if we're still on for tonight."

Bobbie's eyes sparkled as she looked up at him and nodded. "I'm looking forward to it. Dinner is at seven, but feel free to come early if you'd like. I just might put you to work in the kitchen," she threatened him.

"You're on." With an affectionate look at Bobbie, he left the room without a backward glance.

Jessie was grinning. "Dinner at your house?"

Bobbie dimpled with happiness and nodded. "It was my idea. After all, Brian has treated me to several occasions, so it's only right that I pay him back." She reached out and grabbed Jessie's hands, excitedly. "And he *really* wants to come, Jess! Can you believe it? He said yes right away!"

"But of course, he wants to come. He's *besotted* with you. I can tell by how he stares at you when he thinks you're not looking. He wants to be in your company—a lot. Let's face it, Bobbie, he's smitten!"

"Don't say that, Jess. It could bring bad luck." Bobbie sat back with a sigh. "It's just that it's taken me so long to get his attention, I wouldn't want to jeopardize our relationship."

"Has he kissed you yet?" Jessie teased.

"Not yet. He's still shy in that area. But I think he's working up to it and tonight might be the night!" Bobbie's eyes widened. "What should I do, Jess? I want him to kiss me. Is that wrong? Will he think me forward if I kiss him back?"

"Don't worry, Bobbie. If the time is right, it'll feel so natural you'll wonder why you worried. In fact—"

A sudden rumble, then shaking of the building, interrupted whatever Jessie was going to say next. She grabbed her cocoa before it jiggled across the desk and on to the floor. Bobbie wasn't as lucky as the chocolate from the cup she was holding, sloshed over and ran down the front of her dress.

Silently, they stared at each other. Then, by mutual agreement, got up and hurried to the window where the mines were visually in sight. From their point of view, everything looked the same until a tremendous roar, followed by another good shaking grabbed hold of the building once again. Gazing up, they could now see a plume of smoke rising into the air near one of the shaft houses.

Knowing that wasn't a good sign, Jessie ran back to her desk, grabbed her purse and a notebook, and headed toward the door.

"Bobbie, I've got to go! Mitch might still be up there. Run and tell Carl to come quickly and bring his camera. I'll bring the car up front." With those instructions, Jessie raced down the stairs and out the door to the parking lot.

Starting her auto, she revved the motor before driving to the front door just as Carl came leaping out of the building with his camera slung over his shoulder. As soon as he was settled, Jessie gunned it out to the main street and headed toward the bridge. Thankfully, traffic was low with no trolley in sight.

Crossing the Portage quickly, she took a shortcut and headed up hill instead of driving through town. All she could think about was Mitch being caught underground and it would be her fault for persuading him to help.

The tall shaft house came into view as they ventured up Quincy Hill. Already cars and people were milling about blocking the entrance to the mine. Moving closer, she could see a couple of ambulances and firetrucks closer to the opening and as she approached, a policeman halted any further movement, motioning to park her car.

Jessie told Carl to get out and called the officer. After showing the deputy their press credentials, he allowed them to pass and wade through the throng of waiting spectators. Her eyes began a frantic search of the area until they fell upon Mitch, safe with a group of men milling close to the shaft house entrance. She let out the breath she had been holding and sent up a prayer of thanks for his safety. But where was Jacob?

Elbowing her way toward Mitch, she heard snatches of conversation. Timber crew. Second shift miners. Rescue team. Quickly jotting down a few notes, she slipped the notebook into her purse and made a beeline for Mitch.

Scanning the grounds as if expecting her, Mitch wasn't at all surprised to see Jessie rushing toward him. Regardless of the spectators, he opened his arms as she threw herself at him. Jessie cried into his shirt, and he pulled out his handkerchief, dabbed at her eyes and gently brushed off the river of tears rolling down her cheeks. After a few minutes, and with a deep sigh of relief, she took the hankie out of his hand, blew her nose, then shoved the damp mess into the bottom of her purse.

Feeling totally drained, she looked up at Mitch and sniffed. "I was so afraid it was *you* down there and it would have been all my fault for getting you involved in my stupid scheme. I would *never* forgive myself if anything happened to you! Oh, Mitch." Jessie was working herself into a frazzle, again, with her eyes tearing up.

Mitch grasped her hands and drew her apart from the interested crowd.

"Now, Jess, calm down." He tried to reason with her. "You didn't force me into anything. I *chose* to help Jacob and Fannie, so don't feel you twisted my arm." He laughed. "You can't take all the credit, you know."

Jessie sniffed once more. "Well, I was just worried when you didn't show up at the office, especially after we felt the blasts."

"And I'm glad you care enough. But as you can see, I'm just fine. My main concern, right now, is for Jacob. After handing him the note, I watched him enter the shaft house with the other workers and disappear below on the man car. It was just seconds later that the first blast hit, so I don't know how far down they were at that time. The second one came a few minutes after that. Now we're all just waiting to see what the rescue team finds out." He shook his head. "The blast was a big one, Jess. I'm not expecting any good news. If Jacob is safe, it probably means he never got to the fortieth level. The timber crew, working on the forty-first level, were the only workers engaged at the time, so it's most likely the suspect location."

Jessie sighed heavily as she pulled out her pad. It was time to put emotions aside and seek whatever facts were available. "Guess I'd better get to work, then, and start doing my job." She glanced around. "Carl's here somewhere so I need to find him and interview a few people. But first I'll start with you, Mitch. Do you know long the rescue team's been down there?"

Mitch glanced at his watch. "I think it's been about forty-five minutes. An engineer was injured right after he had sent the men down and the ambulance took him to the hospital for treatment. The rescue team went down shortly after that."

"The engineer. How bad were his injuries? Was he able to tell you anything?"

"He had a tough time speaking, Jess. His lungs were filled up with dust and debris, and he had a nasty gash on his forehead that will probably need stitching. Other than that, he was the only one on the main level at the time. He remembers Jacob going below with the others and was scheduled to work somewhere above the timber crew. That's all he could tell us."

Spying a young man heading their direction Mitch lifted his arm and waved. "Here comes Carl, now."

Striding up to them, Carl stopped to put more film into his camera and then pointed it at them. "How about a photo of the two of you to start off with, using the hoist as a backdrop? It could make a great opening to your story."

Jessie thought for a minute, then nodded. "It might be a good idea, Mitch, as I *am* interviewing you, and Carl can take pictures of others as I question them. As they say, 'a picture is worth a thousand words.' But make sure you get approval from those who will be in the photographs, first, Carl. This is a stressful time for all of them and they might not want their pictures in the newspaper."

"Yes, ma'am. Now, move to the right a little. That's it. No, don't look at me, look at each other. That's good. Now, one more just in case." He clicked the button a second time. "Got it! What next, Jessie?" Carl asked as he looked around.

"First, I'll start interviewing the striking miners as some of them may have been caught in a similar situation. After that, I'll approach the groups of families waiting for news. If they want to be questioned, fine; otherwise, we'll just move on." Jessie looked at Carl. "Now, just follow me. As you do, put yourself in their place and imagine how you'd feel if one of *your* loved ones was lost below. Tread carefully and be considerate. No posing them as you did with me and Mitch. Just shoot when you can. After getting permission, of course." With these instructions, Jess headed off with Carl shadowing her footsteps.

Mitch watched them as they worked their way to the strikers. Knowing there was nothing more he could do, he edged his way closer to the shaft hoping the rescue team would appear soon.

CHAPTER 18

Leaning way back, Sid Brewster pushed his chair away from the desk and took a sip of his frothy beer. Grimacing, he stared down into the dark brown ale, reflecting (unfortunately) that it was a lot warmer than Sable's trail. Efforts to locate her whereabouts had been unsuccessful, and his self-imprisonment in the dilapidated old warehouse was getting old. Maybe it wasn't his best move, but as each day passed, he became more obsessed with *her* capture instead of his own.

Well, warmer's better than nothing, he decided as he took another swig and thought back to his predicament. Sable shouldn't have been at his private club where liquor had been smuggled in for his special clients, but her gay flirting and flashy style had kept them coming back for more, paying the high price for his imported booze. He had made a killing as well as connecting with just the right people who vowed to support his cause. With Sable by his side, men had flocked to his den of iniquity to vie for her attention or even one dance with the infamous flapper. Everything had been perfect; well, almost perfect.

Sighing, Sid knew time was not on his side. The longer he stayed in one place, the more likely he'd be discovered as a new intense search for him was in progress, funneling down to Detroit's south side. Apparently, the greedy guard had either become remorseful (very doubtful) or was singing for his own life (most likely). Sid snorted. *You can't trust anyone these days!*

A scraping in the hallway brought him quickly upright. Setting the mug on his desk, he quietly opened the top drawer, pulled out his revolver, and aimed it at the door. Within seconds, a loud knock came from the other side.

"Hey, Sid! It's Vinnie and Eddy. We've got great news!"

Lowering the handgun, Sid pushed to his feet. With the weapon still in his hand, he unlocked the bolt on the door and opened it a crack to make sure no one else was with them.

"Come on in, boys." He peeked down the hallway to be sure they weren't being followed before closing the door and facing his cohorts.

"Well?"

Vinnie spoke first. "We found Sable." Then, he hesitated. "Well, we *sort of* found her."

"What' ya mean, you sorta found her?" Sid blustered. "How can you 'sorta' find someone? Is she still missing, or what?"

Vinnie rushed on. "Well, it's like this, boss. She disappeared because she never *was*!" Sable's not her *real* name. She just used it while going undercover for a newspaper, with you as her prime target.

Sid sat down and looked at him skeptically. "Vinnie, I'm not sure I get ya. If she ain't Sable, then who the hell is she? Don't you think I know a fake when I see one?"

"Yah, boss, but not this one. She had you completely fooled."

Sid slammed his fist against the desk, making it wobble and the boys jump as he bellowed, "*No* one makes a fool out of Sid Brewster! Ya hear?"

Used to Sid's tantrums, Vinnie rushed on knowing it was better filling him in on the whole picture even though the rest of the news wasn't good.

"Sure, Sid, sure. Well, we've all heard of Randall Peterson, CEO of the *Detroit News Press*. He's one of those big shots in this area."

"Yeah, I've heard of him. So what?"

"She's his *daughter*, Sid! Sable is his daughter, and a reporter to boot," he gushed on. "Her real name is Jessica. We got that information from one of our informers"—Eddie coughed—"excuse me, deputies in the sheriff's office who just happened to see her photo laying on the police chief's desk." He shook his head. "It cost us big-time, Sid, every penny we had." Vinnie went on. "Anyway, knowing we were looking for her, he slipped in later that night and went through a file that contained all her information. She was out to get ya, boss," he added mournfully. "No doubt about it."

Sid stood up and paced the floor, absorbing all this information. "But you still don't know where she is?"

Vinnie shook his head shamefully. "No, boss, and we'll need more of the ready to investigate further. We're both all out of funds. What do you want to do next?"

Sid strolled back to his desk and pulled out the old metal box. Bribery took money, but the greedier the better, as they usually were the best rats. Thank goodness he had enough stashed away for times like this. Taking out a wad, he plunked it down in front of Vinnie. "There, that should be enough. Get a hold of that deputy you used. Promise him whatever he wants, but I want results! And fast!"

"Eddy, come here." Sid motioned for his other accomplice to come forward, and pulling out another bundle from the box, handed it to him. "There must be someone on the *Detroit News Press* staff who will have a clue as to Sable's, excuse me, *Ms. Peterson's*, whereabouts. Someone in a bind who could use a little extra. But…choose *carefully*. That turncoat of a guard I bribed while in prison is singing a different tune, so my time here is limited. I'll have to move fast fellas if you don't find her."

Sid looked from one to the other. "Well, what ya wait'n for?"

"Gotcha, boss. We're on our way. Don't worry. We'll find her, wherever she's hiding." Vinnie promised as he grabbed Eddy's arm and hauled him down the hallway.

But where could she be?

As Sid thought back, he wondered how he had missed all the signs. He remembered only the happy-go-lucky, bubbly airhead that had the mark of every other flapper he knew. Yet the more he thought about it, something *had* been different about her, more refined. Maybe that's where the difference had been. Maybe that's what drew the other men to her side.

She played me for a sucker. Well, Ms. Peterson, the game's not over yet.

Strolling to the door, Sid made sure it was locked and securely bolted. Pacing back and forth across the floor, he knew it was time to weigh his options knowing the Feds had picked up his scent and were hot on his trail. Staring at his bleak surroundings, he wondered if prison had been any worse than this. Cursing the turncoat guard, he sat back down and contemplated his next move, mentally and physically. There just had to be *some* place where they'd never find him.

CHAPTER 19

Mitch encircled the hoist, once again, looking for some movement, any sound or sign from the rescuers. Although normally a patient man, his nerves were on edge at the dead silence. Turning his focus from the doorway, he could see Jessie and Carl mingling with the crowd, with Carl taking photos from a discreet distance.

His attention was suddenly diverted by a lone woman running across the field, her gold-colored dress matching the knee-deep Yarrow that she trampled on as she rushed toward him. On her head, a straw-colored hat, tied below her chin in a bow was swathed with netting over and around her head and face.

Curious, he left the hoist. As she approached, Mitch could see her backward glances. Looking in that direction, he saw nothing amiss so continued moving toward her. Seeing her hesitate before approaching the group of women, he waved and motioned her over to join the waiting families. But shaking her head, she stood where she was, alone. With an occasional peek over her shoulder, the woman seemed undecided whether to move backward or forward.

Determined to help her in any way he could, Mitch closed the distance between them before stopping a few yards from where she stood. As he approached, she turned quickly to flee but stood still when he called out to her.

"Miss, is there anything I can help you with? Can I find someone for you?" Mitch offered.

Slowly, she turned to face him, and spoke so softly he had to move closer to hear her reply.

"The air blast." Her voice was thick with emotion. "I heard some men are trapped. Is it true? It *must* be, for I see all the women gathering about the shaft house." She held out her hand imploringly. "Please, I have a friend who worked this shift today and I need to know what's happened to him!"

"Then come and join the others," Mitch invited. "They're all waiting too." He moved to take her elbow, but she cringed and stepped back.

"No, I'm sorry. I can't join the other women. It wouldn't be proper." She looked about frantically. "I shouldn't have come. If they find out I'm missing..." She shook her head, despondently and sniffed. "I'm so sorry I bothered you. It's best if I go now."

As Mitch watched her turn and walk dejectedly across the field, a thought suddenly occurred to him, and he hastened his stride to catch up with her.

"Fannie, wait!" he called out to her.

Startled, she swiveled at hearing her name.

"How do you know my name?" She paused and scanned his face. "I don't know *you*, do I?"

"No, Fannie, we've never met. My name is Mitch," he said gently. He took her hand and continued. "But I *do* believe we have a mutual friend in Jacob. He *is* who you're looking for?"

Fannie withdrew her hand, reached up and lifted her veil to reveal sparkling eyes filled with tears. "How do *you* know my Jacob?" she asked in astonishment.

Mitch blinked. No wonder Jacob was smitten! Petite and slender, with long coppery curls framing her pale face, Fannie was every man's dream come true. Deep emerald, green eyes accented her soft ivory skin, tinged with a peach glow, and the smidgen of freckles scattered across her upper cheeks would entice anyone to count them, one by one. But it was her eyes, radiating her love for Jacob that struck him the hardest. *Oh boy...*

Mitch sighed. Jessie was right. They had to do something.

With regret, he wished he had good news to tell her. "Unfortunately, Fannie, we haven't heard anything from the rescue team," Mitch told her gently as he touched her shoulder. "But come and meet a friend of mine who's going to help you. Her name is Jessie, and Jacob's told her all about the two of you."

Knowing she would be meeting a woman, Fannie moved to pull the netting down across her face, but Mitch shook his head. Holding her hand, he spoke firmly. "*No*, Fannie, you're not going to need that veil any longer. In fact, that's the reason I happened to be here today." At her confused expression, he continued. "I'll explain about that later, but Jacob confided in us his concern for your safety and his fondness for you, as well as your desire to leave your current position. Is that true? I ask because I've known some women in your situation who are highly satisfied."

Fannie nodded, a stray tear rolling down her cheek. "It's true. I love Jacob, and I know he loves me too. But they won't let me leave because the business would lose so much money." She lowered her head and blushed. "I'm not saying the demand for my service is any greater than the others, but I do have many clients who would probably go elsewhere for their needs. Madam says I *owe* her." Fannie sniffed. "I had no place to go when I came here, last year, and no one would hire me. She found me hovering outside an old bar where I was begging for something to eat. She promised me food, clothing, and warmth. I thought her kindness was an answer to prayer." She shook her head in dismay. "Only later did I discover her true nature and what she expected from me in return."

As she spoke, Mitch saw Jessie heading toward them, but so did Fannie. She attempted to break away, but Mitch held on tight, waiting for Jessie to arrive at their side. With her head bowed low and lovely face hidden, Fannie didn't see the bemused look on Jessie's face as she gazed from her to Mitch.

"What's this, Mitch?" Jessie asked playfully. "Have you resorted to brute force in dealing with us females?"

"Jess, this is *Fannie*," he emphasized. An "*oh*" came from Jessie as she looked to Mitch, quickly understanding the situation. *Jacob's Fannie?* she mouthed. He nodded, appreciating her quick uptake. Now, they just needed a safe place to plan their next move.

As though reading his thoughts, Jessie surveyed the area and found more gawkers had arrived on the scene. Firetrucks and ambulances had pulled up close to the shaft entrance, their workers pacing the grounds, waiting for the injured to surface. Over an hour had passed, and there was still no sign of the living, or the dead. It was going to be a long night.

Making a quick decision, Jessie turned to Mitch. "Please take Fannie to my house before anyone sees her." Mitch started to protest, but Jessie was adamant as she fished in her pocket, pulled out a key and handed it over. "I know it's not our original plan, but until we come up with a better one, she needs a safe place to stay, and Tom and Irma aren't ready for her yet." She looked around. "I'll round up Carl and meet you there. Once Fannie's safely inside, you can drive Carl to the office, then meet me at home." She smiled down at Fannie. "In the meantime, Fannie and I will have a nice hot cup of tea and get acquainted."

For the first time, Fannie looked up at Jessie and saw no condemnation in her eyes, only compassion and understanding. Blinking back tears, she only had one question. "But what about Jacob?"

Jessie smile was tender as she put her arm around Fannie's shoulder. "There's nothing more we can do here. Mitch will be checking periodically, as will I. If anything good has come from this, it's *you* being here with us. I'll tell you all about it when we get home, but go now with Mitch, and he'll drive you to where it's safe. Believe me, Jacob would want it that way."

Shooing them off, Jessie watched as Mitch put his jacket around a reluctant Fannie and led her away from the crowd to his car just as Carl walked up behind her.

"What now, boss? We've about covered everything here and I've got some great pictures, especially the one of you and Mitch! Shall I go back and develop them?" Carl offered.

Jessie nodded. "That's fine, Carl. But first, we need to go to my house and then *Mitch* will drive you back to the office."

Carl looked at her knowingly. "Anything to do with that lovely young woman who left with him? Never mind. You don't have to tell me."

"Thanks, Carl." Jessie smiled at him, then, looking at her watch, headed to her car with him tagging along.

When Jessie arrived home, Mitch was unlocking the door, and observing Carl's interested glance, hastened Fannie inside. Shutting the door behind him, he sauntered down the steps toward the car, handed Jessie her key and spoke to Carl.

"Guess it's you and me. Drop you off at the office?"

"Thanks, Mitch. I just got a glimpse of that gorgeous redhead but promised Jessie I wouldn't ask any questions. You'll tell me when you're ready, right?" Carl asked hopefully.

Mitch clapped him on the back. "You bet. And the sooner we get going, the faster it'll be." He turned to Jessie. "I'll check on the mine situation before coming back here. Maybe they'll know something by then." With a quick peck on her cheek and Carl in tow, he got into the auto and chugged back toward the main highway.

Jessie waved him off before turning and running up the steps. Not only was Fannie hidden inside, but as she pushed open the door, she expected to find her home in shambles, again, from the blast. However, except for a couple of items laying on the floor, the house stood in one piece. The blast must have come from a different direction or a lot further underground. Sighing in relief, she turned to her unexpected guest who was waiting in confusion.

"Come, Fannie. Let me take your hat and we'll go into the kitchen and put the kettle on while we're waiting for Mitch." Hating to part with it, Fannie hesitated before handing over the frothy headdress. Jessie placed it on the hall tree and moved toward the kitchen, with an uncertain Fannie following behind her.

"Please sit down while I get this brewing. Mitch never really introduced us, but I'm Jessie. It'll be just a few minutes and we'll have something nice and hot to drink." She turned her head toward Fannie. "Nothing like a strong cup of hot tea to warm you up, right?" Without waiting for a reply, she opened the stove door and placed a large stick of wood into the glowing embers, stirring it briskly with an iron poker. Satisfied when the flames took off, Jessie walked over to the sink, filled the kettle, and placed it on the hottest part of the stove.

"There. That shouldn't take too long." After quickly washing her hands, she reached up into her cupboard for two cups and saucers. "Fannie, right next to you is a canister full of tea bags. Can you grab two of them, please?" As Fannie unscrewed the lid and reached into the container, Jessie brought over the porcelain cups, placing them on the table along with a couple of spoons before sitting down.

Fannie tapped her long red nails on the empty teacup making it clink. "Okay, Jessie. I'm a little confused—no, wait. I'm a *lot* confused. I shouldn't even be talking with you, yet here I am in your kitchen." She paused. "Mitch said you knew about Jacob and me. If that's so, you know what I do. It's nothing I'm proud of, especially since meeting Jacob."

Frowning, she looked Jessie squarely in the eye. "You know this could cause you a lot of trouble. People in this area know who I am; well, at least the *men* do. It could put a black spot on your reputation. Why would you want to take any chances with me?"

Jessie thought about her answer for a minute before replying. "Let's just say I'm a crusader of rights. I know Jacob thinks highly of you and I'd like to think the two of you might have a future together, if it's what *you* want, that is."

Changing the subject, Jessie questioned Fannie. "By the way, how *did* you get out of the house? I heard you were well guarded."

Fannie finally smiled, looking pleased with herself. "Well, the blast shook us up, and after it was over, Madam and her staff were working hard putting everything to rights. While they were busy, a man poked his head in the door and yelled that the blast had caused a cave-in and they needed all the help they could get. So the men who were, ah, visiting, reassembled themselves and as they rushed out the door, I managed to slip away without anyone seeing me."

As the teapot started whistling, Jessie rose and pulled it off the stove. Carrying it to the table, she poured the hot liquid into the china cups and Fannie placed one tea bag into each. Dipping their pouches in and out of the steamy water gave them both time to reflect on their situations.

Fannie was the first to speak. "You know, Jessie, when I ran out of the house, all I could think about was Jacob. I had no idea what I would do next." She glanced around her. "But being here was definitely *not* in my plan." She shrugged. "Not that I had any. Please, don't get me wrong. I do appreciate what you've done, but I can't stay here forever." Pulling up her steeping bag, Fannie placed it on the saucer. Taking a cautious sip, she leaned back with a sigh, fully appreciating the strong flavor. In her "house," tea fed to the girls was always lukewarm and pale. Fannie shook her head. Madam wasn't one to waste money on fripperies.

A commotion on the front stairs and loud knock on the door startled her. But Jessie, placing her hand on Fannie's arm for encouragement, got up and calmly walked down the hallway. When the door opened, Fannie could hear a man's voice and was relieved to see Jessie leading Mitch down the hall toward the kitchen. Good. Now maybe she would know what the game was and what her role was going to be.

Mitch rubbed his hands together and smiled at Fannie. "I hope you girls saved some of that hot tea for me. It's getting mighty chilly out there."

Reassuring him that there was plenty, Jessie walked over to the cabinet and pulled out a masculine mug instead of a dainty cup. Glancing out the kitchen window, she could see dusk was approaching, the clouds turning gold and purple in the distance as the fading sun set behind them. Fannie would have to stay the night, she decided, as she filled the cup with hot water and walked back to the table.

As Mitch joined the ladies, he gave his tea bag a good dunk before turning his attention to Fannie. "First things, first. Fannie, the rescue team came up just as I arrived and there was no sign of Jacob, nor any of the other miners." Seeing her crestfallen face, he hastened to add, "But that might be a good omen. The car had stopped just short of the fortieth level, and thankfully, there was little damage in that area. The men were able to make their way down on foot to the next landing but without any sign of the miners. We don't know Jacob's exact location, only that he was above the caved-in area. He could be trapped on the other side of a rock wall. They shouted hoping someone would hear, but there was no answer. The team was unable to go down any further and will have to use picks and shovels to make their way to the forty-first level where the timber crew was working."

"Does this mean there's a chance that Jacob's still alive, Mitch, and just stuck somewhere?" Jessie asked, wanting to give Fannie some hope.

Mitch took a big gulp of his tea, then set the mug down, wrapping his hands around it for warmth as he leaned forward. "A good question, Jess. Until they find *any* bodies, there's always hope. Tonight, a second shift will go down and start picking their way through the rock. Perhaps we'll hear something in the morning. In the meantime, Fannie, did Jessie explain our original plan for you and Jacob?"

"No, Mitch. And as I was telling *her*, it's dangerous for me to be here. They're probably out searching right now, and if they find me, it could mean trouble for both of us. Madam's not exactly the forgiving type and she's not going to be thrilled that I've escaped her clutches." Fannie looked down at her clenched hands. "Look, maybe it'll be better for everyone if I just went back on my own accord. I appreciate you trying to help me, but I don't think this is going to work."

"*Nonsense*, Fannie. You just dropped into our laps prematurely, so we need time to rework our plans. One way or the other, it'll all work out in the end." Mitch looked outside, gauging the darkness. "Looks like I'd better be getting home. Tom will want an update of the accident, and we can discuss our plans now that you're here." He patted her hand reassuringly. "I'll leave it up to Jessie to go over all the details. I'm sure you gals have a lot to discuss, anyway." Mitch stood up, giving Jessie a lingering kiss on the top of her forehead as she looked up at him, then left without a backward glance.

Fannie looked at Jessie inquiringly.

When Jessie saw the questions in her eyes, she took a deep breath and started in. "Well, here goes. We always planned on getting you out, with a little help from Jacob. He was going to buy you off the floor of an evening."

"But that's a *hundred* dollars! Jacob can't afford that. Besides, I wouldn't let him. It *was* a nice thought, though," she added wistfully.

"You're not to worry about the money. I was going to put up the ante and now I don't have to." At Fannie's protest, Jessie continued.

"*And* Mitch found a new job for Jacob aboveground, so he would be safe. Because of the air blast, though, it just didn't happen the way we planned."

Jessie asked hesitantly, "Fannie, not that I'm jinxing it, but if anything *did* happen to Jacob, would you still consider another job?"

Fannie bit her bottom lip as her eyes swelled up. "I don't like to think about it, Jessie, but Jacob always wanted me to leave…so yes, I would take a different job if I could find one. Do you have something in mind?"

Jessie nodded, tapping her finger on the table. "Here, Fannie. I need help *here*. Most days, and some evenings, I'm off interviewing or at the office typing up notes. I never know when I'll be called in emergencies. If you could keep the house clean and fires lit, it would be a great help to me. You could also take phone messages that I'll return later. Naturally, I'll pay you for your services."

At Fannie's protest, Jessie held up her hand.

"No, I insist. You'll be doing me a great favor as I just can't keep up with everything. Besides, you'll be needing money for clothes and stuff since you left everything behind. Also, for your room and board at the Johns' house." At Fannie's quizzical look, she added. "Oh, I didn't tell you about them, did I. Tom and Irma, with their daughter, Josephine, live next door and run a boarding house where Mitch lives. One of their tenants suddenly moved out so they have a vacant room. Obviously, they weren't expecting you so soon and some cleanup is needed, so that's why you're staying here tonight and maybe even tomorrow."

Jessie waved her hand to the living room. "You'll have to sleep on the sofa until I get the spare bedroom ready, but the stove will keep you nice and toasty."

Fannie sat up eagerly. "I don't mind at all, Jessie. And I'll work hard to keep things nice and tidy. Really, I will!" She continued, thoughtfully. "You see, I was raised in an orphanage until I was eighteen. There was always cleaning to be done, especially for us older girls, but they wouldn't keep us past that age. After hearing about the copper rage, I thought I would find my own 'gold mine' up here.

Didn't think I'd land on my back instead of my feet, though," she said with embarrassment.

Jessie gave her clenched hands a squeeze. "Don't even think about it. But I might need you to be a house sitter, too, as I'm up to my ears with my own problems." At Fannie's curious look, she explained.

"Down in Detroit, I went undercover for a newspaper and put a criminal behind bars. Now he's escaped and is in hiding. I know he's not happy with me. This man has connections and can pay any informer for details on my whereabouts. My dad's been keeping an outlook and will let me know of any changes down there. In the meantime, we've asked everyone to keep their eyes and ears open for anything unusual. But I really can't see him finding me up here. It's not his forte."

Observing the look of apprehension in Fannie's eyes, Jessie continued. "Don't worry. You wouldn't be in any danger, but I wanted to tell you what you'd be getting into with this job. I'll need you to watch out for any strangers roaming around the yard or close to it." She chuckled. "Both Mitch and my friend, Bobbie, think I should get a watch dog." She shrugged. "Maybe it's something I should seriously consider. Would you mind dog sitting too?"

"You just *name* it, Jessie," Fannie said, her eyes shining with enthusiasm. "I'm indebted to you, Mitch and Jacob for having faith in me." She added wistfully, "As for the dog, I've always wanted one, but we couldn't have any where I grew up in. Just let me know what I can do."

Jessie nodded, then looked thoughtful. "Fannie, did you sign any kind of paper when you went to live with your protector? Like for money or time? Anything binding?"

Fannie thought for a moment, then shook her head. "No. There was nothing I can remember. After the first few days, she just told me what she expected from me in exchange for my food, board, and clothing. She kept me well closeted from the other girls for the first day or so, but I never questioned it. As hungry and tired as I was, it felt wonderful just to be warm, fed and have a place to sleep. Once I met the other girls, they seemed happy enough. Everyone gets to keep a small portion of the payment for their services." She added thoughtfully, "In fact, I also had a little money hidden away in my room."

Jessie checked her watch. "Well, it's been a few hours. They've probably searched your room already for any clues to where you could be and most likely confiscated the cash. But if you didn't sign any forms, Fannie, you're not under any obligation to work for them. Let them have the money and move on with your life. We'll call the police if they start harassing you."

She stood up. "Come, now. Let's get you something to sleep in and put the couch in order. We'll make you as comfortable as possible, and hopefully, in the morning, we'll have a better idea of what's happening. Let's think *good* thoughts for Jacob and say prayers for his safety as well as the others'. Like Mitch said, he could be stuck behind a rock wall and just needs to be located. Truly, Fannie, we still have hope."

CHAPTER 20

As the sun was just creeping over the horizon, Mitch pulled into the shaft house parking lot where many vigilant families had returned to the scene, or maybe remained all night hovering around the hot burn barrels. Although the fire trucks had left, ambulances remained, ready to transport the victims as they surfaced.

Mitch headed for the hot coffee he could see being passed around. Walking toward the crowd, he pulled up his fleece lined collar firmly around his neck, then slipped his hands into his jacket pockets wishing he'd worn gloves this morning. As a boy, he'd loved seeing the warm vapor from his mouth rising into the clear air on a cold winter morning. *What ever happened to those days of wonder?* Mitch shivered. *I must be getting old.*

With coffee in hand, he located the exhausted rescue team captain and was told that although the workers had reached the caved in area and three bodies of the timber crew had been found, they were covered with a ton of fallen rock. The next shift just entering the mine would continue trying to extract the victims from the debris. Working with their hands, it could take hours before the first body arrived. Also, four other members of the crew were still missing, as well as the miners located above the blast.

With a heavy heart, Mitch thanked him for the update, then sat down on one of the makeshift log benches. Lifting the coffee mug to his mouth, he contemplated his next move, like what he would say to Fannie and Jessie who were waiting for an answer. Throwing his remaining brown liquid onto the ground, he stood up knowing he was a coward for delaying the inevitable.

About to leave, he heard a shout coming from the direction of the shaft house and everyone started running toward the doorway, carrying Mitch right along with them. Pushing his way through the crowd, he was one of the first to see three men emerge, one of them being supported by the other two. Behind them, a fourth man appeared, walking into the morning sun.

It was Jacob!

Dirty and tattered, Jacob shuffled through the doorway, squinting as the bright daylight hit him. As he joined his three comrades, his eyes searched through the throng of people until finding the one person he was looking for. Reassuring the medical team he was fine, he met Mitch halfway and reached into his pocket, pulling out a crumpled piece of paper. Saying nothing, but holding it out to Mitch, Jacob sobbed, unashamedly, as Mitch took the note from his hand and tried calming him. "Shh, Jacob. It's all right. You're safe now." Putting his arms around his shoulders, Mitch led him away from the boisterous crowd. Yes, they had a reason to celebrate as four of their sons had been returned to them, but seven still lay underground.

Silently, Mitch led a very grimy and exhausted Jacob toward his car, placing him in the front seat. Although he had professed no injury, Jacob was in shock and did what he was told without question. He closed his eyes and leaned back as Mitch slid in beside him. Letting him rest, Mitch leaned behind the passenger's seat and pulled out the gray woolen blanket he kept for emergencies. Spreading it across Jacob's chest and lap, he tucked the edges snugly around him like a cocoon.

"I'll be right back, Jacob," he said softly. Without waiting for a reply, Mitch got back out, quietly closed the door, and rushed back for two more cups of hot coffee, wishing he had some sugar, which was good for shock.

Balancing both mugs, he hurried back to the car, ignoring those who called out to him. A time of reckoning would come later. Right now, Jacob needed peace and quiet and the assurance that he really *was* safe, and his nightmare was over.

Mitch set the cups on the roof of the auto, opened the door, then transferred them to the top of the dash. Jacob turned his head toward him. "My mom. Fannie." Jacob whispered although his eyes were still closed. His body jerked as he coughed hard then laid back against the seat.

"You're going to be the *best* present they've ever had!" Mitch exclaimed as he picked up one of the cups and held it close to Jacob's mouth. "Here, let's see if we can get some of this coffee down you."

Jacob peered up at him through a slit in his eyelids and reached out for the drink. Seeing his hands were shaky, Mitch steadied the base of the cup as Jacob first took a tentative sip, then a second. "Easy now," Mitch advised. Before long, the coffee was half gone, and Mitch placed the remaining brew back on the dash. Jacob sighed heavily as he snuggled deeper into the blanket, fully appreciating the warmth that spread through his body. He felt like he'd been cold forever.

"We'll drive you home, now, so your mom can see you. And, Jacob, we have Fannie at Jessie's house."

"How…?" Jacob began.

"I'll explain on the way over. I promised her and Jessie that I would stop in the morning and give them an update." He chuckled happily. "I can hardly wait to see their faces!"

After pouring the remaining coffee on the ground, Mitch stored the cups behind his seat, started up the car and headed toward the Limerick location where he knew a happy reunion would take place. On the way, he filled Jacob in on Fannie's deliverance and watched him take slow deep breaths, until his body stopped shivering and he relaxed under the blanket.

"When you feel up to it, Jacob, I'd sure like to hear how you made it to the surface. Jessie will want to put it in her editorial too." He smiled at him. "You're a walking miracle, you know."

Hearing a car chug into the driveway, Jacob's mother appeared at the door expecting bad news. She waited, wringing her hands together, watching as Mitch got out and walked over to the passenger side. Opening the door, he helped Jacob out of the vehicle and walk toward his mom. With a loud cry, she raced down the steps and threw her arms around Jacob. Sobbing, she held him tight, laughing and crying at the same time.

Mitch let the family reunion continue for a few minutes, as his brothers came running from all directions. When he cleared his throat, they all turned and looked at him in surprise, as if seeing him for the first time.

"Oh, Mam, I'm sorry. This is my friend, Mitch. And if you can wait, he has some good news!" Jacob exclaimed. He went ahead and introduced his brothers, who were looking at him in awe.

"I'm pleased to meet you all," Mitch said, shaking their hands. "But before we go any further, I think Jacob would like to get cleaned up a bit, wouldn't you?" he asked, looking at him.

With a tired smile, Jacob turned to his mother. "Mitch is right, Mam. Before we talk, I'd like to get out of these grubby clothes, wash up and then have something to eat. Our lunch pails tumbled to the bottom of the shaft yesterday so I'm starving." Looking up at Mitch, he added with a deep sigh, "I can't thank you enough...for everything. I'll be right back, and together, we can discuss your plan."

Mitch watched as Jacob shuffled up the stairs and into the house before turning to Mrs. Pascoe. "Ma'am..."

"Please call me Violet. It seems I'm deeply indebted to you, Mitch." She shook her head sadly. "It's been hard on all of us since my husband passed, but mostly on Jacob as he's our sole supporter. When I heard the blast, knowing he was down there, I thought it was the end for all of us." Her face turned hopeful as she gazed up at Mitch. "He said you have plans for him?"

Mitch smiled at her. "Tell you what, let's heat up some coffee, and by the time it's done, Jacob should be back, and we can go over all the details together." He followed her inside and without being obvious, gazed about the cold, sparsely furnished room. Knowing he'd be helping this family gave him a warm glow of satisfaction.

As he entered the kitchen, he saw Violet hurry and pull out an old cast-iron skillet from the oven. After dabbing her eyes with her apron, she spread some lard around the pan and placed it on the hot stove. When it began to sizzle, she cracked three eggs onto the surface causing them to splatter in the hot fat. Then, reaching over, she checked the coffeepot that was always simmering. Finding it hot, she added two pieces of bread on the stove surface to toast.

Glancing around the kitchen, Mitch could see their coats and hats were neatly hung by pegs on the wall and, as this room was warmer than the rest, concluded it must be the gathering place for the family. He noticed the scratched wooden table in the middle of the room, and the six mix-and-match chairs, four of them now occupied by the brothers. As they eyed him expectantly, he hoped Jacob would make an appearance soon.

"Well, here I am!" Jacob exclaimed, striding into the room with more enthusiasm. Looking refreshed, he took a seat at the head of the table, motioning for Mitch to sit beside him. "I never thought I'd be sitting here, again," he said. "Without that note you handed me yesterday, I never would have made it, Mitch. It gave me *hope* like I'd never had before. I was so excited when I first read it, and then, before we reached the fortieth level, that air blast hit us." Jacob grimaced. "The wind gust blew out our lights, so we were in total darkness for a few minutes before we were able to ignite them again. Rock had fallen all around us, but in the echoing chambers, couldn't tell exactly where. Once we were able to see, though, we found our exit was blocked. My friend, Ray, had a large piece of rock fall on his ankle, but other than that, we were alive." He shook his head, trying to clear the lingering memories, then smiled up at his mom who had approached the table with full hands.

"Thanks, Mam," Jacob said as his mother slid the fried eggs, and jellied toast onto his plate. After she poured coffee into his cup, he grabbed her arm and pulled her down, kissing her cheek. "I love you, Mam."

His mom flushed with pleasure at this unusual display of affection.

"Excuse me, Mitch." Jacob dove into his breakfast like it was his last meal, instead of his first. Sighing with pleasure, he had almost cleaned his plate before asking Mitch if he would like something.

"No, no. Just coffee for me, thanks." Mitch nodded gratefully as Violet placed a large steaming mug in front of him. "This just hits the spot." He sipped from the cup, waiting for Jacob to continue.

After swallowing his last bite, Jacob took a gulp from his own cup and continued. "Anyway, as luck would have it, the ladder was on *our* side, but it was hundreds of feet straight up to the surface. We knew the climb would be difficult, especially with an injured man, but your note, Mitch, it kept me going and the others just followed right along. We used one light at a time and pushed and pulled our way to the surface. I guess you could say you saved all four of us!"

Mitch reddened at his praise and looked down at his coffee. "Well, Jacob, we had it all planned out, as you know, but things took a different direction. Yet here you are and Fannie's safe at Jessie's house."

"Fannie? Who's Fannie?" Violet, with a raised eyebrow, questioned her son.

Jacob looked sheepish. "Guess I never told you about her, Mam. We've been seeing each other for some time, but circumstances… well, it's complicated. Can I just say she's someone special and leave it at that for now? I promise you'll meet her soon."

"Mitch, is she part of the plan Jacob hinted at, this…this Fannie?"

Mitch was cautious. "Well, the Fannie part is *his* story to tell, and yes, it does include her. But the plan also gives Jacob a job safely aboveground."

Violet shooed one of her sons off his chair and sat down beside Mitch. "I would give *anything* to keep my boys safe. Just the thought of the other three heading down there in a couple of years…" She shuddered. "Their dad had to leave school after the sixth grade, but I want something better for my sons. With Jacob working, I hoped they could at least finish school and go on to better jobs, even if it took them down state."

She turned to her son as tears pricked her eyes. "I was always sorry I couldn't do my best for you, Jacob; but when your dad died, I had no choice. We would have starved without your help."

"It's alright, Mam. I knew what I had to do." Jacob reached across the table and took her hand. "And now that Mitch's found me a *new* job, I'll bring in good money and without the danger." He looked around. "Just think, we can finally fix up this old place and for sure, this winter will be warm! My brothers will," he looked at each of them, "*will* finish school. Who knows, one or all of you might go on to college. Right now, I feel *anything's* possible!" He relaxed and leaned back in his chair. "As for me, I look forward to my new job to help support my family and"—he looked at his mom and winked—"possibly a future wife. But only if you approve, Mam."

With that pronouncement, Jacob bounced up and turned eagerly to Mitch. "I believe you have a promise to keep to two pretty ladies who need some answers." He slid his chair back and stood up. Reaching down and wrapping his arms around his mom, he closed his eyes and held her tight before whispering, "I'm so glad to be home, Mam."

Through misty eyes, she looked up at him and patted his arm. "So am I, Jacob, so am I."

CHAPTER 21

Jessie pulled back the curtain from her bedroom window and peered down the road for Mitch. Although he was going to stop at the mine for an update, he should have arrived some time ago. Was that good or bad? The downstairs was quiet, so she assumed Fannie was still sleeping and didn't want to disturb her. *But waiting up here is driving me crazy and isn't going to make Mitch come any faster,* she huffed. *At least I could make some coffee.*

Stepping into her slippers, Jessie shuffled down the stairs hoping not to disturb her new house guest but was surprised to see Fannie fully dressed and sitting on the sofa folding the bed linens.

"Guess we're both getting an early start this morning."

Startled, Fannie looked up. "Good morning, Jessie. Truth be told," she said sheepishly, "when I woke up, I didn't remember where I was."

"Well, with all you've been through, Fannie, that's understandable. But just know that your life is changing for the better, starting today." Jessie held out her arms. "Here, hand me those linens and we'll store them until tonight. Then, we may as well put on the coffee and have some breakfast while we're waiting. No matter what happens today, we'll need to keep up our strength."

Fannie stood up and followed her toward the kitchen. "If only we knew *something* about Jacob, it would make me feel easier. And shouldn't Mitch be here by now, Jessie? I feel like I've been sitting up for hours, not knowing. And what if Madam comes looking for me?" Stopping by the window, she lifted the drape and peered out looking for answers but found none. Sighing, she dropped the curtain and apathetically trailed Jessie into the kitchen.

Jessie, looking over her shoulder as she filled the coffeepot with water, tried valiantly to encourage Fannie. "Come on, Fannie. Remember what Mitch said. No news is *good* news or, at least, something to that affect." After spooning the coffee grounds into the pot and placing it on the stove, she continued. "And if Madam comes knocking on my door, we'll deal with her then. But as I said before, she has no legal hold over you. Did you say prayers for Jacob?"

Fannie nodded. "I'm not used to praying very much, but if God is up there, I hope he heard my prayers on Jacob's behalf. I'm the one who's soiled. Jacob's been nothing but a solid rock for his family. He deserves some help."

"My grandmother used to say God always hears the fervent prayers sent up on behalf of another." Jessie mused. "Funny, I haven't thought of her for a long time. She died before I was ten, just about the time when my dad and mom became busy social leaders. But Granny used to dress me up and take me to church on Sundays and tell me about Jesus. I haven't been to church in a while. Maybe it's something I need to change." She smiled at Fannie. "Anyway, let's think positive thoughts. How about setting the table while I whip up some eggs and ham for breakfast? Does that sound good?"

"I guess. But you'll need to tell me where to find everything. I may as well learn now so I'll know where to put things." She surveyed the kitchen and saw that, although Jessie wasn't the tidiest, she seemed organized.

Jessie pointed to the cabinet closest to the sink. "You should find everything we need in there. Napkins are in the drawer below. Silverware next to that. You'll have more of a chance to explore when I'm off to work." She looked at the clock. "Speaking of work, I'd better call Bobbie—she's my friend and the receptionist at the *Gazette*—to let her know I won't be in until we hear something. I have some notes to organize, so you can get familiar with the house if you're comfortable. Nothing is private, so feel free to check into every room and cabinet. It'll give you something to do while we're waiting."

Whipping up some eggs, Jessie dropped them, along with pieces of ham, into the frying pan and scrambled them together with a little cheese. She checked the oven heat, which was hot enough for toast, and placed two pieces of bread onto the grill and closed the door. Fannie finished setting the table just as the coffee started to bubble.

"Fannie, please flip the toast to brown on the other side. I'll be right back." As Fannie moved to obey, Jessie slipped out of the room, and returned to the living room window. *Just in case...*

But the answer was the same. No Mitch.

Determined not to show her dismay, she planted a bright smile on her face as she walked back into the kitchen. "There, now. You have us all set up and ready to eat. Let's sit down, Fannie, and do some planning. For one thing, we're going to have to find some new clothes for you to wear."

Fannie sat down, but just picked at the food before pushing her place aside and just sipped on her coffee. "I'm sorry, Jessie, but I don't think I can swallow a thing right now. It would just stick in my throat." She put her elbows on the table and leaned her chin on her palms.

"Now, Fannie, you need to eat something. Think of what Jacob would want you to do." Jessie encouraged her.

"Jacob is all I *do* think about and until…"

Her response was interrupted by a hard knock on the front door.

"It's madam. I know it is!" Fannie cried out as she jumped out of her chair.

"Quick!" Jessie whispered. "Go into that little room off the kitchen, Fannie, and stay there until I call for you."

Fannie ran to the area pointed out and closed the door except for a crack to hear what was going on.

Jessie's heart was beating fast as she slowly walked down the hallway. A second insistent knock and she knew the caller meant business.

Peering through the window, she saw, with relief, that it was Mitch on the other side. Glancing back toward the kitchen, she hoped Fannie was prepared for whatever news he might bring.

Taking a deep breath, Jessie opened the door. But now, instead of Mitch, there stood Jacob! Without words, she grabbed his arm and pulled him into the house, then turned to Mitch who was grinning behind him. Jessie threw her arms around him and held him tight. Now her heart was really racing, but with joy.

Releasing Mitch, she put her finger to her lips, then arm in arm, took both into the kitchen.

"Fannie, there's someone here to see you," Jessie sang. *Surely, God does answer, and dreams do come true.*

Cautiously, Fannie opened the door a little wider until Jacob came into view. With a cry, she catapulted into his waiting arms. Holding her close, he whispered words of endearment and encouragement as her warm tears soaked his clean shirt. "Shh, Fannie, it's really me. Do you think I'd give up so easily when I had so much to look forward to?" Rubbing her back, he led her over to a kitchen chair and sat down beside her, never releasing his grip on her hand. Fannie choked, then laughed, staring into the face she'd never expected to see again. Jacob took the napkin from her uneaten breakfast and dabbed at her face; then, kissing her softly, murmured sweetly to the woman he hoped to spend the rest of his life with.

Observing this reunion with deep satisfaction, Jessie turned to Mitch and whispered, "Let's give them some privacy. We'll go into the living room, and you can tell me how it all happened."

Once ensconced on the sofa, Jessie bombarded him with questions. "Where did you find him? Were you part of the rescue? We waited so long for you to come. How did you…?"

"Let's just say Jacob rescued himself, along with three others. Remember that ladder we saw when I took you below?" At her nod, he continued. "Well, he and his friends climbed up on it to the surface. It took so long because one of his workers was injured and they had to move slowly, one wrung at a time. When I was at the mine this morning, I was getting ready to leave without any news when Jacob walked out of the building. He was dirty and tired but looked like a miracle heading my way! He told me it was my note that kept him going. Right away, I took him home so his family could see him, so that's why I was late getting here. Needless to say, it was a mighty happy mother to have her son returned to her. Anyway, I waited while Jacob cleaned up a bit before bringing him over. He couldn't believe Fannie had also been rescued. Now it's up to them to write their own future."

Mitch smiled down at Jessie, who was snuggled against his shoulder. "And of course, we'll help them any way we can."

Jessie looked up and touched his face. "Oh, Mitch, when I first saw you at the door, I expected bad news. But when I saw Jacob, well, there are just no words." She grabbed his hand and pulled him up. Putting her arms around his neck, Jessie brought his head down for a long passionate kiss. "Hmm. You're wonderful, do you know that?" She stirred in his embrace, then, wrapping her arms around his middle, laid her head against his chest and held him tight.

"If this is your response, maybe I should find *more* people to rescue," Mitch teased.

Her eyes glowing with happiness Jessie kissed his cheek as she released him, took his hand, and led him back to the kitchen.

CHAPTER 22

October slipped into November. One more hard freeze and the gold, red, and orange of autumn turned bleak and gray as ominous dark clouds filled the sky and dead brown leaves covered the ground. Soaked by the heavy morning dew, they stuck together, creating a soft mossy carpet for those who trampled upon them. Now leafless, branches shivered, moaned, and cracked together as the brisk northwest winds promised an early winter.

Jessie, appreciating the warmth of her woolly navy-blue jacket, pulled on a red ski cap over her curls and wound the matching scarf she had knitted around her neck. Although the climate between upper and lower Michigan was drastically different, she appreciated the crisp clean air that forever smelled like Christmas instead of the heavy smog that smothered out any clean air Detroit had to offer.

Deciding boots weren't needed, she slipped on her leather gloves, then left the house for a quiet walk through the hills by Lower Pewabic, knowing all was well within her home. It was Saturday, her editorial for the week was complete and Mitch was coming over for supper. Life was good. Looking back at the past few weeks, Jessie pondered the many changes that had taken place.

First, Fannie was a gem and kept everything in spotless order. Sadly, it wouldn't last forever as she and Jacob were planning a spring wedding the following year. Jessie rejoiced with them as did Violet Pascoe. After five boys, she was more than delighted to add Fannie to their household as the daughter she'd never had. Fannie had blossomed as Jacob's mom embraced her, despite her questionable background.

Jacob was ecstatic about his new job, working hard as he toted furniture up and down three flights of stairs every day. But the regular hours, steady salary, and safe working conditions more than compensated for any discomfort.

As for Sid Brewster, he remained lost in the underworld of Detroit. At least for now. According to her dad, his present whereabouts were still unknown. But Jessie knew her life would be shackled forever if she worried about Sid finding her, so it was better to think positive.

Gazing about, she noticed a lack of activity in many company houses, a sign that more of the people had packed up and moved away. Although the strike continued, many had given up hope and found jobs elsewhere. Even the militia had moved back down state, and all that remained was flattened grass where the large tents had stood and the lingering smell of dried horse manure from the corrals. Life went on, except for those who lingered, hoping for a quick resolution and although sympathetic with the strikers, she was quite sure their demands would fall on deaf ears.

Jessie paused, glancing across the field to the shaft house where, after several days, the last remaining body of the buried miners had been released from its rocky grave. She had stood by as the man had been brought to the surface, allowing the family closure as they said their final goodbye. One more funeral, and except for the seven men who had lost their lives, life went on as people picked up the pieces and moved forward.

Absorbed in her thoughts, Jessie failed to see a large rock in her path. Tripping over it, she landed sideways with an *oomph* and rolled into a shallow ditch. Lying on her back, with the air knocked out of her, she gauged her injuries by slowly moving first her arms, then her legs. Taking a deep breath, she was thankful everything seemed to be in working order. *That's what I get for not paying attention to where I was going,* she mused. Satisfied that her only discomfort would be some bruising for the next few days, she got on her hands and knees, and pushed herself upward. *Ugh. Definitely some bruises,* she groaned. And her jacket was filthy.

A sudden blast of wind ruffling through her curls, sent her hat flying to the ground, leaving her head bare. Shivering, she bent down to retrieve it, but another gust sent the cap rolling into a round culvert at the end of the ditch. *Great.* With a sigh, she moved closer, knelt on the mucky ground, and reached into the open duct. Feeling her wooly hat about two feet in, she closed her fingers around it and started pulling it forward until feeling a tug on the other side. Startled, she dropped it, sitting back on her heels as she considered her options. Either leave it or see if it was stuck on something.

Bending over, she peered into the dim interior wishing she had better light. Walking her fingers forward, Jessie touched the garment again when she heard a growl. Now *that* got her attention. Not letting go, but gently bringing the cap toward her, she felt a resistance but persisted, inching the hat closer to the entrance. *Grrr* and a tug. *Grrr* and a tug. Now it felt like a game. Intrigued, Jessie sat back, propped her feet up against the metal rim and kept on pulling. One final jerk and it came loose. Falling back against the ground, she was aware of another fuzzy touch on her hand. Then, a wet slurp.

Jumping up quickly, and jamming the cap onto her head, Jessie heard a scuffing of leaves as the critter scurried away. Curious, she peered into the pipe where two shiny brown eyes peeked out at her. *A puppy!* "Come here, little one." Jessie spoke softly, extending her hand as she tried coaxing it out of hiding.

At the sound of her friendly voice, the pup pushed its nose forward and sniffed at her. Gaining ground, Jessie extended both arms and slowly lifted the young dog out of the pipe, placing it against her chest while stroking it gently. She was rewarded by a soft 'woof' as the pup wriggled enthusiastically, first licking her nose, then her chin. Holding it away from her, Jessie discovered she had rescued a brown male puppy. He was also very thin and very dirty, with a mess of matted fur that was stuck together with burrs. Obviously, he had been alone for some time.

"Now I wonder where you came from and is someone looking for you?" Jessie inquired. Without waiting for an answer, she stood up and tucked the pup under one arm. Opening the buttons of her jacket, she snuggled him inside, unmindful of the havoc he played on her new sweater. Closing the buttons, she started back to her house hoping the puppy wouldn't try to escape. As she glanced down, her maternal instinct kicked in when she saw he was contentedly nestled against her, finding a secure resting place. As the warmth of his little body permeated her sweater, Jessie wrapped her arms around him and headed back up the hill. *Won't Mitch be surprised!* she thought excitedly.

Reaching the crest, she saw Fannie sweeping dead leaves off the front steps. Raising one arm, she waved at her, then cuddled the puppy again.

Fannie dropped the broom and met Jessie halfway across the yard. "What have we here?" she asked, noticing the bulge in Jessie's jacket. Hearing a strange voice, the pup peaked out from under the coat and eyed the new human.

"What we have is a lost little pup that needs some tender care—and a good bath. Whew! He stinks. He was living in a drain culvert when I found him," Jessie said as she pulled him out of her jacket.

"Poor thing." Fannie reached out, stroked his head gently and shook one of his front legs. "I hate to tell you, Jessie, but by the looks of these paws, he's probably going to be a rather large dog when he grows up."

"Well, large or small, we need to take care of him. Are you up to it, Fan?"

Fannie gathered the pup into her arms where he proceeded to wet her face with kisses. "Oh, Jess, he's adorable! What are you going to call him?"

Before she could answer, the puppy, deciding he'd been held long enough, wriggled free, and bounded up the steps into the hallway.

"Well, I guess he knows where his home is." Jessie followed him into the house and hung up her jacket on the hall tree. Nose to the ground, the pup sniffed every corner and wandered into the living room where he spotted the big potbellied stove. Growling, he flattened his ears and circled it warily until a large piece of flaming wood fell into the coals laying on the bottom. The thud of the log and crackle of sparks sent the pup scurrying back into the hallway where he sat on his haunches and woofed. Laughing, Jessie picked him up and smoothed his ruffled fur.

"Let's get this little one into the laundry tub and scrub him down so we can see who he is. It'll probably take two of us." She glanced around her. "We'll need something for a collar and leash, too, to take him outside." She hoped he was house trained but wasn't taking any chances.

After grabbing two aprons from the kitchen, Jessie deposited the pup into the deep laundry tub. As he stood up, bracing his paws on the rim, he barked at them, his long tail wagging, and wondering what new game they were playing.

"At least he's too small to jump out," Fannie observed as she filled a bucket full of warm water, adding soap until it bubbled. She handed Jessie a wash rag, bracing herself for the onslaught of spraying water if the puppy shook, which he probably would.

Jessie tied her apron strings behind her, ready to do battle. "Okay. Here we go." Filling a cup with warm water, she slowly poured it over his back first to test his reaction. The water dripped down his sides and into the sink where it formed a puddle beneath his feet. At first shocked by this new attack, the puppy stood still and looked up at her in question. But when Jessie dosed him with a second cup that trickled down his legs, he focused on the bottom of the sink where dozens of bubbles were floating toward the drain. As he stuck his nose in one, it burst, spraying water all over his face. On the attack now, the pup pounced on the remaining globules with his front paws, splattering water in every direction before giving himself a good shake.

Fannie laughed. "Just as I thought." She used a corner of her apron to wipe off her face, then suggested that she would hold him down while Jessie rubbed him with a bar of soap, which, of course, he tried to eat.

"Come on, fella. The sooner we get done, the sooner you'll get something better to munch on." Slowly pouring the remaining bucket of water over him, she gently scrubbed his fur until foamy, carefully using a cloth for his ears and around his eyes, then refilled the bucket with clear water. This time she used her cup several times, pouring it over him slowly and rinsing out most of the soap. Watching the dark brown water disappear down the drain, she wondered what color he was going to be.

"Fannie, keep holding him a minute while I get one of those big fluffy towels to dry him off." Jessie reached up to the top shelf and quickly pulled down a thick blue bath towel. "Guess this will be his from now on." Wrapping it snugly around him, she lifted him from the tub and set him on top the counter where he proceeded to shake again before biting the end of the towel for a game of tug-of-war.

A sudden knock on the front door broke her concentration, and her grip on the pup. Running down the hallway, it barked furiously at the intruder.

Poking his head through the door, Mitch wasn't prepared for the new arrival and wondered what all the commotion was about. Curious, he began to step inside when the puppy grabbed the bottom of his pants leg and pulled him off balance. Tumbling to the floor, he was accosted by four paws, a cold nose, and a very wet tongue. Gaining control, he hoisted the little dog high above his chest to keep his face dry, although by now his entire body had been dampened by the little scamp. Pulling the pup close to his chest, he started stroking his fur, and lulled into submission, the puppy settled down while Mitch looked up into the laughing faces of Jessie and Fannie.

While holding the dog in the crook of his left arm, Mitch pushed himself up and faced the ladies. "Well, Jess, when I suggested getting a dog for protection, this isn't exactly what I had in mind." He held the pup out in front of him to get a better look. "I must admit, though, I wouldn't have cared for a 150-pounder landing on me. Where'd you get him, anyway?"

Jessie explained how she found him. "Fannie thinks he *will* grow into a large dog, by the looks of his paws." She frowned. "I guess I really should ask around to see if anyone has lost him, but I'm pretty attached already. I'd hate giving him a name and then having his owner show up and take him away."

Shaking his head, Mitch assured her it would probably never happen. "The miners are having a tough enough time just feeding their kids let alone an animal. They probably dropped him off hoping someone would find him. Or he could have belonged to one of the mining families that left and just abandoned him. Either way, it was cruel, so I don't think you should worry about the owner coming after him."

Mitch handed the pup over to Jessie who was reaching out her arms. "Go on, Jess. I think it's safe to give him a name. He seems to have adopted you. And his shrill barking would make anyone think twice about breaking in. Who knows, he *could* end up being a golden retriever or Irish setter by his coloring." He shook one of the paws and chuckled. "I think Fannie is right, Jess. No matter what breed, he is going to be a large one."

Jessie hugged the pup, placing a kiss on the top of his head. "In that case, I'll keep him and call him Bo. In Swedish it means 'to have a household,' and that's *exactly* what he's getting!"

CHAPTER 23

Sid Brewster started his morning as usual, a huge mug of extra strong black coffee with a large shot of brandy. He rolled it over his tongue, savoring its flavor as he looked about his new abode with distaste, convinced he'd hit an all-time low. On the lam, once again, he had been smuggled into Eddie's mother's chilly attic after narrowly escaping capture when his warehouse was raided.

Thankfully, some of his money had fallen into the *right* hands. One grateful cop had been greedy enough to accept the bribe and got word to Sid just minutes before the break-in. Although it had nothing to do with the whereabouts of *Ms.* Peterson, he felt the money had been well spent. Being captured was not an option, especially when they were getting so close. At least he knew who Sable was… or, in this case, wasn't. That girl had gotten under his skin, breaking the barrier he had carefully erected for so many years.

Inhaling the potent fumes, he took another satisfying sip. At least the coffee and his meals arrived on time.

Hearing a clumping up the stairs, Sid set his cup down as he waited for his breakfast to arrive on its usual tray. But to his surprise, it was Vinnie and Eddie who rushed through the door, waving a newspaper.

"We found her, Sid! We found her!" Vinnie gasped, breathless, both from the stairs and announcement as he bolted through the door, followed by a puffing Eddie.

Sid jumped up and grabbed the evidence from Vinnie's hand. Sure enough. There she was on the front page of the *Daily Mining Gazette*, whatever that was—*his* Sable…or was it? He scratched his head as he took a better look at the picture. The photo wasn't face on but angled as she spoke to a gentleman next to her. In her "civilian" clothes, she looked older, more sophisticated. "Are you sure, Vinnie? I mean, she sorta looks like Sable, but without red hair and her flapper dress...I need to be sure."

"Here." Vinnie pointed. "Read the caption below the picture, boss. It says 'Jessica Peterson, *former* reporter of the *Detroit News Press*." He looked up at Sid. "Can't be two of 'em."

Sid carried the paper over to his chair, where a brighter light shined on the grainy photo. He looked up at Vinnie. "You're right. That's *got* to be her. So? Where is she? And where'd you get this newspaper?" He handed the *Gazette* back to his henchman.

Vinnie took the paper from his boss. "This copy came in yesterday addressed to the chief of police and was confiscated by our, ah, agent, who snatched it off his desk during the night. Now let's see... according to this newspaper, she was at a cave-in doing interviews about some trapped miners." He searched the front page for more information before turning the newspaper to the back, then folded it in half and pointed to the fine print on the bottom. "Here it is, Sid. Says this newspaper is printed in Houghton, Michigan, so I'd guess that's where you'd find her." He furrowed his eyebrows and scratched his head. "Never heard of it, boss." He shoved the paper back into Sid's hands. "Any idea where it is?"

Sid drummed his fingers against the table and pursed his lips in thought. "Well, we all know where it *ain't*. There's no mining around here, boys, so it must be up north somewhere. And come to think of it, I did read something about the militia heading to the upper Great Lakes area because of a mine ruckus." He rubbed his chin, then snapped his fingers. "That's it! I've got it!" Sid gleefully smacked the paper on the table excitedly. "This could work both ways, Vin. She's in hiding and I need a place to hide!" He gave a hoarse chuckle. "Kill two birds with one stone, as they say."

He jumped up and paced back and forth. "Eddie, I really appreciate the use of your mom's attic, but it'll be bad for her if I'm found. The sooner I'm gone, the better. By the way, thank her for the great meals she's been delivering, will ya? Especially the brandy!" He delved into his pocket and pulled out a stack of bills. "Here, give her these with my compliments." Then he reached back down and came out with two more large bills. Giving one to each, he added, "And you guys deserve something extra for a job well done. When this is finished, there'll be more of this wait'n for ya."

"Now, go and enjoy the rest of the day, boys. You've earned it! But tomorrow it's back to business. Find out how she got up there and buy me some tickets." Sid handed a few more green backs to Vinnie. "I'd like to take ya with me, fellas, but this is something I've gotta do alone. It'd look too suspicious with three of us nosing around. As just one guy, I can blend in better, camouflage myself, and mingle with the locals. Someone ought to know her." He waved them off. "Get on with ya, now, and enjoy yourselves."

With money in their pockets, Vinnie and Eddie stomped back down the stairs, each thinking of the best way to spend their extra cash. By silent agreement, and grinning at each other, they bounded down the rest of the steps and headed for the nearest Gentleman's Club, where the ladies weren't ladies.

Closing the door behind them, Sid plopped down in the soft oversize chair he'd been given for comfort. Rubbing his hands gleefully together, he started plotting his course. Although he knew it wouldn't happen overnight, it gave him great satisfaction just knowing she'd soon be within his reach. Grabbing his cup, he held it up high. "Here's to *you*, Ms. 'Sable' Jessica Peterson. I think it's about time for us to become reacquainted." In celebration, he added another dollop of brandy to his coffee, thinking, as he sipped it, how sweet his revenge would be. The wait would be worthwhile.

CHAPTER 24

At the shrill ringing of her telephone, Jessie bolted off the sofa and dashed into the kitchen. Glancing at the clock, she knew any call after 10:00 PM wouldn't be good. Breathlessly, she jerked the receiver off its cradle and put it close to her ear.

"Hello?" Jessica held her breath, hoping it wasn't bad news regarding her family.

"Hi, sweetie." It was her dad. Hearing his voice should have made her feel relieved but, instead, caused apprehension.

"Dad! What's wrong? Is Mom alright, and my sisters?" Her pulse racing, Jessie held onto the cord, twisting it around and around her fingers.

"Relax, Jess. Your mom and the girls are fine. I had to call and let you know they found Sid Brewster's hideout, but he'd already bolted before their arrival. Knowing this tells us there's probably an informant in the police department. And unfortunately, that Sid's probably miles away by now." Randall paused. "The worst part, Jess, is that the chief received a copy of the *Gazette* yesterday, and it was gone this morning when he came in. It could have been the mole, but we don't know for sure. We checked all the trash bins and asked around, but no one has seen it. I hate to say it, Jess, but it wasn't the brightest idea to get your picture plastered all over the front page of the newspaper. Who knew the chief subscribed to it because of relatives in that area?" He hesitated. "Jess, maybe you should just come back home and wait awhile until they find Sid."

Before Jessie could reply, Bo, his sleep interrupted by her abrupt departure, came bounding into the kitchen, barking shrilly before jumping up on her.

"Just a minute, Dad." Reaching down, she hoisted the puppy up, settled him in the crook of her left elbow, and held him close to her chest. Balancing both him and the phone became a challenge as he tried raining kisses all over her face. "That's enough, Bo! Sorry about that, Dad. You were saying?"

Randall chuckled. "What's going on, Jess? Sounds like you have a new addition to the family. I know Mitch wanted to you to have a dog and can only hope, after what I've told you, that it's large and vicious."

Jessie laughed. "He's vicious all right. He's killed a few of my good towels, shredded a pair of my slippers, and chewed a spindle off one of my chairs. All in less than a week! Yeah, Dad, he's a killer alright! But it's too soon to tell how big he'll be." She kissed the pup's head and set him back down on the floor.

"Seriously, Jess, something has to be done to protect you from Sid while he's still on the loose."

Jessie shook her head. "Dad, to begin with, I'm not going to become a recluse just because of Sid. We don't know if he's headed here, anyway, and worrying about it would just be a waste of time. Fannie is here daily, and Mitch is a frequent visitor. If he's not here, I'm usually out with him." She reached down and rubbed the puppy's ear, getting a wet slurp in response. "Bo, here, lets me know if anyone comes within fifty feet of the house. He attacked Mitch the first time he tried coming through the front door and pulled him to the ground!"

Randall sighed. "Well, all right, but, Jess, when I heard about Sid, I was about to take the first train out. If you feel reasonably safe, I guess we'll just have to wait and see. But promise me you'll be on your guard. *You* know more than anyone that Sid is notorious in his underhanded dealings and has enough money to buy any official he wants. Don't trust anyone who isn't familiar to you." Then he added thoughtfully, "Come to think of it, Jess, just don't trust anyone who's not *close* to you."

"Okay, Dad. I'd like to say 'don't worry,' but know you will, anyway. I promise to be extra careful. Between Mitch, Fannie, Bobbie, and Brian, as well as the Johns' family, they know what to watch for.

And as for Bo, he may be small, but his bark will make anyone think twice about entering the house."

After a few more fatherly remarks on her safety, Randall hung up and Jessie walked quietly back into the living room. It was late and tomorrow would be a busy day, but she sat down in the rocker, anyway, moving back and forth, considering the possibility, or in her case, probability that Sid was already on his way. Although waves of heat flowed out of the potbellied stove, Jessie shivered apprehensively as she rocked. It wasn't her forte to be scared, but past dealings with Sid's character put her on edge. He wasn't a man to let things drop and was very vindictive to anyone who crossed him. Her dad was right. *She* knew him better than anyone. Most likely, Sid knew she was here and was either on his way, or soon would be.

Bo, as if knowing her troubled mind, jumped up and settled himself on her lap. Lost in thought, Jessie absently stroked his furry head, finding solace in his warmth. Tomorrow was another day. Mitch would have to be informed, as well as Bobbie, Brian, and her other coworkers. Jessie lifted her chin. Although this wasn't a game, she was determined to win. But for now, it wouldn't hurt to double check the locks on her house…just in case.

Coming to a halt, she stood up and set Bo on the floor. "Come on, sweetie. Let's go batten down the hatches." Jessie was suddenly very grateful for her little furry friend as he trotted along beside her. Small he might be and his bark worse than his bite, but no stranger would know that.

Sleeping fitfully that night, Jessie had visions of Sid looming in her head. Tossing back and forth, she finally decided it was too soon to worry as it would take days before he could possibly appear. But instead of falling back to sleep, she arose before dawn, mentally going over her activities for that day and, of course, confiding in her friends.

Arriving at the *Gazette* early in the morning, Jessie filled the coffeepot, waiting for the others to show up. Brian, surprised at seeing her there as he walked in the door, knew something was up, but an important phone call postponed any questions until later. Next, Carl bopped in with some sweet rolls and after making a comment about the early bird getting the worm, grabbed two flaky pastries before heading back to his darkroom.

The door swung open, again, letting a blast of cold air sail into the office. This time it was Bobbie. Taking in Jessie's forlorn face, she walked to the back room, poured two cups of coffee, thoughtfully adding two lumps of sugar and a spoon before handing it to her.

"Thanks, Bobbie." Following her friend, Jessie propped herself against the counter and absently stirred the tiny white cubes until they dissolved before taking a sip of the strong brew. It was sweeter than she usually liked it but now, very satisfying. She drank again, letting the coffee embrace her as it flowed through her body, filling it with warmth and renewed energy. With a sigh of satisfaction, Jessie relaxed, feeling ready to face whatever the day would bring.

Bobbie saw the change in her demeanor. "Okay, Jess. What gives? You look like h—well, you look like you haven't slept in days." Bobbie grinned. "Did you and Mitch have a fight?"

"I wish it were only that, Bobbie." After taking another sip of her sweetened brew, Jessie leaned back against the counter and filled her in on the details.

Bobbie, aghast, set her cup down. "Oh, Jess, if only Carl hadn't taken that picture of you and Mitch! It was the best photo of the bunch, though. And of course, we're so proud of you. But who would have known a copy of the *Gazette* would fall right into Sid's hands? Have you talked to Brian or Mitch yet?"

Jessie shook her head. "Brian was headed for an important phone call but promised to be down as soon as he finished. And Mitch is in another one of those *useless* meetings." She set down her cup and shook her head. "I'm sorry, Bobbie. I shouldn't have said that, but it's been months now. Mitch is frustrated but keeps on trying to negotiate a peace treaty. That deadly air blast only emphasized the need for safer working conditions. They've got to see that."

Jessie picked up her cup, grabbed a glazed doughnut and headed back out to the front office with Bobbie following behind.

Although Brian promised to join them as soon as his phone call was finished, it wouldn't be until noon before Mitch showed up. They often lunched together, so Jessie would fill him in then.

"If Carl hadn't taken your picture with Mitch, this would never have happened!"

"You can't blame Carl, Bobbie. He was just doing his job. And if not him, it would've just been a matter of time before Sid found out where I was, anyway."

As she and Bobbie sat behind their desks, the rumbling of footsteps indicated Brian was on his way down. Finishing her doughnut with a gulp of coffee, Jessie brushed the crumbs off her dress and patted her lips with a napkin.

A minute later, Brian, carrying a large steaming mug in one hand and a jellied confection in the other, sauntered through the doorway and perched himself on the corner of Bobbie's desk, his favorite place. After giving her a wink and an intimate smile, he turned to Jessie.

"Okay, ladies. Give me the scoop. It must be something important for you to be here so early, Jess."

Feeding him the latest information, Brian's light countenance turned into one of grave concern. Not only was she the best reporter he ever had, but she'd become a close friend. Without her, he and Bobbie might never have connected. He owed her and would do his best to protect her.

"Does Mitch know yet?"

"No. He's in a company meeting this morning but will be in around noontime to take me out for lunch."

Brian rubbed his chin, thoughtfully. "Jess, are you sure you don't want to do as your dad suggested and go back to Detroit for a while until this blows over? We'd really miss you, of course, but I wouldn't want you staying here and risking your life. Although I've lived here for a long time, I still don't know any of the police force intimately and couldn't vouch for any of them not taking a bribe. People are people, you know, here in Houghton or in Detroit. Maybe Mitch—"

But just then, the door opened and Mitch, unexpectedly, poked his head in. Seeing them all solemnly grouped together, he quickly shut the door and walked over briskly. "My meeting was cancelled," he explained. "What's going on?" He took Jessie's hand and sat on the edge of her desk.

"Sid Brewster most likely knows where I am." Jessie explained. As she relayed her dad's phone call, Mitch assured her of his protection.

"How, Mitch? How can you promise such a thing? He's *vicious*! And could be dangerous for all of you."

Mitch was quick to reply. "Don't worry, Jess. I've got an idea that I've been mulling over for some time, but now seems like the perfect opportunity to act. First, I'll need to gather some facts this morning, so how about if I come back at noon, as we planned, and we can discuss it over lunch?" He glanced at Brian and Bobbie. "I know I can depend on you to take care of her while I'm gone. Try and make her feel better. We know Sid isn't likely to appear for a few days, so we have time on our side." He lifted Jessie's hand to his lips and after giving it a quick squeeze, jumped to his feet, and headed out the door.

"Well!" Bobbie frowned at the closed door. "It must be something important for Mitch to run out like that. I don't know what he has in mind, but don't worry, Jess. Between all of us, we'll take care of you." She relaxed her countenance. "Now, how about a second cup of coffee and more sugar? I, for one, won't feel guilty about having another sweet roll!"

CHAPTER 25

"Mitch, what a nice surprise!" Randall Petersen grabbed the phone, stood up and stretched, glad to have a break in what was already a busy morning. "Everything okay?"

Mitch hesitated before answering. "Randall, this is probably the most difficult phone call I've ever had to make."

Jessie's dad stopped in his tracks, horrified. "*Jessie...?*"

"No, no, Randall. She's fine," Mitch assured him. "And we want to keep her that way, which is why I called. She told me, as well as Brian and Bobbie, about your call last night, so naturally we're all concerned for her safety." He paused.

"Go on, Mitch. What've you got in mind? You know I trust you to take care of her."

"Thanks, Randall. Like before, I think the best way to keep tabs on her is to keep her close to me. Which is why I called." Mitch took a deep breath, crossed his fingers, and hoped for the best.

"I'd like your permission to ask Jessie to marry me." At Randall's silence on the other end, Mitch rushed on. "I know it hasn't been that long since she and I met, but I do know how I feel about her, and I think she feels the same way. Randall, I *love* Jessie, and promise to take good care of her. This way I can protect her by staying close."

Randall rubbed his chin thoughtfully. "Well, Mitch, I'd like to say this is a surprise, but from all my phone calls with Jess, I know she cares deeply for you. It's in her voice whenever we talk. So although we've never met, yes, you have my permission. I'm sure Lillian will agree with me as she has been trying to get Jessie married off for a long time." He chuckled. "We just never thought it would be someone from up there, although technically you're from Lansing so I guess that doesn't count." He sat back down.

"Okay. So when are you going to ask her?"

Mitch's sigh of relief was audible. "Thanks, Randall. I'm meeting her for lunch and thought I'd pop the question then. It's not the most romantic place, but time being of the essence, I think we need to have the ceremony as soon as possible. Do you mind not being here? We can come down later for a big reception if you like."

"Go ahead, Mitch. Take care of my little girl." He added thoughtfully, "Lillian would probably appreciate a few photos, though, seeing she's missing her daughter's wedding."

"Sure enough, Randall. That is, *if* Jessie accepts my proposal. The *Gazette* has a great photographer who, unfortunately, started this fiasco when he took that picture of us. I'm sure he'll be more than happy to make up for it, although it really wasn't his fault that Sid saw the photo."

After a few more reassurances, Mitch hung up the phone. He made one more quick call, then flew out to his car. The next stop would be a jeweler in downtown Houghton. Checking his watch, he knew he had just enough time to pick out something nice to offer Jessie before heading back to the *Gazette*. Mitch shook his head, still amazed at his good fortune. Then he checked himself. Jessie hadn't said yes yet. Would she believe how much he loved her, or would she think it was only a plot to protect her?

Pulling up by the jewelry store, Mitch took a deep breath before entering, thinking of the magnitude of what he was about to do. Checking his billfold, he was glad for the extra bonus money he'd received yesterday and had gone to the bank early. He was ready. Pushing open the door, he walked in to purchase the most important gift of his life. *Till death do us part.* But he vowed it wouldn't be on Sid Brewster's watch.

Consulting with the proprietor, Mitch gazed at the selection he was offered until he found exactly what he was looking for: a shiny gold ring with one solitaire diamond twinkling up at him through the sparkling glass case. Alongside it were the bride and groom's matching gold wedding bands. He purchased all three. Not every man wore a ring, but he always felt it represented a promise; one he intended to keep.

Exchanging his cash for the little boxes that contained his future, Mitch hurried back to his car just as the church bells struck the noon hour.

Arriving at the newspaper office a few minutes late, he hopped out of the car and raced to the door. *Calm down,* he told himself. Slowly opening the door, he found Jessie waiting for him with a big smile.

"Sorry I'm late, Jess, but I had something to take care of. Ready to go?" He helped her into her coat, picked up her hat and gently placed it on her head, brushing away the few curly locks that peeped out. While Jessie added her woolly scarf and mittens, Mitch turned to Bobbie, who was watching with interest, and winked at her. "We might be a few minutes late getting back, so don't worry." With heightened color and a big grin on his face, he ushered Jessie out the door with a backward glance at Bobbie, who had a speculative look on her face.

"Where are we going, Mitch?" Although he had taken her hand, Jessie had a hard time keeping up. "Slow down a little, will you?" she puffed. "Brian won't mind if I'm a tad late getting back." At her chiding, Mitch altered his stride to match hers.

"Sorry, Jess," he said, grinning. "Can't have you turning into an icicle before we get there." He tugged at her scarf to make sure it was secure. "Is the Douglas House all right with you?"

Jessie stopped in her tracks. "That's awfully steep for lunch, Mitch. Great for special occasions, but I wouldn't mind just having a sandwich at the diner."

"Hey, can't I spoil my girl once in a while?" he teased. "Besides, you know it's pretty quiet in there and we need to decide what to do about Sid." (*Among other things…*)

Jessie's shiver wasn't just from the cold as she recalled last night's phone call. But with her hand in Mitch's, she felt anything was possible. She wasn't going to let *Sid Brewster* ruin a great lunch with her favorite guy.

Smiling up at him, Jessie pointed to the dark heavy clouds hanging low overhead. Snow was in the air. She could smell it and feel it. Just in time for getting into the Christmas spirit. With Thanksgiving next week, she had so much to be thankful for. Mitch, Bobbie, Brian, and the Johns family were sharing the special dinner at her house. Fannie and Jacob would be dining with his mom and brothers. Gazing up at Mitch, she felt overwhelmed at her good fortune.

Mitch glanced down at her. "What are you smiling about?"

She squeezed his hand. "Just counting my blessings. First, my job up here, then meeting you, matching up Brian and Bobbie, then solving Fannie and Jacob's problem and, most recently, rescuing Bo." She chuckled. "Of course, I have to give you credit for *some* of it."

"Well, thank goodness for that!" Mitch was already keyed up, and something stirred inside him at the sound of her laughter. He watched her cheeks get rosy from the frosty air and blue eyes sparkle as she looked up at him. It took all his willpower not to plant a kiss on her little upturned nose, which was now turning red.

Steering her around a clanging trolley, Mitch hustled her across the tracks and up into the restaurant. Although it was lunch time, the dining room was sparsely populated, which was what he had hoped for.

Mitch helped Jessie unwind the long woolly scarf, then removed her coat and plucked the hat from her head. After handing these to an attendant, they were escorted to a window seat overlooking the bustling downtown. Peering out, he noticed how the deep blue/gray clouds were sailing in on the west wind. Maybe gloomy but right now, Mitch felt like he was soaring right along with them.

As the waiter arrived at their table with cold water and menus, Mitch knew, no matter what he ordered, he wouldn't be able to swallow a thing until he had Jessie's answer. Pretending to check the entrées, he fiddled with the boxes in his pants pocket and clenched his hand around them. *What if she says no?*

Jessie, unaware of his dilemma, watched Mitch's face with concern as it seemed to be undergoing a myriad of changes. Closing her menu, she saw him reach below the table, then grasp his menu once again. After repeating this movement a few times, Jessie was curious.

"Is anything wrong, Mitch?" she asked softly.

"No, no. Nothing wrong. Just deciding what I'm going to have." *Liar,* he thought, now fanning his heated face with the menu. "Kind of warm in here, don't you think?"

Jessie put her hand against the windowpane. "I think I feel a cold breeze seeping through. Maybe you're coming down with something?"

Yeah, like a lack of courage now that the time is finally here. Mitch could feel perspiration under his arms and decided it was now or never. "Jessie…"

But just then the waiter came over to take their order, and Mitch groaned inwardly at the lost opportunity. Jessie ordered her favorite hot roast beef sandwich that she knew came with a heap of fluffy mashed potatoes and thick gravy, perfect comfort food for a cold winter day *and* to soothe her troubled mind.

Mitch had no idea what he ordered but handed the menu back to the waiter and tried once again.

"Jess, ah, Jessie…" By now he was sweating profusely.

Jessie, concerned at the moisture drops, leaned over checking his brow for fever. Mitch took the opportunity to grab her hand and hold it tightly in his own.

"I'm *fine*, Jess, believe me. Well, I guess there's no other way of saying this." Mitch reached into his pocket and pulled out a black velvet case. With a flick of his thumb, he opened the lid, displaying the sparkling gem nestled within. Watching her face shock with surprise, he hoped it was a good one.

"Mitch?" Now it was Jessie's turn to feel hot and cold all at once. Gazing across the table, she could see his hopeful expression. "Is this a proposal…because of Sid?"

He shook his head. "Yes, no. Jess, it's not *just* about Sid. I've been thinking about this for some time. And although he's probably hot on your trail, that's not a good enough reason to get married." Mitch rubbed her hand with his thumb. "You *know* how I feel about you," he said softly. "I love you, and I'm pretty sure you love me?" At her nod, he went on, assuring her that his decision was based on his deepest desires and not just the responsibility of keeping her safe.

"Jess, each night I want to have your head on my shoulder when I go to sleep, snuggled up next to me, and wake up with you all warm and cozy in the morning. It's all I've been thinking about for a long time now. You don't know how difficult it's been to leave you at night and go back to my empty bed." He swallowed hard and whispered, "I love you so much, Jess."

Silently, with her eyes glazing over at his sincerity, Jessie held out her left hand to Mitch. He raised it to his lips, kissed her knuckles, took the sparkling diamond out of its resting place, and slid it onto her finger. Just as he thought, a perfect fit. Standing up, he walked to her side and, as she raised her glistening eyes, leaned over and kissed her gently. "Let's make this official, shall we? Jessica Lynn Peterson, will you marry me?"

Although he spoke softly, by now the other patrons had guessed what was happening and watched in complete silence as they waited for Jessie's answer.

"Yes, Mitchel O'Brien. I *do* love you and want to marry you more than *anything* in this world," she whispered, pulling his head down closer and deepening their kiss despite the onlookers.

Mitch felt moisture in his own eyes as he stood up and held Jessie's left hand high so all could see the glittering jewel. Although the room was thin of people, their shout of approval and whistles bounced off the walls. Jessie's face turned a rosy red as she laughed and accepted their congratulations.

As the noise subsided, Mitch resumed his seat and motioned for the waiter to bring over the bottle of champagne he had requested earlier—just in case.

Although the drink was bubbly, it was nothing compared to the euphoria Jessie was feeling as she and Mitch toasted each other, refilled their glasses a second time, and then a third. Brian would have to understand if she came in slightly tipsy. *Well, maybe more than slightly.* She giggled to herself. "Mitch, why don't we take a bottle back to the office so Bobbie and Brian can celebrate with us?"

Mitch grinned, still unable to believe his good luck. "I'm way ahead of you, Jess, and already ordered a second bottle. I think Bobbie knew something was in the air when we left, so our announcement might not be such a surprise to her."

Just then, their entrées arrived, and they applied themselves to the food. Regaining his appetite, Mitch ate with gusto, whatever it was, but Jessie, still high on happiness, just picked at her sandwich and dreamily stirred the gravy around on her plate. There were so many questions yet unanswered.

"Mitch, did you have a specific date in mind for the ceremony? I need to let my folks know so they can prepare for the trip and my mom can start planning. It takes time to put a wedding together, you know, and most of it lands on the bride's side." Jessie smiled winningly.

Swallowing hard, Mitch hesitated a second before answering. "Jess, I spoke to your dad this morning, and he agreed with me that with Sid hovering in the background, it might be better if we get married right away. We can always have a big reception later if you like. As a matter of fact, this morning I also called the justice of the peace here in Houghton, and he can marry us tomorrow."

Jessie choked on the small morsel she had been chewing on. Putting her napkin against her mouth, she stared aghast at Mitch, unable to believe what she had just heard. *Tomorrow? What happened to engagements, wedding plans, dresses, bridal attendants, flowers, and cake? What would her mom say? Come to think of it,* Jessie thought, *that's* exactly *what my mom would say.* Clearing her throat, she took another sip of champagne to steady her nerves before bringing up the obvious.

But before she could open her mouth to protest, Mitch jumped in. "Jess, your dad thinks it's for the best and said your mother would agree. And as for me, you know my feelings. Sid or no Sid, marrying you—well, it's what I've wanted for a very long time." He picked up her hand and smiled at her sheepishly. "I'll just get my wish a little sooner, that's all."

Jessie thought for a moment before answering. Her first instinct was to protest at the high-handed way her dad and Mitch had plotted this hasty wedding without first consulting her. But then, did she really want all the rigmarole of a fancy ceremony or was that just her mother's wish? She knew it would take a lot of time for all the arrangements to be made, maybe months. And when it came down to it, the result would be the same, anyway. Right?

"Let's do it!" she agreed excitedly. Diving into her mashed potatoes, she looked at Mitch and grinned, knowing she'd made the right decision. After all, what more could a girl want than to be married to the man she adored and who adored her!

CHAPTER 26

Grabbing the extra bottle of champagne, Mitch helped Jessie with her coat and hat. Quickly winding the scarf around her neck, he hurriedly buttoned his own jacket and ushered her out the door with Jessie giggling all the way. Mitch chuckled. *Guess champagne can do that to you,* he thought, feeling a little fuzzy himself. Now, to get both safely across the busy street and down the hill to the *Gazette*.

Hanging on to his arm, Jessie gazed up at him, all starry-eyed and Mitch couldn't believe his good luck! Tomorrow she would be his wife, Mrs. Mitchell Patrick O'Brien. He stopped to place a kiss on her upturned face, then blamed it on the brain bubbles, just in case anyone was watching.

Finding their way back to the office without incident, Mitch opened the door to the *Gazette*, and in her haste to get inside, Jessie tripped over the threshold. Giggling, she grabbed his arm to steady herself and waited while he shut the door before walking unsteadily over to her desk and plopping down in her chair.

Bobbie, watching these antics with wide eyes, rose from her desk and without a word helped Mitch remove Jessie's outer gear. Noticing the fancy bottle with the gold label under his arm, she wondered just how much "fun" they had had over lunch and what the bubbly was for.

"You two have something to tell me?" she questioned, looking between them.

Jessie just grinned at her. Then, removing her mitten with a flourish, waved her hand before Bobbie's face, exposing the sparkling gem on her left finger.

With a shriek, Bobbie attacked Jessie with a big hug. Hearing the commotion, Carl came running out from the back just as Brian came bolting down the stairs.

"What on earth...?" Then he stopped. Bobbie and Jessie were in a blubbering embrace and acting like watering pots. Mitch, hovering over them with a silly grin on his face, held a bottle of champagne under his arm. Brian gave a big sigh of relief. *Okay.* Obviously, Sid was not the problem here.

"Come celebrate with us, Brian!" Mitch was exuberant as he waved the bottle in the air. "Jessie's agreed to become my wife. *And* we request the honor of your presence as witnesses tomorrow afternoon at two o'clock at the courthouse."

With that announcement, Bobbie jerked back with an incredulous look. "Tomorrow? Are you *crazy*?"

Jessie laughed. "That's what I thought too. But my dad and Mitch talked it over and decided it was best if we got married right away so I'll have more protection from Sid, *if* he ever shows up. Mitch called the Justice of the Peace this morning and it's all arranged."

"Please, Bobbie," she pleaded. "Please say you'll be my maid of honor, and, Brian, you'll be the best man for Mitch, right? Carl, we'd appreciate you being there, too, to take some photos for my family as they won't be here."

"Sure, Jessie. I'd be more than happy to help considering it was my fault about Sid," Carl assured her, thankful to make up for the trouble he'd caused.

Bobbie frowned. "But, Jess, what about a wedding gown, flowers, cake, reception—you know, all those 'unforgettable' memories that go along with a ceremony?"

"Well, if Brian will give us the afternoon off, we can run over to Gunter's Department Store in Hancock and go through their great line of fancy dresses. We can always grab a cake from the bakery to have after the wedding. And Mitch says we can have a big reception for my family later." Jessie's face was beaming as she looked up at him and reached out her hand. "But after the ceremony, we'd like to have a little party at my, or I should say *our* house, for all of us.

We're going to ask the Johns family and Fannie and Jacob, as well, to celebrate with us."

Mitch took her hand in his and checked with Brian. "So what do you say, Brian, will you stand for us?"

"Yes, of course, Mitch! I'd be honored and I'm sure Bobbie is thrilled too." He looked at her and, at her nod, continued. "But if you gals want to do some shopping, you better get going and save that champagne for tomorrow's celebration. In fact, I'll pick up a couple more bottles on my way home tonight so we can all toast to your happiness." He held out his hand to Mitch and shook it wholeheartedly. "Congratulations, old man!" Walking over to Jessie, he took her hand also. "And best wishes, Jessie," he added softly. After giving Bobbie a special look, he encouraged them to get going. "I can hold down the office for the rest of the day. And of course, Jess, we won't expect you in tomorrow, but will meet you at the courthouse before two o'clock."

Mitch pulled Jessie up from her chair, wrapped his arms around her, and kissed her cheek. "I'll go home, now, and break the news to Tom and Irma that they're losing a boarder. Under the circumstances, I know they'll be delighted to see me go. And it'll give me time to pack up all my things to get ready for the move." He gazed into her eyes. "Until tomorrow..." he promised and walked out the door.

Silence filled the air for a moment until Jessie hiccupped and they all burst out laughing. "I think I need a big mug of strong black coffee before we go anywhere." They all headed to the back room, filling their cups as they discussed plans for the next day. Bobbie knew Jessie's dreamy expression didn't just come from too much champagne and she was happy for both. Sending a coveted look at Brian, she wondered if her time would ever come.

Brian turned and caught her looking at him and, as if reading her mind, gave her a little wink. Bobbie blushed and turned around to refill Jessie's cup, while trying to regain her composure. She watched as he left the room wondering if his eyes held a special message. Bobbie sighed and handed another steaming cup to Jessie. After all this time, her dreams could wait a little longer.

Focusing on the present, she plied Jessie with coffee until they both had enough stimulants to run the 100-yard dash! Grabbing their coats, Bobbie stopped just before walking out the door to answer her jingling telephone. "It's for you, Jess. It sounds like long distance with all the crackling over the wires."

"Oh, great! That'll be my dad checking up on me." She smiled. "He'll be *so* pleased that Mitch and I are getting married tomorrow."

Dropping her coat and purse, she sat down at Bobbie's desk and took the phone from her hands. "Dad? You'll be so excited when you hear—"

"Well, well, well. If it ain't Sable, or should I say *Ms*. Peterson." At her stunned silence, the raspy voice continued. "What's the matter, Sable? Cat got your tongue? I heard you had *plenty* to say to the police." He laughed. "Well, don't you worry. We'll have plenty of time to chat later. *That* I can promise you." The rough voice disappeared with a click as Jessie continued to clutch the phone, staring down at it.

Seeing her ashen face, Bobbie grabbed the phone from her death grip and yelled into it. "Hello! Hello! Who is this?" Disgusted with no answer on the other side, she slammed the phone down and, observing Jessie's shock-like expression, ran to the hallway and yelled up the stairway. "Brian? Get down here. Quick!"

Turning back to Jessie, she sat down beside her and patted her hand. Jess looked up at her, trembling. "Jess, who was that?" Bobbie knew it couldn't have been her dad.

Clambering down the stairs, Brian arrived within seconds and moved to Jessie's side. Looking at Bobbie, he asked what the problem was, but she just shook her head and shrugged.

"Jess, we can't help you unless you tell us what's wrong." By now, he held her other hand while waiting for an answer.

Tears ran uncontrollably down Jessie's face, and she was trembling. "Sid. It was Sid," she whispered. "And he's coming for me."

Bobbie's hands flew to her mouth. "What? Are you sure it was him, Jess?"

Jessie lifted her tear-streamed face and nodded. "Oh yes. I'll never forget that voice, even though it was slightly distorted over the line." She sniffed and let out a sigh. "Well, I guess we don't have to wonder whether he'll find me. He already has."

"What now, Jess? Will you cancel the wedding?" Bobbie's voice was sad and deflated.

Jessie straightened up, her eyes bright with moisture. "Absolutely not! He's not going to spoil *my* special day. Besides, he's the reason we're getting married so quickly." Reaching into her purse, she pulled out a lacy handkerchief, wiped her eyes, blew her nose, and stood up resolutely. "Come on, Bobbie, we've got *lots* of shopping to do *and* a cake to order."

Brian hovered about, uncertain. "What about Mitch, Jess? I think he should be notified right away. Is it alright if I telephone him at the Johns' house and let him know about Sid's call?"

Jessie nodded. "Go ahead, Brian. At least we'll all be on the same page. It'll be days yet before Sid gets here, and hopefully, we'll have a plan in place by then."

Arm in arm, Jessie and Bobbie headed out the door on their quest for wedding attire. Brian stared after them as he rubbed his chin, thoughtfully. This couldn't have come at a worse time. A celebration with Sid hovering in the background put a damper on things. What if it had been Bobbie who was in trouble?

Brian was shocked at his violent feelings. When had all this happened? She had been sitting there for *years*, right in front of his eyes, but he must have been blind. Now she was in his thought's day and night. And it had been Jessie who had opened his eyes to this beautiful girl now within his reach. *Carl's not the only one who owes her something.* One way or the other, Jessie would be protected.

CHAPTER 27

Mitch checked his watch again as he paced up and down the entrance to the courthouse. It was one forty-five and still no sign of the girls. After getting Brian's call yesterday, he'd been ready to camp out on Jessie's doorstep until the wedding, but she'd reassured him that the call was long distance and Sid couldn't possibly arrive for several days.

Where are they? Mitch asked himself, again, crossing the portico.

Watching him, Brian chuckled to himself, wondering if he'd be so addle-brained when his day came. *His day?* Three months ago, he would have laughed at the suggestion that he would marry. But now the idea held great appeal with Bobbie in the picture.

As it was, they had arrived a half hour early because Mitch couldn't sit still. Brian chided him, "Remember, Mitch, a watched pot never boils. You're going to freeze standing out there like that. They'll be here, don't worry." Even as he spoke, Bobbie's car scooted around the corner and into the parking lot.

Mitch dashed into the hallway and retrieved the beautiful bouquet of flowers he had thoughtfully purchased, along with a smaller arrangement for Bobbie. Grabbing both, he bolted to the doorway just as Brian ushered the girls inside, then stopped to stare at Jessie. She was stunning, dressed in a midnight blue coat, trimmed with light brown fur around the neck and bottom. On her head, with a few golden curls peeking out from underneath, sat a matching fur hat. Her face was flawless and, more than anything, he wanted to plant a kiss on those rosy lips. Jessie's eyes twinkled up at him as he appeared to be spellbound.

Her "Are those for me?" broke through his stupor and he hastily thrust the bouquet into her hands. Bending her head to smell the flowers, she smiled up at him in approval. "They're beautiful, Mitch. Thank you!" The bouquet was full of red roses, white chrysanthemums, and baby's breath, with a dark green fern tucked in here and there. "I take it the other arrangement is for Bobbie?"

By now, Brian was chuckling out loud as he retrieved it from Mitch and presented it to Bobbie with a flourish. "You both look lovely, girls." He pulled out a small red rose from each bouquet, placing one in the hole of his lapel, then the other in Mitch's. Holding out his arm, he put Bobbie's hand through it and headed down the hall to the Justice of the Peace.

Jessie watched them saunter down the corridor before turning to Mitch, who still seemed speechless. "I believe it's our turn?" Coming to his senses, Mitch offered his arm. "Jess, I don't know what's come over me. You're *so* beautiful, and I'm the luckiest man alive."

"I'm not sure lucky is the right word," Jessie replied as they strolled sedately down the hallway. "You're marrying a woman with an irrational mobster gunning for her who could affect the lives of everyone else around her." She smiled up at him. "But I'm grateful, Mitch. Grateful for your love, your thoughtfulness, and your protection. *I'm* the luckiest girl in the world."

Brian and Bobbie were waiting for them outside the office door. She had removed her coat and looked delightful in a glistening green silk sheath that brought out the highlights in her shiny red hair. As Mitch helped Jessie with her coat, he stopped for a moment to admire the silky dark blue dress underneath, like Bobbie's, and whistled. "Wow, you girls look breathtaking," he finally said.

"I'll second that," Brian added, giving Bobbie an intimate smile.

Before entering the official's office, the door opened sending a blast of cold air down the corridor as Carl rushed in, breathless. "Sorry I'm late, but the bridge was open, and traffic jammed up." He held up his camera. "I'll just stay in the background and get some photos for your parents, Jess, unless there are some special ones, you'd like me to take. Naturally, one of you and Mitch, along with Brian and Bobbie are priority."

"Thanks, Carl." Jessie beamed up at him before turning to the others. "Come on. Let's get this show on the road."

Mitch opened the door to the Justice of the Peace and as the official glanced up to welcome the wedding party, Jessie gasped and to Mitch's surprise, moved forward with her hands held out.

"Judge Markham! What a wonderful surprise!"

The white-haired gentleman with black robes stood up and, with a beaming smile, walked around his desk to take her outstretched arms. "Jessie Peterson! And all grown up. Let me look at you, girl."

Jessie stood still while admired by one of her father's cronies. He had often visited their home before leaving Detroit ten years earlier, wanting to get out of the 'rat race' as he put it.

"Don't tell me you're the same Peterson gal who has been writing all those colorful editorials for the *Gazette*?" At her nod and laugh, he shook his head. "I should have guessed, knowing your background. Well, Jess, your father must be awfully proud of you, following in his footsteps, although how he let you leave the nest to come up here is beyond thinking." Before she could reply, he turned to acknowledge the rest of the wedding party.

"Well, you may as well introduce me to the groom and your attendants." He shook hands with Mitch, first, as she pulled him forward, then Bobbie and Brian, ending with Carl.

Walking back to his desk, Judge Markham sat down and examined the paperwork before looking up with a frown. "Jessie, this license was applied for just yesterday! I wouldn't be doing my duty if I didn't question your hasty decision and make sure you're doing the right thing. Your dad would have my hide. Marriage is a long-term commitment, you know."

He motioned for all of them to take a seat across from him, while Carl moved to a discreet distance across the room.

As she sat down, Jessie hastened to assure him that it was truly above board, she really loved Mitch and had her father's approval. After giving Judge Markham a brief synopsis of the Sid Brewster situation, his smiling countenance turned grim. He grunted. "Excuse me for a minute." Picking up his phone, he asked the operator for the police department. While he waited for the call to go through, he covered the mouthpiece with his hand and spoke to them. "My sister's son, Michael, is the deputy sheriff for Houghton County. He's one of the reasons I've taken this job, having family close by. If I can't trust my own nephew, I'll hang up my robes and call it quits. Yes, hello? I'd like to speak with Michael Houle, please."

While they waited, Jessie filled her father's friend in on more of the particulars. It wasn't exactly the wedding she had in mind but decided the ceremony could wait a little longer. Right now, the threat on her life was more important than the few words they would speak later. Huddled together, the group waited as Judge Markham spoke into the phone.

"Mikey! It's Uncle Pete. Doing well, thanks. Hey, I've got a situation here that could use your expertise. No, I'd rather not say, right now, but how about coming over in about twenty minutes and I'll fill you in. I'm performing a marriage ceremony and could see you right after." He nodded. "Great! See you then."

Hanging up the phone, he turned back to the wedding party. "Now if you'll please take your places, we'll get started."

Jessie and Mitch stood side by side as the judge read from the official marriage book, with Brian and Bobbie beaming next to them, the latter with joyful tears as she daintily dabbed at the corner of her eyes.

"Do you, Jessica Lynn Peterson, take this man…"

As Judge Markham continued, Jessie, with sparkling eyes, looked at Mitch before replying "I do."

Mitch looked directly at her when the vows were presented to him, and his "I do" was loud and clear.

Rings were exchanged, and the judge pronounced them man and wife. Just as Mitch leaned forward to kiss Jessie, he paused as the door to the chamber opened, admitting a younger man in a policeman's uniform.

"Mikey, my boy, come on in. It's good to see you! We're just about finished here." Looking sheepishly at Mitch he apologized for the interruption. "Sorry about that, Mitch. Please go ahead and kiss your bride." At his words, Mitch and Jessie both laughed, before sealing their vows with a kiss. And then another, as Carl kept snapping pictures. Drawing back, they waited as Judge Markham introduced his nephew.

The look of real concern on Mike's face boosted Jessie's confidence that this was a man she could trust. After reassuring her that a squad car would patrol around the house, at least during the night, he shook hands with all of them as they filed out into hallway. "Please call me with any other information about this character or you need assistance. Right now, I'm heading up your way to check out a domestic disturbance, so I'll make a run through the area and get familiar with your property."

Jessie thanked him for all his assistance and said they would keep him updated.

Before ducking back into his office, Judge Markham spoke to Jessie. "Please give your father my best when you speak to him and tell him how happy I was to officiate at your wedding." Reaching over, he gave her a hug, wishing her all the best, and with a nod at the others, returned to his office.

"Well. That was short and sweet." Mitch laughed self-consciously. "But I guess the deed's done, Jess, and we're officially man and wife." And tonight would be their wedding night. Mitch leaned down and kissed Jessie one more time just because he could, now and forever, and before she could protest that others might be watching. But she just laughed along with him.

Carl posed the two of them for the official wedding photo and then one with Brian and Bobbie. "Got it!" After securing the camera in his leather bag, he sauntered down the hallway and waited for them outside the building.

Bundling up for the outdoors, Mitch and Jessie slowly walked arm in arm toward the front door where Brian and Bobbie had slipped out ahead of them. As they left the building, they were laughingly pelted with a shower of pink rose petals.

As Brian hastened Bobbie to her car to drive them to Jessie's house for the celebration, Mitch helped Jessie inside his car before hurrying around to the driver's side. Starting the motor, he squeezed her hand before shifting gears and pulling out of the parking lot.

Happily, lost in thoughts of their wedding, Jessie scarcely remembered the drive home as Mitch held her hand. What a wonderful day it had been, with even more to come, despite Sid Brewster's threatening presence hovering over her. This was *her* day, and Mitch's, plus she had the anticipation of their wedding night. Although she blushed at *that* thought.

Arriving home, they ran through another gauntlet of petals as Fannie, Jacob, Tom, Irma, and Josie showered them with more of the fragrant pink blossoms. Bo, excited by all the commotion, barked his own greeting, running back and forth between them. Hugs and congratulations were passed all around before Mitch and Jessie found themselves just outside the front door. "Shall we?" With a swoop, he picked her up and carried her over the doorstep, giving her a soft, lingering kiss, winning the approval and whistles from the on-lookers.

Red cheeked, Jessie planted her feet on the floor, looking around in astonishment at the transformation Fannie had created with floral decorations on the beautifully laid-out dining-room table. Sitting on top of a white starched tablecloth, the plates glistened, the silverware shined, and the flowers in the center were flanked by tall white candles. Wedding bells were hanging from the chandelier above, with yards and yards of white crepe paper ribbon stretching across the ceiling from corner to corner.

Jessie, gazing about in awe, gave Fannie a big jubilant hug. "You've really outdone yourself, Fan. Everything looks so beautiful and whatever is cooking smells delicious. I really didn't expect all this but thank you from the bottom of my heart!"

Fannie beamed. "It wasn't just me, Jess. Irma and Josie helped too. I couldn't have done it all without them, given such short notice, that is. Even Tom helped polish up the silverware. Josie took care of Bo, so we were able to work without interruption."

Although the table normally sat eight, a ninth chair was squeezed in to fit one more. With a disregard for etiquette, Fannie had placed Mitch at the head of the table but sat Jessie at his right side instead of at the other end where Tom was now seated. After everyone found their place, Irma and Fannie rushed about the kitchen, then back and forth to the dining room, bringing in the tasty feast they had prepared. Jessie marveled at the variety of the colorful dishes, and exclaimed over the roasted chicken, pork, and beef. The gravy was thick and dark and fresh rolls accompanied the salad greens. Glasses were presented as Brian popped the cork from one of the bottles of champagne.

Standing up, he directed his toast at Jessie and Mitch. "To the bride and groom, our good friends. May your days be richly blessed with love and laughter, mixed with patience, and understanding during times of trial. To Jessie and Mitch!"

At the lifting of glasses, echoes of congratulations were heard with the clinking of the crystal, and well-meant advice was laughingly given on how to keep a marriage happy. Mitch and Jessie entwined their arms as they drank to each other, both thinking of the night ahead and wondering how long their guests would stay.

When everyone had eaten their fill and were champagne happy, Fannie excused herself, then returned with a beautifully decorated three-layer coconut crème cake she had made at Jacob's house, claiming a store-bought cake just wouldn't do the job.

Following tradition, the first piece was handed to Mitch where he took a forkful of the sugary confection and fed it to Jessie without mishap. But she would have none of the niceties and, with a mischievous grin, pinched a large section from her piece and held it in front of Mitch for him to taste. He watched her dancing eyes and leaned forward to receive the gooey dessert from her fingers just as Jessie smashed it onto his lips. His face alight with laughter, Mitch firmly grabbed her hand, pulling her sticky fingers into his mouth, and proceeding to lick the sweetness off each finger, one at a time.

Jessie inwardly gasped at the sensuality of his warm mouth and held her breath as each finger was slowly and deliberately cleaned by the swirling of his tongue. Unable to pull away, she looked into his eyes and saw the hungry passion of one who was anticipating the hours ahead. Meeting him eye to eye, she, too, expressed her desire to be alone with him. *Soon...*she promised.

Suddenly aware of being on display, Mitch eased the tension slightly by taking Jessie's little finger and biting down with a little nip. She yelped, jerking her finger from his mouth, laughing with the others while Mitch took her left hand and kissed the ring he had recently placed there.

As if aware of their heated feelings, Fannie stood up and started to collect their now empty plates. "I think it's time we left these two newlyweds to themselves, once we get these dishes done, of course."

Jessie blushed, aware of their thoughts, but wouldn't dream of letting the others clean for them. "Fannie, you prepared this *wonderful* feast for us, and now it's time for *us* to do the dirty work." She smirked at Mitch. "Besides, how will I ever know if he's going to be a helpful husband or not?" Jessie looked around the table and her heartfelt thanks was conveyed as she stood up and reach down to hug and kiss all those who had presented her and Mitch with this forever memory. A big formal reception had nothing over this!

"We're taking Bo with us, Jess, so you two can have an uninterrupted night," a grinning Josie informed her, giving Jessie another quick hug before attaching the leash to the dog's collar. Sensing something exciting was going to happen, Bo danced about waiting for his new adventure. As they all headed out the front door, though, he stopped suddenly and turned around as if to say "Hey, aren't you coming, Mom?"

Bending down, Jessie gave him a quick kiss on his head, promising to see him tomorrow, then turned to the teenager and hugged her tightly. "Thanks so much, Josie. Please feel free to bring him home any time after breakfast." Then, looking at Mitch, placed her hand on Josie's arm and whispered softly, "On second thought, better make that lunch." With a giggle, Josie led the prancing pup outside and across the yard.

Waving goodbye to their other guests, the door was shut behind them, creating a thick vacuum of silence. Jessie and Mitch stood looking at each other, still unable to believe their good fortune. Moving together without words, they embraced, not hurriedly but as lovers who had all the time in the world. Mitch's kiss was not rushed but soft as he covered her mouth with his own, and slowly sampled the sweetness of wedding cake still lingering on her lips. Despite the almost-winter season, he inhaled the flowery fragrance of her hair, continuing down the side of her neck as he tasted her moist skin. Feeling her shivering response, he drew her closer, wrapping his arms around her waist when she pressed herself up against him, sighing as she moved her mouth against his, meeting one smoldering kiss with another.

Her head in a swirling mist, Jessie moaned softly as Mitch twirled his fingers in her curls, then gasped as he slowly moved his hands down the sides of her body and along her breast. Pulling back, she gazed at him with heavy eyes before taking one of his hands to her mouth, letting her tongue slide around the center of his palm, noting with satisfaction as Mitch sucked in his breath. Emboldened, she leaned up to his ear and blew in softly before nipping at his earlobe.

Where had she learned such things? Surely Sable wouldn't have… no, he reminded himself. This was his Jessie, but two could play this game. Holding her with one arm, he tickled her ribs until she screamed and broke away, laughing before making a mad dash up the stairs. Hurriedly, Mitch locked the front door to ensure their privacy before charging up the steps after her. Slamming the bedroom door behind them, he reached out for Jessie as they shared the most beautiful miracle in their union.

CHAPTER 28

Belching a bellyful of smoke, a steaming locomotive chugged its way through the flat lands of lower Michigan, then decreased its speed as it headed up the steeper terrain further north. Adding more coal to the fire, the engineer checked his dials, gauging the amount of fuel needed to make it over the rolling hills without overtaxing his engine. Schedules and passengers' safety were his main concern, and he was proud of his record.

Checking his watch when they arrived at the last logging town confirmed they were right on time. He had one more water stop before hitting the Straits of Mackinac. There he would turn over the passenger cars to the captain of the Chief Wawatam ferry for their journey across the churning waters. This is where his ride ended although one day, he promised himself, he'd go across the Great Lakes, and see what lay hidden behind the mist on the other side.

Heading toward the back, he grabbed his passenger manifest making sure everyone was accounted for before floating across the water and into the wilderness. Counting heads, he walked down the aisle, observing the various personalities of his riders; a few were couples, but the majority were single men who were passing the time with a poker game. Intrigued, he stood, watchful, placing a mental bet on who the winner would be. After a few hands, his interest piqued as one gentleman continued to win, again and again, although the cards he had drawn were never very promising.

Pretending to write on his manifest, his focus remained on the winner until he determined that the man was cheating. He had to admit, it was slyly done, but cheating all the same. While he was deciding whether to report the card shark, the man looked up and, seeing he was being watched, placed his cards face down on the make-shift table between the benches.

"Ya want something?" His eyes glittering, the man snarled at the engineer while the others looked on.

"No, no," the engineer hastened to assure him. "Just checking the register to make sure everyone was accounted for." He grinned and nodded to the number of coins sitting in front of the swindler. "Looks like *you've* had a lucky day."

"What of it?" the man snorted. "*You* wanna play? I'm sure one of these guys would be glad to sit out a game. He looks like a pigeon ready for plucking, don't he, fellas?" With a raspy laugh and two pudgy fingers, he stuck the stub of an old stogie between his lips, inhaled deeply and blew a cloud of smoke at the engineer and smirked. "Come on, boys, let's get back to our game and let the man get back to his duties." He looked up once again. "You're finished here, *right?*" he asked with a sneer, as if daring him to say otherwise.

Staring into his blotchy face, the engineer opened his register and checked off the man's name. "Right you are, ah, Mr. Smith?" He turned to all the remaining gentlemen and wished them good luck before hurrying down the aisle and into the next car. Not wanting to get involved, he decided to let the men play it out. After all, anyone playing cards should know there was always a chance of losing. Besides, Mr. Card Shark Smith didn't look like the kind of man he'd want to tangle with. *Nope*, he decided. The sooner they reached the Straits, the sooner he could head back home, hopefully in time for his wife's Thanksgiving dinner.

Sid glanced over his shoulder as the engineer exited into the adjoining car. Uneasy at possibly being caught cheating, he decided to let someone else win a hand. He raised the ante and threw more of his cash into the pile. While others groaned at the amount and folded, one man stayed in and called his bluff. Making sure his cards were low, Sid placed them on the table. With a shout of triumph, the other player laid down three jacks, rubbing his hands gleefully before pulling the stash toward him.

Smirking with satisfaction, Sid was thankful that these men were so easy to manipulate. Stubbing out the cigar butt, he leaned back, folded his hands over his belly and addressed the other players. "See, boys? If you'd stayed in the game long enough, maybe that pot could have been yours!" Bemoaning their losses and shaking their heads, they wandered back to their seats as Sid stretched his legs across the wooden crate to the other bench. Watching the scenery slowly drifting by, he was anxious to arrive at the Straits where half of his journey would be complete.

Ever since Vinnie had handed over the tickets and smuggled him onto the train, Sid had been pent up with excitement. But heading out of the city, the terrain had become more and more desolate with nothing to see but leafless trees, dried up fields and thick gray clouds that dipped so low you could almost touch them. Also, to his discomfort, the temperature had dropped with every mile they headed north.

Grabbing his old jacket bunched up beside him and buttoning it up to his neck, Sid moved away from the window and leaned toward the aisle, trying to grasp a little more heat that was filtering out of the smoky little stove in back of the car.

He snorted. This trip had been tedious. In just two days, he was tired of the monotony, the tasteless food and was more than ready to get off this rocking machine. He wondered how Sable had withstood the journey. *Sable, huh! I hope she was miserable, the vixen!* Reaching down and caressing the gun in his holster, he endured one more stop at a water barrel before the train jerked and with a shrill whistle, chugged toward their destination. Hoping the ferry would be more interesting, Sid crouched down, and sliding his hat over his eyes in final resignation, tried to get some shut eye before their debarking in a couple of hours. It couldn't come soon enough for him.

But when the time finally came and he planted his feet on solid ground, Sid was thankful the lengthy crossing was over. Thinking the ferry would offer some relief had been a *gross* miscalculation. The bouncing train had been bad enough, but the large transport ferry had charged into every wave as if doing battle, causing his stomach to roll right along with the undulating water. Although he had never been physically sick, it had been a close call. Now testing his land legs, he swayed a little back and forth until he was certain the earth really stood still.

Staring at his surroundings, he found the hustle and bustle of the docks a relief to the daily monotony of the train, although, he chuckled, his pockets were a little fuller than when he had left Detroit thanks to the gullible riders he'd fleeced.

Jingling the coins, he walked jauntily toward the little town that had emerged along the north side of Lake Michigan. Saint something or other, they called it. Looking over the shoddy wooden structures and black smoking chimneys, he smirked. No saint *he* knew of would be living up here. In fact, gazing just beyond the buildings, he saw nothing but trees and more trees. *Why would she come to this godforsaken country?*

Exuberant in his freedom, Sid raised his arms and stretched, taking in a deep breath of the arctic-like air. Choking as its dryness burned his nostrils, he pulled up the collar of his thin jacket and hastily shoved his hands into its pockets. *Vinnie could have at least checked the weather up here,* he growled to himself. *If Sable's lucky, I might freeze to death before I find her.*

As they had about an hour to kill before boarding their new train for the last leg of the journey, the passengers had been encouraged to stretch their legs, visit the stores, and spend a little of their cash while the fireman shoveled more coal into the open car behind the engine.

Taking another sniff of air, Sid's stomach growled as his nose directed him to one of the shacks that boasted smoked whitefish, trout, and salmon caught daily in the Great Lakes. Salivating, he fingered his change before pulling on the leather strap used to open the thick wooden door. Bombarded by a blast of hot air, his nose crinkled at the pungent smell of smoked fish drying on the walls. Deciding it would be better than the bland fare on the train, he laid down his money and walked out with a large lake trout covered in brown paper.

Finding a wooden barrel to sit on, Sid peeled back the wrapping to get his first taste of the salty fish. Without eating utensils, it would have to be his fingers. With a shrug, he gingerly pinched off a small chunk and placed it in his mouth. *Hmm*...not too bad, he decided, but would have preferred eating the fish without it staring back at him. Losing his appetite, he tore off one more little piece, wrapped the mess up and tossed it into a nearby trash barrel that already smelled rancid. Pulling a handkerchief from his pocket, he wiped off his beard and hands and threw it on top of the fish. Maybe he'd have better luck in one of the other stores.

Walking across the street, Sid poked his head into a larger building. Finding a warm woolly gray jacket and matching newsboy cap with brim and ear flaps, he purchased these along with two red and black plaid flannel shirts, a sturdy pair of tan leather work boots, and some heavy gloves. After adding some knitted socks and a wrap-around scarf, he decided that although his plan didn't include an extended stay, *not if I can help it*, he thought, the investment would be well worth it. After all, he did have to blend in with the locals.

Donning his new jacket and hat, he gazed into the mirror, satisfied to see the reflection of a stranger. Sporting his new mustache and shaggy beard, dyed black to match his wig, Sid puffed up, confident he looked totally different, and ten years younger. *With my new look, I should be able to pass for a commoner*, he thought gleefully. From his experience, if anyone had anything to say, it would be in a tavern. Whether happy or sad, spirits made you talk. Besides, he was looking forward to downing a few well-earned pints himself.

After paying for some dried beef jerky sticks and a bag of peppermints, he threw one of the red and white striped candies into his mouth to camouflage the fishy taste and headed back to the station with his plunder. As he savored the cool spicy flavor, he watched as cars from his train were joined together behind a large locomotive bearing the letters DSS&A. Three or four other engines, facing different directions, also waited their turn for hook-ups. Some were already puffing steam and gyrating like panting horses eager to be off. He didn't care where the others were going if his would take him to Sable.

Seeing passengers streaming back toward the train, Sid ambled behind them watching as the first-class riders lined up by the steps to their private car. Upon hearing a hearty laugh, he looked over as a well-dressed gentleman, taking a few last puffs of his cigar, turned to speak to one of the passengers. Catching his face, Sid thought the man looked familiar, but how he knew him was a mystery.

Cautiously moving their direction, and hoping not to be recognized, he snatched a few snatches of their conversation. Then the word Houghton caught his attention, and he strolled closer to the two men. Bending down, pretending to tie his bootlace, Sid listened as they discussed the pros and cons of the trip.

"I was a news reporter in Houghton last year but left my job for something better," The young guy laughed. "You know how it goes, the grass is always greener… Sure, the pay was good, but I hated the bustle of the city. Too fast pace, too noisy, you know? By the time I discovered my mistake, they'd already hired someone else, so I guess I was lucky getting a new job at the Mining Register in Marquette. The town's a little larger than Houghton but a heck of a lot smaller than Detroit. Maybe one day, if I'm lucky, I'll get rehired at the *Gazette*." He held out his hand. "By the way, my name's Rudy Lahti. My seat's way in the back of the car but I noticed you walking down the aisle occasionally. When we *could* walk, that is." He chuckled. "What a ride, hey?"

Smiling and tapping out the tip of his smoke against the metal car, the older gentleman agreed as he shook hands with Rudy. "You're right about that. I'd say a person must be desperate to take this long desolate ride. As for me, I'm making a surprise visit to my daughter who recently moved into the Hancock area. It's been about four months since I've seen her." He started to elaborate, but before he could continue, the conductor yelled 'All Aboard' and they silently lined up waiting their turn before stepping into the car. Mounting the steps, the cigar smoking gentleman turned behind him to Rudy and said, "Oh, by the way, my name's Peterson. Randall Peterson."

Jerking his head up in surprise, Sid surveyed the two men. Standing tall, he looked Peterson in the face, and except for a nod, the gentleman climbed aboard without recognition.

Exuberant but keeping a low profile, he sedately walked back to his own car. *Sable's dad? How lucky can I get? Both the daughter and the father falling right into my hands! And the local yokel police up here should be easy to handle.* Knowing his suitcase was full of cash to back up his plan, he confidently pulled out his own cigar. At least *this* was something he had in common with Peterson, besides the girl. However, he had to admit, Peterson's Havana smoke smelled a lot better than his.

Maybe I'll move to Cuba when this is all over. Yeah. Somewhere warm and sunny. On this positive note, he climbed into his own car where he saw another game of poker about to commence. If those 'patsies' wanted to part with more of their money, who was he to argue. He grinned as he walked over.

"You men have room for one more player?" Sid shrugged out of his new jacket and laid it back against the seat before sitting down.

"Sure, Smith. I'd like to try and win back some of that cash you took from me yesterday," one of the players jeered. "How about the rest of you guys? Maybe this'll be our lucky day!"

Agreeing, all four passengers settled down for some serious gaming before nightfall. This being their last one, each wanted a chance to recoup their losses before getting off the train.

Sid pulled out his "lucky deck" and plopped it in the middle of the crate. "High card deals?" Knowing he would draw a king, he sat back to enjoy another opportunity of swindling these chumps. He checked up and down the aisle. Hopefully, the conductor wouldn't be back for a few hours, yet.

"Put in your ante, boys and let's play some poker." Shoving some coins onto the table, and cigar in his mouth, Sid settled in for a pleasurable evening. He might even let them win a hand or two.

CHAPTER 29

Jessie's face glowed as she gazed across the table at her husband of one week. Mitch, who was listening to something Thomas was saying, glanced her way and witnessed her besotted smile. He smiled back at her before feeling a sudden kick beneath the table. With twinkling eyes, he turned his attention to Josie, his attacker, who was smirking at him.

Although very fond of Jessie, Josie was pleased to have Mitch's undivided attention, if only for a little while. She missed him terribly and had rarely seen him since he had married Jessie last week. It wasn't jealousy, she knew, just the absence of someone who understood where she was coming from.

Yes, she had parents who loved her, and she loved them; but it was Mitch who really understood her needs and shared with her a world that went beyond the mining community. Even now she eagerly pelted him with questions of living "in the big city," promising herself that one day she would experience it firsthand. Knowing the strike couldn't last forever, maybe she could visit Mitch and Jessie if they moved, although the thought of their absence filled her with melancholy. But then, *maybe*, with Jessie's new job, they would settle here, and all her worrying would be for naught.

Her unspoken thoughts were echoed by Mitch, for although he and Jessie hadn't discussed moving, the unresolved mining strike made him pause, wondering what he was doing up here. Would Jessie want to continue living away from her family and all the comforts she was used to? And what about Sid? Although no further contact had been made, he weighed heavily on their minds. When would he strike and how? Without concrete knowledge of his whereabouts or intentions, they were at a stalemate and could only wait for him to make the first move.

But today was Thanksgiving and they had much to be thankful for. He answered Josie's questions patiently and then fired off some of his own.

"Enough of me. Let's talk about you, Jo. How's school coming? Do you miss me?" At the incredulous look she gave him, he laughed. "Of course, you do. Who else would torment you daily? That's what big brothers are for you know." At her engaging giggle, he asked about school activities and any plans she had for Christmas.

Josie nodded excitedly. "There's going to be a *big* Christmas party, Mitch, haven't you heard? The Ladies Auxiliary is holding it at the Italian Hall on Christmas Eve. It's for all the striking miners and their families, especially the kids, and they'll have games, food and presents for everyone! We're still invited because the mine accident caused Dad's blindness." She looked up at him apologetically. "I don't think you can come, Mitch, but I promise to tell you all the details afterward."

Jessie, who had been homing in on their conversation, interrupted them with a smile. "Don't worry about Mitch, Jo. He'll be able to read all the facts later because I'm covering the party for the *Gazette* as well as taking some photos. Are your mom and dad going to the Christmas party?"

Josie shook her head. "Mom says it's a small space and hundreds of people will be there. She'll stay home and make room for those who really need to go, but Daddy says he'll come with me. He'll be my date! I get to have a new dress just for the party too!" Then she frowned. "I'm not sure how we will get there, though. It's in Calumet, so a bit of a drive."

Jessie reached over and patted her hand. "No worries. If I must be there, you'll both come with me, of course. Mitch can stay home and keep Bo company while I'm gone. Besides, it'll be nice knowing someone there. Most of these people are still strangers to me, so you'll be doing *me* a favor." She leaned over and whispered, "Just make sure I get some of that candy, okay?"

Hearing her invitation, Thomas turned her way with his sightless eyes that were squinting with a smile as he expressed his appreciation. "There you are, Josie. It's all taken care of. Didn't I say we'd get you there one way or the other? I can't thank you, enough, Jessie, as she's been anxious ever since hearing about the party."

"It's my pleasure, Tom. I consider all of you part of my family, especially with you here celebrating Thanksgiving and, of course, this fantastic turkey. I've never cooked one so when Irma volunteered, I couldn't say no." She paused and took another bite of the stuffing. "Irma, what's in this dressing that makes it sweet? It's so delicious!"

"It's the apples." Irma shared her recipe and promised to write it down for Jessie. As the women exchanged ideas, Jessie appreciated these few precious hours surrounded by her adopted family.

After treating themselves to large pieces of Jessie's rich pumpkin pie, topped with thick dollops of whipped cream, the men began discussing the status of the strike and the atmosphere became businesslike. Irma, Jessie, Bobbie, and Josie all headed into the kitchen for clean-up duty and some girl talk.

Bobbie poured some soap into the basin, added water, and swished it around to create bubbles. "Jessie, have you had any more contact from Sid? You haven't said but I know he's got to be on your mind. If it were me, I'd be checking around every corner and over my shoulder every minute."

Jessie gave a troubled look at Josie who was very interested in the conversation, wondering if she should change the subject.

"Don't worry about Josie," Irma said, placing an arm around her daughter. "She knows everything."

"Yes, Jess, and *I'm* keeping a lookout across the yard when I'm home just in case I see anyone sneaking around. That Sid character isn't going to get anything past *me*!" Jessie reached over and gave her a quick hug.

"Well, with all of you watching over me, I feel much safer. Of course, now with Mitch in the house, Sid's going to have to play his cards carefully, if he ever gets up here. And Bo is a great watchdog too." She grabbed a handful of dishes, plunging them into the sudsy water as iridescent bubbles floated into the air. "Naturally I'm apprehensive, Bobbie. I'd feel a lot better knowing one way or the other if he *is* on his way up. At least we could devise a plan of attack." Jessie sighed. "There's not much more we can do than we're doing right now. The police are patrolling the area and we decided to continue living our lives, not around Sid, but without him. We'll just have to wait for him to make the first move."

She turned to Josie. "Would you mind taking Bo out for a little walk? He's been cooped up all day and probably could use some exercise." At the girl's crestfallen face, Jessie grinned. "Don't worry, Jo. If we talk about something important, I promise to let you know, okay?"

With this assurance, Josie reached up on a wall hook for Bo's leash. Sensing it was playtime, Bo danced around the kitchen before settling in front of Josie and lifting a paw. Josie laughed and attached the leash before grabbing her jacket and heading out the back door.

The kitchen was silent before Jessie commented, "I wasn't sure how much you wanted Josie involved in all this, Irma. We don't know what kind of move Sid is going to make and I wouldn't want her or *any* of you getting hurt. Believe me, this man doesn't kid around when it comes to revenge and most likely he'll discover who all my closest friends are." She reached out and grabbed Irma's hand. "Please be extra careful and don't let Josie out of your sight until we know what's what. Sid is very good at playing games and can seem even beguiling when he wants something. He might even approach Josie innocently, pay her compliments on her hair or dress. You just never know." She shook her head despondently. "I'm so sorry I had to involve all of you in my mess."

Irma grabbed a towel and vigorously started drying the dishes that were passed to her. Her face was grim as she rubbed the china plate until it shone before handing it to Bobbie. "Don't worry, Jessie. We'll take care of you, and *no* one's going to hurt my little girl, either. We'll keep a close eye on her. Tom has a few trustworthy cronies at the tavern, too, who know to keep a watch out for strangers. Unless he's well disguised, he'll stick out like a city slicker."

Bobbie reached out and put an arm around both their shoulders and hugged them fiercely. "Hey, ladies, come on. Enough of this gloomy talk. This is Thanksgiving, and we have so much to be thankful for, including what Irma just said. We're all in this together and there's safety in numbers, as they say. He may not know it, yet, but Sid doesn't stand a chance!"

Jessie sniffed. "You're so right, Bobbie. And *I'm* the most thankful just having you guys for my surrogate family." She brushed away a stray soap bubble that had landed on her nose before grabbing a few suds and flicking them at the ladies. Laughing, they continued playfully until the dishes were all put away.

Hanging up the damp towels, Jessie turned to the women. "I think it's time we join the men in the living room. And think positive. They have enough on their plates, especially with Mitch's lack of success with the union. With Christmas right around the corner, I'm looking forward to sleigh rides, skating parties, and lots and lots of hot chocolate and cookies!"

CHAPTER 30

A loud honking horn startled Jessie, shattering the quiet solitude she and Mitch were sharing over breakfast. Setting down her coffee cup, she looked across the table as he lowered the copy of the *Gazette* he'd been reading.

"I don't think Sid would blatantly announce himself by blasting at our door, do you?" Jessie chuckled. She looked up at the clock. But who would be arriving at this early hour? Knowing the answer would remain a mystery unless she opened the door, Jessie started to rise.

"Wait, Jess," Mitch folded the newspaper and set it down on the table. "We'll go together and see who it is. Safety in numbers, you know. Maybe Deputy Houle has discovered something." He grabbed her hand and held it to his lips before leading her to the front door. "Let me go first."

At the end of the hallway, Mitch pulled a curtain back slightly, and taking a quick peek through the side window discovered a stranger standing by the steps. "Well, there's a man out there, for sure, but with a taxi waiting, my guess is it isn't Sid."

Peeking over his shoulder, Jessie gasped then yanked the door open with a shriek. Rushing down the steps she flew into her father's arms. "Daddy!" she cried.

Welcoming his daughter's embrace, Randall wound his arms firmly around her, giving her a tight squeeze. "Jess, my girl," he whispered as he kissed her temple. Then stepping back, he looked her up and down for any signs of abuse or anxiety. Seeing none, he turned to Mitch who was still standing by the doorway.

"And of course, you would be Mitch," he said, holding out his hand.

ON SHAKY GROUND

Slowly descending the steps, Mitch got his first look at his new father-in-law. Yes, here was an older version of Jessie with her blonde hair and blue eyes. He had to admit the man was in good shape for his age, with just a slight graying at the temples. Seeing he was also being given the 'once over' Mitch smiled and reached out to welcome her dad.

"Randall, it's great to finally meet you!" Shaking hands, they looked at each other in approval while Jessie beamed at them both.

"But, Dad, what are you *doing* here?" Jessie looked toward the taxi thinking maybe her mother would pop out. But except for the driver, it was empty.

"Let's get my luggage out so I can pay the man and send him on his way. Then we can talk inside." Although wearing a long winter coat, he shivered as he gazed around. "I must admit, you were right about the cold up here. But where's that infamous snow you told me about?"

"We expect it any day now," she answered, tugging on her dad. "Come on, let's get you into the house." Jessie looked over her shoulder and called to Mitch who was grabbing a large suitcase from the back seat. "Mitch, take care of the fare, please. I've got to get my dad inside before he freezes to death."

Mitch waved them on as he and the driver discussed the price from the Houghton depot. Opening his wallet, he counted out some bills and handed them to the man along with a generous tip. Nodding his thanks, the driver coasted back down the driveway and turned onto the bumpy road.

Lifting the suitcase, Mitch moved toward the door when he heard another vehicle approaching. Turning to see the patrol car making its rounds, he dropped the luggage and waved it over. When the driver rolled down his window to see what was wrong, Mitch stuck his head inside and assured them everything was fine but wanted to let them know Jessica's father had arrived unexpectedly.

Mitch described him. "He's tall and blonde with a little gray in the temples. In great shape too. So if you see him wandering around the property, you'll know it isn't Sid Brewster." He added, "By the way, I just want to say how much we appreciate your surveillance. It makes both of us feel a lot safer."

Mike Houle, who was in the passenger seat, leaned across and assured Mitch that they were happy to keep a lookout and would report any strangers they see in the nearby area. Nodding goodbye, they rolled up the window and continued their patrol.

Grabbing the suitcase once more, Mitch hurried into the house and dropped it inside the doorway. Walking toward the voices, he found Jessie in the kitchen pouring her dad a steaming cup of coffee to warm him up. Randall was sitting at the table and motioned Mitch over.

"Sit down, Mitch. And finish your paper or whatever you were doing before I arrived. As soon as I warm up, we'll talk about why I'm here. Besides missing you, Jessie girl," he said with a wink. "And meeting Mitch, of course. Those phone calls just weren't working for me, so I had to see for myself that you were alright." He looked around the room. "By the way, where's that vicious beast I keep hearing over the phone?"

Jessie laughed. "I'm fine, Dad, as you can see, and Bo usually spends Saturday night with Josie so Mitch and I can have a nice quiet Sunday morning reading the newspaper. It's like a sleepover for Josie with her best friend. You'll love them both when you meet them."

Pulling out an iron skillet from the oven, Jessie waved it at her dad. "Now, what can I fix you for breakfast? Mitch and I were about to have ours when you arrived. How about some bacon and eggs, or, I can make some flap jacks too? Maybe some French toast and ham?" Being so excited at seeing her father, Jessie babbled on.

Randall looked over at Mitch and winked. "Does she give you a full menu every day?"

Chuckling, Jessie slowed down enough to give her dad another hug from behind before dancing back to the stove. "I just can't believe you're here! I'm so shocked and excited. You can have the guest room, which was Fannie's room for the short time she lived with me." She waved a spatula in the air. "So what'll it be?"

In agreement, both Randall and Mitch decided on the flap jacks along with fried eggs. As Jessie got to work, they bent their heads together to share the latest information on Sid. Listening to their conversation, she put her two cents worth in whenever she could without burning their breakfast.

After passing the creamy butter and thick maple syrup, Jessie poured everyone another hot cup of coffee before settling down to enjoy her dad's company and catch up on the latest family news. Reassured all was well, she had a few questions herself as she leaned back with cup in hand.

"Now, Dad, tell me the *real* reason why you're here. Not that I'm not glad to see you but leaving the newspaper at this time of year is very unusual for you. Plus, you're going to be a grandfather, again."

Randall set down his cup and leaned forward, folding his hands on the table.

"I have to admit, your mom and I have been worried sick about you, Jess." He looked across at Mitch, who was frowning. "No slight meant on your part, Mitch, and I know you have others watching out for her too. I just thought maybe if I was here, I could do something. Or maybe I just needed some reassurance that you were all right, sweetie. Your mom would have come, too, but with Allison so close to her confinement, she needed to stay in Detroit. Besides, she knows I can handle everything." He looked seriously between the two of them. "So you haven't had any more contact with Sid? No more phone calls?"

With a shake of her head, Jessie put down her coffee. "I must admit, Dad, I'd feel a lot better just knowing where he was. At least we could prepare, but then, prepare for what? We have no idea what his plans are. Obviously, after that phone call, he knows where I work and how to find me. But as to his plans, your guess is as good as mine." She shrugged. "To be truthful, in the past two weeks, first with the wedding, then Thanksgiving *and* learning to cope with a new husband"—she looked over and smiled at Mitch affectionately—"I haven't spent much time thinking about 'ole' Sid and what he was up to."

"By the way, Jess," Randall put in. "Not to change the subject, but I met a man on the train who had been a reporter for the *Gazette* last year. Said he left the newspaper to pursue another career but found Detroit wasn't to his liking and was coming home. Guess he tried getting his old job back but discovered it had been filled." He eyed her speculatively. "I think he was talking about you, Jess, but I didn't let on that I knew. Just told him I was here visiting with my daughter. He's starting a new job with another newspaper in Marquette, for now, until a position opens at the *Gazette*."

Jessie picked up her empty plate and walked it over to the sink. "Well, Dad, I hate to say it, but his loss is my gain and I have no intention of leaving any time soon. Hopefully, he'll enjoy his new job at the Mining Register. In the meantime, when you men are finished, how about we walk over to the Johns' house and I'll introduce you to Tom, Irma…and Josie." She laughed. "Wait until you meet her, Dad. She's a fireball, and I think you'll see a lot of similarities between us girls."

By this time, Mitch and Randall had finished their breakfast and were patting their stomachs. Both commented on the great breakfast she had fixed. "Always knew you had talent, Jess, but didn't know it was in the kitchen too," Randall teased his daughter.

Gathering their coats, the three headed out the back door, across the yard and over the fence that separated the two dwellings. Hearing an enthusiastic bark, Jessie laughed and pointed to Bo who was dashing across the frozen lawn.

Meeting up with them, Bo came to a halt, and sensing a stranger in their midst, gave Randall a wide berth and a throaty growl. Randall, bending over, gave the back of his hand for the pup to sniff before patting him on his head. Excited to have the extra attention, Bo ran in circles with ecstatic barks before heading to Jessie and launching himself into her waiting arms. Picking him up, she snuggled him under her chin, rocking back and forth. "Hi, sweetie. Did you miss me?" He answered by raining kisses all over her face.

Randall chortled. "So this is your ferocious watchdog, Jess? He would have taken my leg off in another minute or two."

"Sorry, Dad. Guess I've kind of spoiled you, haven't I, baby?" she crooned to the puppy as he sighed and settled in for a little nuzzling.

With a good-natured laugh, Randall rubbed the fuzzy head again before pointing out they were being watched. Jessie glanced over to the porch to see Josie hanging over the rail. "I've got him, Jo!" she called out. "We'll be right there."

Placing Bo back on the ground, Jessie linked arms with her dad and Mitch and strolled toward the Johns' house with Bo bounding ahead of them.

Seeing a stranger with her friends, Josie stayed on the porch and waited for them to approach her. Although not shy in nature, she sensed this man was important and waited expectantly to be introduced. Opening the back door, she shouted for her parents to come out. "Mom, Dad—there's company coming!"

Tom and Irma stepped out onto the landing just as their neighbors arrived. Rushing up the steps to meet them, Jessie explained that her father had come unexpectedly for a visit and wanted to meet them.

Having filled her dad in on Tom's blindness, she wasn't surprised to hear him speak to her friend, first. At the sound of his voice, Tom turned his direction, reached out and shook Randall's outstretched hand with a firm shake. Her dad, turning to the women, let himself be introduced, first to Irma and then Josie, who stood in awe of this big city man who looked a lot like Jessie.

"I've heard a lot about you, young lady. Jessie tells me you two have a lot in common." Josie reddened at his comment but looked happy to have been singled out.

Irma, as gracious as always, shook hands and warmly welcomed him to their home. "I can see who Jessie got her looks from." Pleased at the recognition, Randall spoke of Jessie's birth, and although she hadn't been a boy, was delighted that she had *his* Scandinavian coloring. "And my temperament," he added, ruefully.

"Come on, Dad," Jessie laughed. "I never would have gotten this far without your character. And how could you possibly want a boy when you've got *me*!"

With a twinkle in his eye, Randall looked at her fondly. "I don't know, Jess. But there have been times…"

They all laughed as she jabbed him with her elbow and headed inside, out of the cold.

CHAPTER 31

After being assured by her dad that he preferred to laze around all day and get caught up on his sleep, Jessie waited until Fannie arrived on Monday morning to make the introductions. Knowing he would stay for the week, she didn't feel bad leaving for work but hoped Brian would let her take a day or two off. *In fact, maybe he and Bobbie would want to come for supper one night.* Encouraged by her thoughts, she went on, discussing her normal workday, and answering her dad's questions until Fannie arrived to do the Monday washing.

Delighted at meeting Randall, Fannie offered to stay at home while he was visiting but he wouldn't hear of it. "What? And who's going to clean up this place? Not me! No, you must come as usual, Fannie, and I'll stay out of your way. Besides, Jessie tells me you always have a great supper ready for her when she comes home from the office, and I wouldn't want to miss that!"

Confident that all would be well in her household, she left her dad in good hands, petted Bo goodbye and headed out the door. Looking up at the deep blue/gray clouds in the darkening sky and shivering in the brisk north wind, she wrapped her knitted scarf around her neck a second time and predicted Randall would probably see his snow today.

Arriving at the *Gazette*, Jessie parked in her assigned space and made a quick dash for the door just as a few fluffy white flakes began falling, the wind swirling them across the parking lot.

"Coffee! I need some coffee! She called to Bobbie who was already typing at her desk.

"You're late!" Bobbie teased her as she checked the clock. "But I won't tell. Besides, I'll have you know I have a *very* good rapport with the boss, and he'd probably let you off easy."

Shrugging out of her coat and scarf, Jessie retorted with a bright smile. "Well, I have a *good* reason to be tardy and just might tell you if you'd get that steaming cup I need so badly."

Encouraged by Jessie's good mood, Bobbie, as she headed for the back room, laughingly suggested a few reasons to be late that included Mitch.

"No, but there *is* another man in my life." Jessie hinted mysteriously.

"Don't tell me Sid's made an appearance and all is well between you? *That* would be a miracle!" Bobbie chortled as she placed a hot mug in front of Jessie and sat at the edge of her desk.

"Nope, that would be a fairy tale. The truth is that my dad arrived unexpectedly yesterday and is going to spend this week with us. I just can't believe he's here!" Taking a deep sip of her coffee, Jessie's eyes sparkled as she conveyed her happiness to Bobbie. "He wanted to make sure I really was all right and also wanted to meet Mitch to make sure *he's* all right for me, of course." She chuckled. "Not that it would make any difference. The deed is done—*much* to our satisfaction."

"I was hoping the boss would give me a couple of days off so I can spend more time with my dad. Also, I'd like you and Brian to come over for supper to meet my dad as he's heard so much about you. What do you think? I'll have Fannie make something special."

"Well, Brian was going to come over for supper on Wednesday night. Why don't I ask—"

"Jessica, you're late!" Brian said, coming in with his own mug of brew and pretending to be stern, but she saw the laughter in his eyes.

"You gonna dock me, Brian?" Jessie teased back. "I'll have you know there's a very good reason for my being late."

"Well, let's hear it, then." Brian settled himself comfortably on the corner of Bobbie's desk as he looked at his reporter expectantly.

"The man I love and admire the most—besides Mitch, of course—is currently residing at my house." She looked up at Brian's startled expression and then laughed. "Brian, my *dad's* here! He came in yesterday by train to check up on me. I'd love for you to meet him and have asked Bobbie if you'd like to come over for supper on Wednesday evening."

Brian's eyes widened as he set down his cup. "Even though I'd love supper at your house, Jess, meeting Randall Peterson would be the frosting on the cake. Who, in the newspaper business, wouldn't want to be introduced to someone of his caliber!"

"*Brian*"—Jessie was aghast—"you're not meeting the *president*. He's just my dad!"

"Maybe to you, Jess," Brian replied. "But for anyone in our trade, he's a beacon of success that we'd all like to emulate." Checking first with Bobbie for her nod of approval, he added, "Sure, Jess, you can count on us."

Jessie sighed. "It's just supper, Brian, and Fannie is going make something yummy like she usually does so please don't go putting on a tux or anything fancy."

Vowing he'd be on his best behavior, Brian hastened up the steps to resume his duties and left the planning to the girls.

"I don't know much about your dad, Jess, other than what you've told me. But it's because of him that you're here and I'll be forever grateful. Just think of the changes in my life since you showed up?" Bobbie grinned, took a sip of her cold coffee, then grimaced. "Ugh, let's get a warmer upper."

Sliding off the desk, Jessie picked up her own mug.

"By the way, my dad met a guy on the train who said he had worked for the *Gazette* until last year. Said his name was Rudy Lahti. Does that name ring a bell?" Jessie inquired.

"It should. You have his job." Bobbie, followed by an interested Jessie, strolled into the back room to warm up her drink. Refilling both mugs, she leaned up against the counter and blew into the liquid.

"Rudy was a good worker, young and cute too. Tall, curly blonde hair, and dark-brown eyes. Always had a smile. At one time, I thought maybe he'd be the one for me. But he always had those eyes focused somewhere else. Not that he made many mistakes, but I always took him for a wanderer and wasn't surprised when he decided to leave." Bobbie shrugged. "Guess his new job didn't meet his expectations, though. Did he say what he's doing back up here?"

Adding her usual lump of sugar to the cup, Jessie headed back to her desk before replying. "He started working today in Marquette at the Mining Register but said his real interest was being rehired by the *Gazette*. He knew his old job had been filled so had to take what was available. Thankfully, my dad didn't let on that I was the one who took it over."

Jessie stood up with her coffee and stopped by Bobbie's desk before heading upstairs. "If it's all right with you, I'm going to ask Brian to let me go home early today and maybe all day on Friday. I'd like to give my dad a tour of the town and fill him in on the strike." She looked at her schedule. "I have two interviews, one at one thirty and the other at two thirty and will probably leave from there." She eyed Bobbie. "Is there anything else on the agenda I should know about?"

Bobbie checked her appointments before shaking her head. "Unless something important comes up, you're almost free for today. Go ahead and ask Brian. I can handle the phone calls here."

Freed from any additional responsibilities, Jessie prepared for her afternoon appointments, and after getting Brian's approval, worked through her lunch hour. Then, with a "see you tomorrow" to Bobbie, headed out the door.

Arriving home about three-thirty, the sun had melted away any snow that had fallen and she found her dad playing with Bo out in the backyard; but as soon as the puppy caught sight of her, he lost interest in the game and rushed toward her, barking wildly. Jessie reached down as he threw himself at her and lifted him up.

Randall crowed. "Your dog's fickle, Jess. And after I fed him all those treats! You ungrateful beast."

Jessie grinned. "No, Dad, he just knows his mama, that's all."

Putting Bo back on the ground, they sauntered back to the porch with Bo weaving back and forth between their legs. Hearing the commotion outside, Fannie came out the back door and looked down at them.

"Looks like you need a little distraction. Just a minute. I'll be right back."

Plopping down on the top stoop, Jessie unwound the heavy scarf from around her neck and enjoyed the warm rays of the afternoon sun, knowing these times were short as winter approached. With a contented sigh, she explained why she was home early and happy to announce she'd have Friday off, also. Before they could solidify their plans, the door opened, and Fannie reached out to Jessie.

"Here's a big soup bone for Bo. That'll keep him busy so you can have some quiet time."

Reaching out for the treat, Jessie smiled up at her. "Thanks, Fannie! It'll take him some time to gnaw through this one." She tossed it into the backyard and Bo immediately settled down for a good chew.

"Supper is in the oven and should take about another hour. If it's all right with you, I'll collect my things and head over to Jacob's." She grinned. "Violet's teaching me how to crochet."

"Good for you! I know she appreciates having another woman in the house after all her boys. Go ahead, Fannie. And thanks for fixing lunch for my dad as well as supper. You're a saint!"

Grinning in agreement, Fannie closed the door, allowing them to continue their conversation.

"She's a gem, Dad. I can't believe how far along she's come in just a short time. Truthfully, I couldn't get along without her and she adores Bo. Her madam never came looking for her, probably knowing she wouldn't have a leg to stand on. And by now, I'm sure there's another poor girl taking her place." Jessie shook her head in dismay. "If I had my way, Dad, all those houses would be shut down. But I guess with all the unattached males in the area…well, you know."

She quickly changed the subject and stood up. "How about if I change my clothes and drive you around the countryside and over to the hoist area so you can see what Mitch's up against. At this time of day, there'll still be strikers marching about." She chuckled. "If you're lucky, you might even see a fistfight or two."

Heading into the house with her dad following behind, she added, "I can't begin to describe how scared *I* felt when one of those men hit me with those rotten tomatoes." Her nose crinkled in distaste. "But the experience of going below and meeting Jacob was all worth it, and I'd do it again if I knew it would end the same."

Randall kept his thoughts to himself as she chattered on, but secretly hoped it was something she'd *never* try again. He sighed as Jessie ran upstairs to change, knowing his daughter was one of a kind.

Unaware of her father's thoughts, Jessie hopped down the stairs and grabbed one of Mitch's scarves that hung on the hall tree, along with a pair of gloves. "Here, Dad." She wound the thickly knitted scarf thoroughly around his neck and handed him the gloves. "For all that we both live in Michigan, the cold up here's frigid when the wind comes soaring off the big lake. But I must admit, the dry cold feels better than the seeping dampness in Detroit."

As Jessie called for Bo, he dropped the soup bone and came running. With tail wagging and tongue hanging out, he jumped into the back seat when she opened the car door. Randall climbed into the passenger side just as Jessie slid behind the steering wheel. "Ready?" She shifted gears and headed down the frozen dirt road, bumping toward the shaft houses. It was the beginning of an idyllic week that was shattered when Jessie arrived home from work on Thursday.

"That you, Jess?" her father called from the living room where he was comfortably seated next to the stove, newspaper in hand. "Where've you been? You're late and I was getting worried. Mitch called to check on you too."

"It was just one of those days, Dad," she answered, tiredly, her shoulders slumping a little as she hung up her coat.

It *had* been a difficult day and she'd stayed late at the office waiting for a couple of mining supervisors who had decided at the last minute not to show up for their interviews. "Putting their lives in jeopardy," they'd said when she called them. Dejectedly grabbing her coat and quickly locking up the office, she had peered from the doorway in every direction looking for a shadow or even some strange sound. When neither happened, Jessie had hurriedly climbed into her car, locked the doors, and whisked off home hoping to change into some comfy clothes, grab a cup of coffee or glass of wine and relax by the fire.

Pasting a smile on her face, she walked over to him and settled into the rocker. "As I said, it's been one of those days, Dad. I waited and waited for two people to meet me for their interviews, and they ended up as no shows. Just once, Dad, I wish they would have the *decency* to call me if they weren't coming." She rocked back and forth, agitated, as the rocker creaked. "Guess that's part of the game, though, being a reporter." Jessie grinned at her dad. "I'm sure you've had some experience in that field."

Agreeing, Randall folded his paper and stood behind her, rubbing her shoulders. "Your mom always does this for me when I've had a rotten day. You can't imagine how many times she's done this." He leaned over and whispered, "Of course, sometimes I just pretend so she'll give me a good back rub. But don't ever tell her I said that!"

Jessie laughed. "Not fair, Dad, putting me in between you and Mom. But I guess I owe you one for coming all this way to see me." She stood up. "Now, what has Fannie left us for supper tonight? I'm starved!"

Randall sniffed the air. "I think it's a pot roast with potatoes and vegetables, with an apple pie for dessert." He beamed as he patted his stomach. "Your Fannie is going to make me fat. I know I'll be doing extra workouts at Louie's when I go home." Seeing Jessie's crestfallen face at the reminder he would be leaving, he reached over with one arm and gave her a squeeze. "Maybe your mom will come with me next time. But at least I know I leave you in good hands with Mitch."

Seeing a piece of paper anchored with a glass by the kitchen sink, Randall added, "Oh, by the way, Fannie said there's a phone message for you on the kitchen counter."

Jessie reached over and grabbed the note that sat beneath the water glass. "Let's see…" She looked up at her dad. "Listen to this. A Rudy Lahti called and wants to meet with me tomorrow afternoon at five o'clock to discuss the miners' strike." She frowned. "Isn't that the guy who just started working at the Mining Register in Marquette, the one you told me about?" Jessie looked down again at the note, trying to read between the lines before handing it back to her dad. "And Bobbie also said he had worked for the *Gazette* until last year."

"Sounds like the one I met on the train." Randall nodded as he read the paper. Then he grunted. "Wait a minute. He wants to meet you at the hoist. And he wants to do it at that time of day? It'll be almost dark by then. Jess, maybe you ought to have another talk with Bobbie and make sure this guy's on the level. Sounds like a strange request to me. Plus, how will you recognize him?"

Grabbing the note, Jessie turned it over. Thankfully, Fannie was always thorough when taking notes. "Well, Dad, he's described himself, so I'll know him when I get there. Says he's middle age, of medium height with black hair, mustache, and short beard." She looked up. "Shouldn't be hard to locate him...what are you doing, Dad?" She asked as Randall snatched the note out of her hand and studied it.

"For starters, Jess, the Rudy Lahti *I* met was younger, tall, with wavy blond hair, a real looker." He glanced at his daughter. "Says he wants to meet you late tomorrow afternoon? That's not giving you much time." He turned the note over. "He didn't leave a phone number, either, so you can't call him back and confirm before he leaves to drive up here. *That* means you must show up whether you want to or not." He handed the paper back to Jessie. "Something sounds fishy to me, Jess. Can you call the Mining Register and see if it's the same Rudy Lahti?"

Jessie checked the clock. "Well, they'll be closed for the day by now, so I'll have to do it first thing in the morning. I'd try calling Bobbie, but I happen to know she and Brian are at supper with a movie to follow." Jessie was silently considering all the possible scenarios, and her eyes suddenly widened in horror.

"Dad, you don't think...?"

Randall scratched his chin. "Sid Brewster? It's possible, but only if he was on the same train as me and heard Rudy introduced himself." As he thought back, he remembered something else. "I traveled in first class, so he could have been in coach. You know, the more I think about it, the more it makes sense. When we were in St. Ignace, Rudy and I were discussing his new job at the Mining

Register. Anyone standing around could have been privy to our conversation. But the description on the note doesn't match Sid's appearance, either. Isn't he almost bald and clean shaven?"

Jessie nodded thoughtfully. "Yes, but with all the lapsed time since his escape, he could have altered his appearance. Sid was like a chameleon, Dad, changing at every whim to get what he wanted, making it easy for anyone to be taken in by his allure. He was always vain, surrounding himself with dignitaries and beautiful women."

She smiled whimsically in remembrance. "*Sable* was one of his prize possessions to be shown off. She was his property, adding a mystical presence, enticing unsuspecting men into his web of deceit. She was like the shiny bubbles in his imported champagne, glittering and floating on his arm, drawing in unsuspecting chumps with her promising smiles. She was a prop he used like his free drinks and poker chips."

Jessie looked up at her father. "I'm not sorry for what I did, Dad, no matter what the outcome, and I'd do it again. He was a fake and a bully and *deserved* what he got. But what he has in mind for me...?"

As she became silent, Randal stared at her. It was the first time she had been truly explicit, baring her soul with those details. Gazing at her, he only saw the little girl who had followed at his heels, soaking up all the knowledge she was so thirsty for and wanting to be just like her dad. If he *ever* imagined, for just one moment, that her tenacious drive would place her into dangerous venues, he would have guided her into safer areas. *Or maybe locked in her room until I found a husband for her.*

As if sensing his agitation, Jessie hastened to reassure her father. "Not to worry, Dad. As evil as he was or is, other than using me as a trophy to be paraded around, he never touched me." She shivered. "I'll never forget the look on his face, though, when he caught me spying on him. First, in disbelief that I had disobeyed a direct order by following him as he talked business with some of his operates. Then furious, he yelled and tried to grab me. With knowing too much about his daily operations, I knew I was in danger; but before I could escape, the police raided the joint and I was thrown into jail with a bunch of other women who'd been there."

Jessie continued, but now with a sparkle in her eye. "*That's* when I whispered to the guard that I needed to speak to the chief. I wasn't sure he would believe who I was, but, boy, was I relieved when he called *you*, Dad. Again, sorry you had to bail me out and get stuck in this mess."

Randal chuckled. "It was hard for *me* to recognize you, Jess, let alone the chief! When he called me, I had my own doubts, thinking he was crazy. After all, what dad is going to believe or admit, that his daughter was caught up in the middle of such a criminal act? Then the way you looked…those twinkling blue eyes of yours were my only clue that you *did* belong to me. It took a while to convince him that you were undercover for a story, even though *I* had no clue at the time."

He looked a little chagrined. "For that, he gave me a verbal lashing about the responsibilities of fatherhood. I had to slip a little something under his desk mat to stop the man's grumbling. But when you walked out of the lady's room, with your blonde curls and shiny clean face, looking so innocent, he could understand how anyone could have been duped by your appearance. By the way, Jess, what *did* you do with Sable's attire? Burn it? Bury it?"

Jessie giggled. "Nothing so drastic, Dad. In fact, if you were to check the back of my closet, you'd find her resting comfortably in a box behind the rest of my clothes just in case I wanted to use her for a Halloween party or something. I sort of forgot she's in there. It's been a while since I thought about those days. So many wonderful things have filled my life since then," she added dreamily, "especially Mitch."

Looking down at the paper in her hand, Jessie frowned. "You know, while this message should make me feel apprehensive, it's having the opposite effect. I just want to get this over with. Mitch and I've waited and worried long enough about Sid, wondering if he was really going to come after me and now, I'm ready for the confrontation, whatever it may be. He's taken up too much of my precious time."

Randall looked less optimistic. "Well, Jess, you might feel relieved, but I think I'll stay on for a few extra days while we get this all worked out."

Jessie threw her arms around his neck and hugged him tightly. "Thanks, Dad. If Sid's coming here extends your time with me, all the better. Why don't you—"

"I'm home!" Mitch bellowed as he came through the front door. "I got out earlier than I expected.

"In the kitchen, Mitch," Jessie called, tripping down the hall and meeting him halfway. "*And* we have a mystery to discuss." After throwing her arms around him and giving her new husband a smoldering kiss on the lips, she guided him to her dad, who had waited to give them privacy.

"Hey, Randall!" Mitch shook his hand. "Hope your day was better than mine. Sometimes I wonder why I'm even here. This has been the worst case of obstinacy I've ever seen between a union and employer. Neither side is willing to budge an inch, and it's going to take a miracle or a disaster to wake them up." He turned to Jess. "But what's this about a mystery, sweetie? Maybe it'll take my mind off things." He shrugged out of his coat, threw it over a kitchen chair and headed for the coffeepot.

Jessie, already stimulated by the note, didn't need any more caffeine to fire her up. She grabbed the message off the counter and sat down between the men. "Here, Mitch. What do you make of this?" she asked, passing the note over to her husband.

Mitch wrinkled his eyebrows as he read both sides of the paper, turning it over a couple of times and rereading it. "So? What's so special about his wanting to meet with you, Jess? It isn't an unusual request considering it's happened before." Looking at Randall, he handed the note back to Jessie and raised his cup for another sip.

"The mystery is that *this* Rudy Lahti, as described in the message, is *not* the same Rudy Lahti my dad met on the train. And as they both seem to work at the Mining Register in Marquette, one of them must be lying."

She looked up at Mitch and made a face. "Wanna bet our adversary has finally arrived?"

Mitch choked as his coffee went down the wrong way. "You mean Sid Brewster? You think he's here?" His heart took off at a full gallop as he put down his cup and grabbed her hands. "Come on, Jess, we've got to let the police know right away!"

As he rushed over to the telephone, Jessie pulled on his arm and stopped him in his tracks. "Hold on, Mitch. Not yet. First, we must confirm that the Rudy Lahti my dad met is indeed working at the Register and find out if *he* made the appointment to see me. If he denies knowing anything about it, we know for sure it must be Sid. *Then* we can call in Mike Houle." She checked the clock. "We have about twenty-four hours to come up with a plan."

Mitch closed his eyes, savoring the warmth of his wife as he pulled her into a close embrace, regardless of Randall looking on. This woman meant everything to him and if she was going to be in any danger... *No! It doesn't bear thinking about. We will get through this, and Jessie, and all of us, will be just fine,* he thought to himself. Taking her hand, he led her back to the table where all three began planning how to outfox Sid.

Jessie had a few ideas of her own and as she presented them to the men, they stared at her in disbelief.

"You wanna to do what?" Both Randall and Mitch yelped at the same time.

Jessie sighed. Really, this was déjà vu all over again.

"Come on, guys. Who better to get close to Sid than me? But instead of Jessica Peterson, *Sable* will be waiting for him. He doesn't know we've discovered his identity, so we'll catch him off guard, and she's just the one to do it. I told you about his ego. If he has any doubts at all that Sable was the one who fingered him, maybe he'll be willing to listen to her. A man of his conceit couldn't bear thinking that someone had outwitted him, especially a woman. I'll cajole him into a false security, play on his unsure feelings, then draw him away from the miners for some private talk and head across the field toward Fannie's old house. You guys will be close behind me, so what can possibly go wrong?" Jessie, pleased with her plan of attack, beamed at the two men.

Mitch looked at her and then turned back to Randall. "As I was saying, we need to come up with a plan—"

"Wait a minute! Didn't you heard a word I said?" Jessie, frustrated, stood up and slammed her palms against the table.

"Jess, sweetheart, you can't be serious. Sid Brewster's a thug, a dangerous gamester who's gunning for *you*, and you want to challenge him face-to-face?" Mitch shook his head.

"I admit I must agree with Mitch on this one, Jess. Such a plan that'll put you right in his path is *totally* out of the question." Randall looked pointedly at his daughter, who was starting to look mutinous. Which, he knew from experience, was not a good thing.

Exasperated, Jessie turned without a word and headed toward the front door. Grabbing her coat and scarf, she slammed the door behind her and thumped heavily down the steps.

"Uh-oh. We've done it now." Mitch looked at Randall in concern. "She's got that look." He called for Bo and ran to the front door. "Go get her, Bo! Go get your mom!"

Bo, wagging his tail, leaped down the steps, charging after her at full tilt. Jessie acknowledged his arrival by patting his head, but didn't look back, continuing down the road toward the hills which were always her refuge.

Standing at the doorway, Mitch and Randall watched her stride down the incline, each thinking the same thing. Jess wasn't going to let this go.

"Well? What are we going to do? We both know when Jessie gets like this, it's her way or no way." Mitch pulled on his jacket and turned to Randall. "We're just going to have to find a way to protect her if she insists on pulling a stunt like this. Maybe between us, Bobbie and Brian, *and* the police, we'll muddle through…somehow. Miracles do happen, you know."

Mitch opened the door, letting the brisk evening air flow down the hallway and shivered. It would be a cold one tonight. Already the dusky sun had disappeared behind the purple and gray clouds on the horizon. Faint yellow rays flowed out from beneath them casting a surreal glow on nearby houses. He sighed. Time was of the essence, and he had to find Jessie before total darkness descended on them.

Noticing the partially clothed hall tree, he stated to Randall, "In her huff, she forgot her mittens and hat. I'll let her blow off steam for a few minutes before I catch up to her. There's not much we can do tonight, anyway, until we find out if Rudy Lahti *did* make the appointment." Grabbing an extra pair of mittens, a hat for Jessie, and Bo's leash, he started down the hill.

Randall closed the door thoughtfully. Although Jessie would always be his little girl, right now he was glad to relinquish the responsibility of curbing her to her husband. Like Mitch said, if they all put their heads together, they just might come out of this in one piece.

CHAPTER 32

Today is the day. Jessie shivered more in anticipation than from the chilly morning air as she drove off toward the office knowing Mitch and her dad would arrive together shortly after. The question now was how to play her scenario to Bobbie.

Laying her arms down on her desk and covering them with her head...*that* was Bobbie's reaction to Jessie's plan of attack. Jessie sighed, heavily as she had expected this.

"No, no, no." Bobbie groaned. "I can't believe I'm hearing this."

"C'mon, Bobbie, please don't be that way. I *need* you now. Buck up, get on that phone and verify whether Rudy Lahti *did* try to get in touch with me." Jessie stood in front of her with hands on her hips, frowning in disapproval.

With a sniff, Bobbie raised her head, shaking it with dismay and disbelief. "Jessie, how one woman can come up with *so* many idiotic ways to get hurt is beyond me! But this takes the cake. Let me get this straight. You're going to tackle Sid Brewster, if it *is* him, all by yourself?"

"Don't be silly," Jessie retorted. "Mitch, my dad and the police will be right behind me in case anything goes wrong. As Sable, I really think I can con old Sid into thinking I still care for him, and with that man's big head he'll *want* to believe I had nothing to do with his jail time." She cajoled Bobbie. "Besides, if we don't do anything, Sid will always be a controlling factor in my future, and as you said before, I'll always be looking over my shoulder. I'd rather deal with it now and get it over with, one way or the other."

"It's the *other* that I'm worried about, Jess." With a sigh, Bobbie flipped through her index cards and retrieved the Mining Register's phone number. "Here it is, but I'll bet he's never heard of you."

Jessie sat down at her desk, drumming her fingers on its surface while Bobbie placed the call. Despite her outward bravado, she was half hoping Bobbie would be wrong.

"Are you sure?" Listening to Rudy on the other end, Bobbie looked doubtfully at Jessie. "Well, all right, then. Yes, it was good talking with you, too, Rudy, and I'll be sure to let you know if something opens here at the *Gazette*. Best of luck with your new job, though." After a few more civilities, Bobbie hung up and stared at Jessie in horror and whispered, "It wasn't him."

Jessie slouched down in her chair. "Well, that's that, then." She checked the clock. Mitch and her dad would arrive soon. "Will you please ask Brian to come down, Bobbie? He'll need to know what's going on just in case anything happens." At Bobbie's forlorn expression, she hastened to reassure her. "*Not* that I'm worried, of course. Especially with everyone guarding my back."

With a doubtful look, Bobbie walked slowly up the stairs, thinking with every creaking step she took. There *had* to be some way of talking Jessie out of this absurd plan of hers. Maybe Brian would come up with an idea before Mitch and Randall arrived.

Taking a deep breath and racing up the rest of the stairs, Bobbie burst into Brian's office just as he was hanging up the phone. "That was Mitch. He's on his way here," he said solemnly as he stood up.

Bobbie's eyes grew wide. "So you know."

Brian held out his hand. "Please tell me it *was* Rudy Lahti who left the message and you'll make my day."

"No such luck, Brian." Bobbie was mournful now. "He's here, Sid's here and Jessie...she wants to go after him herself!" she cried, choking down the tears that threatened to strangle her.

Brian walked over to his office door, closing it softly before gathering a shaking Bobbie in his arms. "Shh..." he whispered. "We're going to get through this—all of us—you've got to believe that. We've just got to get our heads together and come up with a course of action. You know Jessie. She's going to do what she wants no matter what we say." Then he added, "Think of it this way: we'll get to see the infamous 'Sable' in the flesh."

Bobbie produced a weak grin as Brian used a large white handkerchief, he always had on hand to dab at her eyes and cheeks. "That's my girl. Now let's go downstairs and put up a good front. Mitch and Randall will be arriving soon, and we can start the ball rolling. Mitch's called Mike Houle at the police station and he'll be joining us, also."

Jessie, hearing the clamor of feet coming down from the stairway, prepared herself for a rebuttal if they had any issues with her plan. Now that she knew for sure Sid was in the area, the anxiety of *not* knowing had been replaced by a courage-driven surge of adrenaline that had her pacing the office floor when the two arrived.

But to her relief, all Brian said was, "Okay, Jess, we're with you. Bobbie and I agree that Sid Brewster must be taken down and now's as good a time as any. We have the upper hand since he's not expecting us to know his identity. We'll go along with this plan, but if *anything* happened to you…" he threatened before going on. "And besides, you'd miss our wedding."

Bobbie stared at him agog. *Wedding? Whose wedding?*

Realizing what he had just said, Brian's face blanched white, instead of his usual red, and his hands grew cold and clammy.

"Bobbie, Roberta, I, ah…just give me a minute. I'll be right back." Brian backed out of the room, then twirled and raced up the stairs, leaving the two women staring after him in astonishment.

Bewildered, Jessie and Bobbie just looked at each other before turning their attention to the stomping feet scurrying back down the wooden steps.

"Ah, Jess, would you please excuse us for a few minutes?" Brian asked her.

Jessie looked back and forth between the two of them. "Sure, Brian. I'll be in the coffee room if you need me." Noticing a small box in his hand, she thought, *Is that what I think it is?* Hoping to give them some privacy, Jessie clanked a few cups and glasses around, noisily, giving Brian the opportunity to complete his task. Looking into the mirror over the sink, she saw him taking Bobbie's hand, bringing it to his lips before offering her the jewel box.

"Bobbie, this...well, this is definitely *not* the time or place I imagined doing this." Brian stuttered with a chagrined look on his face. "But with Jessie facing the danger head on without knowing the outcome, I thought of how *I* would feel if it were you." His face softened and voice lowered. "Bobbie, believe me when I say I couldn't bear anything happening to you."

With that declaration, he held out the tiny velvet case and flicked it open.

Bobbie's hands flew to her mouth as she stared at the round glittering jewel embedded in a gold circle.

With a tender smile on his face, he released the diamond from its satiny enclosure and, reaching for Bobbie's hand, drew her nearer. "Roberta Nutini, will you do me the honor of becoming my wife?"

As if in a trance, Bobbie gazed at Brian in disbelief before she nodded and slowly held out her left hand. But as soon as he slipped the ring onto her finger, she flew into motion and threw her arms around his neck. "Yes, oh *yes*, Brian!"

Now she was crying—*again*. But hoping they were happy tears, Brian lifted her chin with his finger and kissed her softly. At her passionate response, the kiss left him hungry for more and he gathered her into his arms once again. Knowing they could soon be in sight of everyone, Bobbie drew away with a sigh and laid her head against his chest. No more words were needed, at least for right now. Whether or not Brian thought the time was right, Bobbie thought it was *perfect*.

"Jessie!" Bobbie suddenly pulled out of his embrace as she remembered her friend who was hiding in the coffee room. Pulling Brian along with her, she skipped into the break room to see Jessie's smiling reflection in the mirror.

"You saw?"

Jessie reached out and grabbed Bobbie's hand, lifting it toward her face to examine the sparkling jewel. "I'm so happy for you, and you, too, Brian. You're getting a great girl here!" Looking at the glowing couple, Jessie felt a quiver of sadness as she glimpsed their wedding without her if things didn't turn out right. Shaking the negative thoughts from her mind, Jessie chased away her morose feelings by squeezing both friends in a fierce hug.

"Don't I know it!" Brian retorted as he beamed at Bobbie. *How could I have not seen her?* Brian shook his head ruefully as he considered the time they could have shared together. Determined to make up for the past, he took Bobbie's hand, and smiled, knowing they now had all the time in the world.

But did Jessie?

As she coughed to remind them of her presence, an icy blast of reality doused Brian as he remembered today was not only a day for celebration, but retribution. How far would Sid Brewster go in seeking his revenge on Jessie and what could they do to prevent it?

Hearing the rattling of the front door, he looked across the room as two gentlemen entered the office and hoped the answer had just arrived.

CHAPTER 33

With a promise from Mitch not to look until she called him, Jessie reached behind her wardrobe, feeling for a large hat box that held her other personality. Touching a braided rope, she drew it out, and set it on the bed.

Opening the cover, she slipped into the past, gingerly caressing the dress that had been carefully folded up within. Cautiously, she touched the shiny flounces before unfolding the dress and holding it up in front of her. A tremor ran through her as she recalled the last time it had molded her body; just a wispy piece of black silk with a low V neckline and shimmering ruffles that swayed above her knees as she had walked arm in arm with Sid Brewster. It seemed like eons ago.

Shaking her head, Jessie gently hung the dress on a hanger. Returning to the round box, she delved back in searching for the red-haired wig and the glittering multijeweled headband that had been a special gift from Sid when she'd helped him close a shady deal. Without contemplating why she had kept it, Jessie knew it would be useful tonight as she faced her opponent. She grimaced. *Maybe Sid will think I still fancy him.* Knowing the band's matching diamond earrings were in her jewelry box, she reached in her dresser, pulled out the glittering orbs and placed them next to the headband.

The last items retrieved were a pair of real silk stockings, her sequined heels, and a long silver cigarette holder. Now all she had to do was paint her face, blacken her eyes, and get ready to step into her future, whatever it might be.

Without second thoughts, Jessie slowly applied her makeup with deliberation, then adjusted the wig over her blonde curls, pulling down at the wavy red tresses that just touched her shoulders.

Lifting the sparkling headband, she positioned it across her forehead, clasping it in the back before clipping on the pair of glittering earbobs. Reddening her lips, she pouted at her reflection in the mirror before pasting on the heavy black eyelashes. With each step, Jessie began to disappear until, at last, it was Sable who stared back at her.

Releasing the sleek dress from its hanger, she stepped into it and with high heels pivoted in front of the mirror. Satisfied with her appearance, Jessie grabbed the plush mink stole on loan from her mother, who thought every girl should have one…just in case. Placing it across her arm, she smiled grimly. *Well, tonight's just the night.* Thank goodness the temperature had risen into the upper forties, almost unheard of for this time of year.

With a deep breath, Jessie walked down the steps and into the living room where the gentlemen awaited her appearance.

Randal, having seen her in this garb once before, said nothing but watched in amusement at Mitch's shocked reaction while taking in her attire.

"Wow!" Whistling, Mitch slowly sauntered toward her, his wide eyes fully glued on her face before strolling down to check out the rest of her body.

Jessie could feel her face redden under all the paint as Mitch walked toward her but held her head high as she reached for his outstretched hands.

"That old photo didn't do you justice, Jess. No wonder Sid was smitten with you! Come here, gal." Mitch took her hand and twirled her around a few times as the silky flounces flashed with every move she made.

Randall strolled over to join them. "Jessie, you do a father proud. I only wish the circumstances were different." He checked his watch then glanced outside at the muted colors that foretold the coming of dusk and sighed. "It's time, Jess. Are you *sure* you want to go through with this? We could always tell Mike Houle you changed your mind. It's possible they could pick him up, you know."

Jessie shook her head. "No, Dad. It's me he's after, and with his sneaky ways, he could slip into the shadows if he suspected others were looking for him. This way we'll be sure, and if all goes as planned, we'll never have to deal with him again."

With determination, Jessie threw the stole around her shoulders and, after tucking it between her elbows, opened the front door. The twice blinking of headlights between the trees assured her that Mike Houle and his patrol were on board and would be following her every move. Taking a deep breath, she stepped off the porch and onto the road. It would be a ten-minute walk if she took the shortcut to the hoist building, giving her the upper hand by element of surprise, as Sid would most likely be watching for an auto.

Jessie turned off the main road and minced down the rocky path leading toward the mine area hoping not to meet anyone. In her getup, she could be mistaken for one of Madam's girls. *And that's all I'd need right now.* She walked on in silence listening to the bare limbs of trees cracking together as they swayed in the wind. Shivering, she noticed flickers of lights as the usual strikers hovered around the burn barrels, and although she derived a sense of comfort knowing others were around, she was wise enough to know Sid would have secluded himself waiting for her arrival.

Spotting a solitary figure standing at the edge of the parking lot, Jessie knew the time for reckoning had come. But first, she had a few surprises lined up for Sid. Knowing he would have a car and could abduct her, she moved carefully around the lot until she came into direct view on the other side. As she stepped out from the shadows, her movement prompted Sid to see her in the misty rays of the fading sun.

"What the…?" Shaken by her unexpected appearance, Sid sucked in his breath and quickly headed her way only to discover she had disappeared. *Am I seeing things?* Expecting to meet refined Jessica Peterson, he hadn't been prepared for the appearance of Sable. It threw him off guard. Or was his mind playing tricks with what he wanted the most? Ms. Peterson was basically a stranger to him. It was Sable whom he *really* wanted. Seductive, alluring Sable, who had made his life a living hell.

Glancing back at the revelers playing cards and drinking beer, he was certain no one would notice them. Quickly heading to the other end of the lot, he suddenly noticed a shimmering glow floating in the opposite direction. *What kind of game are you playing, Sable?* Hide-and-seek was for kids, and he didn't come here to play. Sable was toying with him instead of fearing him, and that made him furious. Fingering the pistol in his pocket, Sid was engulfed with rage as he chased after her.

Striding purposefully through the barren field, Jessie headed across toward the red-light district. While slowing down a little so Sid could catch sight of her, she spotted another two blinks waiting for her arrival on the other side. She let out a sigh of relief. It wouldn't be long now. Everything was going just as planned. She was confident her scheme would work, knowing the police were just ahead of her and Mitch close behind.

Glancing over her shoulder, Jessie noticed Sid was quickly closing the distance between them and quickened her stride. Hastening toward the beckoning lights, she failed to see an arched tree root half buried in the frozen mud. As the toe of her shoe caught in the woody loop, she tumbled, falling forward, landing facedown and stunned. Seconds later, feeling a boot nudging her leg, Jessie knew with foreboding it wouldn't be Mitch. She lay still; it was just moments before an arm grabbed her, rolling her onto her back and into the face of her worst nightmare.

"Well, now," Sid drawled. "Ain't *you* a sight for sore eyes. Here I was expecting to meet Ms. Peterson, and lo and behold, my Sable appears out of nowhere. Just what were you planning, anyway? To play on my fondness for you?" With a derisive laugh, he reached down and jerked her up until they were face-to-face. "You've made it a lot easier, now, sister, seeing you dressed the way I remember you."

Sid leered at her from head to toe. "I must admit, Sable, you're looking mighty fine for someone who doesn't exist. But then, you always were a looker." He scratched his chin. "You know, if you begged me, I just might drag you back down to Detroit. Could use a little company while I wait to cross the border. Know what I mean?" He grinned suggestively, then shook his head. "But things never turn out the way you plan, especially for you." His face turned ugly, and anger spewed across his face as he shook her violently. "You really messed up my life, girl, and you're going to pay, just like the others who crossed me."

Jessie gulped down her hysteria as her eyes glanced over his shoulder seeking any sign of Mitch.

Sid caught her furtive look and snorted. "I wouldn't put my hope in any of those guys at the mine. They never saw me coming and are so far gone they wouldn't hear if you called, anyway." Sid growled as he pulled out his revolver and shoved it into the center of her back. "Get walking. I want to find a nice, secluded place to conclude my business."

As he pushed her forward into the darkness, Jessie's heart leaped as she saw the familiar lights blinking at her, once again, from across the field but hoped Sid wouldn't get suspicious. What excuse could she invent to keep him moving in that direction? Thankfully, he supplied the answer.

"What are those blinking lights?" Sid motioned that direction with his gun after they had walked in silence for a few minutes.

Jessie had to come up with an answer, and fast. "That's just the red-light district welcoming their clients," she said, hoping he'd believe her.

"A bawdy house, huh? I could use a little extra money right now. Maybe I should just trade you in." Sid paused for a moment and pulled on his scraggly beard. "On the other hand, it could be just the answer I've been looking for. By finding you close enough to *that* place, they could blame any of those guys for getting a little rough with one of their ladybirds." He shoved the gun harder into her back, propelling her forward. "Yeah, this could work. I wasn't sure how I was going to dispose of you once we've finished our little 'business,' and by the time they find you, I'll be long gone."

His coarse laughter taunted her to retaliate with a smart remark, but before Jessie had time to think of a retort, he roughly tore off her headband and earrings, the pain causing her to cry out as he jerked them from her lobes. Removing the mink stole, he stroked it appreciatively before tossing it around his own neck and pocketed the jewels. "You'll not be needing *this* anymore, and these gems will give me the money I need to get out of the country.

Shoving Jessie's arm behind her, Sid pushed her in the direction of the lights. Trembling now from the cold as well as fear, she complied with his demand, thinking wildly of her options. Knowing he was unaware of her marriage to Mitch gave her some satisfaction and hope. If Mitch came from behind, it would be a surprise attack that Sid wasn't expecting. And the closer they got to the lights, well, maybe she could call out. Miracles did happen. *It's not over yet, Sid.* Knowing he loved weakness and got his kicks by seeing people grovel before him, Jessie lifted her chin, pulled back her shoulders and doggedly moved forward, trying to buy some time for Mitch to catch up…wherever he was.

As she plodded along, Sid, unaware of her thoughts, shuffled through the unknown terrain, accepting her silence as obedience. In his concentration, he missed the slight tingling of the ground beneath his feet. But not Jessie…

Oh no. Not now. She moaned silently.

Just hoping to get to the other side unscathed, despite Sid's threatening demeanor, Jessie started moving quickly across the field. But the low vibrating rumble raced toward them and escalated until, with a thunderous roar, she felt the ground give way beneath her.

Taken by surprise, Sid's hands flew into the air, throwing the gun behind him as he scrambled desperately to maintain his footing. Knowing it was her only hope, Jessie tried grasping onto anything that would stop her from falling into the deep pit that had opened beneath them. Managing to throw her arms around a rotting plank of wood, her legs swung until her heel caught on a piece of large rock protruding from the wall. Sid, feeling himself sliding down with the rocky sludge, screamed until his echoing cries faded with a thud at the bottom of the deep chasm.

Stunned, and suspended in midair, Jessie tightened her grip on the wood as she listened for any sound coming from below. Closing her eyes, she prayed someone would have heard his outcry and come looking for her. Although Sid was gone, her precarious position couldn't be maintained for any length of time. The quaking had stopped but the numbing cold was playing havoc with her fingers and threatening her grip.

Mitch, where are you? Taking a deep breath, Jessie tried telling herself not to panic. *He's coming. I know he is*...unless he, too, had been swallowed up by the air blast.

Shaking that last thought from her mind, she tried clasping her hands together, but as she moved, her foot slipped from the wall, once again leaving her dangling in midair. *I love you, Mitch,* she sobbed silently. It wouldn't be long, and she'd be joining Sid in the deep abyss. *He'll get his revenge after all,* she thought bitterly.

Being five feet beneath the surface, Jessie couldn't hear the frantic cries as the two men she loved most were desperately trying to find her.

"Randall, I'm sure they were heading this way when Jessie cried out." A distraught Mitch pointed in the direction of the lights across the field. They both had tumbled to the ground when the blast shook underneath them and were disoriented. "She knew Mike Houle would be waiting for them to cross the field. I saw the blinking lights, myself, just before the blast hit us."

With shaking hands, Mitch struck a match to his lantern, producing a wavy yellow glow all around them. Holding it out in front, he edged forward searching for anything that would indicate Sid and Jessie had come this way. "Wait a minute." Reaching down, he picked up a diamond shaped rock that, when turned over, became a sparkling blue gem.

"This was part of her headband!" he shouted to Randall. Moving quickly, he found two sets of footprints that led straight ahead.

Pulling on Mitch's arm, Randall came to a stop and put a finger to his lips. "Shh. I think I heard something." The night had become still, although a faint rumble could be heard in the distance as the blast kept traveling away from them. Listening intently, both men strained to hear any sound ahead of them. "I'm sure I heard someone cry out—there it is again! This way, Mitch, hurry!"

As they stumbled through the dark, both heard a terrified scream, first loud, then fading a few seconds later. "That wasn't her. I'm sure of it. It must have been Sid. Jess is in trouble, Randall, I just know it." By now Mitch was running across the uneven ground.

"Jess! Jess, where are you?" Mitch was yelling now. If Sid still held her captive, they'd all be in trouble. But he had to take that chance.

Feeling his foot hit something hard, Mitch halted and lowered the light. Not only had he discovered the revolver, but they had come within five feet of a large sink hole. Just a minute more and both would have dropped into the black pit. Sending up a prayer of thanks, he gingerly moved the lantern forward until he could see into the deep cavity. There she was, dangling from an old piece of wood.

"Jess, Jess! Can you hear me?" Mitch knelt and waved the lantern back and forth.

Afraid to move, and with eyes closed, Jessie barely whispered, but it was enough for him to hear. "Mitch, I don't think I can hold on much longer."

Randall peered over the edge, his heart palpitating as he realized the danger his daughter was in. "Just hold on a minute more, Jess." With his soft words of encouragement, a tear trickled down her face, but she was too shaken to open her eyes.

After pulling a rope from his shoulder and tying a knot around his waist, he turned and handed the other end to Mitch. "You've got to go down. Despite my age, I'm stronger than you and can pull you back up. *Hurry,* Mitch! There isn't much time left."

Seeing the wisdom in his statement, Mitch didn't waste time arguing but tied the rope under his arms. "You'll have to pull both of us up, Randall. I'll try and get underneath her so she can wrap her arms around me. It'll leave my hands free to hang onto the rope." Lowering the lantern, he stared into the bottom and shuddered to see Sid lying about thirty feet below in what was probably an old, abandoned mine shaft. It could have been Jessie, and if this didn't work out, they both could plummet to the bottom.

Knowing the plank of wood she was hanging onto wouldn't take any more weight, Mitch set the lantern at the edge of the opening, planted his feet on the side of the hole and started lowering himself down. As he came even with the board, Jess finally opened her weary eyes. "That's my girl. Just a minute more and we'll have you out of here." Mitch climbed down a little further until he was positioned under her. "Now Jess, I want you to climb onto my back like a monkey. Can you swing your legs a little?"

With what strength she had left, Jessie tightened her grip on the board, and little by little, swung her legs until she felt them touch Mitch. As he placed them around his waist, he encouraged her to let go of the plank. "Now, take your hands off the board, one at a time, Jess, and place your arms around my neck."

"I'm so afraid, Mitch," she whispered tearfully.

"I know you are, sweetheart, but we're going to do this together and your dad's going to pull us up. Come on, Jess, just be brave one more time."

Taking a deep breath, she released her hold on the board and wound one arm around his neck. Then, with a prayer, let go of the plank and grabbed onto Mitch.

Her hands were cold and stiff, but she clasped them together around his neck and laid her head against his back. No matter what happened now, they were together. Jessie rested in that thought.

"Okay, Randall!" Mitch called up to the surface. "You can start pulling us up. I'm going to try to climb as you tighten the rope." Bracing his feet against the rocky wall, Mitch moved slowly, careful not to look down. *Come on, Mitch, you can do this.* When one foot slid on loose pebbles, Jessie gasped and hooked her arms tighter around his throat.

"Jess, you're choking me," Mitch rasped. "You've got to trust me. We're going to make it." Jessie loosened her grip just a little and he took a deep breath. The five feet to the top seemed like ten. Inch by inch, they crawled up until Mitch's head appeared above the surface and he could see Randall pulling on the rope, his heels dug into the ground. As soon as they were visible, Randall gave the rope a mighty yank and Mitch landed flat on his chest, feet dangling, but with Jessie still secure on his back. Rushing to their side, Randall quickly grabbed Jessie from Mitch and into his arms. Mitch crawled the rest of the way out and threw himself onto the ground, gasping for breath.

Both Jessie and her dad were sobbing, and Randall's words were muffled but Mitch heard them all the same. "You always promised to take care of her, and you have. I owe you forever, Mitch."

Putting Jessie away from him, Randall checked her over from head to foot. Her arms and legs, full of cuts and scrapes from her fall, were bleeding and she'd probably be bruised, but except for a dirty, tearful face, his daughter stood before him, *alive*. After hugging her once more, he turned her over to Mitch who held on to her like a drowning man. Without words, they stood in an embrace for several minutes before Mitch felt her shiver and realized how cold she must be.

"Come on, Jess. Let's get you warm. I think Mike's car is closer than ours, right now, and we need to let him know about Sid." They walked three across as the two men tried to shield her with their arms. Once again, the lights blinked twice and realizing she was free, Jessie's adrenaline finally evaporated, and she slipped out of their arms and to the ground.

"She's in shock, Randall!" Picking her up in his arms, Mitch cradled her limp body against his chest, almost running across the remaining field while Randall carried the lantern ahead of them. Jessie was moaning, now, and Mitch, concerned about her physical as well as mental condition, whispered endearing words of encouragement. The lights were almost upon them, and he sighed with relief when he saw Mike Houle and his team racing toward them.

Taking in the situation, Mike immediately ran back to the auto and returned with a woolen blanket to envelope her in. Mitch wouldn't let her go but allowed Mike to tuck it all round Jessie as they walked to the auto. Gently laying her in the backseat, Mitch slid in next to her and cradled her head in his lap. Stroking her hair, he filled Mike in with as many details as he knew, particularly Jessie's abduction and Sid's body in the bottom of the shaft. Jessie would have to fill in the blanks when she was able.

Accepting the set of keys Randall held out to him, Mike ordered his men to cross the field and pick up Mitch's auto he had left behind. Because of Jessie's condition, he hurried to the driver's side, and with

Randall in the passenger seat and siren wailing, sped down the hill to St. Joseph's Hospital to deliver an unconscious Jessie.

It was early morning before she awakened to the sound of soft weeping. *Am I dead, then?* Her strength zapped, she was even too tired to breathe. Her arms ached and parts of her legs felt on fire.

As the sobbing continued, she tried opening her eyes and became disoriented as unfamiliar objects came into view. *Where am I?* Hearing a sniff, she slowly turned her head in that direction and groggily focused on the person sitting beside the bed, holding her hand. Recognizing her friend Bobbie, Jessie remained silent but squeezed her hand.

"Jessie!" Bobbie's head popped up, her face streaming with tears. Cupping Jessie's hand with both of hers, she brought it to her cheek and held it there as she stared at her best friend. Jessie opened her mouth to say something, but Bobbie stopped her. "No, Jess. No talking. The doctor said you had to lay still until he came back in to check you over." Another tear slipped down her face. "You were so lifeless when they brought you in. I thought you'd *never* wake up. Just squeeze my hand if you're in pain and I'll call for the nurse."

Jessie managed one word. "Mitch?"

Bobbie smiled. "He's fine. Both he and your dad were here all night while the doctor worked over you. You needed several stitches, Jess, in your legs, but your face just needed a good cleaning and some antiseptic."

Satisfied, Jessie closed her eyes and floated back into a blessed oblivion.

Letting go of her hand, Bobbie stood up and adjusted the warm blanket over her before heading to the cafeteria where Mitch and Randall were having some coffee after their long night's vigil. She shuddered, remembering last night's phone call informing her that Jessie had been rushed to the hospital. She and Brian had immediately driven to St. Joe's where they found Mitch sitting outside the emergency room, elbows on his knees, and hands covering his face. Randall, looking pale, sat beside him but pushed himself up when he saw them enter the ward.

"Is she...?" Not wanting to say *the* word, Bobbie ran forward, grasping his hand, hoping the news wouldn't be what she expected.

Mitch, hearing her voice, looked up with a pale face.

"Bobbie...Brian, so good of you to come." Too exhausted to get up, he leaned back, propping himself up against the wall. "The doctor says she should be fine but kicked us out when they started working on her. He hasn't been back out, so we don't know the extent of her injuries."

He reached up to stretch out his arms but grimaced as both felt they had been pulled out of their sockets.

Just then, the doctor, covered in green scrubs, came into the waiting room. Pulling off his mask and gloves, he filled them in on the procedures that had taken place. "I had to suture several lacerations on her legs, but the scrapes on her face just needed a good cleansing and medication. Except for exhaustion, and possible emotional trauma, she should heal. She's also probably going to be black and blue from her fall and will be in some pain, especially from the stitches."

With this good news, Mitch stood up, finding a new spurge of energy, and wanting to rush into the treatment room. "Can I go in and see her, Doc?"

The doctor shook his head. "I've given her some sleeping tablets because we want to keep her still for a few hours as she recovers. She'll be moved to a private room on the third floor, soon." He checked his watch. "I'd say you can probably visit in about an hour, but don't expect any response from her. With what she's just been through, along with the medicine I gave her, she just needs to sleep. So don't be alarmed if she's unaware of your presence. I'll check on her again in the morning when I come on duty. If you plan to stay with her, just ask the ward nurse for some extra chairs and blankets. Other than that, I'll see you tomorrow." He nodded at them all and walked tiredly down the polished hallway to the exit.

Blinking back to the present, Bobbie rode the elevator to the first floor and hurried into the cafeteria, finding Mitch and Randall seated at a little table, staring into their coffee cups. Surprised when she scurried in, they jumped up in anticipation. Bobbie was short of breath, but a beaming smile covered her face.

"She woke up a few minutes ago and asked about you, Mitch. Before I left, though, she had fallen back to sleep." Bobbie checked them over from head to foot and shook her head. "You might want to wash up a bit before going to her room. If she sees you like this, it'll remind her of what happened last night, and she doesn't need any more trauma. In the meantime, I'll give Brian a call in the office and let him know how she's doing and stay with her until you come in. Hopefully, she'll be awake, again, soon."

Looking at each other, Randall and Mitch had to admit Bobbie was right. They were a mess, and it wouldn't be good for Jessie to see them caked in dirt.

Contented, sleepy and with no worries, Jessie turned over and cuddled under the warm blankets of the hospital bed. Hearing muffled sounds from the hallway, she felt really secure for the first time in ages and refused to think about the events of the prior evening. She only wanted to remember that Sid was gone and would never bother her again. The heavier details would have to wait until she was ready. Right now, all she wanted to do was sleep.

And that's how Mitch found her a few minutes later. It didn't bother him that she didn't acknowledge his presence. Quietly, he took the chair closest to her bed and opened the magazine he had found in the hallway. His hair was still damp from the quick shower he took in the doctor's lounge and without a razor, had a stubble on his face. But he felt cleansed, inside, and out. All their worries were over, and they could start living without fear.

Knowing Randall would be up shortly to share the watch over Jessie, Mitch closed his tired eyes as the lettering in the magazine became blurred on the pages. Slouching in the chair and leaning up against the wall, he drifted away in peace.

Peeking in on them a few minutes later, Randall found both Jessie and Mitch in a deep slumber. Smiling to himself, he sat down across the room knowing that his daughter was in good hands. She would always be his little girl, but now someone else had become the love of her life, and that was the way it should be. It was time for him to go home.

CHAPTER 34

By the second week in December, the holiday season was in full swing—at least for the merchants. Christmas wreaths hung on every door—bells jingled—and the sweet smell of balsam, pine, and cinnamon, wafted in and out as doors opened and closed. It was a time of joy…and a time for filling up their coffers in this season of "goodwill."

As for Jessie, the past two weeks had been a time of healing, both mentally and physically. With the occasional nightmares beginning to fade, she hoped to return to a normal time in her life without looking over her shoulder. Tomorrow she'd be returning to work, adding another milestone in her journey to wellness.

Brian asked if she wanted to write about her escapade, but Jessie shook her head no. It was better forgotten. Sable was gone forever, along with her tattered dress, and would rest in peace. She had served her purpose, Jessie thought with relief, as she burned the hat box in the potbellied stove.

Saying goodbye to her dad two days after her release from the hospital had been difficult. Jessie hated to see him go, but knew it was time for him to return to Detroit, his newspaper and the rest of her family. She and Mitch would be celebrating Christmas alone, as newlyweds should, developing their own traditions.

Mitch had left for a meeting earlier that morning and Jessie felt restless now that her strength had returned, and her stitches had been removed. With an impatient sigh, she pulled back the kitchen curtain and gazed out the window. Overnight a fresh snowfall had covered the ground and trees, the crystals sparkling in the late morning sun. Finally making its appearance while she recuperated, the snow

now covered the rooftops like white icing and, much to the delight of the children, the drifts were growing higher every day.

Hearing their laughter, Jessie decided she would join them as they slid on wooden sleighs, cardboard boxes or even shovels, whatever would take them racing down the hills and tumbling into the fluffy snow at the bottom. She checked the clock. *I could use some fresh air after being cooped up for so long and Mitch won't be home for a while.* Humming a Christmas carol to herself, she threw on her jacket, wrapped a heavy scarf around her neck and plopped on the red ski hat she had knitted for herself while convalescing. Grabbing a pair of gloves and a leash, she called to her dog.

"Let's go, Bo!" He came running and pranced around excitedly until Jessie finally got him hooked up. He was growing up and had filled out, becoming a long-haired rusty colored mongrel that was probably a shirttail relative of an Irish Setter. Despite his uncertain heritage, both Mitch and she adored him.

Smiling affectionately, Jessie ruffled the top of his head before opening the front door. Taking a deep breath, she exhaled and watched in childlike fascination as clouds of vapor floated from her mouth before disappearing into the frosty air. The sky was deep blue, cloudless and she could feel the glowing sun upon her face despite the floating ice crystals. Motionless, Jessie felt a blanket of peace enveloping her. It was good to be alive.

Feeling Bo tugging on the leash, she checked the area before unhooking him. Delighted in his freedom, he ran and dove headfirst into a large snowbank before coming up and shaking mounds of snow off his coat. Laughing, Jessie picked up a glove-full of snow, shaping it into a ball before throwing it into the drift where it disappeared. Enjoying this game, Bo jumped in, again, and pawed his way through the fluff before coming up, triumphantly, with it in his mouth. With a 'good boy,' she reattached the leash and walked in the direction of the shrieking children on the hill.

Noticing the group suddenly change course at an approaching train, Jessie watched as several of them ran alongside the railroad tracks. One little boy suddenly bent over and, with a triumphant shout, held up a black rock for all to see before dropping it into his tattered coat pocket. Curious, Jessie followed them as they scurried behind the chugging engine and her heart warmed to see a fireman wave at the kids while pushing off a few lumps of coal to the ground. *Ah.* Now she understood. A few chunks of precious fuel to heat their stoves.

Jessie, waving at the fireman, smiled and watched the kids frolic until she felt the first sign of a chill. She headed back toward the house with an uncooperative Bo who was tugging on the leash with his legs dug in, not wanting to be shut in again.

"Let's go, Bo. If you're good, I'll give you a cookie when we get back." As she bribed him with the familiar word 'cookie,' he dropped his hold on the leash and panted alongside her, his tongue lolling out.

Coming around the curve, Jessie saw Mitch waiting anxiously from the top step and waved. Bo, catching sight of him, howled, and strained on the leash until Jessie let go, watching him race toward his second favorite person in all the world, dragging the leash behind him. His enthusiastic greeting was physical as well as vocal as he jumped up, placing his large paws on Mitch's shoulders, and giving him a big slurp on the face.

Laughing, Mitch pulled his legs away and walked down the steps to meet Jessie.

"What a beast you are!" Jessie scolded her pet as he danced circles around them. Mitch, relieved at the sight of her, enveloped her in a big hug. "I was worried when I didn't find you at home."

"I wasn't expecting you so soon and was going stir crazy, so I escaped for a few minutes. How'd your meeting go?" she asked, changing the subject. With their arms entwined, Jessie led the way up the steps and into the house.

"It was about as expected. The companies have dug in their heels and the strikers aren't in the mood for any more suggestions from an arbitrator, specifically me." After shedding their clothes, Mitch sat, dejectedly, on the sofa, his legs stretched out in front with Jessie cuddled up next to him, and Bo warming his feet.

"Jess, although we've never discussed it, I think we've always known there was a possibility of me being recalled to Lansing. I've been here for five months without any progress." He pulled her close and planted a kiss on her brow. "Except meeting you, of course."

Wrapping her arms around her husband, Jessie gave him a big squeeze. "Mitch, we're a family now. Where you go, I go. Have you had any hints from your department?"

He shook his head. "Not yet, I've just got this feeling. It'll be the first time I've been unable to finish any job I was assigned to. But this strike is a whole new ball game. It's like they've never heard of compromising and both sides are being totally unreasonable." Mitch bowed his head. "I don't know, Jess. Maybe they'll just end up closing the mines for good."

Jessie was silent for a moment as she thought about the children she had seen earlier. She recalled the patched jackets, hats, and frayed mittens, some too large, some too small, mended and probably passed down from one child to the next. And those few lumps of coal, thoughtfully given by the rail worker, would be lucky to heat even one room in their chilly house. It was hard not to feel despondent when she and Mitch shared a home full of warmth and food, but they were not miracle workers.

"Mitch, you can only do what you can do. You must remember this is not *your* problem, it's theirs." She raised her head up and kissed him on the cheek. "And you *have* done good. Think about Jacob and Fannie, how their lives have changed because of you. His family is warm and fed and the boys might even go on to more schooling. You're not a failure, Mitch. Sometimes we just have to remember that success isn't always what we expect it to be."

Mitch laid his head on top of hers. "How'd you get so wise, Jess? And how did I become so lucky to find you?"

"Keep telling yourself that and we'll get along just fine." Jessie teased. She glanced at the clock. "Time for lunch; and remember Brian and Bobbie are coming over this afternoon to discuss wedding plans. Something to look forward to!"

Putting aside his despondency, Mitch pulled himself together to greet his visitors when they arrived later that day. *Maybe I did have something to do with this*, he thought. *Jess is right. I can't solve all the world's problems.*

Giving Brian's hand a hardy shake and Bobbie a quick hug, Mitch hung up their coats before leading the way into the living room and the welcoming heat of the chubby stove. As they got comfortable, Jessie walked in from the kitchen carrying a tray full of colorful sugar cookies and mugs of rich fragrant coffee.

Brian rubbed his hands together. "Just what we need, Jess," he said as he reached for a couple of sugary treats and one of the steaming cups. "In spite of the sun, it's miserably cold out there today. Although Bobbie shared a blanket with me, that cinder chest turned chilly halfway before we got here." As he stomped his feet with mocked exaggeration, they all laughed, and Jessie suggested they warm their feet by the fire. "Don't be embarrassed to take your shoes off. We're about as close to family as you can get."

Bobbie looked at Brian, who shrugged and grinned, then proceeded to take off his shoes, followed by Bobbie. Seated side by side, they leaned back and pointed their toes toward the radiating heat while Jessie threw a large fluffy blanket over their legs.

"So?" Jessie asked as she and Mitch seated themselves on the couch. "Have you decided on a date?"

Brian reached over and grabbed Bobbie's hand. They already looked like an old married couple, Jessie thought, smugly.

"Sunday, January 25! That'll get us through the Christmas and New Year's celebrations," Bobbie exclaimed. Looking at their surprised faces at the short engagement, she explained, "We just don't see any reason for a long engagement. We're adults with both sets of parents gone so basically on our own." She looked happily at Brian as she squeezed his hand.

Jessie put down her coffee cup and nibbled on one of her cookies. "Will you get married by Judge Markham at the courthouse?"

"No, Jess. No offense but we are going to do this thing right. As Brian and I are both Catholic, we'll have our ceremony at St. Ignatius Loyola Church in Houghton. It won't be a high mass, but a nice Christian ceremony to get started on the right foot." She reached across and took Jessie's hand. "And of course, we want you and Mitch to stand up with us! We haven't got a flower girl, but what do you think if I ask Josie to scatter some petals before I walk down the aisle?"

Jessie beamed at her best friend. "I'm sure Josie would be thrilled to be included. Will you ask Tom and Irma to attend also? And how about Carl? Can I host a reception for you?"

They spent the rest of the afternoon firming up their plans, with a guest list and menu for the reception to be held there at the house. Because Bobbie wanted a traditional white wedding dress, shopping was also on the schedule.

Tilting her head at Bobbie, Jessie walked back into the kitchen to replenish the cookie tray hoping she would follow her.

"What's up, Jess?" Bobbie handed her the empty cups and leaned back against the counter.

"I love you like a sister, Bobbie. But this wedding came up so quick I just wanted to be sure that you didn't have any doubts." Jessie lowered the dishes into the sink, added a few chips of soap and turned on the water. "You know I care for Brian but just want *you* to be certain he's the one."

"Whew! You scared me for a minute, Jess. I thought something was drastically wrong." Bobbie grabbed a dish towel and vigorously rubbed the wet cup Jessie handed her. "I've *never* been so sure of anything, Jess. I know Brian took a while to really see me, but we've known each other for years. Well, sort of. He's always been kind and understanding, fair to those he works with. It's not like he's a stranger." She looked at Jessie, eye to eye. "I love him, Jess and I know he loves me. Why should we wait just for tradition's sake?" She blushed. "Especially at our age if we want to start a family. I mean, we're not old, but if we want more than one…"

"Bobbie! Have you two already discussed this? Mitch and I haven't even gotten that far because of Sid." Jessie grabbed the towel from Bobbie and placing it on the counter, set the remaining cups and saucers draining. Darting a glance toward the living room, she pulled Bobbie over to a corner and, with eyes shining, whispered.

"You know, I could be carrying right now. Even though we haven't been married that long, we've sure had our share of fun." Both giggled, then covered their mouths. "Seriously, Bobbie, with all the problems with Sid, nothing was further from my mind. Of course, it's too soon to tell but now that you've mentioned it, I'll be thinking of nothing else. Oh dear, how are we going to face the boys without looking guilty? They'll know we've been talking about them." They giggled again before joining the men with a new plate of cookies and kernels of corn to pop for later.

CHAPTER 35

"Where do you want me to put this, Jess?" Mitch was holding up a pungent balsam tree they had cut down in the woods, despite the freezing temperatures and a howling northwest wind. Tramping through the snowy woods, they had picked out the most perfect tree for their first Christmas together.

Jessie tapped her chin and surveyed the living room for the tree's place of honor. "There, Mitch," she said, pointing to the large west side window. "It'll look so pretty with the sun shining through." She circled the room and eyed all the colorful decorations they'd purchased from a grateful merchant. Well, maybe it *was* a little overkill, but one had to start somewhere.

A knock at the door interrupted her concentration and she almost dropped the box she was holding. Looking at Mitch, he just smiled, a reminder that they no longer had to fear unexpected visitors. Setting the ornaments down, Jessie scurried to the door to find Josie on the other side.

"Hi, sweetie! Come on in. Mitch and I were about to start decorating the tree and you're just in time to help. Can I bribe you with some cookies and a cup of cocoa?" Jessie put her arm around the young girl and herded her into the living room.

Catching sight of Mitch, Josie danced over to where he was holding up the tree and gave him a big hug. "I *miss* you, Mitch. We hardly ever see you," she scolded, looking over her shoulder at Jessie. "But Mom says newlyweds need some time to themselves. Have you had enough time yet?" she asked wistfully.

Mitch chuckled. "Josie, you tell your parents you're welcome over here anytime. Besides, Bo would miss seeing you. Jessie must start work tomorrow, so he'll need some extra special attention."

"And just remember, I'll be driving you and your dad to the Christmas party in Calumet next Thursday," Jessie chimed in. "I'll be making a big batch of cookies to take along, too, so you'll have to tell me your favorite kind."

Josie hopped from one foot to the other. "I'm so excited!" she cried. "And did you know I'm going to be Bobbie and Brian's flower girl at their wedding next month? She's going to buy me a new dress and I'll be scattering rose petals before she walks down the aisle. Bobbie wants pink flowers and that's my favorite color. Maybe I'll get a pink dress too! Do you think she'll buy me a pink dress, Jessie?"

Mitch and Jessie both laughed as Josie finally ran out of breath.

Anchoring the tree in its stand, Mitch turned to Josie. "Since you have so much energy, why don't you hand me some of those ornaments and help us trim this tree. Do you have a tree at home, Josie?"

Nodding vigorously, Josie handed him a shiny red ball. "We popped some corn, too, and Daddy helped us string it for the tree. Mom and I put the needle through the popcorn, but Daddy could poke it through the cranberries. Please come over and see how pretty it is! Especially with the presents underneath." She blushed. "I know I'm not supposed to peek, but every once in a while, I lift one up and shake it." She shrugged. "So far, I don't know what's in them but it's fun guessing. Are you going to put presents under this tree? Mitch, you should buy *lots* of presents for Jessie, so she'll be happy. Daddy says a happy mom makes a happy home. He must have given her lots of presents, don't you think, because my mom is always happy."

As she paused for breath, Mitch and Jess looked at each other. Josie was right. Not about the presents, but that Irma seemed happy, despite their circumstances. Obviously, she and Thomas had weathered many horrific events in their marriage, bonding them closer together.

Counting her blessings, Jessie reached out to Josie and enveloped her in a big hug. "You're right, Jo. Your parents *are* happy, but

I don't think it's from presents. It's because of who they are and who *you* are. You're the love of their life, don't you know?"

A pleased, beaming Josie moved next to Mitch and handed him the sparkly white angel that he carefully placed on the top of the tree. Despite what Jessie said, Jo was sure Mitch would buy lots of presents. Maybe even one for her?

But as Jessie discovered later that night, there were others who didn't share Josie's sentiments.

While snuggling on the sofa with their after-dinner coffee, Mitch filled her in on the latest news. All the strikers were dreading this coming holiday season, he said. They had no paycheck coming in and the union coffers were quickly drying up. Any money received was used to buy food for their tables, not Christmas gifts. With the long winter months yet to come, the strikers were at their wits end and there was talk about leaving the area.

"They're stubborn and bullheaded, Jess. Even if they caved in now, they wouldn't be any worse off than before the strike. The companies would let them go back to work if they handed in their union cards, but they won't consider that option. It makes my job impossible."

Jessie digested all this dismal information, and, in the morning, it was confirmed by Brian.

He agreed with Mitch. "I had to attend an alliance meeting last night and I'm afraid it was just as Mitch said, Jess. According to an informant, the union is about dry."

He sat back in his chair, flicking a pencil back and forth. "You know, Jess, I am totally against some of the things that are going on. I feel bad for the strikers, but they started it by joining the union. Although I can't fault them for trying to improve their conditions, I must agree with Mitch. They've caused nothing but grief for themselves and their families." He shook his head and leaned his elbows on the desktop. "It's been five months of striking, marching, fighting, and killing. It's *got* to stop. But what it's going to take, I sure don't know."

"Well, there's going to be a Christmas party in Calumet for the kids and their parents. *I*, for one, am going to try and make it memorable, even for one night. I'll be driving Tom and Josie Johns while getting a firsthand perspective for my editorial."

Jessie stood up preparing to leave Brian's office. He also stood, walked her to the door and laid his hand on her arm. "Jess, I know where your heart is. I just don't want you to be disappointed if the result isn't what you expected. The miners have dug in their heels and no matter how bad you want them to win, I just can't see it happening. It isn't what I wish for, either, but facts are facts. Mitch is right. There'll be a lot of losers before this is finished."

Jessie gave him a half smile and a quick hug before heading downstairs. He was her boss, but he was also her friend.

Bobbie saw her forlorn look as she entered the room. "I take it Brian didn't have anything good to say, either. I'm sorry, Jess. He and I discussed the strike many times. He's not taking sides, but considering the facts, the odds lay heavily with the companies. Even if the strike was over, that one-man drill would replace many workers. With special attorneys, money, and time on their side, the companies have nothing to lose, whereas the strikers have everything to lose."

She sighed. "Jess, it's the Christmas season, a time to be joyful. And with the wedding coming up, maybe I'm just not feeling the strike. I'm sorry. I know it's been an ordeal for Mitch and for you." She looked up at the clock. "But despite everything, today's the day I promised Josie I'd take her shopping. School's out for the holiday and Brian's giving me time off to find dresses for both of us." She gave Jessie a wishful look. "Can you come with us and give me your opinion? I saw some beauties at Gunter's when we looked for your dress." She added persuasively, "I'll treat at lunch!"

Jessie smiled. "You know, Bobbie, that's not a bad idea. Just the ticket to take our minds off things for a while. Wait here while I go ask Brian for the morning off."

After their earlier morose conversation, Brian was more than willing to give Jessie the morning off. "Besides, you're still recuperating and should only be here part time, anyway." He waved her off. "Go. Find Bobbie and Josie some nice dresses and never mind the cost. I want my bride to look beautiful on our wedding day!"

After giving him a quick peck on the cheek and promising to be back after lunch, Jessie trotted downstairs to an impatient Bobbie. It was only nine o'clock, time enough to pick up Josie and head back to town.

Josie, of course, was hanging over the porch railing waiting impatiently. After calling goodbye to her parents, she flew down the steps and skipped her way to the car.

As luck would have it, Bobbie discovered the perfect dress as they entered the building, where a woman was dressing a mannequin in a stunning crème colored wedding gown. They waited until she put on the finishing touch by adding a wispy floor length veil. Turning around, she noticed the trio watching her with interest and stepped toward them.

With a big grin, she turned to Josie. "Well, now, are you the lucky bride?"

Josie giggled and shook her head before pointing to Bobbie. "I'm only fourteen. *She's* the one who's getting married, but I'm going to scatter rose petals down the aisle, so I need a new dress too."

"Well, I'm sure we can find something real pretty for both of you to wear." The good-natured lady turned to Bobbie and held out her hand. "I'm Catherine, one of the owners here. I see you're looking at our latest arrival in bridal gowns. This came in on the train just yesterday."

"It's a beauty, Catherine, that's for sure," Bobbie said, gently fingering the delicate veil. She searched for a price tag, but it was missing. "How much is it?" she asked, looking up at the owner.

When Catherine named the price, Bobbie shook her head and dropped the veil. "That's a little beyond my budget, I'm afraid. It sure is beautiful, though," she added wistfully.

"Nonsense, Bobbie! Brian told me to make sure you pick out something you like without worrying about the price. And if he thinks it a little too high, which I'm sure he won't, I'll be glad to donate the rest," Jessie assured her friend.

Walking around the mannequin, she lifted the flimsy veil that shrouded the gown to better see the dress.

"Bobbie, this is perfect for you. In fact, it *is* you!" She turned to Catherine. "Can she try this on for size?"

"No problem. Bobbie, is it? Come. Let's take this into the fitting room and see how it looks on you." She looked at Jessie and Josie. "While she's changing, why don't you two go through the dresses in the girl's department. Sizes go up to fourteen, but we can also check the women's clothing for a lady's dress in a smaller size."

As she spoke, she gently removed the costume and, draping it over her arms with care, motioned for Bobbie to follow her.

"Let's go, Jessie!" An excited Josie pulled on her arm, and they headed across the room toward a colorful selection of dresses.

After sifting through the variety, both decided they were more for little girls than one in her teens. Disappointed, Josie, with Jessie in tow, headed back to the women's section just as Bobbie emerged from the dressing area.

"Wow!" Josie exclaimed. "Bobbie, you look beautiful."

"Josie is right. You look stunning," Jessie remarked staring at her. "In fact, I'm a little jealous. My only wedding and I didn't wear a formal wedding dress. But that's neither here nor there. This dress is *perfect* for you, Bobbie. Let's turn you around in the mirror."

Standing before her friends, Bobbie gazed at her reflection in the large oval looking glass. They were right. Except for taking a little tuck here and there, the dress was a perfect fit. The soft crepe gown had a low rounded neckline, long sleeves and three skirt tiers that fell softly from the waistline to just below her knees. She watched as Catherine slowly positioned the turban hat with a wide scalloped edge upon her head. Yards and yards of floating tulle cascaded over her shoulders and down around her dress, creating just a silhouette of her wedding gown. The veil lengthened to a train in the back, trailing along the floor as she walked.

Bobbie sighed in satisfaction. Jessie was right. It was perfect.

With her head in the clouds, she returned to the changing room where Catherine helped her change into her day clothes. Not wanting to take it off, she looked down one more time and touched the delicate veil wafting about her. Nodding in permission to take it off,

Bobbie mentally calculated the cost, along with a new pair of slippers. Her mother's pearls would do nicely around her neck.

Catherine took down her measurements and carried the wedding attire to the front desk while Bobbie went in search of Jessie and Josie. Finding them in the lady's department, she tried to subdue her own excitement while searching for a dress for her flower girl. In pink, of course.

Joining the party, Catherine mentally sized up Josie and led them to a rack containing party dresses in a rainbow of colors. Caught up in Josie's excitement, Bobbie flicked through the multitude of pretty frocks in the smaller sizes and pulled out a dress of light pink chiffon. It looked innocent enough for a young girl yet hinted at the woman she would soon become.

Josie's eyes widened as she viewed the vision Bobbie was holding up. Never having a fancy dress before, she was awed as she gingerly felt the soft material in reverence. "And I have a matching hat that would work beautifully," Catherine added. "Want to try the dress on?" Josie, speechless, could only nod as she was led into the changing area.

Amused, Jessie and Bobbie followed behind waiting to behold the transformation of a child into a woman. They didn't have to wait long before hearing a happy squeal coming out of the dressing room, followed by a twirling Josie as she stepped before the mirror.

"Just *look* at me!" A beaming Josie pointed to the reflection of herself. The gangly little teenager had turned into a debutante.

Jessie walked around Josie, checking for any reason Tom and Irma would object to the dress. It seemed to fit her without over accentuating her budding figure. She looked at Bobbie, who nodded. The dress looked just right on their emerging butterfly.

Catherine wandered across the room and returned with the headpiece she recommended. It was a crème cloche style hat, small brimmed with a wide pink ribbon encircling the bonnet, ending in a large pink bow on one side. The color was a perfect match. Placing it on Josie's head, the young girl seemed to stand taller and become a young lady in a matter of seconds. Her eyes shining, Josie checked herself out in the mirror, turning this way and that.

"Well, what do you think? Is this your dress, Josie?" Bobbie asked. She had checked the price tag and although not in the range one would normally pay for a fourteen-year-old, she felt the occasion merited the amount. Plus, seeing Josie so ecstatic about a new dress, well, she was more than happy to play a part in decking her out.

"It's the most *wonderful* dress in the whole world! Thank you, Bobbie. I can't wait for my mom and dad to see it." She reached over and hugged her benefactor.

Bobbie turned with a smile to Catherine. "I guess she likes it. You may as well wrap those up so she can take them home. And you can finish my dress alterations on time?"

After assuring Bobbie it would happen, she questioned whether the women would be wearing gloves. As it was one thing they hadn't discussed, Catherine pointed to a variety of styles beneath the glass countertop. After trying on several pairs, it was decided both Josie and Bobbie would wear identical lacy creations that buttoned at the wrist. The owner placed these in a special box for Bobbie to take home and led Josie back into the fitting room to change.

As an excited, giggling Josie emerged from the little room a few minutes later, Bobbie and Jessie looked at each other and chuckled. Where was the suave little debutante they had witnessed earlier?

Gathering up her packages, Bobbie checked her watch and decided they had just enough time for the promised lunch before taking Josie back home.

CHAPTER 36

Bustling around the kitchen, Jessie glanced up at the clock and gasped at the time. She was late! She should have picked up Thomas and Josie ten minutes ago. Grabbing the container of chocolate chip cookies and Carl's camera, she threw on her jacket and headed out to her car.

The Christmas party given by the Ladies Auxiliary of the union was supposed to start at one o'clock with candy and a new pair of mittens for all the children, along with Santa's arriving to distribute presents. Jessie groaned. The clock read twelve forty-five, and it was a thirty-minute drive to Calumet.

Turning around in her driveway, she chugged the short distance to the Johns' house and found Tom and Josie waiting for her outside. Helping Tom to the ground, Jessie walked him to the car, putting Josie in the back seat and her dad in front.

Tom chuckled. "This is the first time I've been driven by a woman. Do I need to be worried?"

Jessie just laughed as she closed the door. "Let me know what you think when we get there, Tom. In the meantime, hang on. Sorry to be late, but the cookies had to bake a little longer."

Traffic was light as they traveled north, and Jessie picked up a little speed. But when they neared the Italian Hall, it became more congested as both automobiles and horse-drawn sleighs vied for close parking places around the building.

After assisting Tom from his seat, she and Josie each took an arm and joined the noisy group of revelers waiting their turn to climb to the top floor where the party would take place. Reaching the front door, Jessie, looking up the stairway, was appalled at the steep narrow steps. As others rushed by, she decided to let them go first, as she and Josie would have to lead Tom up the stairs at a slower pace.

"Tom, the way is steep, and unfortunately, there are a lot of steps. Josie and I will each take an arm while you carry your cane, if that's all right with you."

Tom looked up with his sightless eyes and patted Jessie's hand, placed on his arm. "Lead the way, girls. My nose is telling me there's coffee up ahead that'll taste great with your cookies, Jess."

Step by step, they slowly made their way to the top where they stopped to catch their breath. An attendant, verifying identifications, checked Josie's and Tom's names, but looked at Jessie with suspicion. Only striking miners and their families were allowed at the party... and Jessie looked anything but needy.

Pulling out her credentials, Jessie identified herself, explaining she had driven the family to the party, but also represented the *Gazette*. Consoled as well as ingratiated, the attendant led them to chairs that had been placed closer to the stage.

"Since you're writing for the newspaper, we want you to have a great view of everything that'll take place," she whispered. "Good publicity, right now, will go far with our cause, so please let me know if you have any questions. I see you came with a camera too. Good. Feel free to take any photographs." With a bright smile, she left their side to admit another group who had just arrived.

"Daddy, I wish you could *see* this! The big Christmas tree up on the stage is full of streamers, shiny tinsel and white stuff that looks just like snow. There's a big empty chair too. Do you think Santa's coming?" Josie gushed all excited, before blushing. "Not that I believe in him anymore, but if he has presents…"

Josie's loud voice chimed in with dozens of others, their happy voices creating a cacophony of excitement that bounced off the walls.

Jessie seated Tom next to the aisle and put an excited Josie in between them. Looking around, she noticed babies, adults and kids of every age squeezing into the small area. She and several other women had contributed money to the Ladies Auxiliary as well as offering to bake cookies for the kids. Smelling the coffee, Jessie grabbed her round tin of sweets and discovered the kitchen halfway beneath the stage where women were preparing candy gifts for the children. They eyed her with curiosity but accepted her offering with heartfelt thanks.

Climbing back up, she grabbed her notebook. "Josie, look around, would you, and tell me what you see. You can be my assistant, an extra pair of eyes today so we don't miss out of anything or anybody."

Seeing the celebration through a child's eyes made the scene more colorful and exciting. Josie pointed out several families she knew and again mentioned the decorated Christmas tree and the possible arrival of Old Saint Nick.

Jessie took notes of the decorations, amount of people attending and happy frenzy of the children who were waiting impatiently. Josie could hardly sit still, and Tom was grinning from ear to ear as many friends he hadn't "seen" in a while came over and shook his hand.

Presently, patrons of the party walked onto the stage and began their welcome speeches. But although they meant well, the children became restless waiting for the 'fun' stuff. Even Josie squirmed in her seat until Tom put his hand on her shoulder. On stage, witnessing the fidgety kids, the ladies cut their speeches short and motioned in the wings. At the appearance of Santa, pandemonium broke loose, and children became riotous as they left their seats and selfishly pushed their way to the stage area.

"Me first, me first!" They shrieked as they shoved each other in front of the platform. She grabbed Josie's hand as the young girl stood up. *Wait,* she mouthed above the bedlam.

Hearing the cries of little ones who had been pushed aside and had fallen to the floor, Jessie became uneasy and set her pencil aside. *This is not going well.* Even adults were jostling each other on their way toward the front. With a frown, she pulled an anxious Josie back into her seat.

"Something's wrong here, Jo, and I don't want you getting caught in the middle." She turned to Tom and explained what was happening. "I don't want Josie getting hurt. Despite their good intentions, this party is getting out of hand, fast. Why, the parents are becoming as rowdy as their children." She turned back to a disappointed Josie. "Sweetie, there'll be other times, but right now, you could—"

"Fire!"

What? Jessie sat up straight, wondering if she heard correctly. Looking around, she couldn't see the person who yelled. Others were still piling onto the stage, oblivious to the shout.

"Fire! Fire!"

This time the warning caught their attention, and in an uproar, people began screaming, looking for their little ones. Frantic, the ladies on stage began tossing several of them into the waiting arms of their frightened parents while another lead their way into the kitchen which had access to a fire escape. Most of the hysterical crowd began dashing over to the stairway, pushing their children first. In their wake, Jessie saw chairs flipping over as they stormed their way to the exit, some tripping and falling, while others just stepped over them. Frightened children were sobbing, clinging to their parents as they rushed to reach the exit.

In a cold sweat, Jessie stood up and grabbed Tom's arm, while a scared Josie started wailing next to him.

With his free arm, Tom jerked Josie back into her chair. "Daughter, stop that caterwauling *right* now and sit down. There *is* no fire." He turned to Jessie who was still holding on to him. "Jessie?" he asked urgently. "Do you see any smoke?"

Stunned that he didn't want to leave, she took a quick look around the room. The area was vacating so fast that every detail was in her sight…except for the smoke.

Turning back to Tom, she noticed he had his sightless eyes aimed at the ceiling while he sniffed a few times.

"I'm telling you, Jessie, there *is* no fire."

"How can you be sure, Tom? Maybe it's below us. Maybe—"

"*No,* Jess. I may be blind, but my other senses work overtime, and my nose is telling me someone has played a very bad joke on everyone. Are you *sure* you heard someone yell fire?"

"Not only me, Tom, but all the others who are rushing down the stairs." Jessie stood up and glanced around the room once again. "I still don't see any smoke and the room is practically empty." She looked at the remaining families holding onto their tearful children in shock. "How about if I go and check it out? Maybe some coffee boiled over in the kitchen."

Just as she headed toward the stage, a scream, followed by several cries of dismay made her turn around and rush back across the room. Running to the exit, Jessie was unprepared for the horror that awaited her.

Laying at the bottom of the stairs was a mountain of still bodies. They had piled up, face down, one on top the other, crushing the life out of those beneath them.

"Josie! Come quick!" After screaming for help, Jessie rushed down, pulling at arms and legs, trying to loosen the pressure off those who were suffocating.

Hearing the panic in Jessie's voice, Josie bolted over, watching in shock as Jessie tried tugging the bodies backward. With a cry of dismay, she joined her on the steps and grabbed onto another leg and, jarring it lose, pulled it toward her. As it slid from the pile, the weight of the body caused her to fall backward and land on her bottom. With tearful eyes, she looked pleadingly at Jessie, not knowing what to do next.

At the sound of breaking glass near the kitchen area, they both looked over their shoulders to see men rushing up from below. Unable to use the stairway, they had smashed a back window, gaining entrance into the building. Help had arrived, but Jessie knew immediately that for many, it was already too late.

As Jessie and Josie were pushed aside, the frenzied men worked fast, but it was futile. Slowly, the hallway began filling up with bodies as firemen and others started removing the lifeless forms, starting at the top, and working their way down, one by one. The entry door was finally opened, and rescuers pulled out the remaining bodies. Jessie knew there was nothing more she could do. Exhausted, she turned to Josie.

"Go. Sit with your dad and let him know what's happening." Not wanting to leave her side, Josie just stared at her, but Jessie was adamant. "Go now. I'll be right there."

Jessie solemnly surveyed the area, now looking more like a morgue than a ballroom. Upon the stage, the Christmas tree was still in the upright position. But the rest of the room was filled with collapsed chairs and debris. *Who would have done such a thing? And why couldn't anyone get out the door?* Jessie asked herself. Distressed, she felt too tired and defeated to consider any options. This was not the happy editorial she had planned on writing.

With shaky legs, she made her way back to Tom and Josie, who were anxiously waiting for her return. Right now, all she wanted was to be held by Mitch and escape from this nightmare. Tomorrow was Christmas Day, but no one would be celebrating. Instead, they would be planning their final goodbyes.

Someone yelled that the stairway was clear for anyone who wanted to leave. Feeling overwhelmed and exhausted, Jessie mustered up whatever strength she had left, grabbed her camera and looking through the lens, clicked one more time. Taking Tom's arms, she and Josie descended the steps, trying to forget the scene they had left behind.

Leaving the building and ignoring the police cars, hearses and curious bystanders, Jessie stared straight ahead as she led a quiet Tom and tearful Josie back to the car, where it was time to start the long and silent ride home.

CHAPTER 37

"Shh." Mitch tried comforting an inconsolable Jessie as she sat limply in his lap, his arms wrapped around her. He rubbed her back as she sobbed, reliving the terror of her harrowing experience.

Coming through the door earlier, she had fallen into his arms, crying incoherently, and it had taken several minutes to catch on to what she was saying. Her ghastly account of the details numbed his mind, unwilling to believe that someone could be so depraved.

"*Why*, Mitch? Why would anyone do this?"

Sniffling now, she sat up and as Mitch pulled out a large handkerchief, dried her eyes, and blew her nose.

"Wish I had an answer for you, Jess. But I promise, we're going to get to the bottom of this. If the companies had *anything* to do with it, well, I quit. Being an impartial mediator, I'm not supposed to take sides, but this is the last straw. We know it wasn't the strikers as they would never put their children in harm's way. You said there were adults too?"

Jessie nodded. "Not as many as the kids, though. Mitch, there were hundreds of people in that little room with no way out except the stairway. The children were screaming and running for the steps, followed by their parents. The lucky ones were lifted through the kitchen window to the fire escape. By the time the firemen arrived, it was all over. We tried to do what we could, but it was hopeless."

She shuddered in remembrance. "And poor Josie, in shock, as she desperately tried pulling on a man's leg that was way too heavy for her to move." Jessie let her shoulders droop. "I know we'll never forget, but for those who lost their loved ones, they still have to plan their goodbyes."

Jessie threw her arms around Mitch's neck and buried her face in his shirt. "It could have been *me*, Mitch! If Tom hadn't stopped me, I could have been one of them, buried at the bottom." Jessie closed her eyes and slumped.

"I'm *so* tired, Mitch. Can we just go up to bed? I couldn't eat anything right now, anyway. All I really want is to cuddle with you."

"Here, Jess, let me help you up." He gently set her down and guided her to the stairway. Bo looked up at them expectantly until Mitch invited him along. Racing up the stairs, he landed on the bed, settling himself on the bottom with his tongue hanging out. Jessie had to smile. She may have rescued him, but he rescued her so often with his unconditional love. Sitting next to him, she found comfort in the softness of his fur as she allowed Mitch to remove her clothing and tuck her in under the covers. Sliding in next to her, he gathered her into his arms. Scenes of what she must have witnessed flashed through his mind, and he wondered if either one of them would get any sleep tonight.

That was also Jessie's last thought before she mercifully drifted off and the first thought when she awoke in the morning. She was worn out with sore muscles but had slept. Checking the clock by the bedside, she realized it was still early on this Christmas morning. Glancing over at Mitch, she could see his chest rising and falling slowly, indicating he was still in a deep sleep.

Quietly, she rose from the bed, donned her robe, and slipped into her fluffy mules. Bo, disturbed at her movement, raised his head for a second before laying it back down. It was way too early.

Padding softly down the stairs, Jessie felt her way through the dark hall and into the kitchen where she turned on the overhead light and started preparing breakfast. The aroma of the rich black coffee would bring him down sooner or later. It was their first Christmas together, and they had this day to enjoy in each other's company. *It will be special*, she vowed, *and we'll create new memories together*.

Once the pot was on the stove, Jessie peeked into the living room to find numerous colorful presents under the tree. Surprised, she walked a little closer knowing that Mitch must have tip-toed down the stairs late last night and placed them there. Quietly, she walked into the pantry where her own stash of gifts had been hidden from Mitch's prying eyes. As she placed them alongside the others, the bright colors and fancy bows lightened her heart. Despite the deplorable events of the previous night, today was just for the two of them.

Staring at the angel atop the tree, she wistfully recalled many happy childhood memories of Christmas programs and pondered her own faith…or lack of it? She shook her head. *The Lord knows we need him, especially now.*

With this thought, the angel seemed to glow brighter than the reflecting lights on the presents as she looked down upon them. *Josie said presents can make you happy,* but Jessie knew in her heart, it really wasn't the presents but the thought behind them. With a lighter step, she returned to the kitchen just as the coffee started perking and footsteps sounded on the stairway, along with the clicking of Bo's nails as he hopped down the steps after his master.

"Hmm. Merry Christmas, Mrs. O'Brien." Mitch's soft voice and light kiss on the back of her neck gave her shivers that had nothing to do with the frosty morning. Turning around, she lifted her arms and encircled his neck, kissing him slowly, once, then twice, his unshaven face tickling her nose and cheeks.

"It looks like Santa came last night," she teased looking over her shoulder. "I must have been a very good girl, and by the looks of it, *you* must have been a very good boy!"

With a grin, Mitch bolted to the living room where Jessie heard him rattling a few boxes. "No fair peeking!" she called. "And keep Bo away from the packages too." He wandered back into the kitchen a few minutes later with a sheepish grin on his face. "Come on, Jess. You can't blame a guy for trying!"

Jessie decided to be merciful. "Presents before breakfast? How about we take a cup of coffee and sit down by the tree."

"Don't ask me twice!" Mitch grabbed two cups from the cabinet and set them on the tray Jessie held out to him, along with a pitcher of cream and bowl of sugar cubes. Checking to see if the coffee was ready, Jessie breathed in the heavy aroma with satisfaction and nodded. After pouring the brew into two large mugs, she added them to the tray.

"Bo? Outside?" Jessie knew the presents would keep them busy for a while so now was a good time. Barking what must have been yes, Bo followed Mitch and ran friskily into the snow. Feeling the cold blast of air coming in, she tightened her robe more firmly around her body as she waited for her two favorites.

Hearing Mitch's laughter as he watched Bo's antics in the backyard was like a comforting balm to her soul, soothing the scar in her heart she knew would probably be there forever. Leaning back against the counter, Jessie took a careful sip of the steaming coffee and found that although it was a little bitter, the strong drink was more than welcome on this icy morning. She looked at the clock. It was only a little after eight thirty. Just as she was thinking of her parents, the phone rang.

Setting down her cup, she hurried over to the receiver. "Hello?" Then, she laughed. "Merry Christmas to you, too, Dad. No, it's not too early. I've been up awhile, and Mitch is just putting Bo outside. I miss you too. What's that? Oh, hi, Mom! Merry Christmas. I love you too. Yes, I'll give your regards to Mitch. I can't wait for you to meet him. You're going to love him, Mom! Oh, and before I forget, thanks so much for the gifts you sent. We'll be opening them shortly. How is Allison and my new baby nephew?" After chatting about the family for a few minutes, Jessie asked for her dad to be put back on the phone.

"Is that new son-in-law of mine behaving himself properly?" Knowing Mitch as he did, Randall was sure his daughter would be treated royally.

Jessie laughed. "He treats me like a princess…and I love it! But, Dad, what I wanted to talk to you about was the disaster I witnessed last night. No, I'm fine." She sighed. "Yes, I know. Somehow disasters always find me, but this wasn't one of my makings. I promise."

Randall listened as Jessie related the gruesome events of the Christmas Eve party. "Anyway, Dad, I'm sure you'll be getting this information across the wires soon. I just can't imagine how devastated the families are on this Christmas Day. Yes, I'll be writing an editorial as soon as I get my facts straight. There's a photo I took, too, before I left that I'll send along to you. Right now, I'm just trying to put it all aside and celebrate this day with Mitch. Are the girls coming over with their families? Please give them a hug for me. I know. I miss you all too. I'll give Mitch your best and we'll be in touch. Love you, Dad."

With that, Jessie hung up just as Mitch and Bo came bounding back into the kitchen. Mitch's rosy face was alight with mischief as he held out his ice-cold hands. Jessie just laughed and evaded his touch by handing him a steaming cup of coffee.

He gazed into her eyes; all laughter forgotten. "I love you, Jess." The words were so simple, yet heartfelt as he considered the possibility that she could have been killed. *Again.* Placing his cup on the table, he enveloped her into a massive hug, leaving her with no doubt of his affections.

"Mitch," Jessie hung on with all her might, her head against his chest. Yes, things could have turned out differently, but they hadn't. There was so much to be thankful for.

"C'mon." She playfully tugged his arm. "Let's sample some of this great coffee. I'll slice some fruit cake; add a few cookies and we can open our presents. I'll give Bo one of his gifts, first, to keep him busy."

As if sensing he was in for a treat, Bo raced ahead of them into the living room and straight to the tree where he began sniffing and pawing at the presents. Jessie and Mitch laughed when he finally smelled his gift. Shredding the paper into little pieces, Bo reached in and grabbed a large meaty soup bone and settled down for a good chew.

"Me first!" Mitch shouted as he dove into the presents circling the tree. But instead of grabbing one with his name on it, he pulled out a large package and handed it to Jessie. "Merry Christmas, sweetie."

Taking it from his hands, Jessie hurriedly pulled on the silky red bow and peeled back the shiny green paper revealing a box with Kodak printed on the outside.

"Mitch!" she squealed. "How did you know I wanted one of my very own?" Carefully opening the box, she reached inside and pulled out a black Vest Pocket camera.

"Well, you've borrowed Carl's so often I felt it was time for you to have one too. Just think of all the photos you can take at Bobbie and Brian's wedding! Besides, don't you think a *good* reporter should have one on hand, just in case?" Mitch teased, and pleased that she liked her gift, handed her another.

Jessie put the camera down and unwrapped a sturdy brown leather carry case with strap for around her neck.

"Just in case you don't have a pocket one day."

"I love it...and you!" Jessie reached across and placed a smacking kiss across his lips.

Reaching under the tree, she brought out a smaller gift wrapped in shiny gold and handed it to him. "Merry Christmas, Mitch."

With a boyish grin, he quickly ripped off the paper, and Jessie was pleased at his shocked expression when he viewed his present.

Mitch just looked at her, then down at the watch he had just unwrapped and whistled, "Jess, how can you possibly afford something like this? A Rolex?"

"My dad pitched in, Mitch. It's from the whole family to show you how much they, and I, appreciate all you've done and for saving my life." She looked at him shyly. "Do you really like it?"

"Honey, I don't know what to say. I've never received a gift like this before. A wristwatch is much more practical than the pocket one I've been wearing." Leaning closely, he whispered, "I'll cherish it always. And *some* day, it'll be a great heirloom to pass on to our children."

Jessie blushed and smiled thinking she might already know something he didn't. It was still early, but the signs were all there. January 17, on Mitch's birthday, would be the perfect time to tell him he was going to be a father. They never discussed the possibility of having children, especially so soon, but Jessie hoped he'd be pleased.

They took their time opening the rest of their presents before heading back into the kitchen for a late breakfast. The day was meant for lazing around, both having received plenty of reading material and board games. Their only interruption was a knock on the front door in the late afternoon when an excited Josie arrived to thank them for her gifts. Jessie had to smile. At Josie's age, *all* presents were important.

As the sun set into a crystal haze, and the snow turned blue in the shadows, they became silent, knowing that tomorrow they would be tossed headfirst into reality. But the few remaining hours of the night belonged to them. Taking Jessie by the hand, Mitch led her upstairs where they found comfort, once again, in each other's arms.

CHAPTER 38

Pacing back and forth across the office floor, Bobbie anxiously awaited Jessie's arrival. The news of the Italian Hall disaster had spread like wildfire throughout the grief-stricken community and knowing Jess had attended the party on Christmas Eve, she wanted to make sure she was all right. On top of it all, Jessie had called in yesterday asking for an extra day off, which, of course, she was given.

As she spotted Jessie's car turning into the parking lot, Bobbie expelled a great sigh of relief. Rushing to the door, she flung it open and pulled Jessie into the office, enveloping her in a tight hug.

"Jess, when we heard the news...all I could think about was that *you* were there in the middle of it." She sniffed tearfully. "I can't imagine what you went through, and I don't think I want to. The news is all over. There's even going to be a federal investigation. Everyone's been pitching in with funds to help with burial expenses and providing for these poor families." She was bawling now, her soft heart overwrought with emotion.

Trying to console Bobbie with one hand and draping her coat over her chair with the other, Jessie led her over to her desk and brought out a large handkerchief to stop the flow of tears.

Bobbie grabbed the hankie, mopped her face, and blew her nose before settling into her chair. It was one of the things Jessie loved most about Bobbie. She cared deeply about people, even those she had never met.

"Brian wanted to see you as soon as you came in. Please take a cup of coffee with you, and come to think of it, he probably needs a refill by now. Here, let me get it. It'll make me feel useful." Blowing one last time, Bobbie stood up, and tucking the handkerchief into her breast pocket walked along with Jessie into the back room. Filling an extra cup, she handed it to her with a warning. "Brian's real edgy, Jess, knowing he put you in such a bad situation." She stared down at the cup in her hand containing the steamy brew. "Not that *this* is going to help any."

Jessie hugged her friend. "Don't worry about me. And, Bobbie, it's not Brian's fault. I volunteered." Giving her a pat on the arm and taking the coffee she held out, Jessie started up the stairs, balancing both cups carefully.

Brian, sensing her presence as she lounged in the doorway, placed the phone on its cradle. His face was pale as he stared at her. The phone had been ringing off the hook all morning, each report more horrible than the last. Standing up, he moved slowly toward her with both hands stretched out.

Jessie placed one of the steaming cups into his hand. "I'm fine, Brian, really. Just let me sit down and I'll fill you in on all the details. But before I begin, I want you to know that you're *not* to blame for anything. I volunteered to cover this story, unfortunate as it was."

Brian rounded his desk, sat back down, and took a tentative sip of his coffee, wincing as it burned his tongue. "Jess, I don't know what to say. I feel so guilty. You suffered needlessly, even though you weren't hurt physically. Remember when I hired you, I told you there would be unsavory situations; but I *never* envisioned anything like this. And how's Mitch taking it? I wonder how this is going to affect the strike. But, Jess, more importantly, is he still speaking to me?" Brian shook his head ruefully.

"Honestly, Brian, Mitch doesn't blame you for anything, so cross *that* worry off your list. Right now, we all just need to get through this. If you think about it, it was good I was there because you'll have firsthand information instead of rumors, as well as a photo for Carl to develop that shows the aftermath of the party." Jessie took a gulp of the stronger-than-normal coffee, noting that Bobbie must have added a few extra grounds this morning. Either she'd been distracted or felt everyone needed an extra boost.

Before she could elaborate, the phone rang. Afraid of more bad news, Brian just stared at it until Jessie encouraged him to answer it.

Impatiently, he picked it up. "Mason, here," he barked into the phone. He resented the interruption when they had so much to talk about. "What? Say that again." Brian listened, then put his hand over the receiver and spoke to Jessie. "Well, it's started. The president of the union was shot in the Scott Hotel, kidnapped, and taken to the train station."

Jessie sat up straight, grabbed a piece of paper off Brian's desk and one of his pencils. Scribbling madly, she motioned for him to continue his conversation. This was her job, and it was time to face the facts, no matter how grueling they might be.

"Repeat that again." Brian stared at his phone in disbelief. "An alliance man? Are you sure? Yes, I can have a reporter on it right away. Thanks for calling me, Sam."

"Jessie, that was Sam Bickley, the manager of the Scott Hotel who witnessed the union president being hauled out of his room. He'd like to give you a statement as soon as possible before he forgets anything. I hate to ask, but do you feel up to covering this?"

"Of course, Brian. But what's this about the alliance?" Jessie knew these people were known for their strong disapproval of the strike, with many businesses siding with the companies.

"Several women bystanders from the Christmas party said they saw a man with an alliance button yell 'fire.' Others say the door was barricaded from the outside, so people were trapped on the stairway. We need to get to the bottom of this, *fast*, with the real facts. Take Carl with you so he can take photos if you want."

Jessie grinned. "Thanks to Mitch, I now have my own Kodak camera." She hesitated. "I hate to say it, but I don't relish the thought of going back to the scene of the crime, if you know what I mean."

"You won't have to, Jess. One of the party hosts, Olivia Brown, would like to be interviewed in the privacy of her own home. She's holding a meeting of the ladies who were involved, and you're invited. There might be several opinions so be prepared, Jess. Just try gathering the real facts. We'll sift through them together, later." He wrote quickly on a piece of paper. "The meeting is this afternoon at three o'clock. Here's her address in Hurontown. I drew a little map in case you were unfamiliar with that location." Brian handed Jessie the folded sheet of instructions across his desk. "Will you have enough time to cover both interviews?"

Jessie nodded. "If I leave right now, I should have plenty of time this morning to meet with Mr. Bickley." She stood up and stashed the notes in her pocket before solemnly facing Brian. "This wasn't the Christmas any of us anticipated, was it, Brian." Without waiting for his answer, Jessie turned and walked out of the office.

Hearing Jessie's footsteps hurrying down the wooden stairs, Bobbie sighed knowing they wouldn't have much time for comparing Christmas notes. It sounded like she was off on a mission that Brian must have assigned to her.

"I take it we don't have any time for a chat?" she quizzed Jessie as she came through the doorway.

"Sorry, Bobbie, but it'll have to wait. Brian is sending me over to the Scott Hotel to interview the manager. We just learned that the union president was shot, kidnapped, and put on a train to Chicago." Bobbie stared at her in horror as Jessie continued. "According to Sam Bickley, that is. He was a witness and wants to make a statement. After that, I'm off to see Olivia Brown who was one of the hostesses for the party. She's invited a few other women who helped over to her house, and I've been included."

Jessie frowned. "There are two stories going around right now. Probably, there'll be more by the time I get done with my interview."

Grabbing her coat, her voice wobbled as she spoke softly to Bobbie. "This isn't going away any time soon, my friend. We're all going to need a lot of strength and patience in getting to the truth. Do you think you can make some phone calls for me while I'm gone? Check out some business associates and see what kind of gossip is going around?"

Bobbie's blotchy face brightened. "I can do that, Jess. Thanks for giving me something to do. I'll try and get some facts for you." Bobbie handed Jessie her hat. "Here. Give me a call later on and I'll fill you in on what I discovered." She gave her a quick hug. "Good luck, Jess."

"Thanks, Bobbie. What would I do without you?" Armed with the support of both the newspaper and her best friend, Jessie felt stronger, calmer, and more optimistic as she left the building and drove over to the Scott Hotel.

Parking her car in the large lot, Jessie entered the lobby and handed her card to the male clerk. With wide eyes, he scurried around the counter and escorted her to a back door. "Mr. Bickley is expecting you, miss."

Not wanting to correct him on her marital status, Jessie could only blame herself for not updating her business cards. She made a mental note to do that soon.

The clerk left her standing by the door. She knocked tentatively and hearing a booming 'come in' pushed open the wood paneled door. Whatever she had imagined Sam Bickley would look like, he took her by surprise with his height and muscular build. *Never have preconceptions,* she mused. He was younger than anticipated, without a strand of gray in his black wavy hair. Walking toward him, she gave his office a quick perusal. It was not littered by any means, but decorated with photos, football trophies and other sport artifacts.

"Ms. Peterson?" Smiling, he stood up and extended his hand across the desk.

"It's Jessie O'Brien now. My husband, Mitch, and I were recently married. Please call me Jessie."

"Great! And as you're working for my friend Brian, you can call me Sam. Please sit down."

After shaking hands, Jessie sat across from him and pulled out a notebook from her briefcase. "I understand you witnessed the shooting and kidnapping of the union's president last night. Not exactly something you'd like to remember so close to Christmas. I can sympathize with you, though, as I was present at the Italian Hall Christmas party. It wasn't a pretty sight and one I'm not likely to forget anytime soon."

He nodded, sympathetically. "That makes two of us. It was nice and quiet yesterday until several men came charging into the lobby, late in the afternoon, one with a gun which he held on me until I gave them the room number of the union president. When they stepped into the elevator and headed up, I called the police right away, then ran up the stairway. By the time I arrived, there was a lot of shouting and scuffling in the room. From their loud voices, I gathered the president had refused all the monies collected for the destitute families. But, Jessie, those weren't strikers who were attacking him. In fact, I recognized one of our local businessmen in the group. If I had my guess, these guys belonged to the alliance."

Jessie looked up, puzzled. "Let me get this straight. He was the president of the union which supported the strikers. Right? I had heard that the union coffers were empty so the monies collected would have been a godsend for these people. Why on earth would he turn away the much-needed funds for the miners? And why would it matter to these businessmen? I would think the striking miners would be the ones upset."

Sam tilted his chair back and folded his hands over his chest. "I can't tell you that, Jessie. All I know is these men were very angry about something he had done. Anyway, I'm not sure what happened as the door was closed. I didn't see the actual shooting, but heard the gun go off and the next thing I knew they were dragging him through the door, bleeding, and into the elevator. When they saw me, one of the men said they were taking him to the railroad station, putting him on a train to Chicago and good riddance."

Jessie put her pencil down and sat back. "Sam, do you think this has anything to do with the Italian Hall party? It just seems like such a coincidence that these two things happened almost simultaneously."

Sam pursed his lips thoughtfully. "It would seem so, but there's no way of knowing for sure. Much of this is just 'say so.' As for the kidnappers, again it's just my guess they were members of the alliance, although none of the men were sporting any identification."

Jessie pushed her notebook into the briefcase. "Well, this afternoon, I'm going to visit some of the ladies who hosted the Christmas party to hear their side of the story. If we're lucky, they'll come up with something more concrete that will tie this all together."

Jessie stood up ready to depart and turning to Sam, held out her hand. "This incident and the Christmas party involves so many more than just the miners. My friend, Bobbie, for example, as well as many others, I'm sure, is crushed by these deplorable events. If you think of anything else, Sam, please call me or let Brian know and we'll add it to our files."

"You can count on me, Jessie. And I hope that you'll update me on your findings too. Being on the city council, I can pull a few strings, so if you need any assistance, just let me know." Shaking her hand, Sam walked her to the door. "Let's try and get to the bottom of this as soon as possible before anything else happens."

Smiling at Sam, she said goodbye with a promise to be in touch. Walking out to her automobile, her head was stuffed with conflicting information. If it *had* been an alliance member who called out "Fire!" why would they take the chance of exposing themselves by attacking the union?

Jessie shook her head, hoping more of the gaps would be filled in during her next meeting. But first, she discovered looking at her watch, it was time to meet Mitch for lunch at the diner. Shifting gears, she headed across the bridge to the restaurant where she saw him through the glass window waiting at their favorite table.

Waving her over, he pulled out a chair and kissed her soundly before seating himself across from her. "Well, Jess, I have some news you need to hear. But ladies first. Were you able to meet with Brian this morning?" He held her hand across the table, hoping she would have better news than he had.

Shaking out her napkin, Jessie placed it in her lap and nodded. "Yes, but it wasn't long because the manager of the Scott Hotel wanted to be interviewed. He was present when the men attacked the president of the union and witnessed the bleeding man being kidnapped and dragged out the door."

Mitch nodded. "I heard something about that in my meeting this morning. Guess they threatened him with murder if he ever showed his face again. With their leader absent, many of the strikers are talking about packing up and moving down state for new jobs. But first they need to bury their loved ones. There's talk of churches preparing mass graves as well as a parade of coffins." With elbows on the table, Mitch put his head in his hands. "I can't imagine what those families are feeling right now. Of course, the companies think they've got an edge on the strikers now and won't budge." He shook his head. "Jess, sometimes I wish I had never been assigned to this mess." Then he looked up and added softly, "But if that was the case, I wouldn't have met you."

Jessie reached over and caressed the side of his face with the back of her hand. "I'm so sorry, Mitch, but this whole strike seems like a losing battle. I think the companies could be a little more sympathetic, but I don't see *that* happening. As far as I know, they're not taking any blame for the Italian Hall, either."

Mitch nodded. "You're right about that. And fortunately or unfortunately, the companies told me today my services are no longer needed."

Reaching across the table, again, Mitch took her hands in his. "This poses a problem for us, Jess. What are *we* going to do when I'm finished here? You've only been at the *Gazette* for a few months, but I don't think there's anything here for me to do. Of course," he added with sarcasm, "with the dwindling number of miners, I could always find a job there."

Jessie squeezed his hands. "Don't even think about it! Remember, I said we were in this together, no matter where it takes us. As for me, I've seen enough misery up here to last a lifetime, Mitch, and if it weren't for Bobbie and Brian's wedding coming up next month, I'd probably join the miners and head down south!"

Mitch was silent for a moment as the waiter came over for their order. Upset as he was, he ordered a large hot beef sandwich with a double serving of mashed potatoes, his comfort food. Jessie smiled knowingly at him and decided on grilled cheese with their special homemade tomato soup. It didn't matter what she ate, anyway, as it would all taste the same. Plus, she had to get through the rest of the afternoon.

Her appetite gone, Jessie sat back in her chair as Mitch spoke to the diners at the next table. What *were* they going to do? She could always go back to the *Detroit News Press*, but Mitch might want to live in Lansing. Besides, as finicky as her appetite had been lately, maybe she wouldn't be working at all.

Now *that* was a bright thought, she mused. Touching her stomach below the table, she wondered if a little life was forming in there.

Her monthly had been late, almost two weeks overdue and as she had always been on time, took it as a positive sign. Her eyes misted over at the thought of carrying Mitch's baby within her.

"What's wrong, sweetie?" Mitch looked at her, concerned at the tears in her eyes and the bemused expression on her face.

Not realizing he had finished his conversation with their neighbors, Jessie had to come up with an answer, and fast. Sitting up straight, she took her napkin and dabbed at the corner of her eyes.

"Not to worry, Mitch. I just think a piece of ash floated into my eye. It'll wash out, soon." She changed the subject. "Did you hear anything else from the table next to us?"

They spoke in generalities until their lunch arrived. Mitch dived into his, and Jessie nibbled on her sandwich knowing that if she was indeed pregnant, the baby needed nourishment.

Promising to meet him at home, Jessie left for her meeting with Olivia Brown. No matter who was responsible, the deed was done, and the children were dead.

Later that afternoon, knocking at the door of a large worn company house at precisely three o'clock, Jessie recognized the woman who opened it as the one who had checked her credentials when arriving with Tom and Josie. Olivia smiled, hung up her jacket, and invited her in to meet the rest of the ladies.

"We were just starting to discuss the party before you arrived, and I must admit, there are several conflicting views. As you were there, anything you can add would be appreciated."

After introducing Jessie to the other four women, Olivia motioned for her to sit in the high back chair by the fireplace where she could see everyone at once and asked her to recall the roll she played during the party.

Jessie cleared her throat that was closing on her. "Ladies, I don't know how much more I can contribute. When I arrived with the Johns' family, my main purpose was to take notes for the *Gazette*. While I was writing, I *did* hear someone yell "Fire!" twice before the pandemonium broke out. My neighbor and friend, Thomas Johns, who is blind, prevented me from bolting to the stairs with the rest of the crowd. By sniffing the air, he didn't smell any smoke, and stubbornly refused to let us go. Both his daughter and I stayed by his side waiting for the commotion to die down until we heard a scream and then silence. That was when I ran to the stairway and discovered the gruesome mound of bodies."

The ladies all clucked in sympathy as Jessie continued. "Believe me, it was a sight I'll never forget. I tried pulling one of the bodies off the others and yelled for Josie to help. But despite our efforts, everyone was already dead, either by suffocation or internal injuries."

She looked around the room. "Can any of you confirm that the person who falsely yelled was with the alliance? That's one of the rumors I've heard. Others say the door to the outside had been barricaded. Of course, by the time we walked down the stairs it was wide open."

Olivia glanced at the other women and, at their nod, replied to Jessie. "Without identifying the witness, I can only say that one of these ladies said she saw a man wearing an alliance button. I've also had it confirmed with others who attended the party. But the rest of us were in the kitchen at the time so were unable to identify him. Some say they saw the man, but *not* the button. One thing we all agree on is that it *was* a man wearing a hat, but what happened to him is a mystery, along with how he entered in the first place. No button was found on the premises by the police department, either." She continued with a sniff. "Most of us are familiar with the families who lost their little ones, as well as some of the adults. I do know many of the businesses, regardless of their affiliation, collected a large amount of money, yesterday, to help the grieving families. But the union said the miners weren't allowed to accept anything that didn't come from the union. Of course, now that their president has left the county, maybe that will change."

"I interviewed the Scott Hotel manager this morning who had witnessed the president being hauled out of the hotel, all bloody from a gunshot wound. He thinks the kidnappers were from the alliance as he recognized one of the men. My question is, why would they risk additional exposure when people are saying the man who yelled 'Fire!' was from the alliance? Wouldn't they want to keep that quiet?"

One of the ladies stood up. "I'm Mary Anderson. I think I can answer that question. My husband spoke with both the miners and the alliance. According to him, the union president had threatened to call in the federal government to investigate the party and find the responsible person. Supposedly, the funds collected by the alliance businesses and offered to the union came with a stipulation that the president would publicly exonerate the alliance from any responsibility for the Italian Hall tragedy. It's my understanding he refused to do so and called in the government agencies, anyway." She shrugged. "The attack on the union president seems to verify that the alliance could have been upset enough to railroad him out of town, don't you think?"

The other ladies nodded. It made sense to Jessie as she jotted down all the information. But again, without proof, it was all speculation. *And maybe that's all it will ever be,* Jessie thought to herself. *An unsolved mystery of useless deaths and destruction started by someone with little regard for life.*

The women were silent, each with their own thoughts as Olivia passed around steaming cups of fragrant tea and fluffy raisin scones. After serving the others, she sat down with her own mug and turned to Jessie. "I don't know whether it will help, but the alliance had, in the past, threatened to take the law into their own hands if the local authorities didn't. Running the president out of town could have been on their agenda. But again, it's all hearsay." She rocked back and forth in her chair, sipping thoughtfully from her spicy drink.

Jessie's mind was in a whirl. Too many different opinions. Too many unanswered questions. Too much hearsay. But write she would, not as hard-core truths but suppositions, relying on all the information she received. She had her own opinions, as most of the ladies did, but proving it was another story. And what a story this was going to be. Jessie could see it being relived year after year, based on the tragedy but without any solid conclusions. Soon, the dead would be put to rest but those living would have to go on.

Putting her cup down, she thanked Olivia and the rest of the women for their contributions and prepared to leave. Walking her to the door, Olivia put her hand on Jessie's shoulder. "I don't envy you trying to make sense out of all of this for your article. As I said, each one of us seems to have seen something different." She hesitated. "You're not going to include our names in your article, are you?"

Jessie shook her head negatively. "Not to worry, Olivia. Between you, the ladies, and the rest of the world, one can only guess what happened. None of you will be held responsible for any quotes, I promise you." Thanking her again for her hospitality, Jessie closed the door behind her and slowly walked to the car.

Snow was beginning to fall, silently dusting her coat and head with fluffy white flakes. She stopped for a moment and closed her eyes. In the quiet before sunset, she breathed in peace, knowing what her answer would be to Mitch's question. She didn't, and never would, belong here. Yes, she'd do her best in the coming days to present the facts as she knew them, but now it would be easier knowing it wasn't forever.

CHAPTER 39

"What do you mean, you're canceling the wedding?" Aghast, Jessie stood with her hands planted on her hips as she faced Bobbie the next morning.

"You're not *listening* to me, Jessie! I didn't say 'canceled' but rescheduled. Because of all that's happened, Brian and I talked it over and decided to marry sooner. Why waste another day apart when we can be together? I contacted Father Mark this morning and he has an opening for this Sunday afternoon at three-thirty." Bobbie was beaming.

"But...your dress? Will Catherine have it ready by then?" Plunking her purse on the desk, Jessie had to sit down as she considered this unexpected change of plans.

Brian came into the room just then and put his arm around Bobbie. "I see you told her the good news!"

"Yes, and I'm in shock. But not unhappily so, Brian. I can understand your wanting to be together. I don't know how I would have survived through all this without Mitch. Unfortunately, we still have this week to get through, and it's going to be a rough one."

Rough wasn't the correct word, as Jessie thought back on Friday. A better word was *hellish*, but no words would *ever* describe the spectacle before their eyes. With Mitch by her side, Jessie and twenty thousand other tearful spectators watched as dozens of little white caskets passed by, each carried by four solemn miners. Accompanying them on each side were Cornish and English singers, their voices rugged with emotion as they sang hymns for the departed.

Knowing it was time to do her job, Jessie took a deep breath, removed her camera from its leather case, and shot several photos of both the funeral procession, as it made a slow journey in front of her, as well as those still in shock at what they were witnessing. The lenses became blurry from the moisture in her own eyes, and she stopped more than once to wipe her tears off the camera. Mitch, seeing her distress, handed over a man-sized hankie. She nodded her thanks as she dabbed her eyes and pocketed the linen for future use. Although she dreaded going to the grave sites, her job wouldn't be complete without witnessing the burial itself as well as listening to comments of the bystanders. But it wasn't just her job that kept her there. Jessie felt it was her duty to share in the pain and grieve with the community of mourners.

Protectively placing her arm across her stomach, she wondered how the hearts of those parents could bear such sorrow. As they continued to watch, hearses bearing the adult victims joined the two-mile procession down the road as they headed to their final resting places in the mass graves prepared by both the Catholic and Protestant churches.

After the cavalcade went by, the crowd began filing in behind them, banding together in support for the rest of the journey. Tightening the scarf around her neck, Jessie looked up at the clouds as she felt ice-like snow nuggets pelting her skin. It was like the frigid air and dreary overcast sky were both grieving with them. Taking Mitch's hand, they blended in with the others for the final pilgrimage.

When coming in sight of the churches, Jessie halted, not knowing if she could go through with this, and Mitch looked at her in concern.

"Jess, we don't have to go any further if you're not feeling well. You've done enough just interviewing the witnesses and getting these photos. Carl could have taken them, you know. No one would blame you after all you've been through."

Jessie looked at her understanding husband. "No, Mitch. I must finish this. Even when we get past the burials, it won't be over. Maybe it never will. But while I'm here, I'll gather as much information as I can. Maybe someone overheard something." She shrugged. "I'll never know if I don't persevere. Come." She pulled on Mitch's arm and propelled him forward as they quickened their pace to catch up to the rest.

Mingling with the crowd, Jessie tried to be as unobtrusive as possible while listening intently to all the comments surrounding her. There was silence during the funerals but afterward, as people began to disperse, she heard factors not mentioned before.

"Mitch," she whispered, "I can't believe what I just heard. Now some are saying that hired men were holding the doors shut from the outside. And deputies with star badges were waiting below with clubs in their hands. What do you think about the union attorney who said this incident should now make the companies arbitrate with the strikers? Didn't you tell me they feel they have the upper hand, now, and won't concede to any of the miner's demands?"

Suddenly, the air was filled with the wailing of mothers as dirt was dropped on top of the tiny caskets...one thud, then another. Weeping herself, Jessie felt her stomach lurch and unable to endure any more, she turned to Mitch.

"Please take me home. I can't take any more of this, and I feel really sick, Mitch. I've got all the notes and photos I need, and just want peace and quiet. Tomorrow is another day...for all of us."

Grabbing her note bag and camera, Mitch put his arm around her waist and led her away from the crowd, stopping several times while she vomited, cried, and used his borrowed handkerchief. Laying his chin on top of her bowed head, he had no words to console her but gave her the physical support she needed. Although they hadn't discussed it lately, he was at the end of his rope knowing there was nothing more he could do. And although he would never have wished it, maybe this calamity was the sign they needed to move on.

Finally getting to the car, Mitch sat an exhausted Jessie in the front seat and spread the soft blanket over her. She closed her eyes as he smoothed the hair from her damp forehead but said nothing. This wasn't like the Jessie he knew, and he was concerned. Noticing her ashen complexion, he hurriedly slid into the driver's seat and put the pedal to the floor.

Arriving home, he stowed away the camera and notes, helped her upstairs and tucked her into bed. Bo, with his canine senses, climbed up and laid quietly beside her. Seeing Jessie was already asleep, he patted Bo on the head and told him to stay with his 'mom.'

Kissing her cheek, Mitch headed downstairs and placed a call to Brian explaining that Jessie would not be in for the rest of the day. He filled him in on the details and assured him that being tomorrow was Saturday and Jessie could rest, they would be at the wedding Sunday afternoon, especially as they had both promised to stand as witnesses.

Brian told Mitch not to worry about the reception dinner Jessie was going to host for the original wedding date. "With such short notice, Bobbie and I decided to make reservations at the Douglas House for the wedding party, including Josie, Tom, and Irma. Besides, since we moved the date up, others will be out of town for the New Year's weekend. So our guests have dwindled down, too, which is fine with us. Not many folks will feel like celebrating right now, anyway. Our wedding will be quiet and intimate, with a few close friends and that's the way we want it."

Mitch breathed a sigh of relief for Jessie's sake. She'd been through enough the past few weeks. "Appreciate that, Brian. Jessie's sleeping now, but I'll let her know when she wakes up."

Which was in the early evening, after the winter dusk had come and gone.

Jessie, groggy from her unusual afternoon nap, opened her eyes to find the room dark, although very toasty. Her whole body felt beaten. Recalling the events of the morning, she groaned audibly and pulled the covers over her head, wishing the world to go away. However, her grumbling stomach reminded her that she hadn't eaten since breakfast, as well as losing what she *did* have.

Throwing back the blanket, she sat up shakily on the edge of the bed and slipped into her mules. Bo, aware that she had awakened, decided it was time to play, and nipped at her slippers as she moved sluggishly to the door.

"Come on, you beast. Let's go and see what Mitch's up to."

Mitch, hearing her footsteps, took a couple leaps up the stairs and met her halfway down.

"You slept so long, Jess, I was beginning to worry. Feeling any better?"

Jessie nodded. "Just tired, Mitch, and very hungry." She sniffed the air appreciatively as they headed into the kitchen. "What smells so good? Don't tell me *you* made supper?"

"Well, I had to do something with my time being the cook didn't show up," he teased, throwing his arm around her shoulders. Pulling the lid off the pot, he grabbed a large spoon and stirred the thick mixture, breathing in its steamy herbal fragrance. "Here, taste." He brought the spoon to her mouth. "It's just a pot of stew I threw together from whatever we had left in the refrigerator."

Jessie swallowed the tasty sample and looked at Mitch in amazement before dipping the spoon in for seconds. "How'd you do this? It's fantastic! Now I'm *really* hungry. Would you grab the butter from the frig, please?" Taking down two bowls from the cabinet, she ladled large amounts of the rich beef and vegetable mixture up to their rims. Then reaching for a loaf of Irma's homemade white bread, she lathered four thick pieces and placed them on a tray. *Better make that five,* she decided as she grabbed another one for Bo or he'd never leave them alone. "How about if we have this feast in front of the living room stove where we can put our feet up and relax?"

As they sat sharing a warm blanket over their legs, Mitch relayed Brian's message. "We can always throw a party for them later on, if you like."

After taking several large spoonsful of the rich beefy mixture and wolfing down one piece of bread, Jessie cuddled up close to him. "In a way, I'm glad, Mitch. I must admit, I have been feeling a bit tired the past few weeks, but now this painful day is over, at least for us. It's been one misery after another, hasn't it?"

She sat up and, placing her bowl on the table, searched his face. "Mitch, I've been thinking. Maybe my coming up here has filled its purpose. Meeting you, getting Bobbie and Brian together as well as Jacob and Fannie. Sid is *finally* off my agenda too. Maybe it's time for us to leave."

Waiting for his reaction, she could see his facial expression change to one of surprise. Thinking she had disappointed him, she hurried on. "But it's whatever you want, Mitch." Dismayed that her eyes were welling up, she became weepy, again. "I'm sorry, Mitch, but I'm just so sick and tired of this whole thing."

Gathering her in his arms, Mitch pulled her close and whispered, "I was hoping to convince *you* to leave but you beat me to it." Jessie stared at him through glassy eyes. "Really, Mitch? You're not just saying that?" He chuckled. "I have *never* felt so useless in my life than on this assignment. No, Jess, I'm not trying to make you feel better. I just didn't know how to ask you. Now you've handed me the most wonderful gift on a platter."

Jessie sniffed and with glistening eyes gave him a brilliant smile that lit up the room, knowing she had an even greater gift of love to give.

Mitch gazed at her curiously. "You alright, Jess?" In an instant, she had gone from one of despair to joy. He scratched his head. Maybe it was a female thing. *Come to think of it, maybe her time is coming near.* He nodded to himself. Yup, that was probably it.

"Mitch, what should I tell Brian and when? Before the wedding, after the wedding?" She grabbed his hands. "You know, the perfect answer could be Rudy Lahti if the *Gazette* would rehire him. I understand he'd rather be working up here, anyway." She looked at him in excitement, with all symptoms of tiredness evaporating. "Oh, Mitch, we can start over without all the baggage I was carrying!" She jumped up. "I've got to call my dad—"

"Whoa, Jess. Before we call him, we've got a few things to sort out."

Jessie nodded quickly, barely containing her excitement. But instead of sitting back down, she headed to the kitchen, calling over her shoulder, "Okay, Mitch, but first I'm going to get the rest of this fantastic stew. I feel hungry enough to clean the pot!"

Mitch chuckled inwardly at how a women's emotions can change from night-to-day in just a second. He had a lot to learn, yet, about his wife. But Jessie was right. They *could* start their lives over. The question was where? Would she prefer to be in Detroit by her family, or could he persuade her to live in Lansing?

"Here you are." Jessie returned with the entire contents of the stew, along with more buttered bread and two cups of coffee.

Spreading the feast out on the little table, she sat back down satisfied that their needs (especially her own) were met. "Now, what's on your mind?"

Mitch swallowed hard as he took the last bite of bread and washed it down his throat with a gulp of his coffee. "Well, Jess, the first thing that came to mind is where we're going to live. Do you want to return to Detroit? I'm sure the newspaper would welcome you back with open arms." He winked at her. "Just so you don't bring Sable back to life, of course. Your husband might frown at that a bit."

"Oh. You're right. I guess I never got that far in my thinking. But like I told you before, Mitch, my life is with you wherever you want to be. Would you mind having a wife who works? And if we did move to Detroit, what kind of job could you get there?" Jessie filled her bowl once again before offering the rest to Mitch, who shook his head and smirked as she downed her second helping, tipping the bowl to her mouth to get the rest of the juice.

Reaching out, Mitch took the bowl away from her, placing it on the table. "Don't worry about me, Jess. My company has branches all over Michigan, so I would just transfer to another division. What about you? Do you want to be closer to your family? Lansing is about half a day's drive to Detroit, not too close, but not too far either. We'd still have plenty of time to visit either way."

Her feet well toasted, Jessie curled them up next to her on the couch. "Well, I know somewhere in the Bible it says a woman should let her husband make the decisions. As I don't feel pulled one way or the other, how about I let you decide, Mitch? Maybe I'll become a stay-at-home wife instead of a career woman. Would you mind that?"

At Mitch's big grin, Jessie was glad she hadn't made a preference. Maybe it would be nice to get away from the hustle and bustle of the big city. Even though Lansing wasn't all that small, the outlying areas, with wide open spaces, sounded very appealing—as well as a great place to raise a young one.

"I know my parents are waiting to meet you, Jess, and I think they'd be so happy if we would be settling somewhere close by. And there are some nice places with plenty of acreage just outside the city." Finishing the last of his stew, Mitch placed his empty dish next to Jessie's and pulled her into his lap for a snuggle. Happiness flowed through him and feeling warm inside and out, he was filled with an inner peace he hadn't felt in a long time.

"Okay. Now that we have that part settled, what about breaking it to Brian and Bobbie? Maybe it would be better to wait until Monday, after the wedding. As they don't plan to honeymoon right away, they'll both be in the office. That way, we can all enjoy the celebration on Sunday."

Jessie, feeling tired again, rested her head against his chest and closed her eyes. "Maybe we can finish this in the morning, Mitch? I'm getting all groggy again, after eating your delicious stew, and just want to climb back into bed. Company would be nice, of course." She raised her head and smiled sleepily at him.

Mitch gave her a tender look before taking her hand and hoisting her to her feet. "If that's an invitation, I accept!"

CHAPTER 40

"Bobbie, hold still!" Jessie commanded as she tried placing the veil on her friend's head. Bobbie stopped fidgeting and gazed at her bridal reflection in the large cheval mirror. Josie came dancing over in her pink confection and they both watched as Jessie deftly arranged the multilayer veil, letting it fall around Bobbie's shoulders and down the front of her gown. Reaching for the wispy train, Jessie smoothed it out in back until it touched the floor, trailing after Bobbie as she walked.

Standing back and surveying her work, Jessie teared up. Hearing a sniff, Bobbie glanced behind her reflection to see Jessie quickly wiping the moisture away from her eyes.

"You *promised*, Jess. No crying. This is a day for celebrating. Besides, if you start blubbering, I'm sure I will, too, and mess up all my makeup. Then we'll have to start all over."

Emotions came easy for Jessie these days. She cried when she was happy, she cried when she was sad. And today she was both. Tomorrow she and Mitch would tell Brian and Bobbie they were leaving. Knowing how much she would miss her best friend, Jessie quickly brushed aside a few hot tears as she gathered up a smile for Bobbie. After putting the final touches on the gown by twitching here and pulling there, she pronounced her ready.

Walking to the back of the room, Jessie picked up two delicate flower bouquets and a basket of fragrant rose petals from the table. Heading back to the girls, she handed the basket to Josie, reminding her of her job when walking down the aisle in front of them. Nodding, but too excited to sit down, Josie just paced back and forth and practiced sowing a few blossoms. Bobbie reached out to receive her luscious bouquet of white orchids and pink lilies, both flowers floating in a cloud of baby's breath. Bobbie lifted her hands to smell the fragrant blooms, then taking a deep breath, she turned to the women. "Alright. Let's get this show on the road!"

Jessie picked up her own large bouquet of pink and white carnations, with corresponding silk ribbons dangling beneath, and led the way into the sanctuary. Just before entering, the organist began playing the processional.

"That's our cue," Jessie whispered to Josie. "Just walk slowly down the aisle and scatter the petals all over the carpet. When you get to the end, you can sit with your mom and dad."

Josie grinned, her face flushed with excitement and importance. Holding the wicker basket high in front of her, she began the important job of preparing the carpet for the bride. Fragrant pink petals floated to the left, to the right and down the middle of the aisle as she marched in step to the music.

Following behind, Jessie noticed the huge white satin bows attached to each pew as well as tall vases of white chrysanthemums and red roses, mixed with fresh green ferns, on each side of the altar. She walked slowly toward the men waiting at the end of the aisle, her sleek calf-length dress of rose satin glimmering in the candlelight.

Anxious for Bobbie to appear, the groom and best man stood beside Father Mark, waiting for their first glimpse of the bride. At the end of her walk, Jessie risked a quick peek at Mitch who winked at her before everyone turned their attention to the door.

Father Mark motioned for the small group of witnesses to rise as Bobbie, confident and glowing, started her solitary walk down the aisle toward Brian. Catching his first look of his bride as she entered the sanctuary, he swallowed the large lump caught in his throat. If *anyone* had told him last year he'd be getting married, he would've laughed at the good joke.

Bobbie handed Jessie her bouquet and accepted Brian's hand as they moved up the steps behind the priest. Opening his ceremonial book, Father Mark began reading, "Dearly beloved, we are gathered here..." And with an exchange of the rings, it was done. Brian kissed his bride and hurried her back down the aisle as the small congregation stood up and applauded.

Jessie and Mitch followed the newlyweds into the vestibule, signing as witnesses on the marriage certificate. Standing in line, they all accepted the congratulations and best wishes from their small group of friends who had attended. Before long, people were reaching for their coats, hats and other paraphernalia that would keep them warm as they headed into the frosty air.

"Well," Brian remarked, as the hallway cleared, "that's another good reason to have the earlier wedding. With a larger group, we could've been standing here for hours." He chuckled. "As it is, I get to spend more time with my lovely new wife." Bobbie colored up adoringly when he reached down and kissed her again, while others just laughed. "Come on, everybody!" he cried jubilantly. "I made reservations at the Douglas House for five o'clock and by the time we get there, we should be seated right away. I, for one, am hungry and looking forward to that champagne I ordered."

The small private dining room, which had been reserved for the wedding party, also included Tom, Irma, Carl and Curt Johnson, the chief editor. The long table was covered in white linen with a beautiful white and pink floral arrangement, not unlike Bobbie's bouquet, sitting in the middle with two tall candles on each side. Glistening white china with gilded edges, napkins tied with pink satin ribbons, and sparkling eating utensils decorated the rest of the table. Hanging above, white streamers crisscrossed the ceiling and were joined in the middle by a large crepe paper bell.

Bobbie was amazed as well as pleased. "Brian, how on earth did you manage all this without me knowing? It's beautiful!"

Brian smirked. "I *do* have connections, you know, working with the newspaper. Besides, I wanted you to have a few surprises considering this was such a hurried affair." He pulled her close to his side. "I'm so glad you're pleased, sweetheart. Ah, great! Here comes the champagne."

Two waiters arrived, one carrying a silver urn containing the bottle of bubbly, surrounded by ice, and the other holding a tray of crystal champagne glasses. Placing the container at the end of the table, the attendant attached an opener and suddenly the cork flew into the air causing the foamy liquid to bubble over and flow down the sides of the bottle. Brian laughed along with everyone else. "Better put a couple of more bottles on ice if we're going to lose *that* much."

At the head of the table, he seated Bobbie to his right and motioned for Jessie and Mitch to sit on his left. Josie sat between her parents, with Carl and Curt Johnson across from them. That left the end vacant until Father Mark entered the room and took his place.

After sitting down, Brian motioned for the waiter to pour the bubbly, allowing a small glass for Josie to sip. After all, it was a celebration!

Father Mark gave his blessing on the food and, when served, hoisted his own glass to salute the newlyweds.

"May God bless you and keep you. And may you be filled with love, patience, and respect for one another and remember this day when you took your vows before God and man." Smiling broadly, he added, "Especially when the little ones start coming and your life turns upside down."

Brian chuckled while Bobbie blushed becomingly at the mention of children as well as thoughts of their approaching wedding night still to come. But hopefully, the day *would* come when she and Brian would share the joys of parenthood. They had discussed the possibility, and both considered children a special blessing that would truly make them a family.

They all raised their glasses and toasted the bride and groom, with Jessie taking just a small sip…just in case. Josie, on the other hand, and feeling quite like an adult, took a large gulp, along with everyone else. However, as she swallowed the strong effervescent beverage, she choked and sputtered, grabbing her napkin, and placing it against her mouth with wide eyes. Staring in amazement at the drink in her hand, she concluded that not everything that looked pretty tasted good. Plus, she had bubbles up her nose. Disgusted, she set the glass back down on the table, giving the adults a reproachful look. "How can you drink this stuff?"

The party just laughed and a few seconds later, Josie giggled. "Don't worry about it, Jo; it takes getting used to." Brian raised his hand and signaled the waiter who was hovering in the corner, waiting to assist. And when he asked, "Would you please bring a large glass of root beer for this young lady," Josie smiled at him in appreciation.

More toasts were given until their meal arrived, a thick winter vegetable soup, salad greens and warm fragrant yeast rolls, a stuffed roasted duck with orange sauce, fluffy mashed potatoes, and glazed carrots.

A beaming Bobbie grabbed Brian's hand under the table and squeezed it in appreciation for all the thought he had put into this fantastic celebration. Brian just grinned and filled their glasses once more. Standing up, he held his glass high.

"Friends, I can't tell you what it means to both Bobbie and me to have you all here with us on this joyous occasion. And speaking of Bobbie," he said, looking down at her, "I offer a toast to my beautiful new bride and all the happiness she has brought me. I just pray I'll measure up to her expectations…whatever they may be."

Bobbie's face glowed with happiness as she looked at Brian and lifted her glass to clink against his. "I promise to love and honor you, always." Then she giggled. "However, the obeying part is still up for grabs."

Everyone chuckled, including Brian, as she added, "But I guess I can promise to *compromise* with you." He laughingly agreed as their glasses met and he bent low to kiss her, much to the approval and whistles of their guests.

As they finished, the waiters came forward, removing their now empty plates and replacing them with smaller ones and tiny forks. Approaching from behind, a baker in a tall white hat approached with a delicious-looking two-tiered wedding cake, decorated with sugary pink roses all around the top and cascading down the sides. At everyone's applause, he bowed and placed the confection next to Brian and Bobbie, handing them a special knife tied with a white ribbon. "Enjoy and accept my congratulations!"

After thanking him, they placed their hands together and cut into the luscious dessert with white icing. As was custom, Bobbie and Brian fed each other a little piece of the sweet, moist pastry, and if Bobbie just *happened* to get a little frosting on Brian's chin, it went unnoticed as everyone began demanding a piece of the beautiful cake, insisting they had waited long enough.

Laughingly, they obeyed, carefully cutting the remaining lower tier into larger portions for their guests, as the upper tier would be frozen to celebrate their first wedding anniversary. As the dessert was passed around, a new bottle of champagne was popped to accompany the rich tasting cake.

As more toasts were given, no one noticed the winter darkness slowly settling in, but their light banter across the table illuminated the room brighter than the glowing candles sitting between them.

Jessie's own eyes glazed over as she basked in the warmth of all her friends, knowing it wouldn't be for long. As if sensing her thoughts, Mitch took her hand in his and squeezed it hard.

"I love you," he mouthed.

Grateful that he understood, Jessie blinked her tears away. Mitch would always be there for her. Of this she was certain. Giving his hand a squeeze, she put on a big smile and turned her attention to the revelers.

While everyone continued eating and talking, Brian motioned the waiter over and placed a small envelope into his hands. "For all of you, and please give our compliments to those who prepared this fantastic feast." Grinning, the waiter said it was their pleasure, wished them a happy marriage and bowing from the waist, slipped away.

Brian leaned over to Bobbie and whispered into her ear. Noticing her blush and slight nod, Mitch, in eye contact with Brian, picked up his fork and clinked on his glass for attention.

"Folks, I think it's about time we call it a night and leave these newlyweds to their privacy. As you know, they are forgoing a honeymoon due to moving up the date of their marriage. The least we can do is give them a few more hours to themselves."

As everyone clapped and pushed their chairs back, Mitch, with Jessie by his side, lowered his voice so only Brian and Bobbie could hear. "And you're *not* to come into the office tomorrow until after noon. Is that clear? Jessie will be there to answer the phone and I'll stick around until you come in. I have some calls that I can make in your office. Now, go and enjoy what remains of the evening and we'll see you sometime tomorrow."

Brian clapped Mitch on his back in appreciation and Bobbie gave Jessie a hug. "Thanks *so* much for this extra time," she whispered. "Brian has booked us the honeymoon suite right here for tonight, so we don't have to go any further."

By now, everyone had their wraps on and heading toward the door, called out their final congratulations. Mitch took Tom by the arm and led him to their car, with Irma, Jessie, and Josie following behind. As Jessie looked back, Brian and Bobbie were locked in a passionate embrace, oblivious to their departure. She smiled to herself, knowing this would be a night Bobbie would never forget! Mitch had been right. *As usual. At least let them enjoy this precious time together before we let the bomb drop.* Although she already felt blue knowing the deed had to be done, she was also elated knowing her future was secure with Mitch, wherever they ended up.

CHAPTER 41

"Jessie, we're all set." She looked up as Mitch ambled through the door and into the quiet office. They both had arrived early, amid a winter storm, to take care of any jobs that needed attention, but the phones were unusually silent, probably due to everyone hearing about Bobbie and Brian's wedding and knowing they wouldn't be in the office. Others were probably hunkering down inside their warm homes waiting for a break in the weather. Carl was hiding away in his dark room busy developing all the photos he had taken during the ceremony and the reception, and Mitch had gone upstairs to use Brian's phone to see where he stood with his company. Obviously, he was satisfied. By the sound of his voice, Jessie knew he had good news.

"My supervisor agrees there's nothing more to keep me here. We're free to leave, Jess, whenever you're ready, that is." He looked at her closely before coming around the back of her chair and placing his hands on her shoulders. "*Are* you ready?" he asked softly.

A heavy silence followed as Jessie gathered her thoughts together before looking up at Mitch. "Am I ready to leave? Definitely! Will I miss my work? Of course. Will I miss Bobbie? With all my heart." Her face suddenly brightened.

"Mitch, how about inviting Brian and Bobbie to Lansing for their honeymoon next summer? It would make our parting *so* much easier."

Mitch clapped his hands. "Jess, that's an *awesome* idea! Maybe it'll lessen the shock of our leaving too." He snapped his fingers. "And you know what? We'll buy the train tickets as their wedding gift." He beamed down at her. "Great thinking, Jess!"

Clasping his hands behind him, Mitch began pacing back and forth in front of her desk. "What about you? How long will you need to settle things here? Not that I'm rushing you, but we need to make some concrete plans so I can get reservations for the train and let my boss know when I'll be back."

Jessie put her elbows on the desk and hands under her chin as she thought. "Well, first I must call my dad and give him the good news. He and my mom are going to be ecstatic knowing I'll just be a few hours away. Then, I guess I'll have to let Fannie know I won't need her services any longer. That should be fine as she and Jacob plan to get married in the spring, anyway. And of course, the agent will have to know he's losing a renter; but under the circumstances, I don't think he'd expect me to stay. Mitch, what about Bo? We *can* take Bo with us, can't we?"

"*Of course,* we can take Bo," he gushed. "After all, he thinks he's been sharing *his* house with *us*!" He pushed her further. "How about two weeks, Jess? Can we do it in two weeks?"

After quick consideration, Jessie nodded. "That should give us plenty of time. Yes, go ahead and make reservations on the train and see what accommodations we'll need for Bo to travel with us."

Reeling in excitement, Mitch took the stairs two at a time and Jessie, so lost in her thoughts, was startled when the front door opened and Bobbie, propelled by the brisk north wind, hurried inside. Jess looked at the clock and then at Bobbie, whose cheeks were rosy, red from the icy air.

"*What* are you doing here," she frowned. "I thought we told you not to come in until after lunch. It's only eleven o'clock."

Jessie could see Bobbie was bursting with news and from the looks of it, it was something good.

"Well, spit it out. Something's on your mind," Jessie coaxed her with a smile.

Bobbie laughed. "You know me too well, Jess, but I want to wait for Brian to park the car before telling you." She shrugged out of her heavy coat, pulled off her hat and shook it until several wet snowflakes floated to the floor. "Where's Mitch? We wanted to talk to you both."

Jessie took the damp coat from Bobbie and hung it in the closet. "He's using Brian's phone to make some calls as we didn't expect to see you so soon."

"Well, being he's still upstairs and Brian's still outside, what say we go into the break room and get warmed up with something hot." Bobbie shivered. "Brr. It's wicked cold out there this morning." On their way to the back, she looked over her shoulder at Jessie and asked, "I know it's usually my job brewing the coffee first thing in the morning, but you *did* perk some, I hope?"

"Just follow your nose and you'll get your answer." Jessie laughed as they headed into the back room. "But if Brian is right behind you and with Mitch here, we'd better make another pot. Especially if we've got some talking to do. And grab one of those French crullers for me, please, the kind with the glazing all over it. Carl brought those in this morning but hasn't had time to eat any. As a surprise for you, he wanted to get all those wedding pictures developed before you came in."

"What a sweetie!" Instead of selecting just one of the donuts, Bobbie grabbed the whole box, a steaming cup of coffee and headed back to her desk. Following close behind with her own mug, Jessie inhaled the aroma of the fresh pastries and knew she'd be eating more than just one.

Mitch, hearing the girl's voices, came bounding down the stairs, giving Bobbie a peck on the cheek. "Good morning, *Mrs.* Mason," he teased. "I don't know what you're doing here, but it's nice to see you all rested from yesterday's festivities. Is Brian here too?"

Bobbie, glowing with happiness, informed Mitch that Brian was outside parking the car and would be in directly.

"In the meantime, why not grab a couple of mugs and join us girls," Jessie suggested. "If you hurry, I promise not to devour the whole box of pastries before you guys get back."

"I'm going to hold you to that, Jess. Just keep the lid on and I'll be back in a few seconds."

Stomping the snow off his boots, Brian stepped through the doorway and spied the girls sipping on their drinks. "I hope you saved some of that for me! I had to park the car at the end of the lot and nearly froze walking back." Rubbing his hands together, he joined the girls just as Mitch came in from the back room holding two steaming mugs. After placing one in Brian's outstretched hands, both guys rolled over a couple of chairs and sat close next to their wives.

Brian's face was animated, and Jessie knew he was going to explode any minute with his news. When he looked at Bobbie, she nodded.

"Well," Brian started, "we have some news that *we* think is very exciting and hope you will too."

Mitch put his cup on the desk. "Let's hear it, then. Jessie and I also have something to tell you, but it'll wait."

Putting his hand over Bobbie's, Brian took a deep breath. "Jess, remember when your dad was here, and I gave him a tour of the *Gazette*?"

She nodded. "Yes. He thought you did a great job of managing while Curt was absent. He told me so himself." She looked between Brian and Bobbie, confused. What did this have to do with anything?

"Randall contacted me about a month ago and we've been in touch ever since. Back then, he asked how satisfied I was working here and if I would ever consider moving away. Jessie, your dad has offered me a position with the *Detroit News Press* as chief editor, and I've accepted." When she frowned and opened her mouth to speak, he held up his hand. "We agreed to keep it between us until Bobbie and I had talked it over. I know this has come as a shock to you, and you don't know how many times we wanted to tell you, but until something was concrete, it was important to keep silent."

Jessie's jaw dropped as she stared back and forth between Bobbie and Brian. "Bobbie, you *knew* about this but didn't tell me? I'm your best friend! Then there's my dad whom I speak to frequently and he never said a word. Humph! *He's* got some explaining to do." Jessie was not only confused but a little hurt that she had been left out of the picture.

Bobbie reached over and took Jessie's hand. "I didn't know about it either, Jess. Honest. Until Brian and your dad came to an agreement, there was nothing to discuss. Brian never mentioned it to me. It was only after we decided to get married that he wanted my input. After all, I'd be pulling up stakes, leaving my house and everything familiar." She looked up at Brian, her eyes shining. "What he *didn't* understand was that our relationship changed my outlook on everything. Now he's the center of my world. What I *thought* was important doesn't matter anymore. Can you understand, Jess?"

Jessie frowned, still upset at the deception. But glancing over at Mitch, saw he had a big grin on his face and was trying not to laugh. She was about to ask him, *"What's so funny?"* when the irony of the whole situation kicked in. *Wait a minute. I'm upset because I wasn't in on the secret; yet we withheld our plans to move, hoping not to upset them.*

They were all looking at her, waiting for her response, especially Bobbie who had a worried look in her eyes.

"Shall I tell them, Jess?" At her nod, Mitch came and put his hands on her shoulders.

"We were going to make an announcement today too. My superiors and I agree that there's nothing left for me to do up here. Without a compromise between the miners and the companies, my work is done."

Brian broke in. "Are you telling me that you and Jessie are going to leave too?" Brian's expression held no reproach, just surprise.

"You've got it. We wanted to wait until after the wedding to break it to you." He chuckled. "As it is, Jessie's leaving won't be your problem, after all."

Jessie reached across the desk and covered Bobbie's hand. "You'll never know how much I dreaded telling my best friend that we were leaving. But now, I'm just flabbergasted, and delighted, at your news!"

Bobbie pried her hand loose and ran around the desk to envelope them both in a fierce hug. "And *I* dreaded leaving you behind, Jess. Does this mean we're going to be close neighbors?"

Jessie shook her head. "Well, not *close*, but just ninety miles away in Lansing, so near enough to still visit often on weekends and holidays. I must say I'm still in shock at your news, Bobbie, but just knowing you'll be in Detroit, well, I'm *so* relieved. We'll be visiting my family quite often too." She looked up at Mitch. "At least that's what he's promised me."

Brian turned serious. "All kidding aside, Mitch, when are you planning to leave? It'll take Bobbie and me until the end of the month to get things in order, so we're planning on leaving around February 1. And now I'll have to tell Curt he'll need to fill *two* positions. You know, maybe Rudy Lahti would want his old job back, but he'll have some big shoes to fill when you leave, Jess." Brian smiled at her. "Your dad says we're welcome to stay with them until we find a permanent place. In the meantime, Bobbie will put her house up for sale and we'll decide what we want to take with us."

Mitch grabbed a calendar from Jessie's desk. Flipping over the pages, he pointed to January 15. "We don't have as many responsibilities as you do, Brian, so we're planning to leave in a couple of weeks. Jessie hasn't even told her dad yet as we wanted to break it to you first."

"Speaking of Randall," Brian grinned at Jessie, "he'll probably be overjoyed not having to worry about you working for the *Detroit News Press* again. And *I'm* grateful because I'd be your boss, Jess; and after seeing you in action, I'd be getting gray hairs *way* before my time!"

Everyone laughed, and they continued discussing the move and making plans to visit each other often. Seeing their cups were empty, the guys went into the back room for refills to go with the remaining donuts that Jessie hadn't managed to demolish. Mitch chuckled to himself, remembering all the food she'd put down lately and attributing it to emotional stress. *Well, that'll all be over soon when we leave.*

Turning her attention back to Jessie, Bobbie saw her wink and nod as she placed her hands over her abdomen. *Does she mean...* Bobbie's eyes widened in wonder as she glanced down at Jessie's hands. Jessie quickly shook her head as Bobbie opened her mouth to speak and put her finger to her lips. "Shh." Nodding, Bobbie understood that Jessie hadn't told Mitch about the precious bundle she was carrying.

Jessie's face was glowing. Mitch might attribute it to all the excitement, but Bobbie knew better, and maybe next time it would be her turn. She thought back to her life before Jessie entered it; her independent, self-assured life. At the time, it had seemed fulfilling, but now realized how empty it had really been.

After getting their stamp of approval, Jessie decided the next step was to call her dad and let him know the good news.

"You're gonna go *where?*" Both Jessie and Mitch looked at each other and laughed as they shared the receiver and listened to Randall's tirade over the telephone the next day. Boy, her dad *really* needed to add some new words to his vocabulary. "You heard me, Dad. I'm leaving the *Gazette* as Mitch has been summoned back to Lansing. And speaking of the *Gazette*, Brian spilled the beans this morning. How *could* you keep this a secret from me? Yes, of course I think it's wonderful, especially as they won't be far away from us. But you could have least given me a clue of what was going on. What's that? Ha! Ha! Brian said the same thing. He was glad I wouldn't be working for him. Said I would give him premature gray hairs! Alright. Hold on."

Jessie passed the receiver to Mitch. "Dad wants to get all the details from you."

"Hello, Randall! Yes, you heard right. We'll be heading out on the fifteenth, taking the train. Sorry Jessie won't be coming back to the Press, but it's my turn to have her for a while. We'll be visiting quite often, though, I promise." Mitch laughed. "Yes, we'll be taking the 'beast' with us. Jess won't go anywhere without him, or should I say, *he* won't let her. What's that? Yes, I'm sorry, too, that things didn't work out with the strikers, but you saw what we were up against. I know I gave it my best, Randall, so I don't feel like I'm running off with my tail between my legs." He smiled down at Jessie. "Me too. I look forward to meeting Lillian and the rest of the family. Hold on. Jess wants to say something."

"Daddy, I'm sorry we can't come to Detroit first, but we've got to find a place to live and get settled in. I'm *so* excited! Anyway, you'll soon have a couple of other boarders staying with you. Brian and Bobbie are so pleased that you offered them room at our house until they find a place of their own. Yes, I agree. Brian is going to be a *fantastic* chief editor and I'm so happy you offered him the position.

Anyway, we'll probably see you in about six weeks or so, depending on how fast we can find a home."

Jessie swallowed hard and blinked back a few tears as she recalled the joys and horrors of the past several months. "You know, Dad, despite everything, I have no regrets about leaving my life in Detroit. Coming up here was the *best* thing I ever did. Sure, I found out who I was, but not the way I expected. My life is with Mitch, now, and I couldn't be happier. So many great things have happened in six months, along with a few bumps in the road. Sid is gone, we rescued Fannie, and she and Jacob are getting married soon. I have a four-legged child who adores me, a husband who loves me even more and now I don't have to leave my best friend Bobbie behind. Oh, and yesterday afternoon Rudy Lahti accepted my position, too, so he's happy and so is the *Gazette*." She looked dreamily at Mitch and blew him a kiss while speaking to her father. "I think it was meant to be, Dad. I didn't find a big lumberjack, but someone *so* much better." Jessie laughed. "Yes, he'll have to remind me of what I said when he's in trouble!"

Recalling the conversation with her dad, Jessie couldn't believe the two weeks had passed so quickly. Gazing at the home that had been hers for the past six months, it already looked like an empty shell without her personal affects. Checking it over one more time for any missing articles, she then placed the key on the kitchen counter for the new renter.

Hearing Bo's unhappy bark from his cage, Jessie knew it was time to leave. Stepping outside, she closed the door, not only physically, but on her life there as well. It had been a time full of upheaval and misery, mixed with joy and laughter. She had shared her tears in the sorrows as well as rejoiced in the achievements. Without looking back, she climbed into the front seat of Mitch's car and gave him a tremulous smile. He squeezed her hand, shifted gears, and headed toward the station where the train would depart at noon.

Although arriving early, other passengers were already milling about inside the building as well as on the platform, giving haggard workers instructions for loading their precious cargo. Wooden carts full of tied up luggage were being wheeled down into the storage car.

Mitch and Jessie grabbed their cases and joined the cue. A private sleeping compartment had been reserved ahead of time to ensure their comfort as well as allowing Bo to accompany them. Mitch pointed to the depot where the last of their luggage had been carried off for storage.

"Jess, go ahead and wait indoors, out of the cold. I'll carry Bo inside and then park the car by the loading dock and make sure it gets on the train." He glanced around. "I don't see your car anywhere, so it must already be on it." He blew on his hands. "See if you can find us a couple of hot drinks too." Glancing at his watch he added, "We've about forty-five minutes before boarding, so may as well get comfortable."

Lifting Bo's crate, Mitch placed it inside by a bench so Jessie could sit and keep an eye on him. Thankfully, Bo, confused by all the changes, remained silent except for an occasional growl, and cowered low within his confinement. Reassuring herself that he'd be all right if left alone for a few minutes, Jessie headed across the room where kids were selling drinks and snacks, taking advantage of the travelers while they earned a little money. Standing in line, she could see their thin worn-out clothing as they handed her the purchases, sleeves too short, mittens with holes and caps too large for their tiny heads. Acknowledging their need, she fumbled inside her purse, making sure there was extra money to hand out. It was one last thing she could do for them. Paying double the asked amount, she closed the little boy's hand as he held out her change and shook her head, saying softly, "Keep the change; it's for you." His eyes widened in astonishment as he acknowledged her gift; then, grinning broadly, he touched the rim of his hat in thanks, and pocketed the precious coins.

Jessie settled herself on the bench and reached down to pet Bo, reassuring him that she was still there. Blowing on the hot coffee, she hoped Mitch would arrive before it got cold. Her wish was granted five minutes later as he walked through the door, shoving it hard against the blowing wind.

"I'll have to admit, I won't miss that cold northerly breeze off Lake Superior," Jessie stated as Mitch snuggled up next to her.

Knowing it was almost lunch time, she had purchased a couple of ham and cheese sandwiches to go with their drink. Nibbling on them, she pinched off a few pieces, bent over and fed them to Bo, who was more than happy to gobble them up. Thankfully, a dining car was attached where they would be eating the rest of their meals.

"All aboard!" The conductor, in his faded blue uniform, shouted the familiar phrase as he poked his head through the door. "Time to leave, folks. Say your goodbyes now and find your seats. We don't want to be late." Checking his fob watch, he corralled his passengers who, after multiple goodbye kisses and hugs from their families, finally made their way through the doorway and onto the platform. "First class over here." He pointed to the middle of the train. "Anyone with a berth, head toward the end. The rest of you grab a seat where you can up front."

Mitch and Jessie headed toward the last car and, with the assistance of the ticket taker, stepped up onto the sturdy wooden box before entering the train. The worker hefted up Bo's crate and slid it along the floor where Mitch grabbed onto the open slats and carried him to their Pullman. Jessie handed the man their tickets and, noticing his frayed elbows and cuffs, thanked him with a generous tip for his help. Pleased with her gratuity, he doffed his cap and assured her of his assistance any time it was needed.

An exhausted Bo was fast asleep by the time they stashed away everything in their compartments. Pillows and blankets, stored on the top shelf, were provided for each of them for the coming night. Jessie knew Mitch had paid extra for this service and was so thankful for her thoughtful husband. With a shrill whistle, the train lurched forward, causing them both to grab onto their bunks. Once chugging down the tracks, its gait turned into a smoother *clackety-clack* as it slid down the rails.

Jessie pulled Mitch's arm. "Come on, Mitch. Let's go out onto the balcony in the back. I want to watch as we leave town. Please?" With a grin, he catered to her whim, and swaying back and forth, they slowly headed to the iron railed platform. The sun had come out, and although the acrid coal smoke from the engine burned their nostrils, they stood together watching as the town slipped away. Glancing up over the lake, Jessie could see plumes of black soot rising from the lugging ore trains as they chugged along their daily route. She continued to gaze at the looming shaft houses high upon the Ripley hills until the smoke from the engine obliterated the sight before her. Nothing had changed, except for her. With a sigh, she turned into Mitch's arms and laid her head on his shoulder. "It seems like a lifetime since I arrived, yet sometimes it feels just like yesterday."

Mitch held her tight as he kissed her forehead. "And *we* have a lifetime ahead of us. It's you and me, now, Jess. Just the two of us."

Jessie raised her head and with a twinkle in her eye, placed his hand upon her stomach.

"No, Mitch, now there's the three of us."

Watching the changing expressions on his face, Jessie hoped she was conveying good news. It didn't take long before he whooped, picked her up and swirled her around. Jessie grinned inwardly. *I guess that means he's happy.* Kissing her tenderly, Mitch gently led her inside where they began planning for the biggest adventure of their lives.

EPILOGUE

Two women sat in the shade of a gnarly old apple tree in the late summer afternoon. One held a sleeping baby in her arms while the other was large with child.

Bobbie stood up and leaned back to stretch her swollen body. Waddling across to the bench swing, she sat down with an 'oomph' and pushed back and forth with her feet.

"Jess," she groaned, "you didn't tell me I'd look like an elephant! I'm twice as big as you were at my stage and I've two months yet to go. Brian, of course, says I'm beautiful but what does *he* know."

Jessie just laughed. "But, Bobbie, I wasn't carrying *twins!* What a shock it must have been to discover you were going to have two babies instead of one."

"Shock to *me*, yes," she added wryly. "To Brian, no. He neglected to tell me that his grandfather was a twin."

"Well, believe what Brian tells you. He's only trying to make you feel better because he feels guilty. *He* isn't the one going through a pregnancy. Mitch said the same thing to me when I ballooned up. Besides, when the babies come, it'll all be worthwhile. I promise you."

When the bundle in her arms began to fuss, she rose and joined Bobbie on the swing. With the gentle swaying, two-week-old Alan Mitchell O'Brien was lulled back to sleep.

Pulling a letter from her pocket, Jessie handed it to Bobbie. "Fannie wrote to me just before I went into labor, and I saved it for you to read. She says she and Jacob are doing well and purchased a nice, abandoned home in the Boston location." She sighed and shifted Alan to her other shoulder, patted his back and continued rocking. "But according to her, the hill is beginning to look like a ghost town. Company houses are emptying out fast because miners are heading down state for better jobs. And anyone who does stay has to abide by all the company rules. Remember that one man drill they fought over so relentlessly? Well, it's there to stay." Jessie shrugged. "Beyond shortening the workday to eight hours, the whole strike was just a futile mess."

They sat silent for a while, each lost in her own thoughts of another time far away. Fannie's letter was a reminder that life moved on despite uncontrollable circumstances. But for the two of them, they were both glad to have escaped the hardships and sorrows of the mining community.

At the sound of masculine laughter, their solitude was broken as two gentlemen pushed open the gate of the white picket fence and headed their direction. Jessie smiled and waved at Mitch and Brian before looking back down into the sleeping face of her newborn child, a special gift made of their love. Breathing in his sweet baby scent, she glanced over at Bobbie's expanding body that protected her two little blessings tucked snugly inside. Choked up with emotion, she reached out and took Mitch's hand as the men joined the girls, then relinquished her precious bundle into his outstretched arms.

With the dismal year behind them, she wondered if dark times sometimes entered your life just to make the good times shine even brighter. Watching her husband tenderly cradle their son, Jessie knew that, although life wasn't always perfect, she wouldn't change a thing.

ABOUT THE AUTHOR

Sandy Keranen Grindey was born and raised in Hancock, Michigan, a part of the historical Copper Country in the Upper Peninsula. Her roots deeply rooted in the community, she grew up immersed in folklore as well as truths, providing for the background of this novel. An avid reader, she also enjoys baking, quilting, and working jigsaw puzzles, along with extensive traveling with her husband. Currently, their home base is Southern Florida.

Printed in the USA
CPSIA information can be obtained
at www.ICGtesting.com
LVHW090744030424
776150LV00002B/127

9 798891 122338